Pete's Return

B. J. Baker

PublishAmerica
Baltimore

ISBN: 978-1-61546-484-5
PUBLISHED BY PUBLISHAMERICA, LLLP
www.publishamerica.com
Baltimore

Printed in the United States of America

This book is dedicated to my
husband, and to our daughters, who
are among the brightest and best.

Thanks to:
John for his help and support, and
to my readers who have told me how
much they enjoyed my first novel,
"Pete On Ice," and want to know the
rest of Pete's story.

Prologue

It is the late nineteen eighties, and the Soviet Union has begun to crumble internally. Supporting Communist Cuba and fighting a war in Afghanistan have drained the rapidly dwindling wealth and miniscule monetary reserves of the loosely organized Soviet Union of individual and far-flung countries that were taken by force when Russia was strong. The already stressed citizens of the Soviet Union are nearly sucked dry by the Communist Party, and by cartels, gangs, and criminals who are ruthless, violent and self-serving.

Peter Genchenko, the son of a disgraced and now deceased Russian dissident, is returning to his homeland after competing in the International Winter Games in the United States. He plays hockey for the Red Army Hockey Team, and his team has been victorious in sweeping the games to win first place.

While in the U.S., Peter has let his guard down, and has fallen in love with a physician, the beautiful Nikola Kellman. Dr. Kellman, whom he calls "Niki," has made a positive impact on his life, and he is indebted to her for taking care of him when he falls ill. At first, he believes that she only feels pity for him, but when he finds that she has fallen in love with him, and cares as deeply for him as he does for her, his joy knows no bounds.

Their time together is deeply passionate, but the knowledge that he must return to Russia tempers Peter's joy with sadness. He cannot leave his mother and sister alone to fend for themselves in the chaos that has now overtaken Russia. He has no choice but to leave Niki and go home to his mother and sister. Their lives depend upon his return.

Chapter 1

January 2, 1987 As the Aeroflot jet made its final approach and then touched down in a jolting, bouncing landing at Sheremetyevo Airport, Peter Genchenko gazed out a window in the airplane and thought about the Chernobyl disaster of 1986. Most of what had happened there had been kept from the Russian people, but Peter was returning from the United States where the Chernobyl meltdown had been in the news, and it worried him. He also was very worried about the *glasnost and perestroika* of Mikhail Gorbachev's government. In Peter's lifetime of twenty-three years, there had never been any political openness *glasnost*, or economic restructuring *perestroika,* in the Soviet Union. Back in 1985, many good changes seemed to be coming, but now, two years later, it was apparent that the Soviet Union was on the brink of collapse. Peter felt like a recaptured convict on his way back to a prison centered on an earthquake fault line, or perhaps more accurately, on a China Syndrome hole burned into the earth like that of the Chernobyl disaster.

Peter found that midwinter Moscow was like a black hole. It seemed to swallow light and matter in much the same way as a black hole in space. He was no astronomer, but he knew about black holes; the super cold blackness and immeasurable density of collapsed stars in outer space. Or was it really inner space…*his* inner space, perhaps? The cold that had always clutched his heart, that had melted only with Nikola Kellman, had now returned with a frigid ferocity.

Black…that is my mood, he decided, and Moscow matches my mood. He could see that winter had hardened the city. The snow was still deep, but it had a dark, corrosive crust on top from liquid filth, splashed by vehicles on the road, that turned to ice.

It's a new year…1987. What new kinds of misery will this year bring to me? He had spent a very small part of 1986 with Dr. Nikola Kellman…*Niki*…but it had changed his life forever. He now realized that, although he had been raised in a strange family setting, where outward demonstrations of love were few and far between, he was nonetheless capable of loving and being loved. And for a while, when he was with Niki, the aching, cold place inside him had melted completely.

His voice was hoarse from crying, but he had no shame for the tears he had shed on his long journey home. And now the tears had all become frozen in the cold place inside him.

He hadn't cared what other passengers had thought of him on the various flights he had taken in his return to Russia. It didn't matter to him. Nothing mattered to him, because he had lost Niki. He had lost her forever, he knew, and he could no more have stopped the fountain of tears that had sprung from his very soul because he had to leave her, than he could have stopped breathing. For most of his journey from the United States to Russia, Peter had interacted with very few people. The only exception was the kind stewardess on board British Airways who had fixed him a strong whiskey hot toddy so that he could sleep.

Peter hailed a cab waiting in the arrival area at Sheremetyevo

Airport, and asked the cabbie to take him to the Red Army Hockey Arena. He hated to spend the money, but he had no way of contacting his friend, Misha, to pick him up at the airport. The cabbie had a glum face with a protruding lower lip, and said not a word to Peter. In fact, Peter wondered if the man was completely awake until he quickly put the car in gear, sped away from the curb, and careened around other, less ruined, vehicles.

The cab was so dented that Peter couldn't determine for a certainty whether it was a Lada or a Zhiguli, and it vibrated with acceleration. Peter's thoughts were not completely coherent before he got into the cab, and all the noise and vibration of the ancient vehicle made him feel almost out of control.

His body still ached from his recent abdominal surgery. Being on airplanes for such a long return journey had been almost unbearable physically as well as mentally. But it was the mental anguish of having to leave Niki that hurt him the most. The pain of losing her was deep and visceral.

After more than a month's absence from his homeland, Peter wanted very much to see his mother and sister, and felt that he should just continue on to Lyubertsy, southeast of Moscow, to see them first, but he knew that he had to go to the arena to get his money and to check back in with the authorities. His family needed this little bit of money that he had managed to earn on the hockey circuit that had taken him to America. No, he could not go home without the money. His family's financial situation was much too desperate.

Peter hoped that his hockey coach, Grigory Serov, would be in the arena when he arrived there. He must talk to his coach. He must tell him that he appreciated Grigory's letter of 'confession' regarding the death of Yakov Popov. Yakov was a meddling, hateful little 'team interpreter' who was actually a KGB operative assigned to watch the Red Army Hockey Team when they traveled. Yakov had made Peter's life miserable during the International Winter Games played in the U.S., and had even made an attempt on Peter's life. If it had not been for Niki, Yakov might have succeeded, too. Tears again filled Peter's eyes as he thought of Niki's courage on his behalf. *She saved my life...*

Grigory sent his letter of 'confession' to the fanatic and somewhat lunatic Detective Myers of the Indianapolis Police Department, but Peter believed the confession to be completely false. Peter was considered by Detective Myers to be the prime suspect in the murder of Yakov Popov until Grigory's letter arrived. But Peter did not believe that Grigory could ever have harmed Yakov.

Coach Grigory was a giant of a man who had a temper that boiled over at times, especially so in a tightly contested hockey game, but Peter had never seen him, in all the years that he had known him, do physical harm to anyone. Grigory could be intimidating, to be sure, but Peter could not, would not, believe that he had murdered Yakov Popov, no matter the provocation.

As Peter looked around during his ride to the arena, everything about Moscow seemed different, diminished, to him in comparison with Indianapolis, where there was light, even at midnight, and there were huge buildings with clean windows. And there was clean white snow on the streets and sidewalks.

The Red Army Hockey Arena was no exception to the diminution of Moscow. It looked as if the deterioration of the building had accelerated greatly in the short time that he had been gone. There was now even more debris from the crumbling building outside the entrance. Had it been flammable, some homeless person would surely have cleared it away for a warming bonfire somewhere.

Peter paid the silent cabbie who pointed to the fare displayed on his dashboard. After counting his change, Peter turned and entered the arena through the massive door at the front of the building. Once inside the building, he was surprised at how even the slightest things looked strange to him now. It was as if he could see more clearly, as if he could take in so much more of his surroundings than he had before. This new vision was because of Niki, he knew. She had opened his eyes to so many things. Peter clutched at his chest, where the aching cold began to spread. I cannot think of her now, Peter decided. No, not now.

When he saw Valeria, the arena office manager, he didn't know what to think at the change in her. She seemed softer, and somehow, more...*human.* Or was it that he just accepted who and what she was, and didn't judge her using Yakov Popov, her former lover, as the measure?

Again, it was Niki who had opened his eyes. She had brought laughter and then love into his life. He would never be the same again, he was sure...never. *Not now,* he told himself again, *I must not think of her now.*

Valeria looked at him, eyes wide and mouth open, but without anger or rancor, it seemed to him. She stood rooted to a spot behind the counter until Peter spoke to her.

Peter cleared his throat and in a hoarse voice asked, "Is Grigory here today?"

She shook her head slowly, "Haven't you heard? His heart has given out, and he is bedridden. It happened right after he brought the team back from the United States. It was so unexpected..." Valeria shrugged, and then asked, "How are you doing, Peter? Grigory said that you had to have surgery while you were in the United States. Are you well now? You don't quite look, or sound, like yourself."

Peter was very surprised at the news of Grigory's illness, and was momentarily at a loss for words. "I, uh, lost a few pounds after my surgery, and I am mostly recovered, now. But what about Grigory? Is he going to recover from his heart problem?" Valeria looked down for a moment, "I don't really know, Peter. According to Vladimir, his assistant, Grigory will not be returning as the coach. In fact, just yesterday, Vladimir was made head coach, so I guess he was correct in what he said to me. But you know how he is… Vladimir tells lies when the truth would make a better story."

Peter could not dispute what Valeria had just said, and nodded his head, "I agree."

"Grigory left an envelope with your wages for the games, Peter. Just a moment, and I'll get it for you." She went to a filing cabinet, unlocked it and retrieved an envelope from the top drawer.

Peter was still stunned by the news about Grigory, "Where is he? Is he at home, or in hospital?"

"He is at home. Do you remember where he lives? You can take a taxi there." Valeria handed Peter his pay envelope. "You can also sign this declaration stating that you have returned to us. The Magistrate is away from his office today, but he trusts me to do these things. Anyway, this will save you a trip back into Moscow to fill out the form when the Magistrate is here." Valeria handed a pen to Peter.

"Thank you." Peter was greatly relieved that she did not have a summons for him requesting an appearance at Militia Headquarters to answer questions regarding Yakov Popov's death. He took the pen that

Valeria offered and scrawled his signature on the document. Peter then took the envelope that she held out to him.

As he quickly pocketed his pay envelope, he asked, "Where are my teammates? Will they be skating today?"

"They skated earlier today, and have left until tomorrow. Vladimir is not as strict a head coach of the hockey team as Grigory was. He has other interests, I think, but he likes the prestige of being the head coach. The team has not won a game since Grigory's departure, however." She folded her arms across her thin chest as she spoke.

Valeria had always thought of Peter Genchenko as handsome, with his height, unruly dark blond hair, and the most extraordinarily striking green-gold eyes she had ever seen. She now saw surprise and then sadness in those eyes.

So many changes, Peter thought, and in such a short time. "Well, I'll be on my way." he said quietly.

"Peter…before you go, I want to apologize for the way I treated you before." Valeria hesitated, "I was afraid of Yakov, so I did everything that he told me to do, but I am sorry for it now."

Valeria's apology so surprised Peter that all he could think to say for a moment was, "Spaseeba *Thank you.*" And then he told her, "I owe you an apology, too, for the way that I behaved toward you."

"That's all right, Peter. I deserved your anger. But now I'm glad that you are back with us. And since you obviously didn't have any problems with Customs, or you wouldn't be here, I will give your signed declaration of return to the Magistrate tomorrow. If he wants to talk with you further, he will let you know, I'm sure."

Peter nodded, and again thanked her, "Spaseeba, Valeria. I will see you again…soon I hope."

This may be the end of my hockey career, he thought sadly as he left the arena. Vladimir will never let me play with a team that he is coaching. Peter walked slowly away with the weight of the world on his shoulders.

Chapter 2

Although Peter was torn between getting home to his mother and sister as quickly as possible, and seeing Grigory, he decided that he should first go to see Grigory, because he knew that he would not get another chance to do so in the near future. Peter really needed to talk to him about the letter Grigory had sent to the detective in Indianapolis regarding Yakov's death.

With Vladimir now in charge of the hockey team, Peter understood only too well that he would be dropped from the team roster. There was no question about that. They had never had a good relationship, he and Vladimir, and so Peter was certain that he would never be able to play with the Red Army Hockey Team again. *How will I ever be able to support my mother and sister, now?*

He hailed another cab. It seemed strange to ride in a cab twice in one day. The cost could feed his family for a week, but he was forced by necessity to travel by cab today. Oddly, Peter found that this cabbie was no more talkative than the last. Perhaps all cabbies were silent, he thought wryly. Peter, because he rarely had the money to hail or ride in a cab, had no point of reference in this regard.

When the cabbie pulled up in front of Grigory's home, Peter asked him what it would take to keep him there for half an hour. Peter didn't want to get stranded in Grigory's neighborhood, because many Chechens lived there. By experience, Peter knew that Chechens did not like Russians, and he did not want to get caught in a brawl, at least not in his present, weakened, physical condition.

The cabbie came back with a surprisingly low fee, and Peter agreed, smiling to himself. The cabbie probably wanted to take a short nap, and this way he would earn money even while he was sleeping.

Peter didn't get the chance to knock on the door, because it was thrown open by Grigory's wife, Hoda, a tall Muslim woman of Chechen descent. Her dark beauty had always intrigued Peter.

"Petrosha! Oh…Grigory will be so happy to see you! Come in and welcome to you." She placed her hands together in a prayerful way, and bowed her head slightly as she greeted Peter.

Hoda wore a veil and a long robe-like garment of variegated colors. Behind her, Grigory's daughters, from toddler to young adult, seven in all, stood watching Peter curiously from behind their own veils.

"Let me tell him that you are here. I have to prepare him for visitors now. He can't have too much excitement."

As Hoda walked down a hallway to another room, Grigory's seven daughters began to silently close ranks around Peter, peering at him with huge, dark, and lovely eyes behind their transparent veils.

Hoda rescued Peter from her daughters and took him to Grigory's room, where he found his coach sitting up in a chair, wrapped in a caftan of dark blue. Grigory had grown a thick, dark beard, and was wearing glasses. Peter had never seen him in glasses before and thought that it aged Grigory. He was thinner than Peter remembered him, too. It saddened Peter to see Grigory somehow diminished.

Grigory smiled, "Greetings, Genchenko. So, you are now recovered from your surgery?"

Peter nodded, "I think so, but I probably won't play any more hockey this season." *Perhaps never.*

Grigory slowly heaved himself up from his chair and threw his arms around Peter, clapping him on the back with his huge hands. "Well, the season is almost over, so you are not missing too much ice time." Turning to his wife, Grigory told her, "Bring us something to eat. Men need to eat when they are together, don't they, Genchenko?"

Peter raised a hand, "That's not necessary, Grigory. Besides, I'm not really hungry."

Grigory put an arm around Peter's shoulders again, squeezing his upper arm, "You could stand a little bulking up, Genchenko. You need bulk to play hockey!"

Hoda left the room and returned shortly with a tray full of breads, cheeses, dates, and dried fish, accompanied by a pot of hot tea that she set on a low table in the center of the room. She placed napkins on Grigory's and Peter's laps, laid moist towels beside them on small tables, and served them from the tray and teapot. When the preparations for the meal were complete, Grigory waved a dismissive hand at his wife.

As she departed, Hoda bowed slightly and told them to, "Enjoy."

"You are asking me a question with your eyes, Peter." Grigory already knew what the question was going to be.

Peter hesitated for several moments, and then spoke, "I can't believe that what you said in your letter to Detective Myers was the truth. I won't believe it."

Grigory grimaced in remembrance of what he had done, "But you must believe it Peter, because it is the truth. I didn't plan to harm Yakov. Of course I didn't plan it. I only wanted to frighten, to intimidate him, to throw him off balance. He threatened me and my family, and I was angry, and drunk; a terrible combination. He always accused me of protecting you. Yakov also told me what he intended for you; he would send you back to Russia in disgrace, and he would personally see to it that you were conscripted into the army. He always laughed his hateful little laugh when he described you as a foot soldier in that desolate, horrible country…Afghanistan.

"I had no idea what he was planning for you with Nikita and Josef, but I knew after the attack on you that he would stop at nothing to harm you, or even kill you. He told me to stay out of it, but I couldn't. That's when he told me what he had in store for me and my family. He said that he would destroy me and scatter my family. He said that seven females, *my daughters*, would bring a high price in the white slavery trade. Believe me, Genchenko, he was not making idle threats!"

"He told you he would do these things? I knew he was after me, but I didn't realize that he would threaten you, too." Peter was astounded.

"*Yes, and I had to do something!* But truly, Peter, I did not mean to kill him. I only wanted to scare him so that he wouldn't harm my family. And then, when the detective went after you for Yakov's death, I didn't know what to do. I was stymied. I didn't know how to get him off your back without incriminating myself. I didn't want to spend time in an American jail if I could help it. So…you can see my dilemma." Grigory had a look of supplication on his face, begging Peter to understand and forgive him.

They ate in silence for a while. This was the first real meal that Peter had eaten since he left Niki. *I left Niki.* The thought caused him physical pain and he put down his fork, unable to eat another bite.

Grigory saw Peter's sadness, and wondered what, or more than likely, who, was the cause. He had hoped that the doctor, Nikola Kellman, would take Peter under her wing, and that she would help him. Grigory realized that it had not happened. Peter was here, and not with the doctor in Indianapolis.

With the meal finished, Peter took his leave of Grigory and his family, thanking Hoda for the meal and the hospitality. He then turned to Grigory and thanked him. Grigory's daughters giggled as Peter shook their father's hand.

"If not for you, I wouldn't have been allowed to play hockey, I wouldn't have gotten to travel, or see other parts of the world, and I will be forever grateful to you for those things. Is there anything that I can do to help you and your family?"

Grigory coughed briefly and shrugged, "We are doing well, so don't worry about us. But please, do come to see me as often as you can."

"I'll do that, Grigory…whenever I can."

"Perhaps you can tell me sometime about the doctor, too. I would love to hear about her." Grigory remembered his own surprise at her reaction to Peter when, after his surgery, she had taken his hand and kissed it.

Grigory saw a cloud pass across Peter's face, and then a mask of deeper sadness settled there. Grigory wished that he had not asked Peter about the doctor. He could see that it was not just a passing thing between them.

Grigory put up his big hand, "I'm sorry Peter, I didn't know…"

For several moments, Peter, pierced through the heart, could not speak, but then he took Grigory's hand and held it. "There is no need to apologize. It was the hardest thing that I have ever had to do, leaving Niki; that's what I came to call her. But I had to return to my mother and sister. I had no choice in the matter." Peter shrugged, "And…now I am returned. Yes, the next time I visit, we will talk about the doctor. She's an extraordinary woman, Grigory, and I'm a better man for having known her."

Chapter 3

Upon leaving Grigory's home, Peter approached the cabbie, and could see and hear that the man was sleeping soundly. He envied the man's ability to sleep. With the exception of the hot toddy-induced sleep on the British Airways airplane, Peter had slept only fitfully on his return flights and connections from the United States. Peter awakened the cabbie and asked that he take him to the train station for the final leg of his journey home. He thought about Grigory's condition, and wondered just how serious it might be? Valeria had said that Grigory was bedridden, but it didn't seem so. Peter was hopeful. *Perhaps he will recover.*

It would be difficult to play hockey without Grigory barking orders and encouragement during practices and games, thought Peter. Well, with Vladimir in charge, I won't have to worry about whether or not I'm going to play hockey. Vladimir dislikes me. After all, it was Vladimir who told the police in Indianapolis that they should look at me for the murder of Yakov Popov.

It was Peter's good fortune to be just in time to catch a train traveling southeast out of Moscow to Lyubertsy. From the train, the countryside looked bleak, but in truth, it was no different than any other Russian winter he had endured in his life. Perhaps it seemed colder now because the cold place, the lonely place, inside him had come back with such ferocity when he left Niki.

If Moscow was a mid-winter black hole, how must Lyubertsy be described? Conditions there, Peter knew, were always so much worse than Moscow. The streets were narrower, dirtier, and there was more debris and trash strewn around that never got cleaned up. How different Lyubertsy is, thought Peter, from Indianapolis, Niki's city.

After the train whistled, screeched and groaned its way into the Lyubertsy terminal and disgorged its passengers, Peter stood outside the train station trying to decide what he should do. He couldn't justify the expense of a third taxi ride, and so he shouldered his duffel bag and began walking the four kilometers from the train station to his apartment. He walked much more slowly than he ordinarily might have if he were completely healthy. It had not been that long since he had his surgery. The Indianapolis surgeon who treated him had told Peter that he had suffered a ruptured appendix and had a femoral hernia that were repaired. *If not for Niki, I wouldn't have had such good medical care.*

As he walked, he saw that the snow in Lyubertsy was not as deep as it had been in Indianapolis. Niki had told him that this winter was not typical of the usual weather in her city.

Niki…he would now always think in terms of what Niki had said or done. Peter felt as if he had a gaping hole, through and through, in the center of his chest that would never heal.

Peter was worn out when he reached his apartment building. The steps that he usually took two or three at a time looked endless and steep as he stood before them. He took a deep breath and started slowly up the stairway.

He rested on the second floor landing for a few moments, and continued on until he reached the third floor, and his apartment. Peter used his key to open the door. It's Wednesday, and my mother and Katya are probably at work, he thought. The apartment was dark, the curtains closed, but as his eyes got used to the darkness, he saw that someone was lying on the sofa bed.

"Peter? Is that you, Petrosha?" It was his mother's voice, but it was faint and weak.

"Yes, I'm home. Are you not feeling well?" Peter dropped his duffel bag, went to the sofa bed and knelt down beside it.

"I knew that you would be home today, Petrosha, I told Katya this morning that you would be home today," her voice had a thin, reedy quality to it.

He reached for her hand, and found that it was very warm and dry, "Mother, have you been ill?"

Eda nodded, and with some effort, sat up and put her arms around her son, "I'm so very happy to have you home again, Petrosha."

"Are you thirsty, mother? Have you eaten anything today?"

"I'm not hungry or thirsty Petrosha. I just need to rest. I'm so tired…"

Peter helped his mother lie back on the day bed and covered her with the blanket there. He gently rubbed her shoulders for a few moments, until she fell asleep.

Peter felt a wave of despair pass over him. There was no 'getting back to normal' here after his experiences in Indianapolis. And now, seeing that his mother was ill, he was frightened for her. He tried to think of what to do. Who would listen to him? He did have some money now, but would it buy his mother some help?

Slowly, he walked back to his bedroom, duffel bag in hand. When

Peter pulled the curtain aside, sadness totally engulfed him. Was this going to be the way things would be for the rest of his life; this shabby, threadbare existence? No matter the hope that lived deep inside him for something better for his mother, sister, and himself. And no matter that he would never stop grieving over losing Niki. This is the life I must live, and there is no changing that.

Peter unpacked his duffel bag, placing Niki's wrapped gifts for his mother and sister on the table near his bed. He was surprised to find the new and freshly washed things that Niki had packed for him in addition to his own clothing. He brought one of the shirts to his face and held it there, luxuriating in the softness and sweet smell of the cloth. It was the same scent as the sheets and pillows that they had made love and slept on, and it made his heart ache deeply with longing for what, no…who, was now lost to him.

When Peter checked the bottom of his bag, he found an envelope there with his name on it. His heart leapt as he recognized Niki's handwriting. Quickly, he tore open the envelope and found a letter wrapped around a fairly large packet of American currency.

> My Darling Pete,
>
> It is more than likely that you are reading this letter in your apartment, and I hope that your journey home was not too difficult. I prayed that you would be safe, and that you would find your mother and sister safe, too, when you reached home.
>
> Although I am not physically there with you, my spirit will always be with you, no matter where you are. You are a part of me now and forever. I can't imagine a life without you. I will always grieve your loss, Pete, always.

If there is ever a time that you find that we can be together, I will be waiting for you with open arms and heart.

I love you, now and for always,

Niki

Peter read and re-read Niki's letter several times, and then, with his heart still aching, and tears rolling down his face unchecked, he folded it and placed it in his small treasure box on the shelf for safekeeping. He didn't know how long he sat there on the edge of his bed with his eyes closed. Of two things he was very sure; he loved Niki, and she loved him. It was clear from what she said in her letter that she would always love him, and would always welcome his return.

He looked at the packet of money that Niki had included in the envelope, but didn't know what to do with it. How had the envelope made it through Customs? The Customs Agent had tossed his clothing up in the air with both hands, thrown everything back in the duffel bag, and then slammed it down on the counter. There hadn't appeared to be anything in the bag for the agent to confiscate; nothing of value or profit.

Finally, Peter put the envelope under his clothing that he had neatly placed, everything that he owned in this world, on the single shelf in his bedroom. When he was finished with unpacking, Peter was exhausted, and lay down on his bed for what he thought would be a brief period of rest. Please, God, he prayed, just let me rest without dreaming…my heart can't take any more dreams of Niki right now. Otherwise, it will break into a million pieces.

But he did dream of Niki…her long, dark and silky hair fanned out across the pillow as she looked at him with her gorgeous dark eyes, shining into his soul, warming his heart. She reached to touch his face and gently caressed his cheek with her fingertips. "I love you, Peter Genchenko. Now and for all of my life, I will love you."

Chapter 4

Katya quietly opened the door to the apartment. Her first thought was for her mother, and she went directly to the sofa bed where Eda was sleeping. Katya placed her hand lightly against her mother's cheek. It's warm, so warm. She has a fever. What am I going to do? Fear clutched her heart.

The apartment was quiet, but then there was a sound from the kitchen, and Katya was immediately on guard. As quietly as she could, she crept to the kitchen door and listened. And then she recognized the sound that she had heard. It was the sound of someone, a man, in a deep sleep, breathing heavily.

Her heart beat wildly as she realized that it must be her brother. Peter was home, he was finally home! When she looked past the curtain into his room, he was there, lying across his bed, sound asleep.

Grigory had come to the apartment in late December and told Katya and her mother how sick Peter had been, and that he had undergone surgery for appendicitis and a hernia. Grigory explained that the surgery was the reason that Peter had not returned with the team. He also told them about the doctor who had helped Peter so much, Nikola Kellman. Grigory, who loved embellishing a story, told them, too, that he believed Dr. Kellman and Peter had feelings for one another. "Do not worry about Peter," he told them. "He is getting the very best of care."

Katya folded the blanket on the bed over Peter and noticed that he was holding a shirt, a clean, white undershirt, next to his face as he slept. She went back into the living room, slipped out of her shoes, and sat in a chair. She didn't want to awaken her mother or brother from their much-needed sleep.

Peter heard the sound of someone crying, but couldn't seem to wake up enough to understand what was happening. Was he dreaming again? He raised his head from the bed to look at his surroundings. To his surprise, he was at home, in his bedroom. The crying was not in a dream, and he realized that it was his *sister*...it was Katya, who was crying!

He rolled off of his bed, and the blanket came with him. "Katya? Katya, where are you?"

Peter half-walked, half-stumbled, through the kitchen into the living room, dragging the blanket until it fell from his leg. He saw that Katya was kneeling next to the day bed where their mother was sleeping.

Katya stood and turned to him, eyes filled with tears, "She is gone, Peter. Mother has died, and it's my fault! I tried to get help for her, but no one would listen to me."

"But what about Misha? Surely he tried to help you, didn't he?"

Katya began to cry harder, "He has been gone for more than a week, and I can't find him anywhere, Peter. He didn't say goodbye. Wouldn't you think that he'd say goodbye to me?"

Peter put his arms around his sister, and the two siblings, completely alone in the world now, clung to one another.

The next several days were a blur to Peter and Katya. Peter made the arrangements for his mother's funeral, and he had to give payoffs, bribes actually, to several people just to get a funeral permit. The Party, he thought with derision, reaches into the coffin and taxes the bloodless dead.

Katya and he were heartbroken with the loss of their mother. It was quickly apparent to both of them that she was the glue that had held their little family together. Each new day without her proved it time and again. In the morning, the apartment seemed empty, although there were still two of them there. At night, the rooms were quiet, much too quiet. Peter even wished that he could smell his mother's cigarette smoke again, just to know that she was there.

Eda's funeral and holding time until spring, when the ground could be broken, cost almost the exact amount of money that had been in the envelope that Valeria had given Peter as his earnings for playing hockey in America. Eda's casket was placed next to their father, Ivan Genchenko's casket, even though Peter and Katya had asked that it not be. Their request was completely ignored by the dough-faced manager of the holding facility, who complained loudly in their presence that space in the facility was limited.

Even with the money that Niki had sent home with him, Peter and Katya were going to have a difficult time surviving on their meager earnings without the boost of the hockey money. And, crass as it might seem in light of their mother's passing, the loss of her earnings made their situation even more dire.

The morning following their mother's placement in the holding facility, Peter and Katya were having a breakfast of bread and tea at the small kitchen table in their apartment. Peter gave Katya the Christmas gift that Niki had sent to her, and she was surprised and delighted with the generous gifts of a bright blue silk scarf and fur-lined leather gloves. He set aside Niki's gift to their mother for a moment, and then told his sister, "Katya, Niki sent a scarf and gloves for our mother, too, and they are in a different color. I think that our mother would want you to have them. Will you wear them?"

Katya wiped tears from her eyes and nodded her head, "Da *yes, Petrosha,* I will wear them in honor of our mother."

Peter had earlier decided that he needed to tell Katya about the money that Niki had sent home with him to help their family. He didn't want Katya to worry so much about their ability to survive. One of the things that Katya feared most was homelessness, and she was greatly relieved to hear of Niki's generosity.

Peter told her all about Niki, and how he and Niki felt about each other. Peter wanted Katya to understand the kind of person that Niki was. There were times, he told his sister, that when he was with Niki, he had felt happier than he ever had before in his life. There was great sadness in his voice when he told Katya that leaving Niki was the most difficult thing that he had ever had to accept; that is, before their mother died.

Katya reached across the table and held his hand. "You love her then? She is the one for you…for all time?"

Peter didn't hesitate, "Yes, Katya, and if you knew her, you'd understand, and you'd love her, too."

"That's the way I feel about Misha." Katya looked at Peter with pain evident in her eyes.

Katya told her brother how frightened, and then frantic, she was with Misha's disappearance. When their mother became ill as well,

Katya felt overwhelmed with the responsibility. Katya tried to get her to a hospital, but Eda refused to go, saying that no one could help her. In desperation, Katya walked to three different clinics for assistance, but was turned away from each because none of the doctors would send medication without seeing the patient. Eda was just too weak to go anywhere, and didn't want to be a burden.

Peter told Katya that it wasn't her fault. Their mother was headstrong and stubborn. "Katya, those traits are part of who we are, too. We couldn't have survived what we have lived through until now, if we weren't as strong as our mother."

The decision to seek treatment was their mother's to make, he said, and she had decided not to go to a hospital. He speculated that perhaps she had been ill for some time without telling them, and that when her symptoms became severe, she didn't want to prolong her own suffering.

"When you think back to how long our mother smoked cigarettes, and how much she coughed in the last few years, there may have been something very serious that was going on, and that she was aware of, but didn't want to acknowledge, Katya." Peter stood from his chair and came around the table to put his arm around his sister's thin shoulders.

"I know, Petrosha, but I miss her terribly." Katya used the back of one hand to wipe her tears away.

Even though Peter had begun to feel a sense of desperation about the situation that he and Katya were in, he didn't want to communicate that desperation to Katya. He wanted to protect his gentle sister. She had been through so much when she, alone, had to cope with their mother's illness, and Misha's disappearance. He wanted to spare her as much as possible, and so said nothing of his own feelings.

Chapter 5

Ten days after his return, Peter walked the three kilometers to Misha's apartment from his own, hoping to find Mrs. Preslov, Misha's mother, there. He wanted very much to talk with her. Peter hoped that she would be able to tell him what might have happened to Misha. There were a few pieces of mail at the door, but Peter was not concerned. He picked up one envelope and saw that it was a recent delivery. He hoped that this was a sign that Misha and his mother had been called away, and would return soon. Nevertheless, he knocked on the door several times in the faint hope that someone was there, but no one answered.

Peter started back to work on the following Monday. Although he was still recuperating from his surgery, he ran as much of the distance, five kilometers, to the factory as he could. It came into view on the last kilometer, and he felt as he always had; revulsion. He hated the atmosphere around and in the factory. It was soot-stained, and dirty, and the work was backbreaking. There were solvents, oils and chemicals all around inside the factory, stored haphazardly, and some were even uncovered. There was no thought by the management about protecting the workers. Gloves, masks and goggles were expensive, and people were not.

His job was to stack small axles, slippery with some kind of oil or solvent, on a cart. He would then put the axles on a truck for shipment to an assembly plant in another city. Like all factories in the Soviet Union, this factory had a quota to meet. The closer the deadline for the quota, the more hateful the factory supervisors became. One of the many reasons that this factory never met its quota was that theft was rampant at every level of the manufacturing process.

Theft was a culture in Lyubertsy, a way of life, a means of survival. Peter did not belong to a Lyubertsy gang, even though he had been pressured to do so by several gang members. One memorable time, Peter and Misha stood back to back, fending off attacking gang members. The thing that actually saved them, after Peter had flung the gang leader over a fence head first, was that the militia intervened. Had it not been for the militia, the sheer numbers in the gang would have prevailed, and Peter and Misha would most surely have been badly injured, or worse.

Within moments of Peter's entry into the plant on this particular morning, Antonin, one of the plant managers, came over to him and began demanding in a loud and rude tone whether Peter had seen Misha in the last week, or so. Antonin's dark face became darker with anger, his overgrown gray eyebrows moving up and down rapidly as he shouted at Peter, "I can't keep up with you bastards. First it's hockey with you, and Red Army hockey at that, so I can't complain about it to the authorities. And then Misha, without saying anything to anyone, leaves and doesn't come back. He's not going to have a job when he gets back. You can tell him that when you see him!"

Of one thing regarding Misha, Peter was certain; his friend would never just *disappear*. No, Misha would never do that to Katya. And Misha's mother…he was her only support, her only family. Misha's father had been long dead when Peter and Misha first met when they were only twelve years old.

Peter had the nagging fear that something terrible might have happened to his friend. He began walking the streets of Lyubertsy in early morning and late evening, hoping to see his friend, or, failing that, hoping to hear news of his friend. Peter looked in the places that they had frequented together, to no avail. It was as though Misha had been swept, silently, from the face of the earth.

Already heartsore and sad for so many reasons, Peter became depressed by his failure to find Misha. He feared the worst, but couldn't admit to himself that Misha was gone for good.

Peter went about his daily work in the factory quietly. But as he worked, he listened to the conversations around him, hoping for a word, a tidbit, a sentence about Misha. He wanted to know what others had to say about Misha. But he heard nothing, nothing at all.

After several weeks, Peter knew that something terrible, and final, must have happened to his friend. During lunch one day, one of the most repugnant of the Lyubertsy thugs working in the factory came over to where Peter was working, and grinned an evil grin in his direction. Peter tried to ignore him, but the thug, Zuk, kept getting closer to Peter, who became uneasy and watchful for other gang members.

Finally, the man came close enough so that Peter could grab him by the collar, "What are you trying to tell me Zuk? Are you trying to tell me something about Misha?"

Zuk's features were askew; one cheek, ear, and eye were noticeably higher on one side of his face than the other. His face and neck reddened, and he became owl-eyed, or cock-eyed, or both, as Peter pressed him. Zuk saw the out-of-control look on Genchenko's face, and it frightened him more than he would like to admit.

"I don't know what you're talking about, Genchenko. Let go of me! Let go or I'll..."

Peter grabbed the lower part of Zuk's jaw, "Or you'll what; call your brethren, your fellow criminals? Well, call them. I'd like to hear what they have to say about Misha. If I find out that any of your gang has harmed Misha..." Peter didn't finish the sentence as he heaved Zuk against the wall.

"Shit!" Zuk screamed as he bounced off the wall and onto the floor. He dragged himself from the floor with a painful lurch and ran away, looking back several times to make sure that Peter wasn't chasing him.

That evening after work, Peter ran home, just as he had since he returned to work. When he had to, he walked rapidly through the snow as quickly as he could, resting only briefly when his sides began to ache.

He reached his apartment house and ran up one flight of stairs, walked the next, and ran the third. He was winded when he reached the top, but he surprised himself, because he hadn't thought that he could do it. Since he had arrived home before Katya on this evening, Peter fixed a boiled dinner of cabbage, beets, and potatoes, with a rather dried out stump of bread for dipping. There was no meat to be had, and so Peter did the best that he could with what was available.

Katya looked like a ghost now. She was pale and thin, and there seemed to be a permanent sadness in her eyes. Peter hoped to see some happiness there again, but he didn't know how to make that so. Losing their mother had been very painful for her, and not knowing what had happened to Misha was a terrible burden to bear.

Peter became so worried about Katya's health, mental and physical, that he decided on a plan to cheer her up, and help her to forget the terrible things that she had endured, alone, while he was far away in America. He would take her places…places that she had not seen in a good long while. Perhaps she would then begin to open up to him so that he could help her. The biggest part of Peter's plan, however, was to find Misha. *I've got to find Misha!*

Chapter 6

The next weekend, in another effort to bring closure to Misha's odd disappearance, Peter went back to his friend's apartment. To his surprise, the apartment was empty. The door was slightly ajar and Peter could see that there were no furnishings inside. What has happened to Misha's mother? Now Peter was frantic for news of his best friend. He knocked on the doors of the surrounding apartments, and the few who answered their doors had very little to say. One woman, who seemed to be the apartment house gossip, would only say that an odd-looking man came one evening, and Misha and his mother put their coats on and went with him. She said that she never saw them after that evening. When Peter pressed the woman for more details, perhaps a description of the man who took them away, she slammed the door in his face.

How can I tell Katya that Misha's apartment is empty? And where is Svetlana Preslov? Peter wondered if Misha had taken his mother with him when he left Lyubertsy? Had he really left Lyubertsy?

If so, then why hadn't Misha had the courage to tell Katya that he was leaving? Misha was not like that. No, Misha would never do that to Katya. Now, Peter fully understood that something terrible, and final, had happened to his friend. It made him heartsick for Katya.

Peter continued to work every day, and always met his quota. Every factory worker had a quota. His was a certain number of stacked and carted axles each shift. He felt wooden, almost robotic, as he groped his way through what seemed endless days, without finding anything useful about Misha's whereabouts. There were times when some of the Lyubertsy gang members working in the plant would taunt him, and move around him as if they would pounce on him, and then start laughing uproariously as if there were some joke that Peter wasn't privy to. But they didn't touch him during these 'tests.'

Moving, carrying, and stacking axles was like weight training for Peter. Each day as he went about his job, Peter became stronger. And he was now running to and from work each day without getting winded. Using his old stopwatch, Peter timed himself on these runs, and found that he had now improved beyond what he had usually done before his surgery.

Most nights, Peter fell into an exhausted, dreamless sleep. But always, before he went to sleep, Peter prayed that he would see Niki again, and that Misha would return to Katya. Even though Peter had not been raised to be religious, he nonetheless felt the need to beseech God, because he would completely lose hope, otherwise. Without hope, he knew, life would not be worth living.

As another month went by, there was still no sign of Misha, no clue to his disappearance. Peter tried desperately to find out anything that he could from his fellow plant workers, but no one, at least those outside the Lyubertsy gang, seemed to have any idea of Misha's whereabouts.

Chapter 7

It was now late February, and Nikola Kellman was certain. At first, she thought she had the flu, and then she was sure that she had mononucleosis, but her Mono-Spot test was negative. By the time that she missed her second menstrual period, she knew that she was carrying Peter Genchenko's child. The realization filled her with joy and fear in equal parts.

Nik had no one that she wanted to talk to about her pregnancy; not even her best friend, Stephanie. Her parents were still angry with her over her breakup with Ron Michael, or Myron, as her mother called him. Or was it really that *she* was still angry with *them?* It didn't really matter, because the outcome was the same. She talked to them sometimes, when necessary, but not very often. Mostly, the contacts were civil, or related to family matters that needed some kind of action.

One evening, after a particularly grueling day, Nik received a phone call from her mother. Marina called to tell her daughter that she had found the engagement ring that Myron had given to Niki. "It was on your dresser, Niki. What shall I do with it?"

Nik told her mother, "Just give it back to Ron."

Marina refused, and said, "It is your obligation, Niki, not mine, to give the ring back to Myron."

Completely exhausted after her hard day, Nik said, "I can't deal with it right now, Mom, I really can't. Please…just put the ring away in a safe place, and I'll do my duty when I'm able to."

Nothing seemed to be going right. Nik felt the pariah in class and at work, too. She now taught sports pathology to the new crop of sports medicine residents at I.U. Medical Center. And her boss, unbelievably, was GariBALDi; none other than the most aggravating, stilted, pain-in-the-ass, son-of-a-bitch that ever drew breath. He was getting even with her for spurning his advances last spring. Oh yes, he would be the kind of man who would carry a grudge. He always had extra assignments for Nik, and she knew that she was really doing some of the work that he was responsible for. When he took credit, during faculty meetings, for Nik's innovative ideas, too, it made her want to give up teaching because she didn't want to further Garibaldi's career.

After searching for a job other than, or in addition to, teaching, since mid-January, Nik found a promising position in a hospital-based sports medicine clinic. Surprisingly, she was now doing well there, but she saw Ron, sometimes up close and sometimes at a distance, nearly every day. He always spoke to her, and she returned the courtesy, but the strain of proximity was difficult for both of them.

Nik knew that her mother was right about the engagement ring. It was Nik's responsibility to give Ron back his ring. *I'm a coward*, she thought. *Why can't I just be honest with Ron, and tell him what happened, and that none of it was his fault?* All she knew was that she loved Pete, and had loved him, probably, from the moment that she first saw him. That wasn't her fault, or Pete's, and it wasn't an indication of shortcomings on Ron's part.

The only person that Nik had to confide in now was her friend,

Stephanie, who was also an instructor in the sports medicine program. It was Stephanie who had come to talk to Nik in her condo when she was a total mess after Pete left. Stephanie had forced Nik to get out of bed, and then made her help to clean up the condo, open the blinds, and get everything back in shape again. She also helped Nik into the shower, where Nik wailed and cried while Stephanie scrubbed her and washed her hair. With all of Stephanie's kind attentions, Nik became a functioning human being again. Or was it just that Nik wished she was?

Stephanie Trent was a no-nonsense kind of young woman who had a mind of her own. She came from a very large family of thirteen children. In birth order she was number thirteen, and had become very independent at an early age. Given the psychology of numbers as they relate to birth order in families, Stephanie could have turned out to be quite different than the self-assured, talented, ambitious young woman that she was.

String bean thin, Stephanie was a full head taller than Nik. We are "Mutt and Jeff," she would say, and then laugh, because the taller of the old comic book duo was named "Mutt." She told Nik that sometimes she really felt like a 'mutt' because she was the youngest of a rather large litter.

Restless, and worried about what she was going to do with a baby in the busy downtown area of Indianapolis, Nik put her condo up for sale. She had owned it for only four years, but downtown real estate prices had gone through the roof, and she hoped to get a good price for her condo because she had found an old farmhouse for sale on a beautiful private lake northeast of the city. It was only a few miles from the farm where Stephanie's parents lived.

When Stephanie told Nik about it, they made plans to go see the farmhouse together. The sun was shining on the snow and ice covering the ground as they drove into a long driveway. A large, two-story Craftsman-style white house came into view when they passed a large stand of pine trees. Nik immediately fell in love with the wide porch that wrapped around two sides of the house.

"It's got a veranda, Steph, a beautiful veranda! We'll put chairs and swings and rockers there and we can sit on the porch this coming summer and drink iced tea with lots of lemon and look at the lake." Nik was breathlessly excited by what she saw.

The elderly couple who lived there, Joy and Mason Wright, were delighted to have an interested potential buyer, and showed Nik and Stephanie through the house, proudly pointing out the flawlessly maintained hardwood floors and gorgeous woodwork that they had restored when they bought the house. The area that they called the living room had a high ceiling with the original dentil mold trim. The room was large and Mason said that he had measured it at thirty by forty-two feet when he bought the house thirty years ago. A wide staircase rose to the second floor on the far wall. Bookcases were built into the wall beneath the staircase so that there was no wasted space. There was a huge native stone fireplace covering half of one wall that had an inviting fire that crackled as it burned.

Nik looked around the room, and she could picture Pete sitting by the fireplace, a book in his lap, napping in front of the crackling fire on a winter afternoon. She ached with a deep longing to see him there, and for a moment she had to gather herself before continuing the tour with her hosts. Only Stephanie took note of Nik's momentary lapse, and she touched Nik's shoulder to let her know that she was there for her.

The Wrights showed Nik and Stephanie through the rest of the house, and Nik found that she liked what she saw. One room, in particular, caught her eye on the first floor. If ever there was a place for Pete's red room, this was it. The room was furnished as a guest bedroom, but Nik could envision bookcases full of books, and overstuffed leather furniture, with a large desk in one corner. The view from the three tall windows in the room was nothing short of spectacular. The lake could be seen from two windows, and a wooded area behind the house could be seen from the third.

The kitchen, although dated, was quite functional, and it was furnished with an antique table and chairs. A bay window with a bright yellow chintz upholstered seat looked out toward the lake. The cupboards had glassed-in doors, and Nik liked the idea that she would be able to see what was in each one. There was a kitchen island, too, where cookies, cakes and pies could be prepared, among other things. How wonderful, thought Nik.

The second floor had four bedrooms, one of which was large enough to be a master bedroom. A large bathroom was next door, and Nik thought that the two rooms could be joined by putting a door between them. The other three bedrooms were of a good size. Just right for nurseries, thought Nik. There was a smaller fifth room, too, where she thought a second bathroom could be added when it was needed.

Joy said, "There's a full attic, too. The stairs are behind this door."

Nik and Stephanie climbed the stairs while Joy and Mason stayed on the second floor. Even the attic had hardwood floors! Nik was delighted. There were dormer windows facing in all directions, North, South, East, and West. This could be a wonderful playroom…and she smiled as they descended the stairs.

Nik thanked the Wrights for the tour of their home, "I'm very interested in your house, and I'll send you an offer through my lawyer within the week."

When they drove away, Nik could see in her rearview mirror that the Wrights were giving each other a hug. They seemed to be happy with their prospective buyer, she decided.

Afterward, Nik and Stephanie discussed the pros and cons of the house over milk and cookies at Nik's condo. Although the house was forty-five years old, it was structurally sound, and the woodwork and floors were pristine. If Nik decided that this was the place for her, she could move right in, and make changes while she lived there. The property encompassed the lake, which was nearly fifty acres. Nik loved the idea of living on a lake again.

"I have just one question, Nik. Why do you want to live in a big old house by yourself?" Stephanie was curious.

Nik replied with only one word, "Hope."

For a while, even though Nik had told Stephanie that hope was the reason that she wanted to live in the big old farmhouse, she wasn't really sure why she wanted to buy it. But then, little by little, she came to remember and understand that the old farmhouse was what she and Pete had talked about during some of their 'if only' dreaming sessions. They were deeply in love, alone, and snowed in together at her parents' house during Pete's recuperation from surgery. The realization came to her just before she went to sleep one night, hands across her abdomen, caressing the child within that she and Pete had created during a Midwestern blizzard.

She still called him Uncle Les. Nik phoned Les Barnes the following morning and asked him to put together an offer for the property on the little lake.

"We don't have to deal with a realtor, Uncle Les, because the owners are selling the property 'FSBO.' You know, 'for sale by owner.'"

"What about your condominium, Niki? Are you going to do a contingency buy/sell?"

"I have an offer pending on my condo, and I want you to look at it and tell me if it's okay legally."

"Let's have lunch, Niki…uh, let's see, maybe Wednesday? How does that sound?"

"You name the place; only, it's got to be pretty close to downtown. I'm teaching at I.U.P.U.I. and I also have a job in the Ortho Clinic at Methodist Hospital."

"Well," said Les, "there's always Acapulco Joe's. How's that?"

Nik was quiet for a moment, then answered, "That's okay, Uncle Les. Twelve noon?"

"Yes, twelve noon at Acapulco Joe's on Wednesday. I'll see you there, Niki."

Chapter 8

Monday seemed to stretch before Nik interminably; first the class at I.U., and then the ortho clinic. Morning sickness was taking over her life. When Uncle Les had chosen Acapulco Joe's for lunch on Wednesday, Nik, who had always loved the food there, felt nauseated at the thought of eating Mexican food.

Of course, on *this* Monday, Garibaldi chose to visit her classroom. After class, he told her that she'd have to change her style of teaching, because he thought that she was speaking above the students' ability to understand. To her credit, Nik heard him out quietly, without showing any outward signs of emotion.

Finally, in a controlled voice, Nik said, "You will leave me alone; from this moment on you are going to leave me alone to do my work, *my work*, not yours. I have four reasons for you to do this, and they are, Ann Regan, Trudy Whitman, Laura Brockman, and Sheila Cooper."

Garibaldi's eyebrows were arched so high that it looked as though he had hair, "What…what are you talking about?"

"Each of the four women, whose names I just mentioned, was harassed by you. Three of them have witnesses. You tried to do the same thing to me, but I want you to know that I am seeing my lawyer the day after tomorrow. I'm going to dig a hole for you so deep, that when you fall in, you'll never be able to slither out."

All Garibaldi could do was fume and sputter. He now knew that *she* knew about what he had done in the past.

"You can't..." he began heatedly.

"Oh, yes I can. I don't need you like an albatross hanging around my neck. I am no longer going to do your scut-work, so you'd better start thinking about how you're going to get your own work done."

Nik stood up and walked away from him, brushing her hands together, dusting him off. No more Garibaldi; *how wonderful,* she thought.

Between teaching and her clinic duties, Nik chose to nap rather than to eat lunch. One of the things that she had not realized about pregnancy was that mothers-to-be usually needed more sleep.

Nik found a treatment table in the clinic that was far away from any activity through the lunch hour, pulled the curtain, and fell asleep very quickly.

From a distance, Ron Michael watched Nik as she wandered into the treatment area of the clinic. She seemed to be listless and tired, and he wondered if she might be ill? Working near her, or anywhere in the same vicinity, was painful for him. Even though she spoke to him, and was polite to him, just knowing that she was no longer his fiancée hurt him deeply. It hurt, too, to know that at least part of what happened between them was his fault. He had neglected her, had failed to let her know that she was the most important person in his life. And for that he had paid dearly. He had lost her to Peter Genchenko.

After about one o'clock, patients started to come in for their examinations and treatments. Ron wondered where Nik had gotten to, so he started looking for her. When he found her sleeping on one of the treatment tables, he didn't know what to do. He had just about decided to take it upon himself to awaken her, when he noticed Stephanie Trent coming into the clinic, and walked over to her.

"Stephanie, I need to talk with you a moment." Ron knew that Stephanie was Nik's best friend.

He quickly explained his dilemma to her, and Stephanie agreed to check on Nik. It relieved Ron to know that Nik wasn't going to have a problem now. He didn't wish her ill. A few moments later, to his relief, Stephanie came into the treatment area with Nik in tow. Nik was pale and a little 'out of it,' but he was glad that Stephanie had helped her.

Later in the afternoon, there was a commotion in the clinic, and as senior resident, Ron had to go see what was wrong. It was Nik. She had fainted, and was surrounded by nurses who were assessing her and checking her vital signs. Ron asked one of them to find Stephanie, and then he quickly got the information from the nurses' assessments of Nik. What's going on here, he wondered?

Nik awakened to Ron's face hovering over her, filled with concern. He didn't say a word, because Stephanie came hurrying over with the nurse that Ron had sent to find her. He immediately turned Nik's care over to Stephanie and left the clinic. He couldn't handle what had just happened to Nik, and he had to get away.

Stephanie took Nik home, and after she fixed something for Nik to eat, they sat and talked about what was happening to her.

"Okay Nik, what's going on?"

The sandwich and milk began to revive her, and Nik's weakness and dizziness were subsiding. But she didn't want to have this conversation; not even with her best friend.

Stephanie was assertive, some would even say aggressive, perhaps due to her birth position as the 'last of the litter' of thirteen children. She was always direct, and it was 'take no prisoners' when she began an interrogation.

"Please tell me that you used precautions when you were with Peter Genchenko," Stephanie stood above Nik with her arms folded and a serious look on her face.

"I don't want to talk about this, Steph," Nik was ghostly pale, and her face was a study in sadness.

Stephanie shook her head in wonder, "You're a *doctor*, for God's sake. You certainly knew the consequences of unprotected sex."

"Enough, that's enough, Steph. I can't explain my conduct to you because *I don't understand it myself.* When Pete and I were together, it didn't occur to me that something…would happen. No, that isn't really true. But so much of what happened was a result of the way we felt about each other. We were overwhelmed, but we resisted, we tried very hard, both of us, not to get involved. One night, it just happened, Steph, and then the storm hit, my parents were called away to help when my uncle had a heart attack, Ron was on his way to Chicago, and Pete and I were alone for several days.

"The time we had together was wonderful. And, if you can believe this, Steph, Pete took care of *me*, not the other way around. He was so protective, and even though we didn't have electricity, he managed to keep us warm and well-fed because he started up Dad's generator. Remember, he was only a week and a half post-op, but *he was the one* who kept us safe. We got to know each other as well as any newly married couple on their honeymoon. We shared our histories, our hopes and dreams…everything. If I had it to do over again, I'd do the same thing, except," she wiped tears from her eyes, "I'd follow Pete to Russia."

Stephanie watched Nik's face as she spoke, and began to realize that her friend hadn't done something stupid. No, she decided, what had happened to Nik was something that very few people ever really get to experience. She fell deeply in love with a man who felt the same way about her.

"You're pregnant." Stephanie's analysis was succinct.

Nik nodded and said in a small voice, "Yes, and I'm scared to death. I don't know what I'm going to do without Pete." Huge tears formed at the corners of her eyes and started to run down her cheeks.

"But Nik, couldn't it be Ron's? You were engaged. Maybe...?"

"No, Steph, I'm sure that Ron isn't involved."

"How can you be so sure? Did you and Ron always use protection? It's really possible, if not probable, that the baby could be Ron's." Stephanie was persistent, as always.

Wiping her eyes, Nik sighed deeply, knowing that Stephanie wasn't going to let this go, and so answered candidly, "Ron and I never had sex, Steph. That's why I'm *very* sure that this baby belongs to Peter Genchenko."

Chapter 9

It snowed again early on Wednesday morning. Damn, thought Nik, another obstacle to overcome. At least the snow isn't a foot deep this time. Nik had the luncheon date with Uncle Les written on her calendar, and even though she seemed to be forgetting some important things recently, the lunch with Uncle Les was not one of them.

Her morning was uneventful at the university. The students were cooperative and even helpful when the opportunity presented itself. Nik kept little round crackers in her pocket, and popped them in her mouth at intervals when she felt most nauseated. Morning sickness is really a bitch, she thought ruefully. And one of the best things about this morning is that Garibaldi is nowhere in sight. I hope that I scared the liver out of him! The thought pleased her greatly.

After class, Nik took New York Avenue to Illinois St. to get to Acapulco Joe's. She knew that the heretofore tantalizing scents wafting from Acapulco Joe's were going to give her some problems, so she parked on Illinois Street and stayed in her car until she caught a glimpse of Uncle Les' new little Porsche. She got out of her car and crossed the street in time to meet him at the front entrance of the restaurant.

"Niki, it's good to see you." Les smiled at her and kissed her on the cheek.

"I'm glad to see you, too. I saw your new Porsche and it looks great in red!"

"It's emblematic of my middle-age crisis. What can I say?" He gave her a boyish grin.

Inside the restaurant, they were seated quickly, and after ordering, started the discussion about Nik's proposed home purchase. Nik was doing okay until the cheese enchiladas that she had ordered were placed in front of her. The scent of the enchiladas, that would have made her mouth water only a month ago, caused her stomach to lurch, and she stifled a gag.

Les thought that he had seen the last of the ravages that morning…all day?…sickness could exact on a woman with his wife's last pregnancy. However, he saw Niki turn almost green right there in front of him. As he watched her, she tried mightily to eat some of her lunch, but she faltered.

"Uncle Les, I haven't felt too good today…" She was pale and her hands were shaking.

"I'm sorry about that, Niki, I'll pay the check and then we can talk in the car, okay? Are you up to that?"

"I…think so," and she put her hand over her mouth, certain that she really *wasn't* up to anything but going home and pulling the covers over her head.

Outside, Nik took several deep breaths of cold, fresh air, hoping that the nausea would go away. Les took her by the elbow and steered her toward her car. They both got into the car, and Les waited patiently until she got control of herself.

Gently, he said, "Helen and I have a big family, Niki, so I've seen morning sickness a few times."

To his surprise, she burst into tears right there in front of him. Les reached into a pocket, pulled out a handkerchief and handed it to her.

"Niki, I'm sorry. Just tell me to mind my own business."

She wiped her eyes and said, "Well, so much for keeping my secret a little while longer. My friend Stephanie knew right away, too."

Les wasn't completely surprised by this turn of events after Peter Genchenko's departure. After all, he and Niki's father, Klaus, had checked on her in her condo after she had broken her engagement with Ron Michael and had fled from her parents' home. Peter's return to Russia seemed to be the cause. Niki hadn't known that Klaus or he were in her condo to see about her, and Les had heard what seemed to be heartbroken sobs emanating from the bedroom in her otherwise dark and empty condo. Les knew that Klaus and Marina were very worried about their daughter.

"Niki, I really don't know exactly what's happened, but I think I have some idea. I was in the training room with your dad after I brought Peter and Coach Grigory back from the police station last December. I saw the look on Peter's face when he looked at you. It was very apparent to me that he was in love with you. You had your back to your dad and me, so we couldn't see your face, but if you felt even a tenth of what Peter was projecting, it was a foregone conclusion that the two of you would get together."

Nik wiped more tears from her eyes and looked at Les, "You know, don't you, that Pete had to have emergency surgery, and that Mom and Dad asked him to stay at their house while he regained his health? We were together because of Pete's illness, Uncle Les, but Pete and I tried so hard not to get involved!

"Pete's team departed for Russia without him, Mom and Dad left to help Uncle Karl when he had his heart attack, and Ron went to Chicago to see his parents. It was a crazy time, but all of these things allowed Pete and me to be alone together. And then the winter storm hit. Do you remember the terrible weather we had last December?"

Les nodded his head, "Yes, Niki, I remember the blizzard. Everything stopped; cars, planes, utilities, everything. It was a bad time for everyone."

"For Pete and me…it was a Godsend! If not for the storm, we wouldn't have had the opportunity to truly understand how much we loved one another. Pete's an honorable man, Uncle Les, he really is. And he didn't seduce me or force me to do anything. He's a good man; decent, kind and honest. We talked at length about his obligations to his mother and sister, and I understood that he had no choice but to go back to them in Russia.

"Pete has no idea what's happened to me. If he did, I think that he would be heartbroken that he couldn't be here with me. He's had a hard life, and he wasn't the one who told me that. It was his coach, Grigory Serov, who told me about it. Have you ever heard of Ivan Genchenko, the author?"

Les frowned, "I'm not sure. He's related to Peter?"

"He was Pete's father, and he died just before Pete came to Indy to play hockey at the International Winter Games. He was a Russian dissident who spent the last ten years of his life in prison for his politics. Before that happened, Pete's family was wealthy, but they lost everything when Ivan went to prison. Pete became the head of his family when he was only twelve, and they were forced to move to a place called Lyubertsy, an industrial city southeast of Moscow."

Well, that accounts for Peter's excellent manners and his easy ability to interact with people, thought Les. As he digested what Niki was telling him, he began to understand Peter's dilemma. What a terrible choice the kid had to make; his family or the woman he loved. That's one hell of a decision any way you look at it, he thought.

"Niki, I'm not going to say anything to your parents about your situation. You're an adult, and it's up to you whether or not you want to tell them. I'll help you in any way I can. Just tell me what you need."

Fresh tears came to her eyes, and she wiped them away with Les' handkerchief before she answered him, "I want to buy a farmhouse that my friend, Stephanie, and I found. I don't want to live in my condo anymore. Besides, it's not a place to raise a child. I'd like to have you draw up an offer for the farmhouse and land. My condo has already sold on Monday of this week, and I got more than three times what I originally paid for it, so I'm in good shape there."

"You already sold your condo?" Les wondered if Niki was thinking straight and if she had gotten a fair price for her property? "I thought that you and I were going to talk about that today."

"Yes, I intended to talk to you today about it, but the price I got for my condo was incredible, so I took the offer. I'm really serious about this, Uncle Les. If you want to look at the farmhouse before you write the offer, I can take you out there to see it. The owners are very nice, and you could talk to them directly about what they're asking for the property."

"All right…when would you like to go?"

"I'll call the Wrights and see what's best for them, and then I'll call you. Is that okay?"

"Sounds good, Niki. Uh, who is Stephanie?"

"Stephanie Trent. She's one of the best friends anyone could ever have. She told me about the farmhouse, because it is only a few miles from where her parents live."

"I see. Well, get back to me on visiting the farmhouse, Niki."

"Oh, and Uncle Les? There's one other thing. A doctor, one of my supervisors, is trying to give me a hard time. He's done this to other female medical residents, too, but right now, I can't handle the harassment. Is there something that can be done?"

"What's the bad guy's name?"

Nik had a look of distaste on her face as she spoke the name, "Garibaldi. He's the Acting Dean."

A wide grin began to spread across Les' face, "I know the man socially. He's a real pain-in-the-ass. Uh…I'm sorry, Niki."

But Nik agreed, because her Uncle Les was oh so right, "He's a nasty man, Uncle Les."

"I guarantee you, Niki, that he won't be bothering you again."

Nik's eyes teared anew, "Thanks, Uncle Les, I really can't thank you enough. I'll call you when I can set up a time with the Wrights to see the farmhouse."

Les waved goodby to Niki as he walked to his car. He was very worried about her physical condition because he knew about fainting spells and other unpleasant things that happened to the newly-pregnant woman. He waved at her again as he got in his car. "Take care of yourself, Niki," he called out to her. "I'll be looking forward to hearing from you."

They looked at the farmhouse together the following weekend, and Les found the Wrights to be very nice people. It was a marvelous old house, and he could see why Niki had fallen in love with it. But she would be out here all by herself, and that bothered him.

On the way back into the city, Nik talked excitedly about the house, "Well, what do you think? Is it worth their asking price?"

"Well, they're asking one-ten, but I think you could put your offer at ninety-five to one hundred, and probably buy the house."

Les hadn't seen her smile for some time, but she smiled now, "No, I'll pay the Wrights their asking price. I think they need it, Uncle Les."

"Well, usually Niki, the buyer offers less than the asking price…but if you wish, I'm sure the Wrights will be ecstatic to get what they want out of their beautiful old house. There's a lot of land, a lake, and woods, too."

Nik nodded and patted her abdomen, "I want to make sure that everything's perfect when I bring this child into the world."

Chapter 10

Two months to the day of the closing of the sale, Nik moved into her farmhouse. It was late April, and the multitude of shrubs and trees on the property were beginning to bloom. The Wrights had long ago planted a perennial garden in front of the house, and some of the early flowers, the crocuses and buttercups, were blooming.

Nik hired a moving company to pack, move, and then unpack her belongings. Her only helper was Stephanie. The two of them, with the help of the movers, arranged, and rearranged Nik's furniture in various rooms of the old house until Nik was completely satisfied and comfortable with the way things looked. The English Country furniture that had looked so out of place in Nik's condominium looked right at home in the farmhouse. The only problem was that there was not enough of it to even begin to furnish the house. She had her work cut out for her.

In the living room, Nik and Stephanie sat down to rest and to have a cup of tea, decaf, of course, in deference to Nik's condition. She wouldn't admit it, but she was very tired. To Nik's chagrin, Stephanie did notice how tired she was, and Nik knew that her over-protective friend would certainly comment on it.

Stephanie turned to Nik, "Sweetie, you've done way, way too much work today. Let's go upstairs and make up your bed and I'll tuck you in before I leave."

Nik was resting one hand on her abdomen, and holding a teacup in the other, "That's the best suggestion I've heard today…well, making the bed, I mean…but you don't have to tuck me in."

Stephanie smiled at the way Nik caressed her slightly rounded belly, "Come on, if you don't move now, you're going to have to sleep on this sofa."

"Actually, that very thought occurred to me, too, Steph." Nik's laugh was gentle.

The two friends went, arm in arm, up the stairs. At Nik's direction, Stephanie had earlier put all of the bed linens in the upstairs hall linen closet, and knew exactly where to find everything. She and Nik made short work of making up the bed, and stacked pillows in a cozy arrangement at the head of the bed as they finished.

As they went back downstairs Stephanie asked, "Are you going to be okay tonight? I mean…by yourself…maybe I should stay with you. What do you think?"

Nik shook her head, "No, Steph, I'm going to be fine. I'm not a bit afraid. This house somehow seems familiar to me, as if I had been here, lived here, before. This is a happy place, Steph, a very happy place."

Nik followed Stephanie to the door to say goodbye. "I'll see you tomorrow at the clinic, Steph, and please, don't worry about me."

It was her first night in her beautiful old farmhouse. Nik lay awake looking up at the ceiling, watching the shadows moving there in time with the movement of the curtains at the open windows. The movement reminded her of the music of Chopin. Her beloved music…she would buy a piano and begin playing again. She listened to the spring peepers, tiny frogs that lived in the wetlands near her new home. There were strange creaking noises every now and then from the house, but they weren't frightening to her.

She felt that this was a new beginning. The old Nikola Kellman is gone, she thought. No more midnight oil for studying or writing, no more fierce competitive spirit. Now, I will rest and await the birth of my…our…first child. Pete's and my first child.

She touched her belly gently and said, aloud, "I love you, little one."

Nik had no money worries, thanks to her trust fund, and thanks, too, to the profitable sale of her condominium. Her investments had been very successful, according to her broker, and her trust fund was funded by her shares of Eli Lilly stock that her parents had accumulated in her name since her birth.

Tomorrow, I'll go to see Dr. Leonard again, Nik decided. Her gynecologist was a kind, older physician, and Nik knew that he was the best choice for her obstetrics needs. Kindness and experience; Dr. Leonard had both qualities in abundance, and she trusted him completely.

She felt only a calmness and deep sense of peace as she lay in her bed in her new home. I'll dream of Pete tonight, she thought, and I'll tell him again that I love him.

Chapter 11

Rain and snow, snow and rain, had been the only constants in Peter's life, with the exception of Katya, for months. Tonight, a cold and rainy Friday in April, he ate dinner with his sister, and finally told her afterward what he had learned about Misha's disappearance.

The news was not good. One of the shift supervisors at the factory, a wiry, small, gray-haired man named Vanya, had come to Peter just before his shift was over to tell him that he had heard that Misha and Mrs. Preslov had been killed and dumped into a field outside the city by two Lyubertsy gang members. At first Vanya, who had always behaved fairly toward Peter and Misha, seemed nervous and unsure of what to tell Peter. But then, the story came out of Vanya in a torrent of words and profanity as he told how Misha had fought with Zuk over an attempt at intimidation, or worse, of one of the women working in the factory. Zuk was perhaps the most violent member of his gang, and had threatened to make Misha disappear.

"Within a week," said Vanya, "Misha was gone. No one could find him, Peter, and Zuk, that rotten, pig-ugly bastard, bragged to all of us about how we wouldn't have to put up with Misha anymore."

"But did you tell the militia about what Zuk said before and after Misha's disappearance, Vanya? Surely the militia would at least have questioned Zuk about his threats against Misha?"

Vanya hung his head and couldn't look Peter in the eye. "No, I was afraid, Peter, and afraid for my family, too. And you know as well as I do that the militia probably wouldn't have listened to me, anyway. They have always turned a blind eye to these gang members. I think the militia are as much afraid of them as the rest of us."

Peter put his hand on Vanya's shoulder, "You have nothing to be ashamed of, Vanya. And I have no right to judge you. Your family must always be your first concern, and we both know that Zuk would have found a way to get even with you if you had talked to the militia about your suspicions."

Vanya looked up into Peter's face, and tears filled his eyes, "If I had your courage, or Misha's courage, I would have told the militia...I would have, Peter. I'm sorry, so sorry that your friend is gone."

Katya took the news very hard, as Peter knew that she would, but he felt that she should know what he had found out. She began to cry, with her hands covering her face.

With words interrupted by sobs, Katya told her brother, "I miss him...very much...Petrosha. We...had so much...in common. We...both wanted the same things...a family, an apartment...of our own. He was a good man, such a good man...and he never caused anyone any harm."

Peter put his arms around her to comfort her. He understood how terrible her loss was, because he had lost Niki. But at least he knew that Niki was safe, and that nothing bad had happened to her. Misha's disappearance was very painful for Katya, and the fear that someone had hurt or even killed him had haunted her since he vanished. Peter had lost his best friend when Misha disappeared, but Katya had lost the man that she loved.

Peter and Katya clung to the sad life that had evolved after their mother died. They tried to eat at least one meal together every day so that they could talk about what was happening in their lives. Tonight, Peter wished with all his heart that he hadn't had to give Katya the bad news about Misha.

Later that night, Peter lay in bed, and as always, he wondered about Niki, and what she was doing? He imagined that she was going about her daily routine, happy and carefree. In his mind's eye, he saw her in her white smock, working with her patients, full of energy, and with a ready smile. At times, if he really wanted to torture himself, he would wonder whether she had gone back to Ron, her fiancé? Perhaps they were even married by now. The cold place in his chest would expand with the thought of Niki in Ron Michael's arms. Peter was a reality-based thinker, and he knew that eventually Niki would begin to pick up the threads of her life again. But that knowledge didn't shut off the aching for her, or the pain of losing her. It only made it more intense. And every night, the ache for her, the longing to hold her, was still there, and it was as strong now as the day he had said goodbye to her.

Chapter 12

After the weekend, Peter followed his usual habit of getting to work a half-hour early on Monday. He didn't like to be crowded by other workers hurrying to the factory. Things could happen in a crowd, anonymous things; a knife here, a length of pipe there, could quickly and easily dispatch the unwary target in a crowd.

When he turned the corner of the block where the factory was located, the old brick and crumbling mortar building loomed ahead, as ugly and uninviting as ever. A pall of smoke visibly hung in the air, acrid as always, wisps blowing in the wind. The morning air was cold and damp, causing Peter to shiver. He walked around a corner of the crumbling building, and the first person that he saw was Vanya. Peter saw that Vanya was in a sitting position and leaning against the employee entrance door. His arms and legs were at unnatural angles, his head bloodied, and a large groove of flesh was carved away from his forehead to the bridge of his nose. A length of bloody pipe, the weapon of choice of many Lyubertsy gang members, was discarded on the steps. Vanya, Peter knew, was dead, and he vomited at the sight of the man who must have suffered terribly before he died. Vanya, who had been alive, so alive, when Peter had talked to him last Friday, was dead. Peter felt a terrible guilt and remorse at having involved the innocent man in his search for Misha. Vanya was dead because of him. *It's my fault, my fault!*.

When the militia arrived two hours later, they questioned a few employees, including Peter, and then left the premises. The body was taken away, but the body fluids, the blood, urine, and feces, from the deceased remained smeared on the door, and the stairs leading to the door, of the employee entrance.

Peter felt sick at what had happened to Vanya, and he believed it had something to do with what Vanya had told him last Friday. He was mulling this over as he went into the area where he usually worked. It was a huge, sooty, debris-strewn room with a two-story ceiling. There were multiple chains hanging down from an overhead crane on the ceiling used to lift the sometimes heavy loads of axles and other equipment. Crates and wooden boxes were stacked haphazardly everywhere, and axles were stored in triangular stacks all over the concrete floor of the room.

The area was deserted, as none of the other workers were there, yet. But then Peter saw Zuk and three other members of the Lyubertsy gang coming in through another door. Peter didn't allow fear, however, to overtake him. His senses were immediately heightened, and he became very calm and deliberate.

"Genchenko, we heard that someone's been spreading lies about us, and we wanted to talk to you about that." Zuk smiled as he spoke, but the effect was that of a dog baring it's yellowed teeth.

Peter looked at means of exit, but not for himself. He wanted to make sure that these mongrels would not be able to escape when the fight started.

When Zuk saw Peter looking at the exits in the area, he smiled again, and nodded at his confederates to cover any escape routes, "You're not going to get away without talking to me, Genchenko."

"Perhaps you should consider that *you* may need to escape before we are through here, Zuk." Peter's normally deep voice had a harsh and menacing quality to it.

Peter's reply made Zuk look up sharply and a cunning wariness appeared in his eyes. He quickly looked to make certain that his gang members were still in place. Zuk then pulled a foot-long length of pipe from the back of his trousers and began swinging it through the air, making a swishing, whistling sound.

"Is that what you used on Misha and Vanya?" Peter's voice was low and menacing as he walked toward Zuk. In a few short steps he could smell the man's body odor. Anger began to build to a boiling point inside Peter.

Zuk and his friends all laughed, and Zuk answered, "Yes, it's something that no one can say is illegal. It's not a gun or a knife, but it's just as effective." Again he bared his yellowed teeth in a smile.

Before Zuk realized that he was under attack, Peter picked up a wooden box and hit him in his midsection, knocking him to the floor. Peter then bounded up onto two crates and leapt down on one of Zuk's friends, pinned him down, punched him full in the face, and thus took him, and a few of his teeth, out of the fight.

One of the other would-be attackers made a half-hearted assault on Peter. He actually grazed Peter's head with his length of pipe, but he was soon airborne, and landed painfully in a large pile of axles. The other gang member bolted out the exit that he was supposed to guard. He cowardly left his friends and leader to their own devices.

Zuk was writhing on the floor and holding his chest, when Peter returned to his side. Zuk's eyes were bulging in terror, and sweat poured down his forehead. He tried to speak, but could not. Peter didn't know it at the time, but he had broken three of Zuk's ribs when he had hit him with the wooden box.

Peter pulled Zuk up by the hair so that he could speak into his ear, "You admitted to me just now that you killed Misha and Vanya, and now I will see that justice is done. But first, I want to know where you dumped Misha's body? Misha deserves a decent burial. If you lie to me, I will come after you. Do you understand? *Do you understand what I am saying?*"

With grunting breaths, eyes wild with fear, Zuk answered as best he could, "He's...he's on the Shavarovsky property, near the west building. But I didn't kill Misha! Someone else, I'm not sure who, killed him, and I was told to dispose of the body, that's all."

"And Vanya? Who killed Vanya?" Peter was furious that the one man who had tried to help him find Misha had been killed because of it.

"Edvard, it was Edvard! He was told by someone in Moscow, I don't know who, but he wanted Vanya out of the picture. *That's all I know!*" he whined.

Peter's co-workers slowly came into the axle transport area, looking around fearfully. One of them, a young man named Sasha, his eyes as big as saucers, came up to Peter.

"You're bleeding, Peter. You need to see the health officer. She will probably put some stitches in your scalp. What has happened here?"

Peter hadn't realized that he had been injured, and put his hand to the right side of his head. When he looked, there was blood on his fingers. Still numb with the fierce anger that he had felt during the fight with

Zuk and his cronies, Peter had not felt any pain from the wound.

"Thanks, Sasha, but please, call the militia and tell them to come back. They need to talk to Zuk and his gang about Misha and Vanya."

Zuk put his hands up in supplication, "No, please don't do that, Sasha," he wheezed. "They'll put me in prison. I can't go to prison!"

Sasha spat at him, "Shut up, you swine. You've made everyone's lives in this factory miserable with your bullying and your gangs. Now it's your turn to suffer!"

After he had five stitches placed in his scalp by the factory 'medical officer,' who had no real training in health care of any kind, Peter found a cab and went directly to the deserted Shavarovsky Plant. It had once been the site of a productive manufacturer of automotive parts, but it had been closed for more than ten years.

He searched the filthy, debris-strewn, weed-choked grounds around the west building for two hours before he found Misha. It was the hair, really, that caught his attention; Misha's pale blond hair. There was little left to identify the body, otherwise. And Peter saw the white hair of another corpse, rolled into a bun on the top of the head. Dear God, Peter thought, it's Misha's mother. Why did they kill Misha's mother? On his knees next to the remains of his friend, Peter prayed for Misha's soul, and that of his mother. Peter wept bitter tears as he knelt on the ground. How am I ever going to be able to tell Katya that Misha is really dead?

Chapter 13

Peter was taken to Militia headquarters for questioning after he reported that he had found Misha. He was told by a militiaman that Chief Investigator Marc Terenoff was to be his interrogator. At first, no one there paid any attention to Peter, but then an older investigator who recognized the Genchenko name came into the holding area where Peter was being detained. He asked Peter only two questions.

The first was, "Where were you born?"

Peter answered, "Moscow."

The second question was, "Are you the son of Ivan Sergeivich Genchenko?"

Peter didn't hesitate. "Da, *yes*" he said.

"Ah," said the investigator, who then turned abruptly on his heel and walked out of the room without uttering another word.

Chief Investigator Terenoff opened the door of interrogation room three slowly, where his assistant had placed Ivan Genchenko's son at Terenoff's request. He looked at Peter with hooded, almost oriental, black eyes as he entered the room, closed the door, and sat down in a chair opposite to Peter. Terenoff was a thin, dark-haired man of average height. He did not speak, nor did he move one muscle in his body, while he stared at Peter for several moments.

Finally, he said, "Genchenko?"

Peter nodded, "Da."

Terenoff cleared his throat, and then waited again before speaking, "You could have denied that Ivan is your father, but you didn't."

"Why deny the obvious? You already know that I am Ivan's son."

"Well," said Terenoff, "you seem to have inherited his brass balls, but we shall see."

Terenoff got up from his chair and began pacing back and forth as he watched Peter. He walked behind where Peter was sitting and continued to pace. He watched closely to see if there was a flinch, a tremor, or any sign that Peter was frightened of him. There was none that he could detect. Like father, like son, he thought.

He turned his chair around, straddled it, and sat down in front of Peter again, "How well did you know the deceased?"

Sadness welled up inside Peter as he answered, "He was my best friend."

Terenoff noted the change in Peter's demeanor, "Was there a falling out, an argument between the two of you?"

Peter shook his head, "No, we got along very well. Misha is...was...engaged to marry my sister."

Terenoff's eyebrows went up slightly, "How long did you know the deceased?"

Peter didn't hesitate, "Misha befriended me when we were twelve years old. As the son of Ivan Genchenko, I was an outcast. No one in our school had the courage to be kind to me, except Misha. I couldn't afford to buy books, so Misha shared his with me. When I had no lunch, he gave me half of his.

"Misha was the reason that I was given the opportunity to play hockey with the Red Army Team. He convinced the school coach to let me try out under Misha's name so that there would be no bias against me. It worked, and I wasn't thrown off the team when the Red Army coach found out, because by then, we were winning games. That was the kind of person that Misha was."

The Chief Investigator pondered this answer for several moments. He took out a cigarette, and offered one to Peter, who declined. Terenoff was silent as he lit his cigarette. After he inhaled and exhaled several deep puffs, he turned to Peter again.

There was smoke drifting from his nostrils and mouth as he spoke, "When did you first realize that your friend was missing?"

"I was out of the country with the Red Army Hockey Team last December, and when I returned home, my sister told me that Misha was gone. They were engaged, as I told you, and she was very upset about his disappearance. Our mother was quite ill and passed away on the day that I returned, so my sister and I had to make arrangements for her funeral before I could start to look for Misha.

"I got several warnings from the Lyubertsy Gang to let things go and stop asking about Misha, but I continued to try to find out what had happened to my friend. When one of my supervisors, Vanya, told me that there had been a bad situation between Zuk Belov and Misha, I questioned Zuk. But that didn't lead anywhere. The next thing I knew, Vanya was killed, and I was attacked by Zuk and some of his friends."

"And what was the outcome there?" The investigator was curious as to what this man would say, even though he already knew what Genchenko had done to three of the four men who had attacked him.

"Zuk decided to tell me where I could find Misha's body. And, it was where he said it would be."

"I see," said Terenoff, who was amused by Genchenko's low-key version of what actually happened.

Peter was exhausted by the time Terenoff told him that he could leave. The Chief Investigator stood in the front entrance of the militia headquarters and watched as Ivan Genchenko's son walked away, shoulders square, back straight, head up, without looking back.

When Peter turned a corner and was out of Terenoff's sight, the Chief Investigator returned to his office and called one of his staff, a woman, who specialized in under-cover operations. Lara Danilova appeared in his doorway almost immediately.

"Da? What is it this time?" There was no love lost between Lara Danilova and Marc Terenoff.

Terenoff waved her in and said one word, "Peace."

Lara replied, "A truce, perhaps…" Her bitterness against him had a long history, going back several years to a case the two had worked together that ended badly in the death of an innocent man.

"You have just completed the robbery/murder case against the Chechen mafia soldier, is that correct?"

"Of course, you know that the case is locked down. All I have to do is testify against the butcher, and then I am finished. However, if the Lyubertsy Chief Prosecutor releases my identity, I might not live to work another case." Lara shrugged her shoulders.

"Prakovski is honest, as far as I know," said Terenoff defensively.

"Da…as far as you know…" Lara's lips were tightly pursed, and her arms were crossed on her chest as she stood before Terenoff.

"Sit," he told her, nodding to a chair in front of his desk.

"I prefer to stand."

Terenoff's brows were knit, and he shook his head. "It wasn't a request, Lara."

"That does not matter to me. Now, what do you want?"

Terenoff exhaled audibly, "I have another assignment for you. Do you know the name Ivan Genchenko?"

"Da, who doesn't? But why are you asking me this? You know that Ivan Genchenko is dead."

"Lara, you're not making this easy for either of us. All I want you to do is keep an eye on Ivan's son, Peter. Somehow, the Lyubertsy gang *and* the Chechen mafia have it in for him. I want you to *protect* Peter Genchenko. I have the feeling that he could be the key to slowing the drug trade in Lyubertsy."

"Are you saying that he is somehow involved with the Lyubertsy gang or the Chechens? Is he a dealer?"

"Nyet…nyet…not involved, Lara; targeted. They killed Peter's friend, Misha…uh, Mikhail Preslov, because he may have known or found out too much about their operations, and I believe now that Peter may be next. For some reason, he has angered not only the Lyubertsy gang, but the Chechen mafia hierarchy. Perhaps Genchenko also knows too much, or they think that he does. In either case, his life is in jeopardy, and I don't want anything to happen to him."

"How refreshing, and how different your attitude now is in regard to a man who is innocent. Genchenko must be of some value to you…?"

Terenoff lost his temper and pounded a fist on his desk, "Damn it, Lara! I'm trying to do the right thing, here. *Your* attitude toward *me* isn't going to be helpful to Peter Genchenko. I don't believe that he deserves what the mafia will do to him if they see him as a threat. And…in the meantime, we can keep an eye on gang activity. You agree, don't you, that the Lyubertsy gang activity is out of control?"

Lara Danilova looked down at the floor, contemplating what this case was going to be like. Well, she decided, maybe I can help to save *this* innocent man.

"All right," she finally replied. "I will try to protect Peter Genchenko. The Chechen mafia, unbelievably, still do not know who I am, and neither do the Lyubertsy gangs. I will need to know where Genchenko lives, and where he works. I'll take it from there."

"You will need a backup, Lara. Choose someone from this jurisdiction to help you."

Lara didn't hesitate before saying, "*Nyet*, there is no one that I trust enough to help me on this, except you. I will deal with you directly, even if my instincts say otherwise, or I won't take the case."

"Agreed," said Terenoff. "I will watch your back on this, and no one else will know what you are doing. Of course, you know that this is a dangerous course of action for you, don't you?"

Without answering him, Lara Danilova strode out of Terenoff's office. She knew that this was not going to be an easy assignment. But of course, none of her assignments ever were.

Terenoff watched as she turned and walked away from him. He had always admired Lara. There was no doubt that she was the best at what she did. Although she was an attractive woman, her features, hair and eye color were such that she could blend into a situation and not be recognized from previous investigations. Her height, too, was average; not too short or tall. Perhaps it was her spirit that he found beautiful, in spite of his own married state. Marc Terenoff would never act upon his feelings for Lara. But he could not deny that her obvious disdain for him cut him deeply.

Misha and his mother were buried a week after Peter talked to Chief Investigator Terenoff. Peter and Katya searched, but could find no family members for them, and so they were the only mourners at the gravesite. They had scraped together the money for the burials and a gravestone. Misha deserved that much. On the same day, Ivan and Eda Genchenko were also laid to rest, next to Misha and his mother. The ground was now thawed enough to dig into.

Somehow, thought Peter, it helps to know that these four loved ones…yes, I even loved Ivan…are together, keeping each other company here in this lonely graveyard. After the short ceremony, Peter, an arm around Katya's shoulders, walked slowly with her out of the gates of the cemetery.

Chapter 14

Spring melted, literally, into summer, and Lyubertsy became a prime example of thermal inversion, based on pollution. Sometimes the heat was almost unbearable in the apartment, even though all the windows were raised, and Peter squandered some of his hard-earned rubles on an electric fan.

A new tenant, a young woman named Lara Ivanova, moved into Yelena's apartment across the hall from the Genchenkos' apartment. Old Yelena's apartment had been empty for several months after her death from natural causes.

Yelena was a contentious old woman who disliked Peter for some unknown reason. But her passing, too, added to his sadness. So many changes, he thought. My father, mother, Misha and his mother, and old Yelena, all gone so quickly…in the blink of an eye.

Lara, the new neighbor, spoke to Katya often, and the two struck up a friendship. They sometimes walked together on a Sunday afternoon, mostly for companionship.

Katya told Peter, "I don't feel so alone when I'm with Lara. But she seems curious about you, and asks some odd questions at times."

Peter stopped what he was doing, briefly, to consider what his sister had just told him. "I've seen her a few times, and she acknowledges my presence with a smile, but I haven't really spoken with her. What kinds of questions is she asking about me, Katya?"

"She is good-natured, Petrosha, and she just says that you seem to be an interesting man. She wondered how you like your job, and she also asked whether any of the "Lyubertsy gang," as she calls them, have been causing you any problems? She told me that she has a brother who is involved in gang activity, and she is very worried about him."

"How sad for her and her brother. Once someone gets involved with a gang, it's almost impossible to get out of the gang alive."

Peter was concerned for his sister, and was glad that she had someone to talk to, and at least walk with, once in a while. He observed that Katya resembled a pale ghost as she went through the motions of living. Peter tried to help her by going on outings with her, and took her to the museums in Moscow. Among others, they saw an exhibit called "The Treasures of the Czars" and marveled at the opulence, beauty and decadence, yes, unbridled decadence, of the riches that had cost so many Russian lives. Katya and Peter understood the suffering of the Russian people at the hands of the ruling class. Peter decided that if he looked closely enough, he might see some of the Russian Serfs' blood on the exquisitely designed and rendered pieces. He decided, too, albeit late, that this was probably not the type of diversion that Katya needed.

They visited their old apartment building in Moscow on another outing. Of course, they weren't able to see how their apartment looked inside now, but it seemed to give closure to them, just looking at the building where they had once *had* a family, *been* a family. *Once Upon a Time*...as the fable goes, thought Peter.

He bought train tickets for Tver on a Saturday in late August, and took Katya to see the dacha there where they had spent their summers

79

as children. They couldn't tour the inside of the dacha, but were pleased to find it in good repair on the outside. Their mother's perennial flower garden was still there, and was blooming in a riot of late summer color. Brother and sister sat for a time in the grass on a hill up and behind the dacha, overlooking the lake where they had learned to swim as children. It was pleasant to see the sun glinting off the water, and to watch several brightly-colored sailboats skimming across its surface, tacking back and forth, just as they had seen them in their youth. At dusk, they finally left the hill and hurried to catch the evening train back into Moscow.

Grigory sent a messenger to Peter's apartment on a Saturday morning in mid-September, asking him to stop by the Red Army arena because there was a letter for him there. It took Peter several days to find the time to go to the arena. He asked about Grigory, and was told again by Valeria that Grigory rarely came to the arena anymore because of his health. The one constant at the arena was Valeria.

She retrieved the letter for Peter. "It's postmarked from the United States. I hope it's good news for you, Peter." Valeria smiled brightly at him as she told him, "No one has tampered with your mail, Peter, because I hid it from Vladimir so that the Magistrate wouldn't find out about it."

When Peter saw the handwriting on the envelope, he began to tremble. It was Niki's handwriting. Even though it was in Cyrillic, it was Niki's handwriting. He remembered seeing her physician's progress notes, handwritten, about him when she had wanted to reassure him that there was nothing damaging in those notes that Yakov, Grigory, or Vladimir might misconstrue.

"Is something wrong, Peter?" Valeria couldn't help but notice the look on his face.

Unable to speak, Peter shook his head, and then found his voice, "No...no, but this is so unexpected..."

Peter thanked Valeria and left the arena without talking to any of his former teammates, who were on the ice practicing. He was in turmoil. He wanted to open the letter, but didn't want to do so in a public place. Peter ran as quickly as he could to the train station to take the train back to Lyubertsy.

It was late afternoon when Peter returned home. As he reached his apartment, the door across from him opened and Lara Ivanova stepped out into the hall. She nodded her head and smiled at him. Peter nodded his head in acknowledgement, but his anxiety over the letter in his pocket kept him from stopping to speak to his neighbor.

The apartment was empty as Katya was still at work. Peter knew that she would be home by dinnertime, so he put some water, vegetables, and a scrap of meat to flavor them, on the small stove to cook slowly over a low fire. He then went to his bedroom, pulled the curtain and sat down on the edge of his bed to open and read the contents of the letter from Niki. With shaking hands and clumsy fingers, Peter opened the envelope, pulled out the letter inside, and began to read Niki's words.

Katya came home in a good mood on this Saturday evening. Although the weather had begun to cool considerably, she liked September and preferred it to the heat of summer. Her three kilometer walk from her job was exhilarating when the weather was like this.

Upon entering the apartment, Katya called out to her brother, "Petrosha? Are you here?"

There was no reply, but Katya could hear something coming from the direction of the kitchen. She looked on the stove, and decided to turn off the meat and vegetables cooking there before looking further for Peter. And then she heard a coughing sound coming from her brother's bedroom.

"Petrosha?" she called before pulling back the curtain.

Her brother was sitting on the edge of his bed, rocking back and forth, with tears running down his face. In alarm, Katya knelt down in front of him.

"What is it? What is wrong, Peter?" She reached for his hand, and saw an envelope there.

Wordlessly, he handed it to her, and when she took out the contents, Katya saw a photograph. It was a photograph of a newborn baby, and there was a letter with it.

> My Darling Pete,
>
> It has taken me a week to write this letter. I wasn't sure what to say to you, because we have not been in contact since you left. After getting Uncle Les's advice, I realized that it is important for me to tell you that you have a son.
>
> He was born September 7, and he weighed eight pounds and three ounces.
>
> His length at birth was twenty-two inches, so there is a good chance that he will be tall like his father. As you can see from his picture, he has a nice head full of dark hair. He's a beautiful baby, Pete, and when I look at him, I can see you looking back at me, even though he is dark-haired and dark-eyed.
>
> I have named our son Nicholas Petrovich. Everyone loves him; my parents, my brother Mike, Uncle Les, and anyone who has seen him. Most of all, he means the world to me. I now understand the true meaning of life, because

I hold it in my arms every time that I hold Nicholas.

Our son will be raised in a loving atmosphere, and he will know his father.

I will tell him about you every day, as long as I draw breath.

I love you now, and forever, and I miss you terribly,

Niki

"I have a son, Katya…a son! But I will never be able to see him or hold him, or tell him that I love him."

Peter put a hand to his forehead and wept in deep, hoarse, wracking sobs. He was inconsolable, and Katya understood why that was so. Her brother had no hope of ever seeing, or holding, or interacting in any way with his son. Katya could hear hopelessness and heartbreak in Peter's sobs, and she hugged him as he cried.

Peter slowly wiped his tears away and stood up, "I'm sorry, Katya, I should act like a man, but I don't know what to do now, I just don't know what to do. I would give anything to be with Niki right now, and to be with our son."

Katya understood Peter's grief because she, too, would give anything to see Misha again. She looked at the photograph of the newborn. Nicholas Petrovich, she thought, you are a beautiful child, and if you are anything like your father, you will be a good and honorable man.

Peter answered Niki's letter the next day. His hand trembled as he wrote these words:

Dearest Niki,

If it were humanly possible, I would be there with you and our son. He is beautiful, Niki, and I would give anything to hold him in my arms, and tell him how much his father loves him.

Each night, before I go to sleep, I will pray for our little family. My prayer will be that sometime in this life, we will be together. If there is a God, and I believe that there is, he will be merciful, and will hear my prayer for mercy.

There has not been a day that has gone by since we parted, that I haven't thought of you, and that I haven't wished with all my heart that I could be with you. Now, with the birth of our son, my hopes and dreams will be centered on the three of us; our little family.

Please know that wherever you and Nicholas go, my heart will follow you always.

Peter

From that day forward, Peter carried his son's picture in his left shirt pocket, over his heart.

Chapter 15

It was early on the morning of September 7th when Nik felt a twinge, a slight pressure, in the small of her back. She had been to see her obstetrician the day before, and he had told her that things were going to begin very soon, now. She had decorated the nursery in neutral colors that could be used with either blue or pink, and she smiled at the thought. Putting her hands under her belly, she wondered which it might be?

"Things," the doctor had said. Well, these twinges could be the beginning of "things." Yesterday, I was full of energy. I even put the finishing touches on the room that I call Pete's room.

It was a very masculine room, full of books on the shelves that covered one wall, a massive desk and chair, a gaming table and chairs, a dark red leather sofa, chair and ottoman, and a large coffee table. The window coverings were minimal; tailored valances of dark red canvas, with oak shutters half-way up the windows that opened to the view, or closed if privacy was needed. Nik loved the room, and sat there often, thinking of Pete.

Last night, Stephanie had brought Ron to visit her. It had surprised Nik very much, because she had thought that he would never want to be in the same room with her again, especially so in her very pregnant state. Instead, Stephanie masterminded a reunion of sorts; the three had ended up fixing dinner together, and eating on Nik's veranda overlooking the lake.

Stephanie left after dinner with the excuse that she had to go down the road to her parents' home for a visit, leaving Nik and Ron to themselves. At first, their conversation was very awkward and superficial, and they stayed away from what had happened nine months before. But then, gradually, they began to speak of some of the funny times that they had experienced together before the Winter Games. They both laughed when Ron imitated Garibaldi, the Acting Dean of the Sports Medicine School at Indiana University, warming up to some female resident, rubbing his palms together, and that led to stories of Garibaldi's machinations and behind-the-scenes manipulation of the medical staff that he had assembled during the Winter Games. And then there was a lull in the conversation, and a time for reflection and remembrance for both of them.

Ron looked down at the floor for several moments, and finally looked up at Nik to ask, "Why?"

At first, Nik wanted to tell him that there was no easy answer, but that wasn't true. The truth of what had happened was very simple. From the moment that she had first seen Peter Genchenko, Nik was drawn to him. And Peter had told her that it was the same for him.

In an unsteady voice, Nik tried to answer Ron's question, "I think that I loved Pete from the first time that I laid eyes on him. If someone had asked me, before I met Pete, whether I believed in love at first sight, I'd have said, not a chance. I didn't, I wouldn't, act on my feelings, and I tried as best I could to be professional and aloof. I was engaged to you. I had made a promise to be your wife," Nik stopped for a moment, and then continued, "but I couldn't keep it."

"I still don't understand why?" Ron was looking out the window toward the lake, and then turned to face her, his usually bright blue eyes now sad.

"It's something that can't be explained, Ron. If you and I had had that 'something,' whatever it is, nothing could have separated us. But you know as well as I do that we didn't see eye-to-eye on anything. We never even found time for communication, let alone intimacy. Our engagement was a sort of series of vignettes, and there was no time for anything that might have built a relationship. You, and I, too, were so busy doing what our professions demanded of us, that our relationship got lost in the shuffle."

Ron didn't know how to ask his next question, but he nonetheless tried, "Was it my fault, Nik?"

Her answer was immediate, "No, Ron, nothing could be farther from the truth."

"I've been so angry with myself, Nik, and I've blamed myself for what happened because I neglected you."

"Oh, Ron…no, that's not true! Please don't blame yourself. It was my fault, all my fault."

Ron stood up, unable to tolerate the pain that was building inside him, "I'd better go, Nik. This isn't the kind of conversation that you should be having in your condition. I don't want to upset you, honestly I don't."

Nik stood slowly. She had 'blossomed,' but only around her abdomen. In fact, the term glowing, as applied to beauty and good health, also applied to Nik. Ron took this in as he gazed at her. If it was possible, she was even more beautiful in her present state than she was before.

"I want to return something to you. I'm sorry that I haven't given it back to you before now, but I didn't have the courage, and I didn't know how." Nik's eyes, too, were sad as she spoke to Ron.

She left the room for several moments, and returned with a small, ornate box, "This was your great-grandmother's ring, Ron, and I want to give it back to you."

Nik placed the box in Ron's outstretched hand. Neither spoke as each tried to maintain control over the emotions that this exchange had dredged up.

"Goodbye, Nik," he said quietly.

"I'm truly sorry, Ron. You are a good person, a decent man, and you didn't deserve what I did to you."

The house was too quiet after Ron left. Nik went through the house turning off lights and locking doors. Upstairs in her bedroom, she turned on the television just long enough to watch the news while she readied herself for bed. When she finished, she turned off the television, pulled the thick comforter back and slid between the soft sheets.

A deep sense of loneliness engulfed her as she lay there. The guilt that she felt over what she had done to Ron weighed her down. Nik had always been straightforward and honest, almost to a fault, her mother once told her. Betrayal, that's what it was, really. I betrayed Ron.

But then she thought of Pete, and there was no doubt in her mind that what she had done was done in the name of love. The loss of Pete would never get easier. Now, in the last week of her pregnancy, she wished with all her heart that he could be there with her. Knowing that he would not only led to a deeper sense of loneliness and loss. Finally, Nik drifted off to sleep.

Something awakened her. Was it a noise, something creaking in the house, or some outside noise, perhaps? It was daylight, at least. She felt a sense of relief over that. She looked at the alarm clock; six-thirty on the nose. It wasn't long before Nik realized what had caused her awakening. Yes, there it was again. So far, there was no pain, but she knew that there was something different here. She had experienced Braxton-Hicks contractions for the last month, but her obstetrician assured her that these were just practice runs for the real thing. Well, this may be the real thing, she thought, with some trepidation.

Nik's first telephone call was to Stephanie. "It's time," she said shakily.

An early riser, Stephanie shouted, "Yahoooo! Sweetie, is it for real?"

"Yes, I'm pretty sure," Nik was tentative.

"I'll be right there, Nik."

Nik's second call was to her mother, "I'm heading to the hospital in about an hour, Mom. Stephanie is going to pick me up."

Marina tried to be upbeat, "Oh Niki, this will be a very special day for you for the rest of your life. Your father and I will be there at the hospital when you arrive, dear."

"Okay, Mom…wish me luck."

"And prayers, too, Niki, and prayers."

Nik called her obstetrician and got his answering service, so she left a message that she was heading to Indiana University Hospital. Her bag was packed, and all she had to do was take a quick shower, dress, and wait for Stephanie.

As it turned out, the shower was a fortuitous idea, because her water broke while she was showering. She wondered what Pete would have

89

said or done if he had been showering with her, and it made her laugh in spite of her predicament. In order to put her clothes on, Nik had to wear a towel between her legs to absorb the leaking amniotic fluid.

It was a good thing that Stephanie was calm, because, although she tried, Nik was not. Her teeth were chattering, as if she were cold. But she knew that it was only excess energy, with a little fear mixed in. She sat on two thick towels for the ride to the hospital, and Stephanie kept glancing at her to see if she was doing okay.

At the hospital, Nik's parents were waiting for her. Klaus hugged his daughter first, and then Marina kissed her on the cheek. Both had words of encouragement for her, even though they had a certain level of concern about her wellbeing. Nik was so relieved that she and her parents had overcome their differences regarding her broken engagement to Ron, and her relationship with Peter Genchenko, and she was happy that they were here for her. A volunteer put Nik in a wheelchair, and the group went together to the obstetrics unit where all was in readiness.

"Hi, I'm Susie Ryan, and I'll be your nurse throughout your labor and delivery. You're going to LDR 3, and Dr. Leonard called to say that he will be here shortly."

As it turned out, Susie Ryan and Dr. Leonard worked well together, and Nik was very grateful to them, and to Stephanie, who was her labor coach, for the comparative ease with which she went through the next four hours. When she went into the transition phase of her labor, tears of relief streamed down her cheeks because the pain was not as severe. In fact, she was now feeling the need to push, and Stephanie, Susie Ryan, and Dr. Leonard encouraged her to begin pushing.

It was like a well-choreographed ballet, the labor and delivery, and at the end, when Nik was tremendously relieved to be pushing, she wanted so much to be able to hold Pete's hand through this, the birth of their first child. For some irrational reason, brought on by the stress of labor, perhaps, Nik thought of this baby as their first child, as if there would be other births, other babies.

Ron looked in on mother and baby about two hours after their birthing experience. Nik was sleeping the sleep of the exhausted, and Marina was at the bedside, holding her new grandson.

They were surprised to see each other, and at first, neither knew what to say. Then Marina smiled, and beckoned to Ron to come see her beautiful grandson.

"Oh, he's a big boy, isn't he?" Ron smiled back at Marina as he looked at the baby.

"Niki has named him Nicholas, after my father...her grandfather. Don't you think that's nice?"

"Yes, that's a great name." Ron looked around the room, "Where's Klaus?"

"I sent him to the cafeteria to eat something. He wasn't able to eat while Niki was in labor. Even though he wasn't in the room, he still worried about her pain. He did the same with the births of his own children."

Ron nodded in understanding. He had felt the same way when Stephanie told him that Nik was in labor. "Well, I just wanted to make sure that Nik and the baby were all right. I'd better get going. I've got some patients to see."

"Your flowers arrived a few minutes ago, Myron, and they are lovely. It was nice of you to send them."

"Nik deserves them, Marina. Please tell her that I stopped by."

"I'll do that Myron. Come back later if you can, when Niki's awake. I know that she will want to see you."

As he walked down the hospital corridor toward the elevators, Ron wasn't sure of his feelings. There were so many 'what if' issues that he had with Nik. What if they had never worked the Winter Games and what if they had married, and what if this was their first child, a son? His heart ached for what would never be.

Around eight o'clock that evening, Ron went back to see Nik. As he rounded the corner in the corridor, he could see into her room, and she was lying in bed, holding her son, smiling and cooing at him. Ron stopped as his breath left him for a moment, but he recovered quickly and then continued on into the room.

"Hi, Nik," he said softly.

She looked up at him and smiled, "Ron, it's so nice of you to visit us."

Us…Nik was now an 'us,' with her new little one. Ron slowly walked to the bedside, marveling at how fresh Nik looked, considering that she had undergone natural childbirth just a few hours earlier.

Ron's smile was somewhat sad as he answered, "I couldn't stay away, Nik. Stephanie called me this morning to let me know that you were here."

"Thank you for the lavender roses. You remembered that I love lavender roses, and they smell so sweet."

"You're welcome. When are you going home?"

"My doctor says day after tomorrow, but I'd like to go home tomorrow, if I could."

"Who's going to be helping you when you go home? Is your mother going to be there?"

"Everything's all set. Mom's going to be there for the first week, and then Steph is going to take some vacation time, and spend the second week with me. Isn't that generous of them?"

"Yes, very, but maybe you should think about staying at your parents' for a while. Your house is out in the country, and a new baby can be a lot of stress."

"I've thought of that, and I can go to Mom and Dad's, or call Steph, if I need to, so I think we are going to be okay."

"If...you need help, Nik, you can call me, too." Ron was hesitant, but he wanted Nik to know that he would be there for her if she needed him.

"Thank you for offering, but I think that everything is covered right now. But please, do come to visit whenever you like. I'll always be glad to see you."

"Okay, Nik," Ron said slowly. "Well, I've got to get going. Take care of yourself...and Nicholas."

Chapter 16

Everything went well upon Nik's return home with her son. Marina and Klaus were absolutely crazy about their grandchild, and spent a great deal of time with their daughter and grandson.

I'm spoiled, and blessed, too, thought Nik. With Mom, Dad, and Stephanie, and Ron's help at times, Nicholas and I want for nothing. But her next thought was, of course, that it wasn't completely true, because she knew in her heart that the one person who meant the world to her, that she wanted, needed so badly, could never be with her and their son. She would always mourn the loss of her beloved Pete.

When Uncle Les came by to see little Nicholas, Nik asked him what she should do about letting Pete know that he was a father. "I miss Pete terribly...and I wanted him to be there when I gave birth to our child. But I don't want to hurt him any more than I already have. And I don't know how he will feel if he knows that he has a son."

Uncle Les shook his head for a moment, "It's not an easy situation, Niki, but I can tell you how *I* would feel if I found out that I had fathered a child with the woman I love. I'd want to know. Peter has the right to know about Nicholas, and I think that you should tell him. Yes...it's going to hurt him, but, in a way, I think that he will be grateful that you told him."

Nik wrote Peter a letter about Nicholas that very night, and hoped and prayed that he would understand that she did not want to hurt him. She told him just how much she still loved him, and she cried the whole time that she was writing Pete's letter. Before she sealed the letter, she put a picture of Nicholas in the envelope so that Peter could see how beautiful their son was. Early the next morning, she hurried out to her mailbox, flipped up the flag, and hoped that Pete would know soon, very soon, that he had a son.

Nik received Pete's reply during the fourth week of September. By then, she and Nicholas were happily into a smooth routine, and she had sent all her helpers packing, with invitations to, "visit anytime."

She read and re-read Pete's letter a dozen times, kissing his signature each time. When Nicholas was awake, Nik read the letter to him several times, too, as he cooed and smiled at her.

Nik cried for a week, because she realized that Pete was as lonely for her as she was for him, and that he still felt the same love for her that he had when they were together. She kept the letter in her jewelry box, and read it every morning as she was getting ready to meet the challenges that Nicholas would present for the day. Nik didn't share Pete's letter with anyone but Nicholas. Pete had said they were a family, and indeed, they were.

Time passed quickly, and Thanksgiving was Nicholas's first holiday. Marina and Klaus hosted a wonderful dinner that included Nik's brother, Mike, Uncle Les and his family, and Ron as guests. Nicholas was two months and two weeks old, and he now smiled and showed his wonderful little personality. Nicholas-watching was the entertainment for the afternoon, and he seemed to enjoy all the attention, until finally, with a wide yawn, he fell asleep in his mother's arms.

Duchess followed the baby's every move, and seemed as attached to him as she had been to his father. She lay down next to whomever the person might be that was presently holding Nicholas, and would whine when he was handed off to someone else, as if she wanted her turn, too.

"Mike, would you like to hold your nephew, Nicholas, while I pack up his things?" Nik couldn't help but smile at the surprise on her brother's face.

"Uh…sure. Just tell me what I'm supposed to do. I don't have any experience with these little guys."

Everyone in the room laughed at Mike's discomfiture. When Nik handed the baby to him, Mike sat down so that he wouldn't disturb Nicholas's sleep.

"You're doing a great job with the baby, Niki," Uncle Les was beaming at her.

"He's so easy to take care of. I sometimes think that he's going to start talking soon, because when he sees me his eyes will light up and his little hands will just wave around, but I know better than that. It's just that he seems to pay attention to everything that's going on around him. He is a joy, Uncle Les, and I sometimes wonder what I ever did without him?"

It was time to go home, and Marina helped her daughter pack up for the trip. Marina held Nicholas and rocked back and forth with him until he fell asleep again, then she wrapped him up in his little blue bunting with bunny ears. It made her chuckle because this wonderful little baby, her beautiful grandson, didn't look silly in his outfit. Actually, he looked quite handsome, and she gave him an extra squeeze before she handed him to his grandfather.

Klaus, the proud grandfather, took his turn holding his grandson in his little blue bunting. When Niki told him it was time to go, he kissed his daughter on the top of her head and gingerly handed the baby to her.

There were goodbyes and hugs all around. Mike hugged his sister tightly and kissed her on the cheek.

"Come and see me this summer in San Francisco, Niki. I'll look forward to seeing you and Nicholas. And remember, if you need anything, don't hesitate to ask. I've got so much vacation time built up, that I'm never going to be able to use it all, and I'll jump on a plane and be back here as soon as I can if you need me."

"Don't worry about your little sister, Mike. I'm doing fine, and so is Nicholas. I love you." She stood on tiptoe to kiss his cheek.

Since Ron had brought Nik and the baby so that she wouldn't have to pack everything and drive by herself, he took her home, as well. When he looked over at Nik as they were nearing her home, her eyes were closed, and he realized that she must be worn out. This was her first big holiday, and she hadn't been out very much, except for trips to the doctor for routine baby checkups, and a few trips to the supermarket. He knew that it had been a full day for her.

Ron wished that he could do more than just drive Nik home and drop her off. He realized that she must be more tired than her little nap in the car would indicate. Ordinarily, Nik would be polite and try to make conversation while riding in the car, but she had fallen asleep almost immediately. When he pulled into her long driveway, he waited at the house until she began to stir before he called her name. Nicholas was beginning to awaken too, and was making smacking noises with his tiny fist in his mouth.

"Hey Nik," he whispered, "you're home, and we should get you and the baby inside now. I'll bring the other stuff in after I get the two of you settled in the house."

Nik yawned widely, putting her hand in front of her mouth, "I'm so sleepy…sorry, Ron, I'm like a zombie sometimes when I don't get my afternoon nap with the baby."

After getting all the baby things carried in, Ron sat down in Nik's warm and inviting kitchen while she sterilized water bottles for Nicholas. As they made small talk, he watched her go from one task to the next, and then she bathed Nicholas and put his pajamas on him. During the bath, Nik talked and cooed to her son, and both obviously loved the process. Ron felt as if he was an interloper, a voyeur, but he enjoyed seeing Nik and Nicholas together.

Nik went upstairs to the baby's bedroom to breastfeed him, while Ron waited in the great room, watching the news on television. He saw some footage of the Macy's Thanksgiving Day Parade, and it made him feel melancholy, for some reason. Perhaps it was because he had watched the parade last year with Nik at her parents' home, and they had enjoyed themselves while celebrating their new engagement. He had given her a family heirloom for an engagement ring that day, and he had thought at the time that it was the happiest day of his life. Maybe it was…

"He's sound asleep," said Nik as she came down the stairs.

"That didn't take long. He's a pretty good baby, isn't he?" Ron watched her as Nik came over to sit in an adjacent chair.

"Most of the time," she said, "but he's got a temper, too." She didn't add, "like his father."

"You seem really happy, content, Nik, and I'm glad for you."

With a wistful smile, Nik replied, "Yes, I am. The baby and I, well, there isn't a lot of time outside of caring for Nicholas that I have to reflect on other things. And that's good, I think, for now. One of these days, I'll have to decide what I'm going to do with the rest of my life."

"Is there room for medicine? Do you think that you'll practice medicine again?"

"Oh yes, medicine's in my future. I can't live off my trust fund and annuity forever, so I'm going to have to be gainfully employed at something. Medicine is what I know, so that will be where I put my energy…when I have some left." Nik laughed as she spoke.

"I have a reason for asking about whether you might want to practice again. I'm going to start my own sports medicine clinic, and I want you to come and work with me."

"Wouldn't that make you uncomfortable, Ron? You'd see me every day. That would be like rubbing salt…" Nik stopped.

"No, it wouldn't be like that…truly it wouldn't. Anyway, I'm here now, aren't I?"

Nik nodded and answered softly, "Yes."

Chapter 17

That first Winter, with her new baby, and in her own house, Nik remained independent, although there were times when she became a little concerned when the weather turned bad. But she and Nicholas were safe and secure, and they often had visitors. Nik had made friends with several of her neighbors, and one of her favorite couples was Cindy and Aaron Anderson. They had three daughters, and it was fun to see how five-year-old Serena, nine-year-old Alysse, and eleven-year-old Alexandra interacted with Nicholas, who was becoming a very sociable little baby.

They visited back and forth. Nik would host an early Friday evening meal, and the Andersons did the same, sometimes including other neighbors, too. There were times when the snow piled up in her driveway, but Aaron, or one of her other neighbors with snow removal equipment, never failed to plow her drive. Nik reciprocated with her "Friday evening invitationals," as she called them. Domesticity came naturally to her, and her desserts,especially cakes, began to earn her a reputation as a good cook.

Christmas was now only a few days away. After several weeks of whirlwind shopping with Marina and Stephanie, decorating the house outside and cookie baking, Nik was finally prepared for Nicholas's first Christmas. She also put candle lamps in all of her windows, and thought of Pete. Someday...someday, Pete will be with us. And somehow, the candles, shining into the winter darkness, helped to keep her hope alive.

Marina and Klaus came to celebrate Christmas at Niki's house, and brought Duchess with them. They were going to stay for several days at her invitation. Together, they decorated a blue spruce that Klaus had ordered from a nearby nursery to be delivered to his daughter's house in a large container. He wanted her to have a live tree for her first Christmas with Nicholas, so that she could have it planted on her property in the Spring. On Christmas Eve, they spent an hour on the telephone with Mike, who said he'd rather be where it was snowing on Christmas. Yes, they had a wonderful, family, white Christmas, watching Nicholas messily tearing opening his presents. They sang carols by the fire, and ate too much, way too much, of Niki's great cooking.

The only thing missing, no, the only *person* missing, thought Nik, is Pete. Although nearly a year had passed since they had said goodbye, her love for him had not cooled, had not faltered. In a certain sense, Nik had built a life around the one man who was missing from her family circle. She had decorated her home to suit what they had talked about when they were together, and she was living in that home as if he would return to her one day.

The months sped by so very quickly, and there were signs of spring everywhere. Crocuses were poking their beautiful blossoms out of the once-cold ground in the perennial garden in front of Nik's home. Easter...I can't believe it's Easter already, thought Nik. For this holiday, she and Nicholas stayed with Klaus and Marina. They attended a Russian Orthodox Mass, and came home to one of Marina's delicious Russian dinners. Mike called at five to wish them all a Happy Easter and each took their turn talking to him. Mostly, the topic of conversation was how much Nicholas had grown, and, "when-are-you-coming-home-for-a-visit-Mike?"

Nicholas, at seven months, was a busy little boy who was pulling himself up to a standing position on whatever piece of furniture he could get his little hands on. Duchess always sat nearby, one front paw crossed over the other, watching him as if *she* was the proud mama. Ron stopped by to visit Nik and Nicholas in late May to talk about Nik's return to medicine. He was getting everything ready for his Sports Medicine Clinic, and he wanted to know if Nik was still interested in working with him, and with Stephanie Trent, who had also agreed to work in his clinic.

"I've talked to my Mom about looking after Nicholas when I start working in the clinic. She tells me that she can't wait to have him."

"Then you've made the decision, Nik? You're going to work in the clinic?" He was smiling widely.

"It's time to get back to the working world, Ron. And I know that Nicholas will be in safe hands with my parents."

"Do you have a timeframe, yet, Nik? I don't want to push you...but I'm hoping to be up and running in the next month or so."

In July, Nik began working three mornings a week at Ron's sports medicine clinic. It was like a whole new world to her. She had some misgivings about being able to communicate with someone, anyone, older than a ten-month-old, but she managed. And she was delighted that Marina, Klaus, and Nicholas were having a wonderful time together. Nik was grateful that busy little Nicholas was thriving and loving every minute of his grandparents' spoiling.

After the first month of Nik's employment, Ron sat down with her to give her an initial evaluation, "You're doing great, Nik. I couldn't ask for a better doctor here. A lot of the patients are requesting you. Did you know that?"

"It surprises the heck out of me, Ron. I wouldn't have believed that it would be this easy to get back into practice. I can't thank you enough."

In September, Nik and Stephanie planned a wonderful first birthday party for Nicholas. They spared no extravagance, and even hired a clown. The Andersons and several families from church were invited in addition to Marina, Klaus, Uncle Les' family, and Ron. Uncle Mike, as usual, called long distance to wish his nephew a happy birthday. Mike also surprised everyone by singing "Happy Birthday" to his little nephew over the telephone.

Everyone was taking photographs. The kitchen and dining room were constantly lit with flashes of light from busy cameras. Stephanie captured one of Nik with Nicholas in his high chair, a little party hat on his head, eating his cake, or, more accurately, wearing his cake, and holding a tiny pair of ice skates that his father had sent to him.

This will be the perfect photograph to send to Pete, thought Nik. Each month, they exchanged letters, and had done so since the birth of their son. Pete wrote that he considered them his letters of hope, but Nik called them love letters.

Chapter 18

Peter went as often as he could to the Red Army Hockey Arena to vist with his former teammates. He missed playing the game, but he also missed the camaraderie that they had all shared. One of his closest friends on the team, Ilya, confided in Peter that the team was not doing well on the road. Ilya told Peter that they were becoming an embarrassment to the 'powers that be' and that Vladimir really didn't know what to do to revitalize the team.

"Vanya, Dmitri and I have told Vladimir again and again that he should bring you back onto the roster, but he is as stubborn as he is stupid."

"That sounds a little harsh, Ilya, but we both know that Vladimir is nothing like Grigory. If Grigory was still your coach, he'd be very tough on all of you, and you'd start winning again." Peter wished that he could help the team.

"Why don't you go in and have a friendly chat with Vladimir for old time's sake? Maybe he will swallow his pride and invite you back. What could it hurt?" Ilya shrugged his shoulders.

Ilya's suggestion seemed ridiculous to Peter, but he didn't want to insult his friend, and so answered as kindly as he knew how, "I guess I could do that. Katya and I really miss the extra money that my hockey playing gave us. For a little while, we were saving some of my hockey earnings. Now, well, it has been difficult for us."

Peter was loathe to speak to Vladimir about returning to the team. He and Vladimir had never had the rapport that Peter had shared with Grigory. I can't beg, he thought. Vladimir would love to see me grovel and beg. But Peter knew that Katya's safety should be more important to him than his pride. *I must swallow my pride and beg for reinstatement on the team.*

"Hey, Peter!" Mikhail threw open the weight room door. "Did you know that Vladimir has been trying to reach you? I think he's been told by someone higher up that we had better start winning more games, and your name came up. He really wants to talk with you."

"No, I wasn't aware…" Peter spoke and then fell silent, but a small bit of hope began to swell in his chest. *Can this be true?*

"I just saw him in the office, and he asked me whether I had seen you recently. If you're interested, and I hope to heaven that you are, you should go in right now and see what he's willing to offer you. We've got one hell of a schedule starting next week, and we've got to start winning again." Mikhail hooked a thumb over his shoulder in the direction of the arena office.

I have nothing to lose, thought Peter. "Thanks for letting me know this, Mikhail." Peter turned to Ilya, "And thanks to you, too, for pushing me in the right direction."

Ilya smiled widely at Peter, "We all need a little pep talk now and then, my friend, so get going!"

Peter's heart was in his throat as he tapped on the door to Vladimir's office. Somehow it didn't seem right. This office had been occupied by Grigory, and, irrationally, Peter wanted Grigory to answer the door.

"Enter!" Vladimir was a man of few words, as well as few thoughts.

Peter turned the door handle and walked into the office, "Mikhail said you were looking for me…"

Vladimir's eyes narrowed as he looked at Peter. "Well, Genchenko, you are just the man that I wanted to see." He looked Peter up and down. "Are you recovered completely from your illness and surgery in America?"

Peter replied with only one word, "Da…"

Vladimir leaned back in his chair and placed a fist under his chin. "Really? Well, let's see how you can skate. For all I know, you may be out of shape and beyond help. Why don't you come in tomorrow afternoon and work out with the team, say around two o'clock? Maybe I'll have a place for you on the team roster if you look good during the practice."

Peter thought about it for a moment, and then replied, "No, I think you have a place for me now, and I want my salary doubled. When Yakov Popov was in control of the team, he forced Grigory to pay me less than anyone else on the team. By doubling my salary, you will only be paying me what my teammates have been earning all along. I'll come to the arena tomorrow, but you will have to tell me *before* I practice with the team whether you want to pay me a fair salary. I already know that you need me to come back to play for the Red Army Hockey Team."

Peter didn't wait for the stunned Vladimir to respond. He walked out of the office and waved goodbye to Valeria as he passed her on his way out of the building.

Peter knew that he had taken a gamble when he made his demands of Vladimir, but it couldn't be helped. He had not had to beg…no, he had been in control, and his pride was intact. But he fervently hoped that his gamble would pay off. He would know what his fate was to be tomorrow afternoon.

Peter slept well that night after he told Katya how he had bluffed Vladimir. "Perhaps it won't work, Katya, but I cannot allow Vladimir to put me under his thumb. I want to play hockey, I really do, but I'm not going to crawl on my hands and knees for anyone."

"It's going to be all right, Peter." Katya's smile was gentle. "You have such a great talent...I know that you will do well."

The Assistant Minister of Sports, Boris Malenkov, a large, balding hulk of a man, was in the arena stands when Peter took the ice to practice with his former teammates. It had surprised Peter when he recognized the man, and he was puzzled as to why someone of such rank would come to a practice game?

Vladimir had immediately come running to Peter when he had first entered the arena and blurted, "You will have the salary you requested...now get suited up!"

It was as if Peter had never stopped playing with the team, even though there were many new faces. Arkady, Ilya, Mikhail, Boris, Dimitri, Vanya and Slava were still there, but Peter was introduced to several more: Stas, Yuri, Gavriil, Nikolai, Roman, Georgii, Aleksander,and Alexei. Peter was excited by the number of players now. *Sixteen,* he thought, *there are sixteen of us!* There had only been six players on the Russian team when they had won the International Winter Games in America. Only six because of players' injuries, and of course, what Josef and Nikita had done when they had tried to kill him. For a moment, he thought of Niki, and his heart sank. But I must play well now...I can't think of Niki right now...

107

Vladimir divided the players into two teams with eight players on each team. Two players would be rotated out into play for each team as Vladimir saw fit. This was an exhibition game in honor of the visiting Assistant Minister of Sports.

Peter and his teammates mostly ignored Vladimir's hysterical directions and shouted strategies, with his tall, emaciated body nearly bent double at times. Instead, Peter took control of the game, and the coaching. In spite of the number of new players, they all played a lively and very rough game. And…Peter Genchenko could still skate rings around everyone else on the team. No one could catch him as, time after time, he went for the goal and scored as some of his teammates assigned to the other team mightily opposed him to no avail.

After watching more than an hour of mayhem on the ice, Boris Malenkov heaved his bulk into a standing position and waved Peter over to him, "You will rejoin the team, and you will be team captain." He turned to Vladimir who stood next to him, and poking Vladimir in his bony chest with a meaty index finger said, "Do you understand what I have just told this athlete?"

All that Vladimir could do was nod dumbly in acquiescence to Assistant Sports Minister Malenkov's question.

Peter was back on the team, and would again assume the duties of team captain.

Chapter 19

Peter was just returned from a hockey exhibition tournament in Norway, and Katya was very happy to have her brother at home. "It was too quiet in the apartment without you, Petrosha."

Peter hugged his sister tightly, and then held her at arms' length, "Are you well?"

Katya smiled and nodded, "Yes, I'm doing well now, but I did miss you very, very much while you were gone. Lara was kind and kept me company while you were away. She told me that she has finally gotten a job, and you won't guess where…"

"Should I try to guess, or will you just tell me?" Peter held his head to the side and grinned at Katya.

"When you return to your job, Lara will be there, too. She is now a bookkeeper at the factory where you work."

"Really?" Peter was mildly surprised that someone like Lara Ivanova would take a job in such a place. By his own observation, she seemed to be…above that sort of employment. From the few times that he had spoken with her, Lara's speech indicated to him that she was well-educated. And of course, he couldn't understand, either, why she lived in this shabby apartment building where he and Katya lived.

"I have some letters for you, Petrosha."

Katya handed him two letters that Niki had sent, and he immediately sat down to read them, even though he was weary from his flight. Each letter contained photographs of Nicholas, and it amazed Peter how quickly his son had grown.

"Isn't he wonderful, Katya?" Peter handed the photographs to her.

"These were taken on his first birthday, and look at his little hat and all that cake he has smeared on his face." Katya couldn't help but laugh.

In another picture, a smiling Nicholas held up the birthday gift that his father and Aunt Katya had sent to him. Niki was standing behind him, obviously enjoying the tiny pair of ice skates that Nicholas was holding.

Peter studied the picture for a very long time. My beautiful Niki, and my handsome son. Opposing emotions fought inside him; sadness and joy. There was sadness because of the distance that he was from his son and Niki. But there was joy, too, at just being able to see them in the photographs that Niki sent.

While he was traveling with his team, Peter wrote to Niki, and his letters were filled with the sights he had seen, the people he had met, and he ended each with a vow of the unchanging love that he had for her and Nicholas. He always found time to write. In fact, there were times when he couldn't wait to sit down and put his thoughts on paper for Niki and their son. Even though he had other obligations, Niki and Nicholas always came first.

Since Vladimir had asked...begged?...him to come back to play hockey with the Red Army Team, Peter had traveled to Germany and to Norway. He hadn't realized how much he had missed playing and traveling, until he was asked to skate again. His teammates, especially Ilya, were ecstatic that Peter was back with the team. And Peter was thrilled, too, because he could still play the game he loved.

Peter was the missing cog in the Russian team's wheel, although he would never admit it. But they began to win again with Peter Genchenko on the roster. Grigory, who no longer traveled with the team, nonetheless was a presence when it came to handing out recognition. And he did so, even to Ivan Genchenko's son. Grigory's influence, and his contact with Assistant Sports Minister Malenkov were the main reasons that Vladimir had relented and asked Peter to rejoin the team. And of course, there was that little issue of actually winning games. Vladimir was desperate to win games. Peter was instrumental in helping the team to win, no matter the opponent. His teammates loved him. But, as always, Peter had to return to his other life off the ice. What would it be like, he wondered, if he could play professional hockey and not have to worry about having enough money to survive?

The morning after he returned from his hockey travels, Peter easily jogged the distance to his job at the factory. Now when he entered the building, he always said a quiet prayer for Vanya, the man that the Lyubertsy gang had killed. Somehow, the marks left by Vanya's body had resisted the elements. There were still traces of dark blood on the employee entry door. Will they ever wash away?

Just inside the door, Peter saw Lara Ivanova, who seemed to be waiting for someone. "Hello, Lara..."

She was startled when Peter spoke to her, but she recovered quickly. "Hello, Peter. I...I was wondering where I should report this morning. Georgi told me to come to his office, but I couldn't find any directory..."

"As far as I know, there is no directory, but I do know where

Georgi's office is. Follow me."

"It's very kind of you to help me, Peter." Lara sounded relieved.

"This factory can sometimes be…" he hesitated before continuing, "unsafe for a young woman. If you have any difficulties, please let me know. There is much gang activity here, and some of the workers who are gang members can be bullies. Don't let them intimidate you."

Peter's words surprised Lara greatly. He wants to protect me, she thought. And, even though the reverse was true, *she* was here to protect *him*, she somehow felt safe in his company. Lara understood that Peter Genchenko would come to her rescue if she needed him.

"Georgi's office is down at the end of this corridor on the right. Can I help you with anything else?"

Lara shook her head, "No…but I thank you very much for your assistance." She was acutely aware of Peter's presence, his closeness to her, in the narrow corridor. She had never before been so *taken* by a man. And she realized that he had no clue about his effect on her. Was there such a thing as 'benevolent neutrality' she wondered?

Chapter 20

On the third evening that Peter was at home after his last hockey tournament, he had a surprise visitor. It was dinnertime, and he and Katya were enjoying a better than average meal, thanks to his hockey earnings, when there was a knock at the door. Peter got up from the table to answer it, and was surprised to find someone from his past, Natalia, standing there, clutching a small child in her arms.

I haven't seen Natalia since she told me that she didn't want to see me anymore,, and that she was going to marry a man from Moscow. The years, he now saw, had not been kind to Natalia.

"I'm sorry, so sorry to bother you Peter, but, I need to talk with you...*please*." There was desperation in her voice.

"Yes, of course, come in." Peter was so surprised to see her that he didn't know what else to say.

Katya came from the kitchen, wiping her hands on a towel, "Natalia...it's so nice to see you."

Natalia burst into tears at the sight of her old friend, and the child she was holding, a toddler girl, began to cry as well. Katya looked at Peter in dismay.

Peter got Natalia to sit on the daybed, and offered her a glass of tea, and a piece of honeyed bread for her child. He also gave Natalia his handkerchief, and she wiped her child's tears, and her own, away. Natalia was silent for several moments while she sipped the tea, and gave some to her daughter.

"This is my daughter, Lydia. Sergei and I," she looked at Peter sadly, "have only one child."

After several swallows of tea, Natalia was more calm, and began to tell Peter and Katya her story. Natalia's husband, a Party Member who was, until six months ago, working in Moscow as an investigator assigned to the Chief Prosecutor's office, was dispatched to look into matters of theft and embezzlement in the factory where Peter worked. Natalia, her husband, and daughter were now living with her mother, who was a retired physician, and living on a pension in the same apartment where she had always lived.

For reasons unknown to her, Natalia's husband's personality began to change since moving to Lyubertsy, and she was now afraid of him, because he had threatened, in a fit of drunken rage, to kill her, his daughter, and her mother. She knew that he was angry and frustrated, but she didn't know why, and she didn't know what to do.

"There is something going on in the factory where you work, Peter. When Sergei was drunk a few weeks ago, he started ranting about the Lyubertsy gang's involvement in drugs at the factory. He said that three people had even been murdered at the Moscow Chief Prosecutor's insistence in order to cover up what was going on because the Prosecutor was profiting from the sale of drugs in the factory. He also told me that he was afraid that he would be blamed, banished from Moscow, if he did not handle the situation in Lyubertsy the way the Prosecutor wanted him to handle it. I don't know what he meant by that, he was very angry, but I could see that he was also frightened."

Natalia's story immediately caught Peter's attention, because of what had happened to Misha and his mother, and to Vanya.

He quietly asked Natalia, "What can I do to help you?"

She looked up at him, her eyes wide and pleading, "Sergei wants to go back to Moscow, Peter, but he can't if the problems at the factory aren't taken care of. Will you help him? But *please*, don't let him know that I asked you. He's been so angry, and I don't know what he might do to us."

"I'll do what I can, Natalia, but what about you? Is it safe for you and your little one to go back to your mother's apartment?"

Natalia shook her head, "No, but I have to go back. Otherwise, my mother might catch the edge of Sergei's anger."

"Stay here for the night, and then you can go back in the morning, Natalia." Katya gently patted her friend's arm as she spoke to her.

Natalia shut her eyes tightly, and tears slid from the corners, "I can't. He would be terribly angry tonight when he gets home if I weren't there. In fact, I must go back right now."

Peter insisted on walking Natalia back to her mother's apartment, "You've carried your little one some distance already, and I can carry her on the way home."

Natalia begged Katya to go with them because she was afraid that her husband might see her with Peter. "Please, Katya, I don't want Sergei to get the wrong idea about Peter. My husband's temper is very frightening to me and my little Lydia," she kissed the child's cheek, "and my mother is afraid of him, too."

"Of course I'll come with you. But isn't there some way that Peter and I could convince your husband that he should…treat his family better? What kind of a man terrorizes a woman and child, his own flesh and blood, after all?" Katya was shocked by Natalia's story.

"He wasn't always this way, and I think that his drinking makes his anger worse. If I could only find a way to get us all back to Moscow…" Natalia's tears flowed anew.

Peter, carrying Lydia, and Katya, arm-in-arm with Natalia, arrived at Natalia's mother's apartment. When she opened the door, Natalia was visibly relieved to find the apartment empty and quiet.

"My mother is probably at the kiosks, buying something for our dinner…" Natalia's voice sounded tentative, but hopeful.

"Will you be all right, Natalia?" Peter was concerned for her and for little Lydia.

"Da," she replied. "Sergei, if he is not at home now, will probably not come home until after midnight, if his previous behavior is any indication, and we will be in bed, asleep, by then."

"I'll watch Sergei in the factory, Natalia, and I'll try to help him. You and your little one…if you need anything, *anything,* please let me know. It is the least that I can do." Peter, whose life Natalia had once saved with the help of her physician mother, had shared a close and loving relationship with her at one time. He now felt badly that she was in harm's way.

Chapter 21

Days, weeks, and months, passed quickly by. Peter was ever mindful of the dangerous atmosphere in the factory as he watched Sergei's activities whenever he could. He wanted very much to discover what had really happened to Misha, and why, and he believed that this man might provide the answer.

One night in late March, when Peter had worked extra hours at the factory, he saw Sergei walking alone toward the dimly lit back parking lot. As he walked toward Sergei, Peter saw five men come out of the shadows at a corner of the building and run toward Sergei from behind. One of them, Peter saw, had something in his hand, and when he got close to Sergei, the man raised a length of pipe to strike him from behind.

Peter ran shouting toward them, and Sergei just missed what might have been a killing blow to the back of his head. In the ensuing melee, Sergei joined Peter against the attackers, but they were seriously outnumbered. Just when things seemed to be at their worst, one, and then another of the gang members cried out. One grabbed a shoulder and the other a knee as each fell to the ground. There was no time for puzzlement on Peter's part...only relief. There was no loud report that might indicate a firearm, but *someone* had to be using a gun. *A gun with a silencer?* Who would have such a weapon?

The attackers were soon routed after the gunfire started, and the three who remained standing dragged their fallen comrades with them as they retreated.

Peter searched the darkness around the parking lot, but could not see anyone nearby. The gunman was nowhere to be seen. But he caught a glint of light reflecting off metal at a third floor window of the factory that overlooked the parking area. It was only visible for a second or two, and then disappeared. Had he really seen something?

Sergei, too, looked up at the dark windows of the factory, following Peter's gaze. "Why was I attacked? Did you see who they were?" Sergei put his hand to his head, and it came away bloody. He looked at Peter, who had his own cuts and bruises, and put his hand on Peter's shoulder.

"How can I thank you? I think you saved my life." Sergei staggered, and leaned against his car, his breath coming in ragged gasps. "Was someone shooting at me…at us…too?"

"I'm not sure about anything right now, but the five men who tried to harm you could have been from one or another of the Lyubertsy gangs. As for the shooter, I think that if he had wanted to do harm to you or me, we would not be standing here right now. We would be wounded, or worse…dead on the pavement."

"But why did you get involved? Were they trying to get you, too?"

Peter hesitated before answering, "I have many enemies in the Lyubertsy gangs, but these men were not after me this time. Actually…your wife asked me to look out for you. I think she knew that something like this was possible, because she lived in Lyubertsy for most of her early life, and she understands that someone from Moscow would be looked upon as a threat by the gangs."

"Who are you, and how do you know my wife?" Sergei was startled by Peter's admission.

Peter again hesitated, trying to decide whether to tell the man the whole truth about his previous relationship with Natalia many years ago, but then he realized that it would only cause more problems for her. Natalia didn't need more problems.

"My sister and your wife are friends. They went to school together here in Lyubertsy. When you brought your family here, Natalia was afraid for you, and she came to ask my sister and me if we could help her to protect you."

The cold early spring air made both men shiver momentarily, as it picked up and moved the light dusting of snow that had fallen earlier in the day, causing it to swirl around them. They stood looking at one another, each taking the other's measure.

Finally, Sergei said, "I owe you my life, and I should know your name."

"I'm Peter Genchenko. And, before you ask…yes, I am Ivan Genchenko's son."

Peter's revelation surprised Sergei, and it showed on his face. At first he didn't know how to respond. Sergei knew a great deal about the elder Genchenko. He had read Genchenko's files when Sergei was working for the Chief Prosecutor in Moscow.

"Genchenko…yes, I know the name. I have worked for the Chief Prosecutor in Moscow, and your father is legend. Is he still in prison?"

Peter looked down as he shook his head. "No…my father died…of pneumonia, at home, in December of 1986."

Sergei was thoughtful, "Oh, I didn't know that Ivan had died. His imprisonment was accomplished on false information. Of course, I think that you already know this. He was a very stubborn, and very angry man. For several years, I did not even know that he had a family."

"Sometimes," Peter said ruefully, "I think that *he* didn't know, or didn't care, that he had a wife and children."

"A man is foolish if he does not acknowledge his family." Sergei again looked thoughtful as he spoke.

"Yes, family is everything in this difficult life. A man who has a family that loves him is rich beyond measure." Peter spoke quietly, philosophically, emphasizing each point that he wanted to make.

Sergei bowed his head and then finally, after several moments, looked up at Peter. There were tears in his eyes as he again thanked Peter for helping him. "Without your help, I think those men might have killed me."

"We must look out for one another, Sergei. The Lyubertsy thugs are mostly cowards who run in gangs. Without the strength of numbers, they won't try to harm you again. I will watch your back, and you can watch mine. Do you agree that we should help each other?"

Sergei's answer was a fervent, "Da! *yes!*"

Lara Danilova, or Ivanova, as she was known to Peter and Katya, watched Peter and Sergei from her car as they talked. She wished that they would just leave, get away from this very dangerous place. Lara had used her silenced service revolver from the third floor window of the factory that overlooked the parking lot. Had she not done so, she was fairly certain that Peter, and the man known as Sergei, could have been seriously or fatally injured by the Lyubertsy gang members. She didn't like this assignment, and told Marc Terenoff so each time she reported in to him. However, she realized that Peter Genchenko was in danger every time that he came near this dump of a factory. Why would such a man, who seemed to have everything going for him, looks, intelligence and charisma, stoop to working in a Lyubertsy factory?

When Peter finally got to his apartment that night, Katya was still awake, and she was worried. She had been pacing the floor until he arrived.

"Petrosha, you've been hurt!" Katya's hands flew to her face.

Peter's forehead was lacerated, and his knuckles were bloody. There were streaks of blood on his coat and hat. Katya ran to the kitchen to grab a cloth. She dampened it and returned to her brother. Peter had taken off his hat and coat, and was sitting forward on a chair, elbows on knees, when she returned to the room.

"I'm all right, Katya. Natalia's husband was attacked tonight, and I helped him to fight off his attackers. Well, we didn't do it alone. Someone was there with a gun, and he used it to disable some of the gang members. Anyway, after the gunfire started, the gang just disappeared."

Peter told her that he and Sergei talked at length after the attack, and Sergei had given him some insight as to the Lyubertsy gang's involvement with the sale of drugs, and that Sergei had found that the Moscow Chief Prosecutor was more than likely involved in Misha's and Vanya's deaths, and Misha's mother's death, too.

"Sergei said that he couldn't prove what he told me, but he was very sure that this was the way things had happened."

Katya was stunned with this news, "But Peter, *you* are now in danger, too. Now they will come after you again!"

He nodded, "I agree, but if the Chief Prosecutor in Moscow is involved in drug sales, and had two men and an old woman murdered to cover up his involvement, I want him to pay for his crimes. I want him to pay for Misha's death."

"Sometimes, I still can't believe that my Misha is gone forever." Katya began to cry quietly.

Peter wearily wiped the blood from his face with the cloth that Katya brought to him, "I know, Katya, because I, too, find it hard to believe that I will never see him again." Peter put his arms around his sister to comfort her, and wondered if this sadness and misery would ever end for them. *Please Lord, have mercy on us.*

Two months passed without any sign that the Lyubertsy gang was going to try to do harm to Peter or to Sergei again. The two men shared information at least twice a week about their findings. Sergei told Peter that he was stymied because so many factory documents had been destroyed, and he didn't think that he would be able to connect any of the pieces of information that he had, aside from the embezzlement and theft issues that he had been sent to investigate in the first place by the Prosecutor.

Chapter 22

The seasons changed, it seemed to Peter, too quickly. Spring had come, and then summer passed without incident into late August. When Sergei was abruptly called back to Moscow, Peter found himself in the dark as to how to proceed against the Moscow Chief Prosecutor. After mulling his options over and over in his mind, Peter decided to talk to Chief Investigator Terenoff about the things he had learned so far. What can it hurt, he wondered? He understood that he was going out on a limb in contacting Terenoff, but what other course of action did he have? Peter wanted, needed, the truth about what really happened to Misha, and he was willing to take risks to find the truth.

"Genchenko," Marc Terenoff's hooded black eyes stared at Peter from behind a scarred desk heaped with stacks of paper, "what brings you here again?"

Peter took a deep breath, "I'm either foolhardy, or brave, or perhaps a mixture of the two, but I have a story to tell you. I want you to listen carefully to what I have to say, and I fervently hope that you are not a close friend of the Moscow Chief Prosecutor."

Marc Terenoff lit a cigarette, inhaled deeply and exhaled slowly, the smoke enwreathing his face. He smiled, "As a matter of fact, I consider myself to be one of Vasiliy Arnov's..." he hesitated for several moments, "worst enemies. He is the reason that I am banished to this shit-hole of a city."

Relief welled up inside Peter, and he took a chair across from Terenoff without invitation. He was quiet for a short time as he gathered his courage, and then he began to tell the investigator his story.

Peter told Terenoff that he and his friend, Misha, had many run-ins with Lyubertsy gang members over the past several years. There were times when, had it not been for the intervention of the militia, Peter and his friend might have suffered extreme bodily harm, or worse; death. The animosity of the gang members toward them stemmed from the fact that he and Misha had interfered many times in the gang's 'business' of intimidation, rape, theft, and selling drugs.

Usually, Peter and Misha were together when they were in and around the factory, but when Peter traveled with the Red Army Hockey Team, Misha was vulnerable to attack by gang members. He had often told Peter of the 'exciting' things that happened to him when Peter was away playing hockey, and Misha had the scars to prove it.

When Zuk, the gang leader, and some of his gang members had attempted to harm Peter upon his return from one of his trips, Peter was able to extract some information from Zuk about Misha, as he had earlier told Investigator Terenoff. Zuk had told Peter that "someone in Moscow" wanted Misha eliminated because he had found evidence of an illicit business connection between the Lyubertsy gang and that, "someone in Moscow."

Peter told Terenoff that it wasn't until he met Sergei, who *worked* for the Chief Prosecutor in Moscow, that more pieces of the puzzle were added. Sergei had found evidence actually *linking* the Chief Prosecutor with the Lyubertsy gang and drug sales, and Sergei believed that the Prosecutor had ordered the murders of Misha and his mother, and then Vanya, to cover his tracks.

"Why would this man, this Sergei, tell you something like that?" Terenoff's dark eyes bored into Peter's.

"I helped him when he was attacked by some Lyubertsy gang members armed with lead pipes," said Peter. "After that, Sergei and I formed a friendship of sorts. He was very angry that the Moscow Chief Prosecutor had sent him to Lyubertsy on a wild goose chase to cover up, rather than uncover, the Chief Prosecutor's criminal activities in Lyubertsy. And when Sergei found out more than he was supposed to, he realized that he and his family were in grave danger because of it."

Terenoff nodded, "And so he confided in you. Well, Genchenko, you aren't telling me anything more than I already know. I have been gathering evidence against Arnov for several years. Until you handed Zuk to me on a silver platter, I was at a dead end. Now, it seems, I have someone else, your friend Sergei, to assist me. Spaseeba. *Thank you.*"

Peter left the militia office and headed for home. He was unsure about the effect his story had on Terenoff, but he was glad that he had gone to him, anyway. Peter hoped that what he told Terenoff would be helpful in proving that the Moscow Chief Prosecutor was involved in criminal activity, and that there were at least three murders that he had ordered to cover up his involvement with the Lyubertsy gang.

When Peter got to his apartment building, he noticed a large, black Zhiguli automobile idling out in front. As he reached the front steps, someone from the car got out and called to him.

"Genchenko! I want to talk to you…I have something for you." The man, a hat pulled down that obscured his face, gestured for Peter to come nearer to him.

He was stocky, short, and powerfully built, Peter could see. His style of dress didn't appear to be Russian. It looked more…Chechen, thought Peter, because the cloth had a sheen to it, and the lapels of the jacket were wide. This was the style that Chechens preferred, and they always wore black or gray. This man was dressed all in black.

Peter had a sense of déjà vu as he stopped at the entrance to his apartment building, "Who are you, and what do you want?"

The setting, sans snow, reminded Peter of the time, many years ago when he was fifteen, that he had been shot by what he later discovered were probably KGB operatives. For this reason alone, Peter quickly went up the steps and entered his apartment building, closing the door behind him. As he looked out through the window on the door, to his dismay, he saw Katya approaching the building from the opposite direction that he had come.

The man was still standing next to his car, and then Peter saw him glance at Katya. The next few seconds were a blur to Peter, because he reacted without thinking.

He nearly pulled the door off its hinges as he ran out of the building entryway, "*Katya!*"

She smiled and waved, not noticing that the man standing near the car began moving toward her. Peter tackled him at a dead run, and both men fell to the ground. Peter pinned the man's arms at his sides, and felt a gun in a shoulder holster. The man struggled, spewing obscenities at Peter.

"Katya," Peter shouted, "get into the building, *now!*"

There was a second man, who was now getting out of the car on the other side, and Katya saw that he had a knife in his hand. She knew that Peter had his hands full with the first man, so she began to scream, causing people to look out their open windows. Some of them actually began shouting at the would-be attackers. In all the noise and confusion, the man with the knife got back into the car and shouted at his partner in crime to get back in the car. There was a 'ping,' then another 'ping,' and the windshield of the car disintegrated.

The Chechen, a startled, and then frightened look on his face, broke free of Peter, wrenched the rear car door open and dove in, while he shouted at the driver to get moving. Peter lay panting on the pavement, watching the car speed away. Gunshots…silenced gunshots…he had heard the odd, muffled noises, and had seen the windshield of the Chenchens' car shatter. Where had the gunfire come from?

When they were safely in their apartment, Katya spoke in a shaking voice, "I knew that they would come after you, Peter. Now you are their target because you know too much!"

Peter hugged her to him, "I will take care, Katya, please believe me. I want to be able to protect you, so I won't do anything foolish, I promise you."

Late that evening, long after Peter had gone to bed, Katya sat at the kitchen table writing a letter to the only person that she could think of who might be able to help her brother. She knew that what she was doing would more than likely separate them forever, but she would rather have Peter gone somewhere safely than lose him to the same criminals who took the life of Misha. Her hand shook as she put pen to paper, and she fervently hoped that her written English would be good enough to convey how desperate her brother's situation really was.

Dear Nikola,

My beloved brother is in terrible danger, and I fear for his life. There is no one to help him here, and even if there were, there is nothing to be done.

Those who would harm Peter are far too powerful to be thwarted.

The reason that Peter is being pursued is that he has tried to find out what happened to my fiancé, Misha. Peter has gotten too close to the truth about Misha's death, and so has become a target, himself.

Please help him, Nikola. I know how he feels about you and little Nicholas.

He loves you both dearly, and lives from letter to letter, cherishing each one that you send as if it were a lifeline, keeping his hope alive.

Peter was attacked outside our apartment building this evening. If it had not been for the warm weather and open windows and the intervention of our neighbors in surrounding apartment buildings, he might have been seriously hurt or perhaps even killed.

My brother means everything to me. He is my only family now, and I cannot bear to lose him to violence at the hands of these wicked men.

Hurry, please hurry! Come to Lyubertsy as quickly as you can. I do not know when, or how, the next attack will come. I pray fervently that you will come to help Peter.

Yours,

Katya

Chapter 23

Late summer, my favorite time of the year, thought Nik as she drove home from her parents' house with Nicholas. She loved the warm summer weather in late August, and had the windows down in her car so that the late summer air, fragrant with end-of-the-season flowers, could come in. The sky was bright blue and almost cloudless, and the temperature was only eighty-two degrees, unusually balmy for August.

My son is going to be two years old next month, she mused, and turned to smile at him in his car seat. Nicholas smiled back at her and clapped his hands. Her child amazed her. He had begun talking at eight months, and was talking in sentences by nine months of age. He had rapidly become bilingual as Nik taught him to speak his father's native language, but sometimes he mixed his languages when he talked to her.

"I'm hungry, mat, *mother,*" Nicholas told her.

"Skora, *soon,* my son, we'll be home in no time."

The evening went quickly as they played and read together. Nicholas loved his Dr. Seuss books, and recited the text from memory as his mother read to him. This was their routine, and it was a wonderful time for Nik. And, small as he was, Nicholas now helped his mother set the table for dinner by placing the napkins next to their dinner plates.

After Nicholas was fed, bathed, and in bed asleep, Nik cleaned the kitchen and then sat down at her desk to look through the day's mail. It had been a long day at the clinic, and she was tired. This was the time of day that she thought about Pete, and what he was doing. His letters were as good as any short stories that she had ever read. His ability to describe characters, to seemingly bring them to life, was extraordinary. But it was the *contact*, the reaching out to one another with the written word, that was so important, and she eagerly looked forward to Pete's love letters, because they kept her starving heart from breaking.

Nik would not, could not, ever stop missing him, she knew. Sometimes her mother, or her friend Stephanie, or even Ron, would tell her that she needed to get on with her life. In her heart, though, there was only Pete, and there was always the hope that they could be together again. Nik was not a dreamer. She was a realist. But in her heart, she hadn't given up on Pete.

She breathed a deep sigh. Oh well, chores had to be done, and there was no one else to do them. Wearily, she sorted through the catalogues, junk mail, and the few bills in her mail, and then found an unusual envelope.

Nik was familiar with the envelopes from Pete; the postmarks in Cyrillic, and the unusual stamps from Russia. But it was the handwriting…it wasn't Pete's broad script. It was written in a more feminine hand. For a moment, Nik felt a stab of fear. Has something happened to Pete?

Quickly, she opened the envelope and read the letter, and then read it again in disbelief. Her heart raced and she felt a rush of panic. Nik knew that Pete's circumstances were not very good, and she worried about his health and safety, but the letter that Katya had written told her that his very life was in danger.

For most of the night, Nik paced, trying to think of what she could do. Her first impulse was to get on the next flight to Kennedy Airport and on to Moscow. But she knew that she needed to have a plan before going to help Pete. Otherwise, she might do more harm than good. And, of course, there were passports and visas to be applied for and obtained. *How can I possibly get to him quickly enough to help him?*

Nik, in a quandary, sought comfort and sanctuary in the study she had created for Pete. She stretched out on the sofa there and finally fell asleep. The last thing she heard was the grandfather clock in the entry hall chiming three o'clock.

Nicholas whispered in his mother's ear, "It's breakfast time, mat *mother,* it's time to wake up."

Startled, Nik sat bolt upright, "Oh…my…gosh…Nicholas, I think we've overslept!"

But when she looked at the clock, it was only six-thirty. Nik breathed a deep sigh of relief, and lifted Nicholas up into her arms.

"Come on, little man, we've got things to do."

It took forty minutes to get herself and Nicholas ready to go, but she was able to get everything done, including breakfast and her shower, in record time. Ordinarily, Nik showered before her son was awake, but today was an exception, so she brought his favorite toys into the dressing area, left the bathroom door ajar, and jumped into the shower.

The traffic at seven-ten wasn't bad this morning, and Nik thanked God for that. They got to her parents' home at about the same time that they ordinarily would have, and that gave Nik a chance to talk to her father about Katya's letter.

Klaus sat quietly pondering the issue and then looked up at Nik, "Well, Les Barnes is well-connected politically. He is a friend of

Senator Martin Saylor, and I think that it would be a very good idea to get some help if you are really going to go to Russia to help Peter and his sister."

Marina, holding Nicholas, told her daughter, "I can go with you Niki, if you like. It isn't a journey that one, especially a pretty young woman, should make alone."

"Right now, I don't know what I'm going to do, but I have to do something quickly. Katya wouldn't write to me like this if something weren't terribly wrong."

When Nik arrived in the clinic, only Ron was there. The first patients were scheduled for nine o'clock, so Nik had some time to talk to Ron about what she should do regarding Katya's letter.

"I barely slept last night after I read Katya's letter. Pete's in danger and I don't know what to do to help him, but I know that I have to go to Russia."

"Hold it a minute, Nik. Slow down. What did she say in the letter?" Ron didn't even like hearing Peter Genchenko's name, so he wasn't in any mood to be very helpful in the matter.

Nik took the letter from her pocket and handed it to him, "I have to go to help him, Ron. When you read this letter, I think you'll understand why."

Ron stared at the envelope for a moment before opening it. He handled it gingerly, as if it might be covered with contagion.

He began shaking his head, "What the hell does she expect you to do? If he's really in big trouble, why don't they just go to the police?"

Nik's angry reply took Ron by surprise, "That's the *most ignorant* thing that I've ever heard you say. You have no idea what they're dealing with. Not the politics, not the law enforcement, or lack of it, not *anything*! Haven't you read newspapers, books, or anything on totalitarian states? He's Ivan Genchenko's *son*! Do you think that anyone will raise a hand to help him?"

She grabbed the letter from Ron's hand and stomped out of his office. Stephanie was just coming into the clinic and immediately read the situation. For a moment, she glared at Ron, and then followed Nik.

When she caught up to her, Stephanie said, "Hey, Nik, you look upset. Is there something wrong?"

Nik shook her head and kept walking, "I don't want to talk about it."

Stephanie fell into step with Nik, "Let's go for a cup of coffee before the patients start coming in. Is that okay with you?"

The letter slipped from Nik's shaking hand, and Stephanie stooped to pick it up. Before she handed it back to Nik, she saw that it was from Russia. The stamp was unmistakable.

"Trouble, huh?" Stephanie handed the letter to Nik and put an arm around her shoulders.

Nik looked down at the floor, "*Big* trouble, Steph. Very big trouble."

As they sat sipping their coffee in the snack bar of the building, Nik, who was calmer now, gave Katya's letter to Stephanie to read.

When she finished it, Stephanie's eyes were wide, "Son-of-a-*bitch*! What are you going to do?"

"I thought that Ron might have some ideas, but he doesn't even begin to comprehend what Pete's life is like. I can't blame him, really. He hates Pete because of me, even though it was my fault. Men are strange creatures."

"Well, yes, they are," Stephanie wrinkled her nose and smiled at Nik.

Nik looked at her watch, "I've got a few minutes until my first appointment, so I think I'd better call Uncle Les. Maybe he will know what to do."

"Good idea, Sweetie. If you're a little late, I'll cover for you."

When Stephanie came back into the clinic without Nik, Ron approached her, "Where's Nik? Isn't she going to work today?"

Stephanie gave him an arch look and repeated what Nik had said to her over coffee, "Men are strange creatures."

"What the hell does that mean?" Ron's hands were on his hips, and his exasperation showed on his face.

"It means, Ron, that Nik was asking for your advice, your help, your kindness, in a matter near and dear to her heart, and you blew her off. Now, if you still cared about her, even if you feel like the jilted lover, you'd pay attention to what she has to say. That's the mistake you made before, and you haven't learned a damned thing."

Ron's face reddened, and his jaw dropped. When Stephanie turned and walked away from him, he was still speechless.

Nik's telephone call to Uncle Les bore fruit. Well, at least it gave her hope that she might be able to do something for Peter outside the regular diplomatic channels, because it would otherwise take months to get a visa to the Soviet Union.

"Our Senator in Washington has always been a straight-up kind of guy, Niki, and I think he might be able to help you. But I've got to caution you, that this isn't going to be just a walk in the park. If Peter has gotten himself into trouble with the law in Russia..."

"It's not like that, Uncle Les. His sister's letter says that he has found some incriminating evidence of wrongdoing in the higher levels of government, and that he's now a target. I'm so frightened for him, and

I wish that I could leave right now to help him!"

"Okay, okay Niki, try to calm down. Let me put out some feelers, and I'll call you back. You said you're in the clinic today?"

"Yes, but I think that I'll leave after I've seen my patients. I should be finished about one-thirty. Maybe you should just leave a message on my answering machine."

"All right, Niki. I'll see what I can do for Peter."

Nik was composed and quiet when she returned to the clinic. She donned her white lab coat and went to work.

The one communication that she had with Ron was that she would work through lunch and take the rest of the day off.

"Okay, Nik," Ron said quietly. "Will I see you tomorrow?"

She nodded without looking up, "I'll be here. I wouldn't do anything to cause problems for my patients."

Chapter 24

It had been more than two months since Ron had talked to his father. They didn't communicate often, because, though neither would ever admit it, they were cut from the same cloth. Both of them had challenging, time-consuming professions; Ron's was medicine, and his father's was banking. And both used the same all-out approach in everything they did, including their personal lives.

Ron knew that his mother had long since given up on trying to change his father, help him to relax, make him more amenable to the more frivolous side of life. His father labeled anything that did not apply to his chosen profession as "frivolous." Was that why Nik gave up on me, sooner, Ron thought, rather than later, as is the case in my parents' marriage?

His father always answered the telephone with a, "Yes?"

"Uh, hello, Dad, how are you?"

"Fine, I'm just fine. And you?"

"I'm fine, too." Ron's usual eloquence was always squelched in any conversation with his father.

"Well, Myron, what's on your mind?" Ari didn't mince words.

Ron hesitated, and then said, "I, I…have a favor to ask of you."

Ari cleared his throat. He always 'harrumphed' when he was

annoyed or disapproving. "Well, what is it? Is your clinic in the red? I thought things were going well for you there."

"It isn't money, Dad."

"I see. So it must be something very important, if it isn't money. Otherwise, you wouldn't be calling me."

"You have friends in high places in Washington. I need two passports and visas for the Soviet Union as soon as they can possibly be gotten. Within the next two or three days would actually be when I need them."

His father was silent for a moment, "Why on earth would you possibly need something like that?"

"I'm trying to help a friend, Dad. It's the most important thing that I have ever done in my life, believe me. I have never asked you for anything before…not even college expenses. I've always worked or had scholarship money for my education. But in this instance, because it's life and death, I will do anything you ask in order to help my friend."

"Will this put you or your friend in danger? You need to think this thing through, Myron."

"I have, Dad, believe me, I have."

Abruptly, Ari ended their conversation. "I'll call you in the morning, Myron. I can't promise you anything, but I will do my best to help you and your friend."

"Thanks, Dad, thanks so much." Ron felt a small bit of the weight of guilt lifting from his shoulders.

Just after midnight, Ron's bedside telephone rang. He was wide awake, lying in his bed, looking at the clock, and hoping that he could help Nik…and Peter Genchenko, too.

"Son, I need the identities and other identifiers of the two persons who need passports and visas to the Soviet Union. I also need current photos as soon as possible. Well, instead of sending the information directly to me, I have a Secret Service fax number for you to send the information to. You'll have passports and Soviet visas awaiting pick-up in the federal building in Indianapolis tomorrow afternoon if you can get the required information to the right people by nine o'clock in the morning."

"I don't know what to say…"

"That's all right, Myron. You sounded pretty desperate when you called, and I decided that you wouldn't have asked me for help if you didn't really need it. But you must promise me that you and your friend will be careful. Can you do that? Russia is not a good place to visit, especially when there is trouble. And…there is your heritage, Myron, so be very careful."

"I understand, Dad, and I can assure you that I…we…will be very careful."

Ron didn't hesitate. He called Nik immediately, "I'm sorry to awaken you, but I have some wonderful news. We have a little bit of leg work to do between now and nine in the morning, but you've got two passports and visas for the Soviet Union that will be issued in the afternoon if we can get the information in on time."

When Nik started crying, Ron's heart ached for her, and he wished that he could be there to comfort her. He waited until she got control of herself, and continued, "I'll travel with you, Nik, if you want me to, but if you want someone else, we've got to contact them now so that they can get the information to us quickly."

In an emotion-laden voice, Nik answered, "I don't know how to thank you, Ron. I just don't know how…"

"I'm going to get dressed, and I'll be over as soon as I can, okay?"

"Yes, I'll put on a pot of coffee."

"I'll be there in less than thirty minutes."

Ron threw some clothes into an overnight bag, grabbed his toiletry kit, and hurried out the door of his north side apartment.

"What made you change your mind?" Nik, still red-eyed from crying, met him at her front door.

"Men are strange creatures," he answered with a smile.

Ron told Nik how he had called his father to see if Ari's connections could help her and Peter Genchenko. It surprised Nik that Ron spoke Pete's name, but it lifted her spirits.

"Can I go with you, Nik? I'd like to make up for what I've done, or, more accurately, for what I haven't done. I'd really like to help. Peter's sister sounded desperate in the letter. After I thought about it for a while, I realized that she wouldn't have written to you if her brother wasn't in danger."

"Can we take Nicholas with us?" Nik's eyes were still sad.

"I think so. He won't need a visa, just a birth certificate and a photograph, since he's less than five years of age."

Nik poured coffee into the two cups setting on the countertop, "I'm going to need this to stay awake."

Ron looked at her and marveled that, even though she was in the midst of turmoil, and was probably very stressed and sleep-deprived, she was still beautiful. Her hair was tousled, and she had pulled on navy sweats, but she couldn't have been more lovely. *I've really missed out on everything with Nik, but at least I can help her now...*

"My father said that we will need birth certificates, social security cards, proof of residence, and our voter registration cards. We also need current photos. I think I'm okay on all of these. What do you think?"

Nik swallowed a sip of the hot coffee, "I've got them too, and I also have Nicholas's birth certificate."

"To save time, and to maybe get a little sleep, I've got some clothes and my overnight bag in the car. If I can bunk on your sofa, we can get an early start together."

When Ron stood, Nik stood, too, and hugged him tightly, "I can't tell you how much this means to me."

He patted her shoulder, "It's okay, Nik…I think that I'm beginning to understand."

Nik carried sheets, blankets, and a pillow down to Ron, and helped him make up the sofa into a bed. Nik yawned widely and Ron followed suit. Then they both laughed.

"Get some sleep, Ron. I'll set my alarm for six o'clock."

"Okay Nik. I'm not going to have any trouble falling asleep this time."

Nicholas was the best alarm clock that his mother had. At precisely five-thirty, he bounded into her bedroom and jumped on her bed.

"We have a surprise visitor, Nicholas. Let's go downstairs and wake him up!"

Nicholas's face became a study in excitement and curiosity, "Who is it, mat *mother*?"

"Come and see, little one, come and see," Nik wrapped her robe around her, tied the sash, stepped into her slippers, and picked her son up in her arms.

Nik let Nicholas awaken Ron, and then she went into the kitchen to put together a quick breakfast of oatmeal, fruit, and toast.

Within minutes, Nik called from the kitchen, "Okay guys, breakfast is ready."

Ron came into the kitchen with Nicholas on his shoulders, "We're here, and we are *hungry*."

After breakfast, Nik ran upstairs with Nicholas and got him ready for his day with his grandparents while Ron showered.

When Nicholas and Ron were ready to go, Nik quickly showered and dressed, grabbed her passport information, and joined them. After running her information by Ron, he told her that she had everything that he could think of for their passports and visas.

They dropped Nicholas off at Nik's parents, and told Klaus and Marina briefly what they were about to do. Nik's spirits were high, and even with her parents' cautionary advice, she wasn't dissuaded. She would go to help Pete, no matter what.

"I've got to at least try to help Pete. He means the world to me, so I've got to try."

Klaus watched curiously as Ron patted his daughter on the shoulder, "I'm going along with Nik and Nicholas," Ron said, "because it's better if Nik has some help on the trip. It's a long flight with two or three lay-overs, so it's best if I can be with them."

Ron opened the clinic early, and immediately faxed all the information to the Secret Service fax number that his father had given to him. To his relief, the fax 'beeped' back, telling him that the information was received.

Next, he went to work on getting airline tickets for the trip, "Nik, what are we going to need for the return trip?'

"If Pete agrees to come with us, we're going to ask Katya, too. I'm hoping against hope that she'll want to come, because if she doesn't, I don't think that Pete will leave her."

"So, we'll need our two tickets, plus whatever they'll charge for Nicholas, on the way over, and then four adults and one child on the return? Is that right?"

Nik nodded animatedly, "Yes, and we've got to pray that Pete's pride won't get in the way." She concentrated for a moment, and then continued, "But I don't know how we're going to get passports and visas from their government so that they can leave the Soviet Union."

When Stephanie came into the clinic, Ron brought her up to speed, "Steph, do you think that you can handle the clinic for the next few days or so? Nik and I are going to Russia to see if we can help Peter Genchenko."

Stephanie looked at him archly, "You are? Well, something pretty big has happened between yesterday and this morning, hasn't it?"

Ron laughed, and relished his answer a second time, "Men are strange creatures."

"Damned right they are," said Nik, joining them.

"What happened?" Stephanie was curious.

Hands in pockets, Ron attempted nonchalance, "I called my father, and he started the ball rolling, so this morning, we've sent our passport and visa information, and we should get them back sometime this afternoon."

"Well, your father must have some pull with someone…right?" Stephanie was impressed.

"I'm not sure who he contacted, but he called me after midnight to tell me that we could go if we got the information in early enough."

"Ron called me right away, and I couldn't believe it. Now all we have to do is find some way to get passports and visas for Pete and his sister, so that we can get them out of Russia."

One of the clinic telephones rang and Ron went to answer it. He came back to Nik and Stephanie,

"It's your father, Nik, and he says that your Uncle Les is trying to get in touch with you."

Nik hurried over to the telephone, "Dad? Does Uncle Les have something for me?"

"I think he does, Niki. He said that there were diplomatic channels that were opened for you regarding Peter Genchenko. You can call Les at his office this morning."

"Thanks Dad! I'll call him right away."

When she dialed the number, Nik's hands were trembling. Please, please, please God, let the news be good.

"Niki, I've got great news for you! There are arrangements for Peter Genchenko and his sister to get U.S. visas if they want to come to America. Senator Saylor has cleared everything through diplomatic channels, and things should go well for all of you."

"That's wonderful, Uncle Les! Ron's father has already arranged to get passports and visas immediately for us here, and Ron's going with Nicholas and me, so we're going to leave in the morning if we can."

"That's great, Niki, and I hope that everything goes well. Do you think that Peter will come back with you?"

"Uncle Les, I hope to God that he does! From what his sister said in her letter, Pete's life is in danger."

At three-thirty that afternoon, Nik and Ron went to the Federal Building on Pennsylvania St. in downtown Indianapolis to claim their passports and visas for their trip to the Soviet Union. The bureaucrat who assisted them kept asking questions as to how and when they had made their applications for their documents, but Ron and Nik only smiled and thanked him for his help as they signed for, and gathered, their papers.

Chapter 25

Nik called her brother, Mike, in San Francisco to let him know what she was about to do. Of course, she knew that he might try to talk her out of going to Russia to help Peter, but she believed that his opinion about what she was going to do would be helpful. She had always depended on her big brother Mike.

"Hello…" Mike sounded as he always did, relaxed and in a good mood.

"Hi, Mike, are you busy right now?"

"I'm never too busy to talk to my little sister, Niki. What's up?"

"Well…I'm about to go to Russia with Ron to help Pete and his sister, Katya. We are going to bring them back to the States where they will be safe."

Mike already knew what had happened between Niki and Peter Genchenko before, and he hesitated for a moment. "What's wrong, Niki? Has something happened to Peter?"

"No, Mike, not yet, but his sister wrote a letter to me, and she is frightened for Peter's safety."

"But how can you help them, Niki? It takes a lot of time to get all of the papers you'll need together."

"Uncle Les and Ron's father, Ari Michael, have already cleared the way for us, and we could leave for Russia as soon as tomorrow if we can get everything, including packing, arranged."

"Are you serious, Niki? It's dangerous to do what you are planning to do. What if you need help when you get there?"

"Uncle Les somehow has seen to it that the Foreign Service and the U.S. Embassy in Russia will take care of everything. We will even have a military escort, so don't worry. We'll be okay."

"What do Mom and Dad have to say about this? Surely they have some misgivings over what you're going to do?"

"Actually, Mike, after they read Katya's letter, they understood how serious the situation is for Peter. They've given me their blessings about this whole thing."

"Okay…" Mike said slowly, "but please, please, be careful. Or…I could go with you…maybe that's the best thing for me to do, Niki."

"No, Mike, there's no time for you to fly here from California. And you have a business out there. You can't just drop everything and come running after me. Don't worry; Ron's going with me. He wants to help Pete, and I am so grateful for his help."

"All right, Niki…I know how you are when your mind is made up. Tell Mom and Dad to keep me posted on how things are going."

"I will, Mike…and I love you."

"I love you, too, Niki, and I hope that you can help Pete and his sister."

For several moments after they hung up, Nik felt sad, but she understood Mike's need to help her. My big brother wants to protect me, she thought, just as he always has.

Nicholas was asleep for the night when Nik began packing. Her closet doors were open and she was pulling clothes out, checking them over, and then putting them in her 'to go' pile, or 'to stay' pile. She realized that the 'to go' pile was becoming far larger than she should pack, so she stopped to take stock of where she was.

The last piece of clothing that she took from the closet was the lab coat that she had worn during the International Winter Games. The tri-color logo was emblazoned on the front pocket. What a time to come across this old thing…this is where it all started. She hugged the lab coat to her for a moment, irrationally thinking that some trace of Pete, perhaps his masculine scent, might still be there.

There was something in one of the pockets. Nik reached in and pulled out two business cards; one from Sheldon Levin, and the other from Marty Pelham. As she looked at the cards, more than two years old now, she began to have a wonderful thought. I should call them, just to see if they're still interested in Pete. She mulled it over, and decided that she really should call one or the other in the morning. What can it hurt?

When Nik finished packing, she hurried into the shower, quickly scrubbed her body, washed her hair, rinsed, then toweled herself off. Her nightgown was hanging on a hook on the back of the bathroom door, and she pulled it on over her head. Mentally, she went through all of the things that she had had to do, ticking them off on her fingers. Okay, everything is done…now it's time to get some sleep. But it took her more than an hour of tossing and turning before she could get comfortable enough to sleep. Her heart was racing…I'm going to see Pete…I'm going to see Pete again!

The next morning, Nik called Sheldon Levin. As she dialed, she wondered if he would even remember her.

"Levin, Smart, and Strong," the voice answered, "how may I help you?"

Nik used her most authoritative 'medical' voice to ask, "May I please speak with Sheldon Levin? This is Dr. Nikola Kellman calling."

"One moment, Dr. Kellman, I'll see if he's in."

"Hey, Nik! How are you, and how's the doctoring business?" Sheldon Levin's voice had lost none of its strength and exuberance.

"I'm great, Sheldon. Doctoring's good, and how are you?"

"Couldn't be better, Nik. Business is hand over fist."

"Have you seen Marty Pelham lately?"

"As a matter of fact, yes, I have. We got together three weeks ago in Chicago. I'll bet you'll never guess who we ended up talking about? Hint…he was the one that got away."

Without hesitation, Nik said, "Peter Genchenko."

"Jackpot! You win, Nik."

"Well, Sheldon, I'm flying to Russia to visit him this week, and I think he's going to come to the U.S. for a while."

Sheldon boomed, "My next call is going to be to Marty! How can I reach you, Nik?"

"You can call me…do you still have my number?"

"Yeah, I have your number right here in my rolodex."

"I'll be in Russia for some time, Sheldon, and I'm not sure how long. You can call and leave a message, and I'll get back to you."

"Great, that's great Nik. Marty's going to be ecstatic over this one."

When Nik, Nicholas, and Ron took their seats at ten-thirty that morning on the American Airlines 747 for the first leg of their journey to Russia, Nik thought of Sheldon Levin's excitement over Pete's return to the U. S., and it gave her hope that, somehow, everything would work out.

Their flight east was mostly quiet, but upon their arrival at Kennedy, they only had forty minutes between connections, and for a short time, Nik panicked, thinking that they might miss their flight. But Ron commandeered a motorized shuttle, telling the driver their tale of woe. They had been passing Nicholas back and forth as they hurried through the terminal, laden also with three carry-on bags that contained their things, and Nicholas's things, including toys and books.

On board the small transport, they traveled rapidly between gates, and made their connection in the International Gate with time to spare. Ron tipped the driver, thanked her, shook her hand, and then he hurried after Nik and Nicholas.

They were on another American Airlines 747 for their trans-oceanic flight to Great Britain. Nik and Ron sat on either side of Nicholas, the better to 'tag team' to meet his needs. Nicholas was unusually fussy at the beginning of their flight, and Nik explained to Ron that little ones, babies and small children, had difficulty equalizing the pressure in their ears during flight, causing pain and upset.

"I've studied up on pediatrics since before Nicholas was born. Babies and children are amazing little creatures, but their ears, with short, straight Eustachian tubes, don't adjust to pressure changes very well during flight."

After a nice warm lunch, which eased Nicholas's ear pain, Nik snuggled with him to encourage him to nap. Ron covered them with an airline blanket, and gave them pillows to rest their heads upon.

"Sweet dreams..." He leaned over and kissed Nicholas on the cheek.

All they saw of London was Heathrow, and by this leg of their journey, all three, but especially Nicholas, were very tired. Ron had a pass to the British Airways Elite Club, and they spent their afternoon in comparative comfort, out of the mainstream…maelstrom?…of people and noise. There was even a small, soft bed available for Nicholas that Nik rocked gently from side to side as she and Ron sipped on cups of hot tea. Soon, Ron, too, was sound asleep. Before Nik settled in for a nap, she asked the attendant to notify her when her flight was two hours from boarding.

"I always worry that I'll sleep through an important appointment or departure," Nik told her.

"Oh, quite right; I know how worrisome that can be. You are on Flight 9517, destination Moscow?"

"Yes, and I think that we will need a little time to freshen up before we get on board another airplane."

"Well, have no concern…I will call you two hours before your flight time. Will you need a transport to the gate?"

"*Yes,* that would be wonderful. My son is small, and little ones can really be a handful in a big and busy airport."

Nik leaned back in her comfortable lounge chair, and soon joined Nicholas and Ron in a much-needed nap. She tried to get her mind around the coming reunion with Pete, but she was too drowsy to think straight, and so gave herself up to sleep.

True to her word, the attendant in the Elite Club awakened Nik two hours prior to her flight time. Nik gently stroked Nicholas on his cheek until he opened his eyes. He smiled at his mother and yawned.

She then called, "Ron, it's time to wake up. We need to get ready to catch our next flight."

Ron's nap had refreshed him too, and he nodded at Nik, "Okay, I think I'm going to make it now with this little nap."

There was some turbulence early in their flight to Moscow, but it cleared after less than an hour, and the dinner service was on time. Nicholas ate much better than he had on the other flights, and this relieved Nik's concern that he wasn't getting enough to eat and drink.

During the meal, Nicholas surprised his mother with a question. "Will papa know me when I see him?"

Nik, with eyebrows raised, looked at Ron before turning back to answer her son, "Yes, he will know that you are his little boy. He has lots of pictures of you, Nicholas, and whenever he writes letters to us, he talks about you, and how much he loves you. You know that he does, because I always read his letters to you."

Chapter 26

Sheremetyevo Airport was overwhelming. It had taken the better part of two days to get to Moscow, and the three travelers were nearly worn out. Nik and Ron were relieved when they saw a man in an American military uniform, a Marine, holding a sign that read, "Nikola Kellman."

"Dr. Kellman? I am Master Sergeant Ryan Garringer. I've been instructed to transport you to the American Embassy, and after your business is conducted there, I'll take you to your hotel." The Marine stood erect in the military tradition, and seemed the epitome of what a Marine should be.

"Oh, thank you. We are so grateful for this special attention."

"You are welcome. You have some very influential friends, Dr. Kellman, and I have been given instructions to facilitate your visit in any way that I can. I will be at your disposal for as long as you are in the Soviet Union. Your luggage is already in my vehicle, so we can be on our way if you like."

They found that there were actually two Marines at their disposal. Their driver, Master Sergeant Zachary Garringer was just as professional and friendly as his brother, who had met them inside the terminal.

Master Sergeant Zachary Garringer welcomed the three visitors to

Moscow, "I'm sure that my brother has told you that we are responsible for you, and also the people that you have come to see, so I will just reiterate that we are at your disposal throughout your visit." His smile was broad as he spoke.

At the Embassy, Nik, Nicholas, and Ron were introduced to the staff and were given their visas, with special instructions as to the way in which things were done in the Soviet Union. The Attaché who addressed them, John Ray, was very polished, and assured them that he would do everything in his power to see that their visit was productive, safe and secure.

"And how are you acquainted with Senator Martin Saylor, Dr. Kellman? Are you a relative?" Mr. Ray was very curious as to the connection because of the strict instructions he had received to make the doctor's visit as trouble-free as possible.

Nik gave him an enigmatic smile, "He is a friend of the family."

"I see. Well, the Senator wanted to make certain that you were given every benefit and assistance available from our Embassy here. Our Station Chief, Charles Leonard, is out of the country, but we expect him to return next week. If your party is still here, he wants to have a dinner for you."

She fervently hoped that they would not be. That would mean that there was a delay in bringing Peter and Katya out of the Soviet Union. And it would also mean that they might not be able to go home with her where they would be safe.

Nik was outwardly calm, "Thank you. It would be quite an honor for all of us to be dinner guests of the Chief Consul of the American Embassy in Moscow."

Their Marines took them to the Metropole Hotel, where Nik and

153

Ron registered for a suite of rooms. They had decided before they left the states that they could easily be three or more weeks in Moscow, awaiting the release of Peter and Katya, so the suite of rooms had to have three bedrooms and three baths. After much discussion, mostly in Russian, with Nik taking the lead, they ended up with the penthouse, where there was a sitting room, kitchenette, three bedrooms, and two baths. It was a compromise, but they knew that it was the best they could do under the circumstances. The Garringer Marines assisted them with their luggage and accompanied them to their suite of rooms.

In the penthouse, Nicholas ran from room to room, inspecting the premises, as if he might be looking for someone…his father, perhaps?

Nik and Ron took a few minutes to unpack, and to freshen themselves and make a change of clothing for themselves and Nicholas. And then they were ready to go. By this time, Nik had begun to shake with anticipation.

"Okay, everyone, I think we're ready for the trip to Lyubertsy. What time is it Ron?"

"Do you want local or 'real' time?" He looked out a window to check the position of the sun.

Nik put a hand to her hip, "What do *you* think?"

The Marine named Zachary laughed politely and told them, "It's half-past two locally. By the time that we take you to Lyubertsy, it's going to be about four-thirty to five o'clock. Will that work with your schedule?"

"That will be excellent timing." Nik, though tired, could now allow herself to believe that she would see Pete very soon, and the excitement was building within her.

The ride to Lyubertsy was mostly quiet, with a few excited outbursts from Nicholas when he saw something unusual. He saw a man on the road with a horse-drawn cart, and talked about the "horsey" for several miles.

Lyubertsy was exactly the way Pete had described it to her; an industrial city, down on its luck, with soot and debris everywhere. Both Marines cautioned their charges to be alert to their surroundings.

"This city has a well-entrenched gang of more than three hundred members," Zachary told them, "and we don't want anything to happen to any of you, so be careful."

"We'll escort you to and from the building, and if any trouble arises, please use this," said Ryan.

He handed a radio telephone to Ron, and explained its use. He told him that it wasn't really a telephone, but it was the next best thing, and it always worked, since it didn't depend on wire connections; only radio signals.

"I believe this is the address that you gave us, Dr. Kellman." Ryan looked up at the old building that was in disrepair, and crumbling at the edges.

It's just as Peter described it. Nik was sad to think that this was how Peter and his sister, Katya, had to live.

The old stairs creaked and moaned as Nik, Nicholas, and Ron climbed slowly upward. Stale food odors drifted from apartments, and assailed their noses. There was a musty smell from the stair treds that probably came from the deterioration of the paint and the wood beneath...and a thick layer of dust.

Nik tapped gingerly, once, twice, a third time, on the door to apartment 3C. Her hand was shaking as she knocked at the door. *Will Pete answer the door?* Her heart was pounding with excitement. Ron

155

stood behind her with Nicholas in his arms, and wondered the same thing.

The door opened slowly, and a tall, slender, dark blond young woman stood there, almost transfixed. Her beauty startled Ron, who also noticed a deep sadness in her lovely green-gold eyes.

"Katya?" Nik's voice faltered.

"Nikola…*Nikola*! You have come to help my brother. I thank God for your kindness!"

Katya threw her arms around Nik and held her for several moments. Nicholas, who had wriggled out of Ron's arms, tugged at their skirts until his mother bent down to pick him up, and then introduced him to his Aunt Katya.

"This is Nicholas Petrovich, your nephew, and this," she said, turning to indicate Ron, "is Myron Michael, our Guardian Angel."

"Come in, please come in. Peter will be so surprised, so happy to see you!" Katya wiped tears from her eyes with her long, slender fingers as she spoke.

Peter was observant and cautious whenever he left or entered his apartment building. He had begun to slip into a deep and hopeless depression after the Chechens tried to harm Katya. His greatest fear was that something terrible would happen to her. He blamed himself for their desperate situation now. If he hadn't been so aggressive in looking for Misha's murderers, perhaps Katya might still be safe.

On this late afternoon in early September, Peter approached his apartment from a different route. He had been doing this every day since the confrontation with the Chechens. He also made sure that Katya understood that she, too, should always be vigilant, and should not take the same routes to and from work each day.

He was startled to see a large, black American car with American diplomatic plates parked in front of his apartment building. There were two men inside the car dressed in what seemed to be military uniforms. He could read the make of the car across the trunk. It was a Cadillac. Could this be just another ruse to catch him unaware? Chechens favored Mercedes, BMW's, or large American cars, and he knew that diplomatic plates could easily be stolen or forged.

Peter went around and behind an adjacent apartment building, and then circled back to a side entrance to his own. Characteristically, he took the steps two and three at a time until he reached the third floor landing, and his own apartment.

He and Katya had worked out a special knock, based on the Morse Code, that they changed every day. She was an apt pupil, and they used short nouns, dog, cat, cow, pig, and so on, to make the process as easy as possible.

He tapped today's word, cat, and then put his key in the lock. As he entered the apartment, he heard a man's voice, and froze. He could see that Katya was in her chair, and she looked up as he came in.

"Petrosha, we have visitors." She smiled at him and began to stand.

When Peter saw who was sitting on the daybed, a look of surprise and then deep hurt passed across his face. There was Niki, sitting with Ron, who held Nicholas on his lap. It was so unexpected, and at first, Peter thought that they looked like they were a family. *Are they together, now?* Peter could barely breathe.

Nik felt as if her heart might stop as she saw him come through the door. Her throat was dry, and she was unable to speak. She had thought of this moment for a very long time, had prayed for it, and now that Pete was here, right in front of her, she was almost paralyzed with emotion.

Katya recognized the hurt look on her brother's face, realized that he might be misinterpreting what he was seeing, and said, "Petrosha, wait, let me explain."

But Nicholas was the first to act. He slipped from Ron's lap and ran to Peter.

He tugged at Peter's pant leg until Peter bent down on one knee, and then in perfect Russian said, "Papa, I am your little boy."

Nicholas put his arms around his father's neck, and Peter stood up with him, embracing his son. Peter's eyes were tightly closed against the tears that were threatening to spill from them. A sob escaped Nik's throat, and she joined them. Peter put an arm out and enclosed her within the circle. Nicholas patted his father's shoulder, and kissed his cheek.

"Niki, dear God, Niki…and Nicholas…dear, merciful *God!*" Peter's voice was hoarse as he held onto them tightly.

As Ron watched them, he let go of the anger that he had harbored against Peter for so long. He now began to understand what Nik had told him nearly two years ago, about her feelings for Peter. It was very evident that there was a deep love between them. He and Nik had never felt that way about each other.

Katya went into the kitchen and Ron followed her, wanting to give Nik and Peter their privacy in this most heartfelt and intimate reunion. Katya wiped tears from her face with shaking hands.

In halting English she told him, "I know that…if it were not for my brother, you would probably…be married to Nikola. He told me about what happened when he was there with his team in your city. But you must believe that my brother is a good and honest man. He never meant to hurt anyone, but he ended up hurting everyone, himself included."

Ron groped for words, "Nik told me everything, Katya, and I don't hold any ill will toward Peter."

Katya continued to tremble, and tears streamed down her face. "Please take my brother with you. I will probably never see him again, but I want him to be safe. *Please* take him with you," she begged.

Ron tried to comfort her by putting his arms around her while she got control of herself. He looked around at the spare, but very clean, surroundings, and knew why Peter had come back to Katya, and why he would not leave without her. It was unimaginable to Ron that she could survive, alone, in this setting for very long.

"It's all right, Katya. I finally understand everything, I really do, and Peter's coming with us."

Ron turned to see that Nik and Peter, his son still in his arms, were talking, and that Nik was wiping the tears from Peter's face with her fingertips. They had all regained their composure, more or less, and Nik beckoned for Ron and Katya to come back into the room.

"How? Why?" Peter struggled for words. "I am so happy to see you. I cannot express to you how much. In my entire life I have never been so happy!"

Peter put a hand to Nik's face, and leaned over to kiss her. Nicholas clapped his hands in delight, and reached up to kiss his father's cheek.

"Let's sit down and talk about why we're here." Ron took the lead, "We can't waste any time because of the danger to both of you."

Peter, Nicholas on his lap, and Nik, as close as she could get to them, took the daybed as seating, while Ron and Katya sat on chairs next to each other. Ron told Peter and Katya how the arrangements to travel, and the obtaining of documents for Nik, Nicholas, and himself, had been achieved by special means. He also told them that there were U.S.

visas awaiting them at the American Embassy. Although he didn't see any reasons for delay on the part of the Soviets regarding passports, Ron wanted to point out to Peter and Katya that there might be problems.

"But we are ready for whatever comes our way. What Nik and I need to know, is whether you want to come with us?" Ron looked directly at Peter.

Peter put his hand to his forehead and when he looked up there was anguish in his eyes. He began to stand up.

He doesn't know that we're here for Katya, too. Ron was about to speak again when Nik tried to clarify what they wanted to do.

"Wait, Pete…hear Ron out. We want *both of you* to come with us. We want Katya to come, too." Nik held Peter's hand tightly.

Peter lifted Nicholas into Nik's lap, stood, took Katya's hands in his, pulled her up from her chair, and then hugged her, "Will you go to America with me…with us…will you?"

Katya's smile was radiant as she now understood that she was included. "Of course, yes, I'll gladly go with you!"

Ron was back to the business at hand, "Okay, we've got that bridge crossed. Now, we've got to pack up your things, and take you to the hotel. We're at the Metropole in Moscow, and we have a suite of rooms; a place for everyone. We are going to stay as long as it takes to get your passports and visas, and then we'll go back to the States. What do you think?"

Peter looked around the shabby little apartment that had been his home for more than fourteen years, and knew, that in spite of the difficulties he had experienced in growing up here, he would miss it. He could almost see his mother, standing in the kitchen doorway, nodding her head, and telling him to go.

"This is your chance," she would say. "You deserve more than this place. Katya deserves more. So, go with the woman you love, and your son, to a place where you will be safe. You and Katya will be safe, and I can rest in peace."

Peter bowed his head briefly, and then looked into his Niki's beautiful eyes, "I am free now, to be with you and Nicholas. And Katya will be with us, too."

She stood on tiptoe, put her arms around his neck, and held his eyes with her own, "*Yes*, we'll all be together."

It didn't take long to gather their belongings; there were so few. Peter used his sports duffel bag for his, and then helped Katya pack her things in their mother's old ornate valise. The last thing that they did was to turn over the tablecloth on their kitchen table, so that they could collect their savings, the rubles taped there. Other than these few things, there was nothing else that they wanted to take with them.

Ron couldn't believe the truly desperate circumstances in which Peter and Katya lived. And yet, he could see how much they meant to one another. He wished that he had that sort of connection with his own brother, Zeke. Perhaps affluence promotes alienation, he thought. But after this experience, Ron was going to make the effort to reconnect with his brother. Of this, he was very certain.

Nicholas had fallen asleep on the daybed amidst all the activity. And when Peter saw him, he knelt down beside his son and gently touched his cheek. Ron watched them from the kitchen door. Father and son together, he thought, and they'll be together from now on.

Nik helped Katya do a walk-through of the apartment to check for anything that might be left to take. They started in Peter's room. Nik looked at the gray-green walls and wondered what color they had started out to be? From now on, she thought, Peter and Katya's lives will be different. They deserve so much more than this, and they're remarkable for having survived so long in such a place. As she looked at Peter's bed, she realized that, as small as it was, his feet must have dangled from the end of the bed when he slept there. This odd thought made her heart ache for him.

Peter, with Nicholas in one arm, locked the door to his apartment for the last time, and put the key in his pocket. He was unaware that Lara, his neighbor across the hall, opened her door and watched as he and the others with him descended the stairs.

Lara Danilova immediately used her radio telephone to contact Chief Investigator Marc Terenoff, and her message was cryptic, "The party is on its way to the hotel."

"Good…a job well done," was Terenoff's reply. "I will see you in Moscow tomorrow morning."

When they all reached the first floor, Peter handed Nicholas to his mother, and went to the caretaker's apartment and tapped on her door. A small, bent woman with white hair came to the door. She was barely higher than Peter's waist.

"Anya," said Peter, "Katya and I are leaving our apartment, and we want you to have the furnishings there. I also want you to have two months' rent so that you won't lose anything because of us. I'm sorry for such short notice, but we must leave quickly." Peter handed her all of the rubles that he and Katya had taken from under their tablecloth.

Anya brushed tears from her eyes with the back of one gnarled hand and nodded. "Petrosha," she always called him by his nickname, "I saw what happened to you the other evening, and I know that you and Katya will be safer somewhere else. I thank you both for your help and kindness over the years, and I will miss you and Katya very much, just as I miss your mother, Eda."

Peter bent down on one knee and kissed Anya's cheek. "And I thank *you* for your good heart and kindness, too. Goodbye, Anya." Peter stood and headed for the door and the beginning of his new life.

Once inside the embassy car, Katya and Peter were introduced to the Garringer brothers, the Marines assigned to them. Peter thought it interesting that these military men were brothers, and was impressed by their ability to speak his native language.

Out of curiosity, he asked them where they had learned to speak such flawless Russian, and they replied, almost in unison, "Indiana University."

Nik smiled and asked, "You're from Indiana? Oh my gosh, what part?"

Again in unison, the brothers answered, "Fort Wayne."

On the way back to Moscow, everyone became quiet for a time; each with his or her own thoughts. Nicholas stretched out across his mother and father's laps and took another nap. Peter reached for Nik's hand, put it to his lips, and then held it against his chest, near his heart, as she looked into his eyes. Before long, Nik leaned against his shoulder, and she, too, fell asleep.

Ron's head nodded and he made a valiant attempt to make conversation, but sleep overtook him and he was the third of the tired travelers to put his head back to nap. Then, of the passengers, only Katya and Peter remained awake.

"Petrosha, are you happy now?"

"*Da,* Katya. But I'm afraid that this is a dream. There's such a sense of unreality. I've dreamed of this reunion from the moment that I had to leave Niki, and now it is here."

"I wrote to Nikola after the two Chechens tried to attack you," said Katya. "In fact, I wrote the letter that same night."

"You did…? I had no idea. But that was just a short time ago, Katya. How did they get here so quickly? Passports and visas sometimes take weeks, or months, to obtain, even in the United States."

It was the quieter of the Garringer brothers, Zachary, who offered an opinion, "Pardon me for eavesdropping, but one answer to your question is that Ryan and I got our orders directly through the Foreign Service, and they came from Indiana Senator Martin Saylor's office."

Peter asked, "Does that mean that there were some special circumstances under which they were able to get their documents so quickly?"

Zachary looked back with a raised eyebrow at Peter in his rearview mirror, "Oh yes, there were some very special circumstances involving you and your sister. Dr. Michael's father, Ari Michael, the financier, and Dr. Kellman's friend, Lester Barnes, made it possible for them to come to Russia."

Ryan agreed with his brother, "You must have a lot of 'pull' back in the States, Peter. Otherwise, we wouldn't be assigned to you and your sister. Dr. Kellman and Dr. Michael really moved mountains of red tape to get you out of here."

Katya said softly, "I can't believe our good fortune, Petrosha."

Momentarily, Peter was at a loss for words, "And I am grateful…so very grateful to both of them for helping us."

Peter looked at his sleeping Niki and smiled, fully understanding now, that she and Ron had worked so very hard, pulling strings and begging favors, to come here to save Katya and him. As he had from the beginning of their relationship, he marveled at Niki's strength and sense of purpose. *How very fortunate I am to have such a woman love me.*

Chapter 27

The Metropole Hotel is beautiful, thought Peter, as their car pulled under the portico. He knew that it was quite famous and very much in demand by foreign travelers, but he had never been inside the building. He also knew it to be an old hotel, circa the early 1900's. His father used to speak with disdain of the new Finnish owners who renovated the hotel mid-century, furnished it with exquisite antiques, and made a world-class hotel out of an aging ruin.

"They are not Russian," Ivan would say of the Finnish owners. "What do they know of Russia? Only a Russian has a Russian heart!"

Peter and Katya tried not to gawk at the gorgeous antique furnishings in the lobby, and the lavish styling of the appointments, but they couldn't help themselves. It was a magnificent hotel.

The Garringer Marines again helped their charges with their luggage, and soon the group was heading to the penthouse. When the door to their suite was unlocked and opened, Peter was not prepared for the sumptuous luxury inside.

Katya went to a window, gently pulled the heavy silk and brocade draperies aside to look out, and said in an excited voice, "There is the Bolshoi! We can see the Bolshoi from our hotel."

Peter joined her, "Yes, and Red Square is in that direction." He pointed to the east.

Ron laughed, "Well, that settles it. Katya gets the room overlooking the Bolshoi."

She turned to him, her face glowing with excitement, "Such a wonderful thing, to see the Bolshoi from my room. I'd never have thought that this could happen to me."

Nicholas ran to his father, and Peter scooped him up into his arms, "Look at the beautiful view, Nicholas. This is a wonderful place."

Nik watched them from a short distance, and she felt a rush of love and happiness as she saw the ease with which father and son interacted. Her decision to make this journey had been the right one, she knew. How could she not have come when Pete was in danger? In his apartment, when he first put his arms around Nicholas and her, she felt whole again…complete.

Zachary, military cap in hand, stood in the middle of the sitting room and addressed the group. "If everyone has everything that they need right now, Ryan and I will be heading back to the Embassy. Two other Marines will be available to you until we return tomorrow morning. Marine Lieutenant Cynthia Fleming and Lance Corporal Stephen Thomas will be right outside your door this evening and throughout the night. Keep your radio telephone turned on, and in a place that you can reach it quickly if you need to use it."

Ron told Zachary, "Thank you both very much. We all appreciate your help." He rubbed his forehead for a moment, and then continued, "In the morning, we're going to need to go to the Hall of Records to begin the process of obtaining passports for Peter and Katya. Do you know what time the offices open?"

"I think that everything in that area opens by nine in the morning, and your appointment/appearance is already set for that time. We will be here at eight-thirty to escort you there. We will also wait for you to conduct your business, and then bring you back to your hotel," replied Zachary.

"That's great," said Nik. "We can get an early start."

Since it was nearly eight o'clock, and way past Nicholas's dinner time, they all agreed to have room service sent up, rather than trying to find a restaurant. Ron deferred to Katya and Peter in regard to ordering their dinner.

"What sorts of things appeal to you? What are your tastes?" Katya wondered if Nikola and Ron would like Russian cuisine?

"Nicholas likes chicken, and so does his father," Nik replied with a smile. "I like fish, and if I'm not mistaken, Ron likes nothing better than a good steak, cooked medium rare." Just the mention of food caused Nik to remember how little she, Nicholas and Ron had eaten on this day. And she also believed that Peter and Katya hadn't eaten very much, either.

"If you want to be adventurous, Katya will order a perfect Russian meal for us." Peter was smiling at his sister.

Katya blushed and looked down for a moment, "I would be very happy to do so, if you wish."

Ron picked up the telephone and dialed for room service. "Here you go," he said, and handed the telephone to Katya.

Katya was very efficient. She ordered salat iz pomidor *tomato salad,* bifsteks *beefsteak,* kur'iitsa *chicken,* kambala' *flounder,* ris *rice,* bulochki *rolls,* mas'lo *butter,* and svyok'la *beets;* enough for everyone to sample the different tastes of Russian fare. Her choice for sladkoye *dessert* was tort *cake,* and she ordered an assortment of beverages to complement the meal.

"Pete, would you like to help me bathe Nicholas while we wait for dinner?" Nik held Nicholas in her arms.

"*Yes*, but I'll need some instruction on the process." Peter was delighted at the thought.

Nicholas wriggled out of his mother's arms, took his father's hand and led him to the bedroom where they had put their luggage. He pointed to the bathroom door. "It's the bathroom, papa," he said in Russian.

"You are a wonderful boy, my son, and thank you for helping me," said Peter, laughing.

Nik put pajamas out on the bed. "We'll dress Nicholas in his 'jammies' for dinner. He's pretty good at his eating skills now, so he won't get too messy."

Peter's hands were actually trembling at first as he began to bathe his son. He knelt by the tub, scrubbing Nicholas and rinsing him clean. A sense of wonder filled his soul. *My son, I am bathing my son.*

Nik sat on the bed, watching them through the open bathroom door. Just looking at Peter's broad shoulders filled her with longing. He's thin, so thin, and he's been through so much, she thought. Again, her heart ached for him because of the bad times that he had struggled through since they parted. She didn't know the full story of what had happened to Katya's fiancé. Nik realized that what Pete had done to find out who had harmed his friend, his sister's fiancé, had been courageous.

Peter lifted Nicholas from the tub dripping and slippery, and Nik got up from the bed to help him towel their son off. The towel was so large that it wrapped Nicholas three times around, and when his father began to unwrap him, he spun slowly in a circle, giggling and laughing.

Peter's eyes met Nik's, and he bent to kiss her, "Thank you. I want to be able to do this for our son from now on…well, at least until he is able to bathe himself," and he laughed gently.

The doorbell was melodious. Its chimes hummed for several seconds after they were struck. Were the notes from the overture to Tchaikovsky's "Swan Lake?" Nik thought so, and smiled at Peter, who nodded his head and smiled back at her.

"Dinner!" squealed Nicholas.

Cynthia and Stephen, their evening and night Marines, looked in and introduced themselves, "We will be just outside your door if you need us." Cynthia waved at everyone.

"Thank you, so very much," said Nik as she waved back at Cynthia. "Would you like to join us for dinner?"

"Oh…no, Ma'am, we can't do that, but we thank you very much for your kind invitation."

The waiter put a tablecloth on a round table that he had wheeled in, and set it with china and silverware. After he put five chairs around the table, he placed the platters of food on its surface, poured the beverages, and invited the guests to their meal.

Peter felt another surge of unreality as he took his seat at the table next to his son. Is this truly happening, or is it just a dream? Katya was to his right, next to Ron, and Niki was on the other side of Nicholas. My little family has been extended, Peter thought, looking around the table. He was so happy to see Katya smiling and conversing with Ron. He hadn't seen her smile, truly smile, since Misha had disappeared.

Nik complimented Katya on her choices for dinner. She was pleased that Nicholas was eating very well. He hadn't done so during their lengthy flights, but now his appetite had returned. It made her happy, as well, that Pete seemed to be enjoying his dinner. When Nik glanced over at Ron and Katya, she saw that they were talking, and this, too, pleased her. Katya was shy, so shy, and yet Ron had gotten her to talk, had drawn her out. How wonderful…

They all talked animatedly during the meal about how to best approach the 'powers that be' in the Hall of Records. Toward the end of dinner, Peter seemed to have the best insight into what they must do.

"We cannot second guess what the person who ultimately makes the decision about Katya and me will do. We can only pursue our documents as diligently as we possibly can, and hope for the best. In the end, I think we will prevail, but no one is going to make the way easy for Ivan Genchenko's son and daughter."

Katya agreed, "Even though Ivan is gone, and is no longer a threat to anyone in the Kremlin, just the mention of his name makes Communist Party Members bristle. Peter is correct in what he says, because he and I have had to deal with our family name time and time again. When our mother was alive…" Katya was quiet for a moment, and then began again. "When our mother was alive, she especially had problems heaped upon her by those who despised Ivan."

Ron wanted to reassure them, "No matter how long it takes, we will continue to work for your freedom. Nik and I discussed many of what we thought were foreseeable pitfalls, but you and your brother, having lived with the…uh…stigma…of your name, certainly know much more than we do."

Nik spoke with a sense of purpose, "Senator Saylor and Ron's father have set no timetables on what we are doing. If it looks like it will take months, rather than weeks, I will have my visa extended for as long as it takes. Peter, you know that I will not give up on this, and I want Katya to know it, too. Even if Ron has to go back to the states to check on his clinic, Nicholas and I will be here with you. We are not leaving until you two can come with us. We are family, and I…we," she nodded at Ron, "will not abandon you."

Peter stood from his chair and took Niki's hand, pulling her up into an embrace. As he held her, he whispered in her ear, "My beautiful, courageous Niki…I love you so very, very much."

Ron took Katya's hand at the table and gave her a reassuring smile. "Don't worry, Katya. I have a feeling that everything will be okay."

Katya's eyes brimmed with tears as she nodded in agreement. "Yes…it will be 'oh-kay.'"

When the meal and discussion were over, Nik washed Nicholas's face and hands, and got him down from the table. "He likes to have a book read to him after dinner. Would you like to read to him Pete?"

Peter stooped and picked up his son, "That would be wonderful, Niki. What does he like to read?"

"Oh, he likes "Cat in the Hat," "Green Eggs and Ham;" any Dr. Seuss book will do. They're in his luggage, just inside the first zipper."

Peter gave her a quizzical look, and she told him, "Trust me, he really loves Dr. Seuss."

Soon after the second reading of "Green Eggs and Ham," Nicholas was rubbing his eyes and asking to go to bed. His father took him into the bedroom, where Nicholas brushed his teeth in the gleaming and well-appointed bathroom, and then put him into a little bed tucked into an alcove of the larger bedroom. The small bed was an antique made of wood with whimsical bear carvings on its four posts. A soft blue velvet duvet with a matching pillow sham embroidered with bears covered the bed. Peter pulled the covers down, waited for Nicholas to snuggle into the soft bed sheets, and then pulled the velvet duvet to his chin.

"You're supposed to kiss me Papa…right here." Nicholas pointed to his cheek.

Emotion flooded through Peter, and for a moment, he couldn't respond, but then he smiled at his son, kissed him on the cheek, and wished him a good night.

In the dining area Nik and Katya cleared the table and placed the dishes back on the cart left by the waiter. Nik told Katya that they probably could have called the waiter back to do the clean-up, but it was quicker this way.

Katya replied, "I hate to sit and look at a messy table."

Nik smiled, "I agree. This way, we can put the cart outside our door, and someone can take it down when they are available."

"Good thinking," said Ron, nodding his head. "And is anyone as sleepy as I am?"

"*Yes*, I'm just about to fall over. I think I'll say goodnight to you two now, and go see whether Pete was successful in getting Nicholas to sleep." Nik was fading fast.

"Goodnight," Katya said softly as she moved toward her room.

"Sleep well," Ron replied.

Nik found Peter kneeling beside Nicholas's bed. She tiptoed over and knelt down beside him.

"He's asleep," Peter whispered, putting an arm around Nik's shoulders.

Nik looked up at him, "Are you ready for your shower before bed?"

A surge of excitement ran through Peter as he whispered, "Very much, Niki…I've thought many times about our showers together. You will join me?"

For a moment, she hesitated, and there were tears in her eyes as she replied quietly, "Yes, because I've often thought about our showers, too."

Gently, Peter lifted her to her feet, put his arms around her, pulled her to him, and kissed her tenderly.

"Niki," he whispered against her ear as he caressed her, "It's as if we haven't been apart. I didn't know if you would still love me after such a long time, but I thank God that you do. And you must know that my feelings for you are as strong now as they have ever been."

"Yes…I know, and I feel the same way, Pete."

In the bathroom, they shyly undressed for their shower. Peter told her that he was ashamed for her to see him in such a shabby condition.

"I feel badly that my clothes are so ragged," and he looked down at the floor.

Oh, he's so thin, thought Nik, as she saw that she could almost count his ribs. She put her arms around him and lay her head against his chest. "I love you, Pete, and to me, you are beautiful."

"You are unchanged," he said. "Even though you have given birth to our son, you are the same as you were when I last held you."

His hand spanned the width of her slightly rounded abdomen. Nik placed both of her hands over his, as the warmth of his hand began to radiate throughout her body.

Their shower was one of remembrance and reawakening, and of slowly unfolding passion. Peter's hunger for her, and his physical strength, ignited the fire in her response. They traveled back in time to a remembered passion, to the beginning of the deep and abiding love they still had for one another.

"Is this possible, Niki?" Peter whispered to her as they made love. "It is as though we have never been apart. If I am dreaming, I don't ever want to wake up."

"This is real...*we are real*, and we are together again...from now on, we will be *together*," she replied breathlessly as she and Peter moved as one toward a complete and deeply satisfying release.

"Nothing has changed, Niki, nothing," whispered Peter. "We are one, you and I...*one*."

Later, dressed in the pajamas that Nik had packed for both of them, they checked on Nicholas.

"Our wonderful, beautiful son, Niki," Peter whispered. "I am so grateful...I can't express how grateful I am to be kneeling here with you, watching Nicholas sleep."

Nik put her arm around Peter's waist and quietly replied, "We will have many nights like this with our son, my love; a *lifetime of nights like this*."

After several moments of watching and listening to their son as he slept, they crept quietly over to their bed and crawled under the soft sheets and blanket. Peter put both arms around Niki and pulled her close to him. They fell asleep, cuddled together, almost immediately.

Chapter 28

It was only five o'clock in the morning, but Ron was wide-awake. He lay in bed wondering if he had made the right decision in coming here? There were so many conflicting emotions running through him. It was painful, even now, to see Nik with Peter. How would he ever be able to accept what had happened before, when he had lost her to Peter Genchenko? And now, even though he had willingly helped Nik to come so far to save Peter's life, and that of his sister's, what was happening now?

Finally, at about six-fifteen, he decided to get up and get dressed. He could take a walk, or get some breakfast, or find *something* to do. He just didn't want to lie in bed anymore and think about Nik and Peter.

Ron was surprised to find Katya in the kitchenette, drinking a cup of hot tea. "You're an early riser."

Katya, sitting at the table in her pajamas and robe, was startled, but then smiled and said, "I slept well last night. My bed was comfortable, and the linens were soft and fresh."

The teapot was still hot, so Ron poured a cup of tea for himself. "Mind if I join you?"

It took a few moments for Ron to overcome Katya's shyness, and they talked quietly for a while. Ron was curious about the living circumstances of Katya and Peter, and she told him a little about what their lives were like after their father's imprisonment many years ago. Ron realized that he had underestimated the courage and resiliency of the Genchenkos.

"There isn't a sound coming from their quarters," said Ron, nodding toward the bedroom where Nik, Nicholas, and Peter were still more than likely sleeping.

A small, light laugh escaped Katya's lips, "I have never seen my brother quite as tired as he was last night, and I'm sure that Nikola and Nicholas were exhausted from their journey. But aren't you still tired as well?"

"A little, I guess, but I'm hungrier than I am sleepy. Would you like to go to breakfast with me?"

Katya's beautiful and expressive eyes brightened. "Yes, I would like that very much."

Ron waited as she went into her room to dress. In just a few minutes, perhaps fifteen, no more, Katya came out wearing a white blouse with a little lace at the collar, a black skirt, and a pair of low-heeled black pumps. Her hair was pulled back from her face in a soft chignon, and she had put pearls at her ears; her only adornment. She was stunning in her simple outfit.

The Marines on duty outside their suite spoke briefly to Ron about where he and Katya were going, and he explained that they were going to breakfast. One Marine, Cynthia, went with them, and the other stayed behind at the door to their suite of rooms. They took the elevator down to the mezzanine where there were several restaurants to choose from.

In the elevator, there were pictures of antique shops located in the hotel complex, and this became a topic of conversation for Ron and Katya. Cynthia remained quiet during their descent.

"I was overwhelmed when we first entered the hotel last evening. The Metropole is known for its beautiful antiques and furnishings, but I had never been inside the lobby, so I wasn't prepared for just how magnificent this old hotel is." Katya was still wide-eyed about her surroundings.

"Nik and I took the advice of her parents and uncle when we chose the Metropole. We tried to find out which hotel in Moscow would best suit our needs, but Marina, Nik's mother, told us that the Metropole was the *only* place to stay."

Ron noticed that Katya was causing a bit of a stir as they walked along the mezzanine. Heads turned, whether male or female, to look at her as she passed by, but she was oblivious of the attention. When they reached an interesting restaurant, Ron was smiling widely at the attention that Katya was getting. They invited Cynthia to join them for breakfast, but she declined, telling them that she would stay just outside the entrance to the restaurant.

They talked easily throughout their meal, and Ron was struck by how sweet and genuinely warm Katya really was. She asked him about the United States, and whether she and her brother would be accepted there. Ron assured her that they would both do well, and that she should not worry.

By the end of breakfast, Ron and Katya felt comfortable in each others' company, and had begun to build a level of trust. Ron was happy in her presence, much happier than he had been in a very long time.

Peter was drowsing between sleeping and waking, and he lay there thinking about his fantastic dream. In it, he had been with Niki and their son, and he and Katya were going to go to America with them. Oddly, Ron Michael was going to help Niki to bring Peter and Katya there. But then, two cold little hands touched his face on either side, and Peter's eyes flew open.

"Papa," whispered Nicholas, "I'm cold. May I snuggle with you and *mat*?"

"*Da*, my son." With the thrill of joy coursing through him, because this was no dream, Peter lifted Nicholas into the bed.

Peter looked over his shoulder, and Niki was there facing toward them, sound asleep, breathing quietly. He turned, holding Nicholas, and put his son between Niki and himself. And then he pulled the blankets up to keep them warm. Nicholas giggled, and snuggled up against his father.

When Katya and Ron returned from their breakfast, Peter, Nik, and Nicholas were just getting a start on their day. Nik had ordered Peter's favorite, an American-style breakfast of eggs, bacon, and toast from room service, and Nicholas was using a fork to stab pieces of scrambled egg that he popped into his mouth with a flourish, causing his parents to laugh with delight.

"You two must have had breakfast here in the hotel," Peter said between bites of egg.

"We were both awake very early, Petrosha, and Ron invited me to dine with him in one of the restaurants downstairs. It was a wonderful experience. I have never eaten in such fine surroundings," and she began to talk about the colors, the upholstery, and the gleaming china and crystal used in their meal service.

Ron beamed as Katya described the décor and atmosphere in the restaurant, "It was really quite nice, and the food was excellent," he added.

All of a sudden, Nik put a hand to her forehead and said, "Tomorrow is September 7th. It's Nicholas's second birthday!"

"We sort of dropped everything when we made our plans to come here, didn't we? I'll bet that your mom and dad were planning something special for Nicholas until they heard what we were going to do." Ron was surprised that they had forgotten Nicholas's birthday in the rush to rescue Peter and Katya.

Peter smiled when he told Niki, "Katya and I sent his birthday present three weeks ago, because we knew it would take forever to get to the U.S. I guess Nicholas will have to open his gift when we get home." *Home, yes…when we get home.*

"But we will have a wonderful birthday party for him here tomorrow, too," said Katya, as she gently touched the top of her nephew's head.

Nicholas threw his arms in the air and called out in his little voice, "*Happy Buffday!*"

All four adults were reduced to laughter. And Peter, still laughing, picked up his son and took him into the bathroom to wash his face and hands. Peter then brought Nicholas back out into the sitting area quickly with his clothing and shoes in hand.

"It is time to get ready for today," said Peter.

Ron told him, "Our Marines are in the lobby. Katya and I saw the changing of the guard when we came out of the restaurant, and we talked with the Garringer brothers a few minutes. They are very impressive young men."

"They are that, and more," agreed Peter. "I know that we are all safe when they are in charge."

Katya and Ron dressed Nicholas while Nik and Peter hurried into their bedroom to dress for their meeting with the Magistrate in charge of emigration at the Hall of Records. Dressing a two-year-old child ordinarily might be a challenge, but Nicholas was cooperative, and when they finished tying his shoes, he wanted a book read to him.

In their bedroom, Peter embraced Niki, and kissed her deeply, "I love you so very much, and I hope that today will go well for us."

Nik pressed her face against his chest and then looked up at him, "It will go well, my love, I just know it will." *Oh God, please make it so…*

They were very quick in dressing; Nik in a tailored gray pantsuit and Peter in his one (and only) best outfit, a black shirt and pants. They were ready to go before Katya had finished reading Nicholas's book to him, but he didn't protest. There was too much excitement in the air, and Nicholas, as young as he was, understood that today would be a special day.

Peter picked his son up as Nik stuffed a change of clothing, some snacks, a few toys, and the radio telephone into a small travel bag. He then took Nik's hand in his free hand and they hurried out the door behind Ron and Katya.

Marine Master Sergeant Ryan Garringer seemed to be standing at attention as he greeted them in the lobby, "Zach has gone to bring the car around to the hotel entrance. We're good on time, and you should be early for your appointment."

Nik was apprehensive, but didn't share her feelings with Pete. Her earlier words of optimism were beginning to seem distant. She didn't want him to know that she was afraid of what might happen when they requested his and Katya's passports at the Hall of Records.

Chapter 29

In the Embassy limousine Peter held a very quiet Nicholas on his lap, and reached for Niki's hand. She attempted a smile for him, but her smile was unconvincing. He tried to remain outwardly calm, but his thoughts were racing. Peter fully expected that things would *not* go well today. Given the history of the Genchenko family, his expectations were low.

Peter glanced at his sister and recognized that Katya was nearly paralyzed with fear. She sat next to Ron, and Peter saw that her hands, clasped in her lap, were shaking. When he saw Ron reach over and gently place a hand over hers to reassure her, Peter deeply appreciated Ron's kindness toward Katya.

"This is it, folks…the Hall of Records," Zachary told them as they pulled up to the front of the huge, old gray stone building.

"I'll go inside the building with you, but I'll have to stay outside in the hall while your business is being conducted. The Magistrate contacted our Embassy and gave them a set of rules, one of which is that they do not allow foreign military staff to witness Soviet Government legal proceedings." Zachary looked at each of them for emphasis. "Do you have any questions? Okay…if not, then let's go inside. Ryan is going to stay here with the car."

Ryan smiled and waved at them, "I hope all goes well for everyone today."

With Zachary in the lead, they easily found the room where they were to meet with an official from the *Byooro,* the Bureau of Emigration. Zachary opened the door for them, stepped into the room and checked to see if anyone was there. The room was empty, but it was more than fifteen minutes before their appointment time.

"Go ahead and take a seat inside, everyone. The Magistrate is scheduled to be here shortly." Zachary was an optimist. "I'll be waiting outside in the hall."

Peter thanked him, and then began to take stock of his surroundings. As was his habit in such a situation, he was in a heightened state of awareness, and he was looking for a means of escape if they had to leave quickly. There must be another way in and out, he thought.

It was a large room with a high ceiling. The paint on the walls and ceiling was beginning to peel, giving the room the appearance that it was melting in the late summer heat. Draperies at the two tall open windows were gray and dust-covered. An old and very battle-scarred desk sat on a raised platform between the windows. Above the desk a large hammer and sickle hung askew. The only thing setting on the desk was a calendar on a stand, turned outward, with the date, September 6, 1988, displayed in large Cyrillic characters. Six rows of pews, like those found in a church, were on either side of a narrow aisle leading to the old desk. Peter led the way to the front of the room. No one felt like talking, and so they quietly followed him and sat down together on the first row pew. Peter held Nicholas, and put a protective arm around Niki. Katya sat next to her brother, with Ron on the other side of her.

Try as she might, Katya couldn't stop shaking. Ron put an arm around her shoulders, and she turned to look at him. Although she didn't speak, her eyes conveyed her gratitude for his kindness.

A door opened at the right side of the room adjacent to the elevated desk. A thin, stooped, gray-haired man came into the room, and immediately, without speaking, took a seat behind the desk. For several minutes, without acknowledging the presence of the people in the pew in front of him, he adjusted his flimsy, and slightly askew, glasses and shuffled papers back and forth.

Finally, with one last adjustment to his glasses, he looked up and glared directly at Peter. "Come forward with your petition."

In spite of the feeling of dread that clutched his very soul, Peter stood, outwardly calm, and walked to the desk, his papers in one hand. He was carrying Nicholas, and Nik followed behind him, her heart in her throat. They stood in front of the desk, waiting for the official to recognize them.

"I want the *petitioners only* to stand in front of my desk. All others must step back. Are there any foreign nationals in this group?" The official's voice dripped with sarcasm.

"This is my family, and they will stand with me."

Peter's voice was strong as he replied to the Magistrate. He then turned and beckoned to Katya to join them. At first, Katya didn't, or couldn't, stand up.

Ron stood, took her hand, and said, "I'll go with you."

The official's face reddened, and he told Peter, "No matter who you think you are, *I* will have the last word here."

"I don't think so!" A voice boomed from the back of the room and startled everyone.

Marc Terenoff came slowly toward the gathering, the soles of his shoes s-s-slap-slapping against the floor tile. Peter looked stricken, and he pulled Niki and Nicholas closer to him. Katya shrank back against Ron, who put both arms around her.

"And who are *you?*" The official, who had been angry before, was now furious.

"Chief Investigator Terenoff of the Lyubertsy Prosecutor's office," he responded, holding up his badge. Terenoff's hooded eyes took in Peter and Katya, and he nodded at them. And then those dark eyes settled on Nicholas, Nik, and Ron. "Dr. Kellman, and Dr. Michael," he said, "and this handsome young man is your son, Genchenko?"

Peter's throat was constricted, and he was momentarily unable to speak, but he made a supreme effort, "Yes, this is my son, Nicholas."

"You are a hard man to keep up with, Genchenko, but I've had someone watching you, protecting you, since you last visited my office." Terenoff actually smiled as he spoke, "I'm sure you wondered why the Lyubertsy gang and the Chenchens never came back to finish what they started with you?"

The official could stand it no longer, "What is going on here?" he shouted. "You have no right to interrupt these proceedings, no matter who you are! You have no jurisdiction here. I will report you to the Moscow Chief Prosecutor!"

Terenoff turned back to the official, "You must hurry if you are going to do so, because he has been arrested this morning on suspicion of murder, theft, and drug dealing, among other things."

This pronouncement left the official speechless, and he started to get up from behind his desk.

"*Sit down,*" Terenoff said in a commanding tone. "You are not finished here."

"Papa, can we go home now?" Nicholas put his head on his father's shoulder because he was beginning to be uncomfortable with the level of emotion in the room, although he didn't understand what was going on.

Terenoff gently patted the child's back, "This will be over very soon, little one."

As it turned out, Katya and Peter got their passports very quickly after Terenoff took over the proceedings. When the little group went out into the hallway afterward, their Marine came up to them to see what had happened.

Terenoff asked, "Which of the Garringer Marines are you?"

Zachary stood ram-rod straight and looked Terenoff in the eye. "I'm Marine Master Sergeant Zachary Garringer. And who are you?"

"Join us in the corner over here, and you'll find out everything you need to know." Terenoff indicated an alcove off the main hallway.

As they gathered in the alcove, someone else joined the group, "Hello Katya, Peter..." Lara Danilova nodded first at Katya, and then at Peter.

Katya's surprise was evident as she reached out to take Lara's hand, "Lara...?"

"*You* were our protector, Lara?" Peter was astounded.

"I was...but it looks as if you don't need my services anymore." Lara glanced at Marine Master Sergeant Zachary Garringer and smiled at him.

"You were the one who helped Sergei and me...and also helped me with the Chechens? Niki, this woman saved my life twice, and she saved Katya's, too!"

Peter gave Nicholas to a wide-eyed Niki and then took Lara in his arms, *"I can never thank you, enough, Lara!"*

Niki was surprised by the look on Lara Danilova's face as Peter embraced her. Lara closed her eyes for a moment, and then stood back and looked up at him. Her eyes were still bright with tears as Katya reached for her and hugged her, too.

"You both knew this investigator as Lara Ivanova," said Terenoff. "I wanted only the best person for the job, and I chose Lara. She didn't disappoint me. The fact that you and Katya are here today, Peter, is probably due, in great measure, to Lara's skill."

Nicholas held his arms out to his father, and Peter again took his son in his arms. Nik then stepped forward and also put her arms around Lara Danilova.

"I'm Nikola Kellman, Nicholas's mother. I don't know what to say other than, thank you...I can't thank you enough for protecting Peter and Katya." Now all three womens' eyes were wet with tears.

Terenoff cleared his throat, "I know that your party has much to do to get ready to go to the United States, Peter, and I probably won't have any contact with you again. If you have any questions, I will be more than happy to answer them for you now."

"Da," said Peter as he turned back to Terenoff. "You said that the Moscow Chief Prosecutor has been arrested?"

"He has," Terenoff nodded and smiled widely, "and it was due, for the most part, to the information that you provided."

Katya, who was again standing next to Ron, asked, "Does this mean that the man responsible for Misha's death will be brought to justice?"

"He was arrested this morning, and charged, among other things, with ordering the murder of Mikhail Preslov...your fiancé. Several

Lyubertsy gang members were arrested, too, and they have been telling us a great deal about how their criminal network is set up, and who their bosses are."

"It turns out," added Lara, "that one of the Chechens who attacked you needed medical treatment after the windshield shattered in his face. He was an excellent source of information, too."

Terenoff turned to Zachary, "I am the Chief Investigator for the Lyubertsy Prosecutor's office." He offered his hand to the U.S. Marine.

"How did you know who I am?" Zachary was curious as he shook the investigator's extended hand.

Terenoff raised his eyebrows, smiled, and replied, "We have our ways of gathering information, but that doesn't matter. We have been watching Genchenko's every move for several weeks. When he was attacked by the two Chechens in front of his apartment, we apprehended them less than a mile away, as they sought medical treatment. This prevented them from returning to finish what they started. But we weren't sure that the Genchenkos were out of danger, because at that point, we didn't know who had sent the Chechens, so Lara maintained her surveillance. Then Dr. Kellman, Dr. Michael, and Peter's son arrived yesterday, transported by you and your brother Ryan, Marines stationed at your American Embassy here in Moscow. Lara was quick to let me know what she had observed. By last night at around eleven o'clock, after we finished questioning the Lyubertsy gang members and the Chechens that we had in custody, we had enough evidence to ask for, and receive, a warrant this morning for the arrest of the Moscow Chief Prosecutor."

Peter shook his head in wonder, "You have been very busy, Investigator Terenoff."

Terenoff cocked his head to one side and again smiled widely at Peter, "Yes, you could certainly say that, but Lara and I were happy in our work!"

Nik, in spite of what seemed to be a cordial discussion between Peter and the Investigator, began to feel a sense of foreboding, "Will Peter be detained in order to testify in court? Does this mean that he won't be able to go with us when we return to the United States?"

Katya gave a small cry, "No, please, Peter must go with Nikola…"

"It's okay, Katya, I don't think that they can keep Peter here." Ron tried to calm her.

Terenoff recognized the fear in Katya's voice and saw it on Dr. Kellman's face, too. "Don't worry." He held up one hand, "Peter won't have to testify. We have many witnesses, and it wouldn't be helpful, even now, to put Ivan Genchenko's son on the stand to testify against the Moscow Chief Prosecutor. But there is another side to this story, and I want Peter and Katya to know about it."

What Terenoff told them next was unbelievable. "Vasiliy Arnov, the Moscow Chief Prosecutor, was responsible for smuggling your father's books from the Soviet Union. His only motive, so far as we can tell at this point, was to profit from the sale of Ivan Genchenko's books."

"Arnov," said Peter, as recognition dawned on him, "it was a man named Arnov who sent my mother, sister, and me away from Moscow after Ivan was arrested. Mother said that Arnov laughed at her when he told her we had to go to Lyubertsy."

"That is typical behavior for Arnov. However, Yakov Popov was the name of the man who actually got Ivan Genchenko's writings out of the country. He was Arnov's assistant, *and lover,* for several years, and

Popov visited your father often while he was in Lefortovo Prison."
Terenoff's hooded dark eyes fixed on Peter.

Nik put her hand to her mouth, "Pete, it was *Yakov,* the man who
tried to have you killed!"

Peter put an arm around her, "That answers many questions, doesn't
it?"

"Is there something more that I should know?" Terenoff looked
from Peter to Niki and back.

"Yakov was the KGB agent assigned to the Red Army Hockey
Team when we traveled outside the country. He almost succeeded in
getting me killed when he used two of my teammates to attack me. If it
hadn't been for Niki, he might have gotten the job done. I thought that
he was just my father's enemy, and that he wanted to harm me because
of that."

Katya took in a deep breath as Peter talked to Terenoff. She hadn't
known of the attempt on her brother's life when he was in America.

Although Ron was not fluent in Russian, he nonetheless saw the
effect of this conversation on Katya and gently squeezed her hand.
"Don't be frightened," he whispered.

"Once our investigation is completed, and we have looked into
Arnov's finances, Genchenko, you and your sister will receive
monetary reparation for the theft of your father's books." Terenoff was
full of surprises.

Peter shook his head as he thought that there was no way that he and
Katya would ever see the first ruble of monetary reparation from Ivan's
books. He told Marc Terenoff, "Thank you for telling us what really
happened to Ivan's writings, but this sounds like what the Americans
call a 'long shot.' I will not hold my breath, or lose a minute of sleep

over Ivan's books. In life, he was not kind to his children, so I don't really believe that Katya and I will ever receive anything positive from Ivan now that he is dead."

"I understand your bitterness in this matter, Peter, but perhaps sometime we can compare our childhood experiences, and you may find that yours were no worse than mine." Terenoff's smile now seemed rather melancholy. "Goodbye Peter, Katya, and the rest of you. I wish you all a happy and successful life in America. And perhaps, too…who knows?…we might meet again, considering that 1989 has been a terrible year for the Soviet Union. There is tremendous pressure to take down the Berlin Wall, and that is only one of the harbingers of collapse that we face right now."

"It's true…I have followed Gorbachev's career, and have seen the signs of collapse everywhere. Take care of yourselves." Peter's face was somber as he nodded to Terenoff and then Lara.

"It's time to go, Peter. There are several things that we need to get accomplished before all of you," Zachary made a sweeping hand gesture, "are ready to head west."

There were more hugs, handshakes, thanks and tears, and then Marc Terenoff and Lara Danilova stood and watched as Peter, assisted by the Marine, shepherded the group toward the door.

Master Sergeant Ryan Garringer got out of the government vehicle to assist them as Peter's group reached the parking area, "Well, that didn't take long. Everything must have gone well…?"

"You can't imagine how well, Ryan," Zachary replied with a grin. "I'll fill you in later."

That evening at the hotel restaurant, a celebration was held, which included birthday cake for dessert. Nicholas had several birthday gifts, plush toy animals, and a miniature wooden train, hastily bought and gift-wrapped at GUM, the huge department store in Moscow. He gleefully unwrapped his gifts, one by one, and squealed with delight at each. Peter and Nik had invited their Marines to join the party for dinner, and they accepted. By nine o'clock, however, the party was winding down. The events of the day had been stressful, and the next few days of travel would be even more so.

Peter thanked the Garringer brothers and told them that everyone would be catching an airplane at two in the afternoon the next day for the beginning of their journey to the United States. Ron had called British Airways after they returned from the Hall of Records, and had activated their V.I.P. tickets for their flights.

"Your Marines from last evening will be watching over you tonight. Zachary and I will be here at nine in the morning in order to get you to Sheremetyevo on time. It's a busy place, and it's good to get there early," said Ryan, who reached out and shook Peter's hand.

"I can tell you without reservation that we will all be ready to go when you arrive." Peter also shook Zachary's hand and thanked him for all that he had done on their behalf.

"You are welcome, Peter, and I speak for Ryan, too, when I tell you that we are very pleased with how well things went today." Zachary liked happy endings.

Ron and Katya sat at the table in the kitchenette, sipping hot tea and talking. After the day's ordeal in the Hall of Records, they were trying to unwind a little before bedtime.

Peter put his arm around Niki's shoulders as he bid them goodnight, "It's been an amazing day, and we are going to turn in. Good night to you both."

Niki yawned, her hand covering her mouth, "We'll see you in the morning."

With Nicholas bathed and in bed, sound asleep, Peter and Niki packed as much of their belongings as they could in anticipation of their busy day of travel the next day. Peter held his passport in his hand, and looked at it for several moments.

"I still can't believe that this is actually happening, Niki. There is such a sense of unreality…"

She put her fingertips against his lips. "Hush," she whispered, and kissed him.

The warm water sprayed on their bodies from several showerheads in the spacious marble-floored shower. As he lathered Niki's body with the fragrant soap, Peter knew that it would be the most wonderful shower that he had ever experienced, because he was free now, and Niki and their son were here with him. His heart quickened. *I am free to go with my family to America!*

When it was her turn to lather Peter, Nik stood on tiptoe to wash his hair, and then worked her way downward to his neck, chest, arms…but she wasn't able to complete his bathing. Peter gently lifted her onto him, and pressed her against the shower wall, his strong arms surrounding and supporting her. They moved together, coupled, in the warm and gentle spray from the showerheads, all the while giving voice to their love for one another.

Nik sat on the edge of the bed as she set an alarm for the morning. Peter, his head resting on his pillow, watched her and waited…ached…to put his arms around her. Together, they had checked Nicholas before coming to bed, and found him fast asleep, cuddling his plush birthday toys, a Siberian tiger and a Russian bear.

"Come here, Niki," Peter called to her, his arms open.

She crawled into the soft, very comfortable bed and into Peter's arms. He enfolded her in his arms, his heart swelling with happiness. *My Niki, my beautiful Niki...*

"Goodnight, my love." Her voice had a gentle, familiar lilt, and it was like a special music to Peter's ears as she came to him.

He pulled her close against his body, lying behind her, and asked in an emotion-filled, husky voice, "Will you marry me?"

She turned, her eyes wide and luminous, and kissed him, "Yes, Pete...with all my heart, *yes*!"

They lay together, holding one another, their joy almost palpable. Niki fell asleep within minutes, just as she had when they were alone together for those few short days in Indianapolis more than two years ago. This resurrected feeling, something that he thought he would never experience again, *the return of happiness,* felt strange to Peter, and he realized with more than a little surprise that the cold, aching place inside him was gone. It had completely melted away. With Niki's soft and warm, and very dear body nestled against his, Peter finally fell asleep.

Early the next morning, Nicholas came quietly to their bed, climbed in, pulled up the covers, and cuddled up against his father.

Chapter 30

The Garringer brothers were in the hotel lobby waiting for them at nine o'clock sharp, and all went smoothly. Surprisingly, it was Peter who rallied everyone, and made sure that all the arrangements were in order.

Ron didn't mind, really, because he was now smitten with Katya. He realized that his interest might not be reciprocated, at least not now, but he couldn't help himself. Ron had a buoyant and ever-hopeful spirit. *Maybe this is the way things were meant to be.*

Peter watched the way Ron was behaving toward Katya, and he was very happy that this man had taken an interest in his sister. Perhaps it was too soon after Misha's loss for this to be happening from Katya's viewpoint, Peter knew, but it was nonetheless wonderful that someone, other than himself, cared about her.

Niki noticed too, and she and Peter discussed the possibilities, "This is great, Pete, and I would never have guessed that it could happen."

"I have worried for a long time about Katya's safety and happiness if something should happen to me, but now I see that Ron could be there for her." Peter smiled in agreement with Niki.

In the boarding area at Sheremetyevo, the Garringer Marines waved goodbye to their charges. "Hope your flights are smooth," they said in unison, and then looked at one another in surprise and laughed.

Nicholas would not let his father out of his sight, especially when they boarded the airplane. He put his arms around his father's neck tightly, and didn't let go until they found their seats. And then he held his father's hand until the airplane took off.

Although their flights were very long, the little group made every connecting flight without problems. Nicholas cuddled alternately with his father and his mother to read books, eat, or sleep. He seemed to have fewer problems traveling home than he had during the journey to Russia.

By the time that they landed at Kennedy, Katya was resting her head on Ron's shoulder while they slept. This pleased Nik very much, because there was going to be another happy ending; she was just sure of it.

Klaus and Marina were there when Niki, Peter, and Nicholas, followed by Katya and Ron, came straggling off the jetway at Gate 9 of the Indianapolis Weir-Cook Airport.

"Welcome home everyone!" Klaus kissed and hugged his daughter, gave Peter a bear hug, and hugged Katya and Ron, too. Then he picked up his grandson and held him high for a moment before clutching Nicholas to his chest for a long hug.

Marina was laughing as she watched and waited her turn. When Klaus handed Nicholas to Marina, she kissed him and told him how much she had missed him.

"I missed you, too, *Babushka*." Nicholas melted his grandmother's heart with a beautiful smile.

Niki introduced Katya to her parents, and Klaus hugged Peter's sister again as Marina patted her shoulder.

Klaus beamed, "Well, let's get on the road. I know that you are all anxious to get home."

One by one, the exhausted travelers climbed into Klaus' van, and Duchess, who had been waiting patiently in the van, was now overjoyed to see Peter. Even though Klaus tried to get her to sit in the back of the van, she kept climbing over the seats to lie on the floor at Peter's feet. Peter told Klaus that he was glad to have her there. By the time Duchess got her way, everyone in the van was laughing at her insistence on being with Peter.

Nik was laughing as she told him, "She loves you, Pete. What can I say? She has the memory of an elephant."

Peter smiled and nodded, "Love is a wonderful thing." He looked into Niki's eyes as he spoke.

Much to Klaus' surprise, all of the luggage fit in the back of the van with very little effort. He happily drove them all to Niki's house in spite of the heavy traffic on I-465. It was a wonderful homecoming.

Klaus and Marina had thoroughly cleaned Niki's house, although it hadn't really needed it, filled the refrigerator, and prepared a dinner for the weary travelers. They wanted to make sure that there would be very little to do, at least for the first few days, after Niki's return.

Niki, with Nicholas in tow, took Peter, Katya, and Ron on a tour of the house. When Peter saw the study that Niki had prepared for him, he was surprised and very touched.

"Niki, it's just as we spoke of it, even to the smallest of details. You did this for me?" Peter was sitting in the large desk chair with Nicholas on his lap.

"Yes, all of it was," Niki knelt down in front of him, "for you."

Peter caressed her cheek with his fingertips. He was filled with emotion as he whispered a heartfelt, "You never gave up hope that we would be together, again, did you? Thank you, Niki…for waiting for me."

As she watched them, Katya was very happy for her brother and his beloved. Shyly, she turned to look at the beautiful view of the lake from the windows of Peter's study. Ron was by her side, smiling down at her.

Peter and Nicholas stayed downstairs with Marina and Klaus while Niki took Katya to her bedroom. Ron followed along because he was interested to see what the décor was like on the second floor, and, more importantly, he wanted to be near Katya.

"Peter told me that you loved flowers and that your favorite place as a child was the dacha at Tver overlooking the lake. Pull the curtains aside." Niki touched Katya's hand, and then held it.

Niki had decorated Katya's room in soft shades of yellow and lavender with white furniture. It overlooked a colorful perennial flower garden and the lake. The surprise and happiness on Katya's face showed how much she loved the room.

"Oh Niki, it's so beautiful, so very beautiful." Katya's eyes filled with tears.

Ron was grateful to Nik for making Katya feel at home. And he realized, too, how important it was to him that Katya would feel at home here.

Marina called up the stairway, "Dinner is on the table…"

It was a joyous dinner, a homecoming in every sense of the word, even for Peter and Katya, who had never been in this house before this wonderful night. Marina and Klaus did their best to make everyone comfortable, and Marina's cooking was absolutely delicious. For this special meal she had fixed a roast beef dinner with all the trimmings; an

American meal. They dined at the huge antique dining table that Nik and Stephanie had found on an antiquing expedition. It was perfect for this family gathering, this family meal.

When dinner was over, there was a birthday cake for Nicholas and two large and beautifully wrapped birthday presents. Nicholas, his eyes as big as saucers, wanted his papa to help him with his gifts, and Peter was very happy that his son had chosen him. He got down on the floor with Nicholas to open the gifts. Duchess lay down next to him as though she might help with the unwrapping. The first, and largest package was a rocking horse that Nicholas immediately jumped upon and began to ride. Peter coaxed him to help open the second package, and Nicholas obliged, pulling the paper in big swatches away from a box that contained large and colorful wooden building blocks that his father and Aunt Katya had sent for his second birthday. Nicholas and his father used the blocks to begin assembling a skyscraper in the great room in front of the fireplace.

"My son," Peter said happily as he held Nicholas on his lap, "I think that you may become an architect someday."

Niki agreed, "He does seem to have some aptitude, Pete. You may be right." Her heart was light, and she believed that she had never had a happier moment in her life than this, except for Nicholas's birth.

When the festivities ended, Klaus, Marina and Duchess, who were all reluctant to leave, took Ron back to the airport to pick up his car. Ron told Katya that he would visit the next day to check on everyone. He asked her if she needed anything, and Katya, smiling, told him that she wasn't sure of anything at the moment.

"Okay, but I'll come and see you tomorrow to check on how things are going." Ron wished that he could be more eloquent, but for the first time in his life he felt awkward and at a loss for words.

"It's time to get Nicholas ready for bed, and we can do his bath while Katya unpacks her things, Pete." Niki had just started the dishwasher in the kitchen as she talked to Peter. When she turned and looked directly at him, she could see how fatigued and pale he was. *So thin, he's still so thin.*

"Are you okay, Pete? I know that you're tired, but you're awfully pale, too."

Niki came over to where he was sitting on a kitchen stool at the counter with Nicholas on his lap. He smiled down at his son and ruffled his hair.

My beautiful Niki, he thought. Is this a dream? Am I really here with you and Nicholas? He was overwhelmed with emotion, and took a few moments to answer Niki.

"It's hard to believe that I'm…here with you and our son, and Katya, too. So much has happened so quickly, and I feel…mixed up. Maybe it's just that I'm tired?"

"*Yes*, you are tired, but you can believe that you are here with your family, Katya, Nicholas, and me. We are all safe and sound, and most important of all, we are together."

Niki put her arms around her men, and kissed both of them on the cheek, "I love you both, so very, very much."

Nicholas patted his mother's cheek and said, "I'm sleepy, mat *mother*. I don't want to read a book tonight."

Niki laughed gently, and so did Peter. Nicholas had just turned two years old, but he was like a little old man. Peter carried his son up the stairs while Niki turned off the lights in the kitchen and living areas. She checked the doors to make sure that they were locked, as was her habit, before going up the stairs, too.

Katya was already in nightclothes at the head of the stairs, "I will say goodnight to everyone now, because I'm not sure how much longer I can stay awake."

Nicholas, in his father's arms, reached over and gave Katya a hug, "G'night, Aunt Katya."

It didn't take Niki very long to get Nicholas ready for bed. He seemed anxious to get into his own bed after so many nights away from it.

"Pete, would you like to put Nicholas into bed?"

"I'd love to do it," Peter reached down and picked Nicholas up in his arms.

After tucking Nicholas into bed, Peter sat on the floor beside his son's bed. He looked around the room. There were airplane mobiles that hung from the ceiling, and stars, too. It was a wonderful boy's room, full of toys and books on shelves. And there were pictures of Peter, dressed for hockey, and in streeclothes, too. Niki had promised him that she would make sure that Nicholas knew his father. She had kept her promise. Peter's heart swelled with love and happiness.

When Nicholas was asleep, Peter stood up and found Niki in the doorway, watching them. He put a finger to his lips, and then took her by the waist, holding her close for a moment. She put her hand in his and led Peter out of Nicholas's room and down the hall to their bedroom.

Peter stood inside the doorway of the bedroom that he would share with his love. The large room was done in soft shades of blue and gray. The floor was hardwood, with thick, dark blue, throw rugs scattered about. The windows were dressed with layered white sheer curtains that moved in the breeze from the four open windows. A quilt pieced in a star pattern of light and dark shades of blue covered the bed, with shams in blue and gray. The furniture was Colonial Williamsburg cherry, except for one piece.

The antique sleigh bed positioned between two windows took his eye immediately, "Niki, where did you find such a beautiful bed? And the wood…is it cherry?"

"It was my one extravagance. It's an authentic cherry wood sleigh bed, and I bought it from a dealer in St. Petersburg."

"Russia? This bed came from St. Petersburg, in Russia?" Peter was astounded.

"Yes, and it was authenticated by a friend of mine who is in the antique business. She said that it is a museum-quality piece, and that it is definitely Russian. I wouldn't have my love, my very Russian love, sleeping on something that wasn't Russian. You have a brave and strong Russian heart and spirit, Peter Ivanovich Genchenko, and I love you for those things, and so much more."

On this night, this wonderful night of homecoming, they bathed together in the Jacuzzi that Niki had installed in the master bathroom near the shower.

"This is better than a whirlpool, Niki, much better." Peter slowly sank his tired body into the warm, bubbling water.

"I did this for you, Pete. In each step of the remodeling process, I thought of how you would react to what I was doing. I think this Jacuzzi is just what the doctor ordered," and she laughed softly. "I'm glad you like it. We will have many, many baths, memorable baths, and showers, too, in this room."

Peter nodded his head and smiled at his love, "Yes…many baths and many showers, Niki. We will be, as you say, 'squeaky clean' all of the time." And he reached for her...

When they were completely relaxed and, as Peter predicted, 'squeaky clean,' they slipped out of the Jacuzzi, grabbed two huge towels from a cabinet, and toweled each other off. Peter was quicker than Niki as they pulled on their nightclothes. Niki's foot got caught in one leg of her pajamas and Peter grabbed her arm to steady her. They both began to laugh at her predicament, as Peter lifted her up in his arms.

"It's time for bed, Niki," he said in a soft voice.

He carried her over to the sleigh bed, gently placed her in the middle, and then got in beside her. Peter pulled up the sweet-smelling sheets and blankets around them. Niki lay her head against Peter's shoulder, talking to him about wedding plans, "What do you think about the last Saturday in October as a wedding date...?" But she didn't hear his answer, as she fell asleep in mid-sentence.

Peter chuckled, and kissed her forehead lightly, "Goodnight my love, my Niki, and sleep well."

At first morning light, Peter got up quietly, so that he would not awaken Niki, dressed, and went downstairs after checking to see that Nicholas was still asleep. He wanted to walk by the lake for a while.

Niki's...no...*our* home, is a beautiful place, he thought. But he knew that the difference, the change from his life in Lyubertsy, would take some getting used to.

Peter took a deep breath as he stood on the porch, leaning on the railing. The air was cool and fresh as he filled his lungs. Slowly, he descended the veranda steps and walked through dew-covered grass toward the lake. He startled a deer that was getting a drink of water there, partially hidden by reeds and cattails. Peter was in a state of awe as he walked. A week ago, he could not have dreamed of being here in this lovely place with Niki, Nicholas, and Katya. *Home…I am home, now.*

He continued his walk all the way to the woods, a quarter mile or more. It was wonderful to be here experiencing this glorious morning of the first full day of his new life of freedom in America. The sun was rising from behind the trees across the lake, and Peter Ivanovich Genchenko's heart swelled with joy at the sight.

Chapter 31

Niki watched from their bedroom window as Peter walked near the lake. She leaned her elbows on the windowsill with her chin in her hands, and tears flooded her eyes. How many times had she looked out this window, wishing, hoping, *praying,* that someday Pete would be here with her, and that she would be able to watch him from this very window? And now he is here…Pete is really here!

Niki and Katya had breakfast preparations well underway when Peter came back from his walk. Nicholas was standing at the door, watching for his father, and began laughing when he saw him coming up the steps.

"Papa, I see Papa!" Nicholas was excited.

As Peter came into the kitchen, he picked up his son, kissed Niki's cheek and hugged Katya, "What is for breakfast? I am starved."

"There are so many delicious things, Petrosha. Where shall I start?" Katya's face was aglow with happiness.

"Steak and eggs with whole wheat toast coming up. Who wants orange juice?" Niki held the pitcher aloft.

It turned out that they all wanted orange juice. Nicholas said the blessing as he sat on his father's lap, rather than in his own chair, "God is great, God is good, let us thank him for our food. Amen."

Later in the morning, Niki took time to listen to her telephone messages, *"Pete, come and listen to this message!"* She was elated over the recorded message.

Peter was sitting cross-legged on the floor in the great room with Nicholas while Katya read a book to them. Niki's tone caught his attention immediately. He quickly got up and came to her.

"What is it, Niki? Is there a problem?"

"No, Pete, it's something truly wonderful…listen," and she played a message from Marty Pelham.

"Hello, Dr. Kellman, this is Marty Pelham. Sheldon Levin told me that Peter Genchenko would be in the U.S. soon, and I'd like to talk to Peter about hockey. You can reach me at (212) 555-5555 during office hours from nine to five through the week, and my home phone is (212) 555-1212. I'm really excited that Peter's coming back, and I'm sure that I can place him with one of several NHL teams that could really use someone like him. Anyway, please call me. I haven't been this excited since I first met the great Teril Ruchoi!"

"Are you interested, Pete?" Niki looked up at him hopefully.

Peter looked dazed, "Yes, but is there really a chance that I could play hockey here?"

"Didn't you hear the excitement in Marty's voice? Do you know who Teril Ruchoi is?"

"I know of him, yes…but there is no comparison between Ruchoi and me. He is a fantastic athlete, and he can make goals like no one else I have ever heard of…" Peter's voice trailed off.

"And so can you, Pete, *so can you.*" Niki threw her arms around his neck.

In the afternoon, Ron came by and asked if he could take Nicholas to a movie. A Disney movie was playing at a theater near the Fashion Mall, he said, and he knew that Nicholas would enjoy it. He also asked Katya if she would like to go with them, and, to his readily apparent delight, she agreed to go.

Everyone went out onto the porch, or as Niki called it, the veranda, and Peter and Nik stood at the railing to wave goodbye to the moviegoers. Nicholas, sitting in his little car seat in the back seat of Ron's car, was bubbling over with excitement as he waved goodbye to his parents.

Back inside the house, they laughed together about the smoothness of Ron's plan to get Katya to go to the movies with him. They agreed that his plan had been ingenious, and that Nicholas would benefit, too, because he loved movies; especially animated Disney movies.

Peter took Niki by the hand, and they went into his study where they sat on the sofa holding hands. They began to talk about Peter's options regarding hockey. One of the most important things to him, he told her, was that he wanted to get back into shape so that he could play well.

"I want to be able to give the best performance that I can for whatever team I might get the opportunity to play for," his face was serious as he spoke to Niki.

"Uncle Les told me that you would be welcome to practice with our local Indy team. They're not NHL, but they really are good. They'd give you a workout. And Uncle Les said, too, that he could arrange for ice time for you, so that you could practice on your own if you wanted to."

"You are full of surprises, Niki," Peter smiled at her and brought her hand to his lips.

"The next thing that we need to do is call Marty Pelham, Pete, and it wouldn't hurt to include Sheldon Levin, too. They are going to be key to your playing with a good team."

Peter agreed, "Yes, I think that they could be helpful, but I'm still mystified as to why they think that I am good enough to play on a professional team."

"All of the International Winter Games were videotaped, Pete, and I have them right over here." She got up to pull the tapes from a bookshelf, "Let's look at them for a little while. I think that maybe you'll understand why Marty and Sheldon are interested in you after you see some of these tapes."

Niki activated the television and VCR in the room, and put in one of the tapes. It was the game against Canada. Peter watched it in rapt silence as Niki glanced from him to the television screen and back, trying to gauge his reaction. Throughout the afternoon, as they snacked on leftovers and drank iced tea, they watched segments of all of the games that Peter had played in.

When they finished, Niki asked him, "Now do you see why Marty is ecstatic over having the opportunity to place you with a professional team?"

"I have never before seen what you have just shown me," Peter was shaking his head in disbelief.

"You are unique, Pete, you have a gift, and I want you to have every opportunity to do what you love to do."

At Niki's gentle insistence, Peter called Marty, who was so excited to be talking to him that he dropped his telephone. "Ooops! Uh, sorry, I'm just a little, uh, excited. Peter, how long are you going to be in the U.S.?"

"I am here on a visa now, but I will also apply for a green card. I hope to become a U.S. citizen as soon as they will let me apply."

"That's the best news that I have heard in a very long time, Peter! When can I talk with you face to face?"

Peter hesitated, "Well, Niki and I are planning to be married in late October, so it would probably be best if we agreed on a date after that. We aren't quite sure if our wedding will be the third or last Saturday in October."

"Hey, send me an invitation…Sheldon, too. You and Dr. Kellman…that's great, Peter, really great! Congratulations to both of you."

"Thank you, Marty. I feel like the luckiest man in the world right now. And to show you just how special my bride-to-be is…she has arranged to have me practice with the local team so that I can get back into my best playing form. I'm going to be practicing starting tomorrow, and working out on their ice. I want to be ready to compete as soon as I can, and this is the best way for me to do it."

"Sounds like a good plan to me. I'm going to send some of your stats and info that I compiled on you during the Winter Games in Indy to teams that I know are looking for someone like you. Is that okay with you?"

"*Yes,* and I thank you again, Marty. I appreciate anything that you might do on my behalf."

"Okay, Peter. I'd like to be your agent, so please don't sign with anyone else until I can talk to you about what you want in terms of earnings and a contract. When you start practicing with the local team, agents are going to come to see you. I can guarantee you that will happen."

"You have my word, Marty."

"That's all I need Peter. I'll see you at your wedding!"

Peter's excitement was boundless when he got off the telephone, "*Niki*, Marty says he wants to be my agent. Can you believe it?"

"It's wonderful, Pete, so wonderful. I know that good things are going to happen to us from now on."

"*Us*," Peter said, "yes, to *us.*" He picked his Niki up, whirled her around, and kissed her.

"Wow…you really know how to make a girl dizzy with love, Pete." She looked up at him and laughed.

"Always," he said. "I will always want you to be as dizzy with love for me, Niki, as I am with you."

She smiled and replied, "Since we're talking about love, let's talk more about wedding plans, Pete. I'll fix some more iced tea, and we can sit down and discuss some of the things we want in our ceremony."

As they sipped their tea, Niki told Peter that she was pretty sure that her mother would more than likely want to have a big wedding for them. Niki, however, wanted something small, something 'intimate' that wouldn't be such a big production.

"What do you think, Pete? Do you have some ideas about what you want?"

Peter's smile was slow, "Yes, I do. It would be wonderful to be married in a formal religious ceremony. You are your mother's only daughter and I think that she would want to do something special for you. I remember that my mother talked often about what she would like to do for Katya when the time came for her to marry."

"So…you'd wear a tuxedo, and stand at the front of the church…in front of all those people, while I walk down the aisle with Dad?"

"Yes, I would do that, and it would be the most wonderful thing that has ever happened to me, watching you come down the aisle to be my wife."

Niki was delighted with Peter's reaction, "Well, that settles it. You and I are going to have to suffer through the whole, long, drawn-out affair…the big wedding. But are you sure, absolutely sure that it's what you want to do?"

"Absolutely, my dearest Niki, absolutely." Peter's eyes held a tender expression as he gazed at her.

Chapter 32

It was definitely going to be a late October wedding, and Marina wanted to fill their beautiful, old, Russian Orthodox Church with friends and relatives for her daughter's wedding. Time was short, and she knew that she and Niki had their work cut out for them.

Peter was working out with the Indianapolis hockey team three times a week and loving it. Between workouts with the team, he used the training set-up that he and Niki had put together at home for his weight-lifting and exercise program. He was beginning to feel stronger and much better about his skills on the ice.

The Genchenkos, including Katya, who spent a great deal of time with Nicholas, were busy in many spheres, preparing for a wedding and getting Peter in shape to play professional hockey.

Klaus had beamed with pride when his daughter told him about her wedding plans. "My beautiful daughter is going to get married! How wonderful, Niki, for you and Peter. I am very happy for both of you, and for Nicholas, too." He bent and kissed the top of his daughter's head.

"Marina…are we not the luckiest parents in the world? Our daughter will be the most beautiful bride anyone has ever seen!" He put his arms around his wife and gently hugged her to him.

"Well, Klaus, I think that you, we, may be biased on that subject, but it is true that Niki will make a beautiful bride." Delight danced in Marina's eyes.

"I haven't called Mike yet, but I wanted the three of us to be together so that we could all talk to him."

"That's a grand idea, Niki. Let's do it now." Klaus was eager to call his son and share the good news.

Niki made the call, "Hi, Mike…what's new with me? Well, I'm glad that you asked, because Pete and I have set a date for our wedding…Yes…I'm very excited!…Dad wants to talk to you, and then Mom, too…Yes, I love you, too. Pete will be calling you soon to officially ask you to be his Best Man…Oh, yes…he's very excited with all of this, too…well, here's Dad…" Niki handed her father the telephone.

While the Kellman men were conversing…shouting?…their excitement quite apparent over the good news, Marina and Niki made a date to go shopping for Niki's wedding dress.

And then it was Marina's turn to speak to her son…"Isn't this the most wonderful news you have ever heard, Mike?…Yes, Niki is so-o-o happy!…She says that Peter will call you this evening to make your invitation to be Best Man official…Yes, I love you, too, dear…Goodbye."

Because they had very little time, Marina, Niki and Katya worked together on a guest list and all other aspects of the wedding. With Peter's blessings, they chose the color scheme, a soft blend of fall colors, and carried it through to the invitations, flowers, decorations, cake, and table settings for a sit-down dinner for the three hundred-plus guests who would be invited to the festivities.

"You are the three most important women in my life," Peter told them, "and I know that you will all work well together to prepare a most beautiful wedding ceremony." He grinned and bowed.

Niki curtsied, laughed and said, "Thanks, m'lord."

When Niki gave the final guest list to Marina, she and Katya worked for two days to get the invitations out as quickly as possible. It was a wonderful way for Marina and Katya to really get to know one another.

It made Marina very happy when her daughter took Katya and her to shop for a wedding gown. Niki was no-nonsense, and knew what she wanted. They 'power-shopped' three wedding boutiques and she decided on a gown that she found in the third shop at the Fashion Mall. Marina and Katya loved Niki's choice. It was a champagne-colored silk bombazine gown that became voluminously full from a tiny waist, and it had long, fitted sleeves. There were seed pearls sewn around the scooped neckline that dipped low in back to a large, softly draped bow. The train of the gown was elegant, but not showy, as Marina said, and it could be 'bustled' for easy movement and dancing at the reception.

"Oh, Nikola, you are so beautiful in your wedding gown!" Katya was as excited as Marina over Niki's choice of gowns. "My brother will be overwhelmed by your beauty."

"I truly hope so, Katya…I want to please him." Niki looked at her reflection in the mirror and smiled. *Pete will like this wedding gown; I just know he will!*

Marina asked Niki if she would wear the wedding veil and pearl-encrusted crown that she, herself, had worn for her wedding to Klaus, and Niki had agreed immediately, much to Marina's delight. And after a brief debate with her mother, she decided to wear her shoulder length hair in a chignon. This met with Marina's whole-hearted approval, as she had always thought that her daughter looked beautiful with her hair pulled back from her face, exposing the elegant and lovely length of her neck.

Katya, too, agreed that Niki's upswept chignon would be perfect with Marina's crown and veil. "This is all so wonderful. I did not know how exciting such a time as this could be. Thank you, Niki and Marina, for including me in your plans. Perhaps one day, this experience will prove to be most helpful."

Niki thought about what Katya had just said, and decided that Katya was thinking about Ron when she talked about this experience perhaps being helpful in the future. *Wouldn't that be lovely?* The week after Niki had found her wedding ensemble, she, Katya and Marina shopped for the bridesmaids' gowns. Niki wanted Katya to be her maid of honor, her friends Stephanie, Susan, and Sarah to be attendants, and her neighbor's daughter, Serena, to be her junior bridesmaid. Niki had decided to go all-out in the preparations for her big wedding. Pete had said that this was what he wanted, and her mother, she knew, was very happy about it, too.

They literally struck gold, the gold of a maple tree in the fall, when they shopped at a boutique shop in the Broad Ripple area. The bridesmaid's dress was simple and elegant; a floor-length sheath that skimmed the body, with a kick-pleat at the back for ease of walking. The silk shantung cloth draped across the bodice fluidly, with one strap across the right shoulder. Katya, otherwise unadorned, was nonetheless stunning in the dress. Niki was sure that her other bridesmaids would also look beautiful in the dress. And, she decided, this would be one bridesmaid's dress that could be worn again.

"How can this be so easy?" Niki asked her mother and Katya. She was very happy with their success in finding the perfect bridesmaid's dress and immediately called her bridesmaids and Serena's mother to let them know when to come in for their fittings. She told each of them, "the quicker, the better" because of time constraints.

One afternoon, more than a week after their earlier shopping expeditions, and when Katya was shopping with Ron, mother and daughter had a heart-to-heart talk about the appropriateness of Niki's having a formal wedding in light of the fact that she had already borne her intended husband a son. Niki brought up the subject, because she really wanted to know how her mother felt about the situation.

Marina's answer was short and to the point. "Niki, those who care about you and your family, and those who love you dearly, will have no criticism about your choosing a formal wedding to celebrate the love that you and Peter have for one another. Those who might criticize you or decide not to attend because they don't feel that you should have a formal wedding under the circumstances, do not fall in either the first or second categories, and therefore, do not matter."

One of the last things that Marina, Niki and Katya did before the wedding date was to go shopping for a mother-of-the-bride dress. They found the perfect dress in the first shop that they tried, much to their surprise. It was a sunset-colored full length sheath dress with a matching jacket in a satin material. They bought the dress on the spot, and told the saleswoman that Marina would do the alterations herself, because of the pressures of time regarding the approaching wedding.

After their quick success with the mother-of-the-bride dress, Niki, Marina and Katya went to the best cake-maker in town; Chandler's on North Meridian. Niki had said that she wanted at least three layers, and wanted to incorporate her chosen fall colors in the cake decorations. Mrs. Chandler was very helpful, and showed them more than thirty pages of fall wedding cakes.

Katya found a cake that had four layers, and a small, top layer, that seemed to meet all of Niki's criteria. "What do you think of this one, Nikola? Perhaps it is too 'old world,' but I truly like it."

"Oh…that's it; that's the one! Katya, it is so gorgeous…" Niki put a hand to her mouth in awe. "I love it. Mom, do you like this one?"

"Perfect…it is perfect!" Marina kissed her daughter, and then Katya, on the cheek.

Peter and Niki visited a florist to choose the flowers for their wedding. Again, fall colors prevailed. Peter liked the gracefully draped flowers that had a modest spray above, then tumbled down the front of the bride's and bridesmaids' gowns in a profusion of gold, red, and orange, with green foliage and vines.

The florist, a middle-aged woman, told Peter, "You have a wonderful sense of color and design, Mr. Genchenko, you really do," and gave him a warm smile.

Niki chuckled as they left the shop, "I think she was giving you the eye, Pete. She really liked you."

"It's my animal magnetism, Niki, nothing more." He squeezed her hand gently and smiled at her as they hurried toward their car.

The following day, when Niki came to pick up Nicholas, Marina told her daughter that she would hire a chef who could handle all of the food ordering and catering, including the champagne and wine, for the reception. Niki gave her mother carte blanche with the food and drink because she knew that Marina could envision and direct a spectacular wedding banquet.

"I love you, Mom, and thanks so very much for all of your help!" Niki kissed her mother's cheek, took Nicholas' hand and waved goodbye. "We are meeting Pete, Katya and Ron for dinner at St. Elmo's at six, so we've got to get going."

Chapter 33

Peter, coffecup in hand, watched the gorgeous, peach-colored sunrise from the broad porch of his home on his wedding day. The late October morning sky was bright blue and almost cloudless. The crimson sun tinged the sky around it pink, adding a new dimension of color. He breathed in the fresh scent of the lake, filling his lungs deeply. As he gazed at his surroundings, he marveled at the profusion of colorful fall perennial flowers in Niki's gardens, and the red and gold foliage of the trees. Birds called melodically from the tall trees skirting the lake, and waterfowl, ducks, geese, and a pair of swans floated silently on the lightly wind-rippled surface of the water.

This is a beautiful beginning to a wonderful day, thought Peter. He raised his coffeecup in a toast to such a spectacular sunrise as this, on the most important day of his life. Happiness, *joy*, a sense of belonging to someone, belonging in this place, filled his heart to the brim. From this day forward, Nikola Kellman will be Nikola Genchenko, my wife. He spoke their names aloud, smiling as he did so. "Mr. and Mrs. Peter Genchenko…at last."

Niki was inside the house, getting Nicholas's wedding clothes together. She and Katya were going to drive to the church together, and Nicholas would ride with his father and his Uncle Mike, who would pick them up soon.

Peter was amazed at Niki's ability to organize everything that they needed for their wedding ceremony. He helped her as much as he could, but weddings were mostly a woman's province, he knew. Niki seemed to be able to think of everyone's' needs. But there was something that she didn't know. He had a special surprise for her on this, their wedding day. His little secret made him chuckle with anticipation…

Not long after Peter and Katya had first arrived in their new home, Katya was unpacking her things from her mother's valise, and had found a small, flat bag in the lining of the valise. When she opened it, she found that the contents were a ring and a pair of earrings. She showed them to Peter, who was speechless for a moment, and then he reminded her of the story that their mother had told them about the early days in her marriage to their father.

"This is our great-grandmother's jewelry that Ivan gave to our mother when they were first married! I can't believe that Mother was able to keep the ring and earrings through all of our Lyubertsy miseries…" Peter was amazed at his mother's ingenuity and tenacity.

"Petrosha," Katya spoke quietly to her brother. "I think that it would be wonderful if you gave this beautiful ring to Niki on your wedding day." She held up the multi-faceted ring to catch the light and it shined with rainbow colors from the many stones; diamonds, rubies, and emeralds.

"Yes…that's a fantastic idea!" Peter's eyes brightened, "I can give Niki something unique and precious, something from our family, when we marry. I want this to be a surprise for her, Katya. This will be our wonderful secret…and the earrings should be yours. We will both have something of great value from our family. I think our mother would be very happy with this arrangement, don't you agree?"

Katya's smile was radiant, "Yes, Petrosha, I know that this would have made her happy for her children. She was saving these things for us for a very long time."

Peter was pensive and quiet for a few moments, and then replied, "Yes, Katya, I think she was. I truly believe that she was, and it wasn't at all easy for her to do so."

On the day of the wedding, Katya, as Maid of Honor, was dressed in the soft gold silk sheath that Niki had chosen for her. Stephanie, Susan, and Sarah, as Bridesmaids, and Serena as the Junior Bridesmaid, were wearing a lighter shade of gold in the same style sheath as Katya's. Each wore a few fall flowers pinned in their upswept hair that coordinated with the bouquets that they would carry during the ceremony.

All of the young women got along quite well, and teased the bride, who took it good-naturedly, about whether or not the groom would be late for the ceremony. And then it was time to help Niki into her wedding gown and veil. Marina was there to help her daughter into her beautiful wedding dress. Tears filled Marina's eyes when Niki's dress and veil were in place.

"So beautiful, my Nikola, you are so beautiful in your wedding finery," she told her daughter. "And all of your Bridesmaids are beautiful, too." Marina smiled and nodded at each of them.

"Thank you, Mom, you have been wonderful to me, and to Peter, Nicholas, and Katya through everything…" Tears formed at the corners of her eyes.

Susan offered Niki a handkerchief that she kept in her bodice for just such an emergency, "No tears, Niki…no tears are allowed on your wedding day…at least not until after the ceremony." And all of the women in the room laughed together.

Peter was the typical nervous bridegroom. Dressed in a pleated white shirt, cravat, black tuxedo, vest and cummerbund, with his hair tamed somewhat, he looked like an ad in "Gentleman's Quarterly Magazine," but the butterflies in his stomach belied his cool exterior. He paced from one end of the dressing room to the other, back and forth, back and forth.

Finally, Mike Kellman, Peter's Best Man, took him by the arm and led him outside for a breath of fresh air. Ron, Tom, and Mickey, who were groomsmen, along with Wesley, the junior groomsman, followed Peter and Mike outside into a courtyard resplendent with colorful fall flowers.

"Pete, you've got to lighten up a bit," Mike patted him on the back and grinned at him as he spoke.

Tom, Ron, and Mickey agreed with Mike's assessment, nodding their heads in unison.

"Yes, and if you don't," said Ron, "you're going to fall over in there." He hooked a thumb toward the church, "I've seen it happen before."

Seven-year-old Wesley told Peter, "My Dad said that it's not easy to get married, and I think he's right."

This comment brought laughter and, again, complete agreement among the older groomsmen.

Peter also nodded in understanding, "I know…I know, but this is the most important day of my life, and I'm a little, uh, scared, I guess."

Tom and Mickey, who had been Peter's Athletic Trainers during the International Winter Games in 1986, and had remained friends of Niki's, both laughed at Peter's current behavior, because he had always been 'cool' when he played hockey.

Tom, who had recently married, put his big arm around Peter's shoulders and said, "It's gonna be okay, Pete. All you have to do right now is settle down. After the ceremony, you'll feel great, and that's a promise!"

Klaus, with Nicholas in his arms, joined them from a side door in the church, "How is everyone doing?"

"Well, Dad, Ron, Mickey, Tom, Wesley and I are doing great, but Pete's a little 'iffy', I think."

Klaus clamped his large hand on Peter's shoulder, "Don't worry Peter. Every man who is about to be married is nervous, I mean gut-wrenching nervous, before he says his vows. It's only natural."

This pronouncement made Peter laugh as he reached for his son, "I see. Well, I get the point. I'm not the first groom to get…what is it you say?…butterflies, in my stomach."

It was time for the ceremony to begin. Flowers filled the church, releasing the wonderfully heady perfume of romance into the air. All of the guests had been seated by Ron, Tom, Mickey or Wesley. The organist had played a moving and powerful medley of the favorite sacred and classical music of the bride and groom, that included compositions by Mozart, Bach, and Beethoven, as the guests awaited the ceremony. Sunshine streamed through the stained glass windows of the church, creating a mosaic of beautifully bright colors on the walls, ceiling, floor, and assembled guests, and an expectant hush fell over the assemblage.

Peter, Nicholas, Mike, Ron, Tom, Mickey and Wesley entered through a side door and took their places to the right of the sanctuary. All of them, including Nicholas, were smiling as they faced the guests.

In a few moments, the bridesmaids began to walk gracefully down the aisle to the organ strains of Handel's "Water Music" to take their places on the left, opposite the groom and groomsmen. Katya caught Peter's eye and smiled encouragement at him as she turned to face the guests with Stephanie, Susan, Sarah and Serena.

A string quartet began to play Pachelbel's Canon, and Niki slowly started the walk down the long aisle toward Peter. It seemed that she was floating on a cloud; she glided so lightly along, holding her father's arm. Her smile was radiant as she looked directly at Peter and Nicholas from the moment that she started down the aisle.

Peter's heart turned over. A vision, my Niki is a beautiful vision, he thought, as he swallowed hard.

Nicholas stood with his father at the front of the church, waiting for his mother to reach them. He hopped from foot to foot in anticipation of what would happen next. His Uncle Mike patted him on the head lightly, and Nicholas turned to look up at him and smiled. Uncle Mike smiled back.

Klaus proudly stood at the front of the church, holding his daughter's hand until Peter stepped forward and took the hand of his wife-to-be. Peter then led her up the steps toward the altar. Niki handed her bouquet to Katya as she and Peter paused before ascending to the wedding altar where the Priest awaited them.

Marina and Klaus sat, rapt, in the left front pew with Irina and Karl Kellman as Niki recited her vows with Peter. It was apparent to Marina and Klaus, as they watched their child and the man she had chosen to wed recite their vows to one another, that these two young people were very much in love.

Niki looked up at Peter as they stood in front of the Priest, and her face was glowing. They shared a secret that increased their happiness on this day. Their second child, conceived, no doubt, in Moscow, was on the way.

When it came time for the exchanging of the rings, Mike came forward to hand Peter the ring for Niki. As Peter spoke his vows, he put his great-grandmother's ring on Niki's third finger, left hand. She looked down at the ring, and then up at Peter, her eyes wide with surprise and delight. He smiled and nodded his head. He could see that she remembered the story that he had told her about his mother and father when they were newly-weds, and his great-grandmother's ring.

Katya beamed, and Ron noticed that something, he didn't know what, had happened. And then Katya looked at him and smiled. Ron's heart, at that moment, was ensnared, and he was as happy as he had ever been in his entire life.

Niki put a wide gold band on Peter's ring finger as she made her vows to him, "With this ring, I thee wed..." Her eyes, bright with unshed tears, never left his as she repeated the words of the Priest, her vows, to Peter.

At the end of the ceremony, Mr. and Mrs. Peter Genchenko and their son, Nicholas, in his father's arms, came up the aisle to the triumphantly repeated music of Pachelbel's Canon, their faces wreathed in smiles. The receiving line formed in the narthex of the church, and Peter, still holding Nicholas in his arms, had never before seen so many people who wanted to shake his hand, kiss, or hug him in congratulation.

During a lull in the lineup of congratulatory guests, Niki tugged at Peter's sleeve until he bowed to listen to her, "You took me completely by surprise, Peter Genchenko. The ring is beautiful, and it was your great-grandmother's engagement and wedding ring, wasn't it?"

"Yes," he smiled down at her, and kissed her on the forehead, "it was my great-grandmother's, and my mother's ring, and now it is yours because you married into our family."

The reception went smoothly at the Geist Country Club. The dinner was superbly cooked and served, due in great part to Marina's and her chef's management. The meal and service were lavish, lovely, delicious, and completely in keeping with the gorgeous wedding ceremony.

Marty Pelham and his wife, Diane, and Sheldon Levin and his wife, Elaine, sat with Niki and Peter for several minutes after the formal dinner, discussing how Marty's search was coming in regard to openings for Peter with NHL hockey teams.

"Detroit is very interested, and so are Chicago and Pittsburgh. I gave all of them the video footage from the Winter Games when you were here, and they liked what they saw. All three teams can really use someone like you, Peter."

"I don't know how to thank you, Marty…and I want you to be my agent. Niki and I," he took her hand, "have talked about it, and we have a great deal of confidence in you."

"That's great, Peter, that's fantastic! I'll do my best for you." Marty's face was red with emotion.

"I can vouch for Marty, Peter. He's as great an agent as he was a scout, and you won't be sorry." Sheldon seemed as happy as was his friend.

Stephanie came hurriedly to the table, "Hi everyone…" She waved a hand in greeting, "Marina said that it's time for the bride and groom to do a little dancing."

"That's okay, go dance with your lovely bride, Peter. You're sure a lucky guy, and you two make a very handsome couple. I'll be in touch with you very soon." Marty shook Peter's hand.

Peter wanted the same band that had played at the 1986 International Winter Games dinner dance to play at the wedding reception. There was a soft place in his heart for the band that had made that evening in 1986 so magical. On that night, Niki had worn a beautiful red dress and red heels, and she had danced with him. Yes, Peter wanted that same band, because he had captured Niki's heart on that night, and she his.

Ron had winced a little when Katya told him about Peter's choice for the wedding reception music. He really didn't have anything against Garibaldi's nephew, the bandleader, but Ron was no fan of big band era music. But as he thought about it, he reconsidered, because he knew that he would be able to dance with Katya…and big band music meant dancing close together.

The bride and groom requested "Moonlight Serenade," for their first dance. It was one of the songs that they had danced to in 1986, when they first realized that they were falling in love. This time around, Peter didn't have to pull Niki closer to him, because she got as close to Peter as her wedding gown would allow.

As Peter embraced Niki…*his wife*…the music moved him now as it had before. Happiness flooded through him. He put his lips to his wife's ear and whispered, "My beautiful, brave Niki…dreams really do come true, because here we are, you and I, husband and wife…at last!"

Niki tilted her head upward, smiled brightly, and repeated his words, "Yes…at last!"

Their guests applauded as the handsome couple moved around the dance floor, and the wedding party joined in the dance. Marina and

Klaus, Uncle Karl and Aunt Irina, then followed the wedding party onto the dance floor. Katya and Mike, Stephanie and Ron, Susan and Tom, Sarah and Mickey, and Wesley and Serena were paired up for this first dance of the wedding party with the bride and groom.

"They make a beautiful couple, don't you think, Marina?" Klaus, who was holding Nicholas as he and Marina danced, was very proud of his daughter at this moment. And now he finally understood how much Niki cared for Peter.

"Yes, Klaus, they look perfect together." Marina thought briefly of the first time that she had seen them embrace and kiss, and of her trepidation at the time, but she was glad now, to know that they were now together.

Katya danced with Mike, and Ron danced with Stephanie, as was the custom for the wedding party for the first dance with the bride and groom. But Ron soon 'cut in' on Mike, and Katya smiled brightly at him. Stephanie didn't mind; she had big, handsome Mike, and she really liked Nik's big brother.

Mr. and Mrs. Genchenko's second musical selection was an instrumental version of Elvis Presley's "Can't Help Falling In Love." Peter sang the words of the song to his new bride, much to her delight. When the wedding guests realized that he was singing, the ballroom became quiet so that they could hear the groom sing to his bride. At the end of the song, the wedding guests stood and applauded.

Marty and Sheldon clapped their hands and whistled...and their wives joined in...at least for the applause.

A grinning Pete laughed and bowed low, then gathered his wife to him for their third musical selection, an instrumental version of Ann Murray's "A Love Song." Niki sang the words to Pete, as the wedding guests stood and applauded again, and it was Niki's turn to bow.

As the wedding guests joined the newlyweds and wedding party on the dance floor, Klaus, still holding Nicholas, danced with his lovely daughter. They posed briefly for the photographer. "I am so very happy for you and Peter, Niki. It's the most wonderful thing that could happen for Nicholas, too, and your mother and I want you to know that we love all of you very much." Klaus kissed his daughter on the top of her head, just in front of her tiara, as Nicholas patted his mother's face.

Marina and Peter paired for a dance. Looking up at him with a warm smile on her face, she said, "You and Niki make a lovely couple, Peter, and you have made Klaus and me very, very happy. We want you to know that we welcome you into our family wholeheartedly, and with a great deal of love for you and Katya."

Peter's throat tightened with emotion at Marina's pronouncement, "Thank you, Marina. I am glad to be a part of your family. And thank you for including Katya, too." He bent and kissed his mother-in-law on the cheek.

The music stopped as Peter danced with Marina, and then started again, "Peter, my sister, Irina, would like to dance with you…but she's too shy to ask. Shall we dance by her table and scoop her up?" Marina laughed.

Irina, who greatly favored her sister in looks, was indeed shy, but she beamed when Peter invited her to dance with him. "It was so nice of you to ask me to dance, Peter. I'm sorry that Karl and I haven't gotten to meet you before now, but I'm sure you know of his illness."

Peter charmed her, "I want to get to know all of Niki's family, Irina. The only close relative that I have now is my sister, Katya, and I am happy to join Niki's family." Peter hesitated a moment, and then asked,

"Is your husband, Karl, doing well, now?"

"Yes, he is…but he tires easily. I have to watch him closely, too," she smiled, "because he always wants to be busy. He always has a project of some sort."

Uncle Les cut in on Klaus and Nicholas to dance with Niki. "Wow, Niki, you two kids look *fantastic* together on the dance floor. I'm happy for both of you, and this is a great 'happy ending,' isn't it?"

"It's beyond my wildest dreams, Uncle Les. And I want to thank you again, from the bottom of my heart, for helping me when Pete needed me. You and Dad, and Ron's father, Ari Michael," Niki nodded toward where the Michaels' were sitting, "probably saved Pete's life, and Katya's, too. I thank you for myself, and for Nicholas. Just look at him…he's on his father's shoulders now, and he's having a wonderful time!"

Niki's next partner was her Uncle Karl, who smiled down at his niece. "Today is the most important day of your life, Niki. Your Aunt Irina and I are very happy for you."

Looking up into her Uncle's face, Niki could see the remarkable family resemblance to her father. "Thanks, Uncle Karl. I'm so glad to have you here, and healthy again."

"Being here with our family to celebrate such a wonderful occasion means everything to me, Niki."

Niki stood up on tiptoe and kissed her Uncle's cheek, "This is a lovely party, isn't it?"

"Yes, my dear, it certainly is," Karl replied with a broad smile.

Marina came to take her daughter's hand, "If you don't mind relinquishing the rest of your dance with Niki, Karl, it's time for her to throw her bouquet."

Karl nodded at Marina and smiled, "Perhaps she will dance another dance with her old uncle later."

All three laughed together, and then Niki and Marina headed toward the bandstand where the band was now leaving to take a break. Niki climbed the stairs and stood on the bandstand to throw her bouquet as the ballroom lights became brighter. The drummer in the band stayed behind for the tossing of the bouquet, and did a loud drum roll to catch everyones' attention.

"Ladies…all of you single ladies," Niki called into the microphone on the stage, "come on up here, and let's see who catches my bouquet for good luck!"

A large group of giggling young ladies formed a line in front of the bandstand. Niki turned her back to the room and threw her bouquet backward, over her head. Immediately, there were squeals of delight and applause. When she turned to face the ladies, she was very happy to see that Katya had caught her bouquet! A good luck omen, thought Niki. It's truly a good luck omen…

Peter came bounding up the stairs to the bandstand and took his wife's hand, "I have been told by your mother that I must take the garter from your lovely leg and toss it to a group of the unattached men among our wedding guests."

Niki touched his face lightly with her fingertips, "This is going to be fun!"

Again, the drummer gave a loud drum roll before Peter, who had been coached by Mike Kellman, called to all of the unattched male wedding guests to assemble for the garter toss.

"Gentlemen…*start your engines!*"

Peter tossed the garter over his head to the bachelors standing behind him, and quickly turned to see who the lucky man was. Mike Kellman grinned a devilish grin at him, and, holding the garter high above his head, shouted, "Gotcha!"

Peter had to laugh, because he remembered that Niki had once said the same thing to him, when she realized that he could speak English after he had just arrived in Indianapolis for the International Winter Games. Everything, all his history with Niki, harkened back to December of 1986. *That's where it all began...*

"There is just one more photo op," their photographer, Maddie Meyers, a tiny, dark-haired, dark-eyed beauty, told them. "We've got to do the traditional cutting of the cake photo, and then you can both have fun and mingle with your guests the rest of the evening. I'll still be shooting photos of the reception, too, at random, but this is your last 'required' photo."

Wedding guests gathered around the happy couple as they cut their spectacular wedding cake, Peter's hand over Niki's, according to tradition. One of the best photographs of the entire wedding and reception took place when Niki playfully put a daub of frosting on Peter's nose as she fed him a piece of the cake, and he returned the favor. Maddie's photo of Mr. and Mrs. Genchenko cutting their wedding cake was priceless.

Ron, proudly holding Katya's hand, led her to his parents' table to introduce her to them, "Mother and Dad, this is Ekaterina Ivanova, Peter's sister."

Katya smiled at Ron's effort to be polite and formal in front of his parents, "Everyone calls me Katya, and I'm very happy to meet you both." She offered her hand to Miriam, and then to Ari.

Ron's mother's eyes brightened as she saw how her son was acting toward this young woman. Perhaps he was truly in love this time?

"Myron has told us that your mother was born in Poland, and that she attended school there."

Miriam was well aware that this young woman's mother was Jewish. Myron had told her some of Katya's family history, and she had seen how important it had been for him to put Katya in a good light. It was truly wonderful how things worked out, sometimes, she thought.

"Yes, my mother was born into the Warsaw Ghetto. Her uncle was the Rabbi at the Synagogue there when she was born."

This comment got Ari's undivided attention, and Ron was very surprised at his father's interest. Ari, a smile on his face, animatedly invited his son and Katya to join them at their table to "sit and chat" for a while.

Peter, again on the dance floor with his wife, with Nicholas between them, noticed that Ron had taken Katya to sit with his parents. "Look, Niki, Ron is introducing Katya to his parents. This may be a good omen. What do you think, my dear wife?"

Niki smiled up at her husband and nodded, "I agree, Pete…something wonderful is going to happen for Katya and Ron…I just know it!"

Nicholas put his head on his father's shoulder, "I'm very sleepy Papa."

Peter and his wife chuckled at their son's comment.

Chapter 34

Marina and Klaus were designated sitters for Nicholas after the wedding reception. He was going home with his grandparents, and although he would miss his parents, he loved to stay overnight with Babushka *Grandmother,* and Dyedooshka *Grandfather.*

Niki's brother, Mike, came to say goodbye to his sister and her new husband. "I wish you two the best…the best of everything. I'm going to be heading home tomorrow, but I have promised Nicholas that we will have breakfast together, pancakes of course, in the morning at Mom and Dad's." He bent to kiss his sister on the cheek, and then shook Peter's hand. "I hope to see all of you soon."

At a late, or more accurately, early, morning hour at the end of their wedding reception, with farewells and best wishes still ringing in their ears, Niki and Pete were taken by limousine to the Westin Hotel for the weekend. Marina and Klaus had given them a weekend in the Honeymoon Suite as a wedding gift.

This time, Niki didn't tease the bellhop who escorted them to their room, but she squeezed Pete's hand and shared a smile of remembrance with him, regarding another bellhop, more than three years ago, that had been 'snooty' toward them on the way up to the concierge level of the Westin, which had been the designated hotel for the Winter Games in 1986.

When they were settled in their room and had tipped and dismissed the bellhop, they both gave a deep sigh of relief, and put their arms around each other. It had been a long day, and longer evening, and now they were alone, wonderfully and completely alone…just the two of them.

Peter's fingers were clumsy as he tried to unbutton the back of Niki's wedding gown, "Mrs. Genchenko, they have put tiny buttons on your gown, and I am having great difficulty…"

She turned toward him, her laughter like music, "I love to hear you say that, Pete. It's so wonderful to be Mrs. Peter Genchenko!"

He kissed her, and somehow they managed to get her out of the wedding gown. He slipped the straps of her petticoat from her shoulders and let it fall to the floor. Niki had already taken off her veil and tiara, setting them aside carefully, because they were her mother's.

She pulled one sleeve of Peter's tuxedo jacket, and then the other, down his arms, letting the jacket fall to the floor. Next, she unfastened his cummerbund, and then his tie. Peter took the cue and pulled off his trousers quickly, and then the stiff white shirt of his formal attire, both of which landed on the floor next to the jacket.

They stood face to face, and she looked up at him, as he pulled her close with only the briefest of underwear fabric between their bodies…and then they slipped out of them.

Peter Genchenko kissed his wife once, twice, a third time; each kiss increasing in urgency, as his need for her overwhelmed him. He picked her up and placed her gently on the bed. Niki scrambled to pull the duvet and bedsheets down as Peter climbed into the bed.

And then he was in her. Peter thought that his heart might burst with happiness. He could not get enough of her; this wonderful, beautiful, courageous woman of his. "I dreamed of marrying you…so many times…of having a family with you…and my dreams came true…they came true," he whispered to her as they made love.

As for Niki, her world, torn apart when Pete had left to return to his family in Russia, was now completely reassembled into the most wonderful life with him that she could imagine.

That night, neither of them could sleep, and they talked for hours about some of the things that had happened to them while they were apart. Niki told Peter how much she had wanted him to be there to hold her hand while she was in labor with Nicholas.

"Stephanie was my labor coach, and I didn't really have a bad time at all, but my heart ached for you to be there. I wanted so much for you to be there…to see our child come into the world. "

"Niki," Peter began, his voice filled with emotion, "I truly wish that I could have been there to help you and to see the birth of our first child. I will forever carry the sadness inside me because I wasn't there."

Niki put her fingertips on his lips, "Hush, Pete, there was nothing that you could have done differently at the time. You had to go home to your mother and sister. And you didn't know that we had created a child."

He put his big hand across her abdomen, "This time, I will be there, Niki. We will have this child together."

They didn't stay the whole weekend at the hotel. Neither could stand being away from Nicholas that long. In the morning, the desk clerk was very surprised when they checked out a day early from the Honeymoon Suite.

He asked them, "Were there any problems that we might have helped you with?" And then, realizing his faux pas, he blushed a bright crimson.

After checking out of the hotel, Peter and Niki laughed all the way to their car. "The poor man was mortified!" said Niki. "When he realized what he said and how he said it, I think he could have crawled under the counter."

"He had a way with words, Niki, he really did," laughed Peter.

Niki had already called her mother and asked her to get Nicholas ready to go home. "Mom, we just couldn't be here without Nicholas. Pete and I talked last night, and we've decided to go to Disney World, and we're taking Nicholas and Katya with us. No one has ever had a honeymoon like the one we're going to have. If you'd like, you and Dad can come with us, too."

Marina and Klaus begged off the invitation, saying that Duchess would hate to go back to the kennel. "You know how spoiled she is, Niki. She doesn't know that she is a dog."

The Genchenko family, Pete, Niki, Nicholas, and Katya, went to Disney World for a most unusual honeymoon. They stayed in a large suite of rooms in the Polynesian Hotel for a week, enjoying the pampering and entertainment there and the daily fun at the amusement park. Even though Nicholas was small, he loved everything about Disney World, and he *really* loved Snow White.

Katya was nearly overwhelmed by the crowds, rides, especially Space Mountain, and the multitude of shops with everything from food to toys and clothing. She bought a gift for Ron in the shop where hand-blown glass figures were made. It was a delicately wrought sailing ship, and she hoped that he would like what she had chosen for him.

Niki and Pete became 'coaster junkies' during their week-long adventure, and rode all of the challenging, exciting rides that they could find, some wet, some wild, some mostly upside down.

Katya told them often, "You are both soomasshyedshee *crazy.*"

They stood, dripping wet, their clothes and sandals soggy, in front of Nicholas and his Aunt Katya on their last full day in Disney World. She laughed when they hugged her and then Nicholas, getting them a little wet, too.

"Go on, you two. Nicholas and I are enjoying ourselves, and we were even dry, up until now."

"Don't you want to do some of the bigger rides, Katya? I can stay with Nicholas while you and Pete do some of the rides." Niki wanted Katya to have some fun, too.

"Nicholas and I are having a wonderful time, Niki. This is my very first time in an amusement park. I am with my wonderful little nephew, and he is very entertaining. And besides that, Peter knows quite well that I do not like high places. I'd rather be close to the ground."

Peter hugged his sister again, and whispered in her ear, "Thanks, Katya. Having you and Nicholas with us on our honeymoon is a most extraordinary experience."

Niki and Peter headed for the next scary ride holding hands, and running like excited children. Nicholas and his Aunt Katya stayed with the 'kiddie rides' and had their own extraordinary experiences, too.

As the afternoon progressed into evening, Peter sat holding his very sleepy son, waiting for Niki and Katya to finish shopping in one of the Disney stores. He puzzled over his good fortune. It has only been a short time since Niki brought Nicholas and Ron to rescue Katya and me, thought Peter. Yet here we are, Niki and I, married, and in this fantastic resort with Nicholas and Katya, enjoying ourselves, with more than enough to eat, and a world of opportunities ahead of us. He marveled at this complete change in his life…to love someone so much, and to have that love returned in full measure. Life takes many pathways, and I am so grateful that my life has taken this one. He kissed Nicholas on the cheek and ruffled his hair gently with one hand. My son, my wonderful son, he thought, and then smiled as he gathered Nicholas closer to him. We will be going home tomorrow. The thought of home, the Genchenko family's home, brought tears of joy to his eyes.

After their week of sun and fun, some of them sunburned, some of them tanned, and laden with souvenirs and gifts, the Genchenko family started for home. When they were settled on the airplane, Nicholas, who was completely worn out from so much 'fun' slept comfortably on his father's lap for most of the flight. Niki and Katya took the opportunity to talk and and rehash their amazing adventure. It made Niki very happy to know that Katya was warming to her, and that they could talk so easily.

At five-thirty that evening, Ron was waiting for them at the Indianapolis airport. He laughed out loud when he saw the sunburned, rag-tag group.

"Well, did you have a good time?" He had his hands on his hips, and his face was wreathed in smiles.

Peter hoisted Nicholas onto his shoulders, "We all had a great time, but I think that Nicholas enjoyed himself the most."

"Yes, it was wonderful, Ron." Katya stood in front of him, a huge smile on her tanned face.

Ron took her hands in his and told her, "I'm so glad that you're back. I really missed you, Katya."

Peter and Niki exchanged glances and slow smiles. It was truly a blessing to see that Katya had someone who cared for her besides her very small family.

On the way home, they all talked at once, telling story after story about their adventures in Disney World. Ron nodded his head as he tried to follow what was being said, and still manage to concentrate on his driving.

When they got home they ordered pizza, and Ron was invited to stay and eat dinner with them. After a happy and uproariously fun dinner filled with stories and anecdotes about the honeymoon, Ron and Katya cleared the table while Pete and Niki got Nicholas bathed and in bed.

"I want Papa to give me my bath, Mama, and maybe you can read a book to me." Nicholas' eyes were heavy-lidded as he looked from one parent to the other.

Peter picked up his son, and carried Nicholas like a football under his arm, laughing, into the bathroom. Niki could hear the two, still laughing, over the sound of the water running into the tub.

Downstairs, Katya invited Ron to sit with her in the great room when they finished cleaning the kitchen. She brought the gift that she had chosen for Ron and gave it to him.

"It's a beautiful sailboat, Katya...*thank you.*," Ron was touched by Katya's thoughtfulness, and reached for her hand.

When Peter and Niki came downstairs, Katya and Ron were sitting next to each other on the sofa in the great room, talking quietly, and holding hands.

Chapter 35

The next two weeks were busy for Peter as he began to get back into playing form with exercise, weight training, and treadmill workouts. Niki managed his return to training, and carefully plotted his strength training needs to maximize results without injury.

Peter's mornings started at five o'clock, when he would stretch and then jog three miles, rain or shine. He and Niki had put together an exercise room with free weights, an all-purpose exercise machine, and treadmill, where he worked out two hours twice each day. She had insisted on a whirlpool, too, because that was an important part of keeping Pete in good shape, and without pain.

If they hadn't put the exercise room in their house, Peter's training regimen would have necessitated a great deal of daily travel into, and out of, Indianapolis to one of the gyms there. With the exercise room at home, he could spend more time with his wife, son, and sister, and he loved it.

On the ice at Market Square Arena with the Indy hockey team, Peter practiced on Tuesday and Thursday afternoons, and he always got a good workout with the team. Uncle Les and Klaus made the practice arrangements with the Indianapolis hockey team for Peter, and they also came often to watch him practice. For his part, Peter was very grateful to Niki's father and Uncle Les for their efforts on his behalf.

Peter found that Marty Pelham's predictions about scouts and agents coming in to watch him work out and play hockey were accurate. There were often two, and as many as five, scouts and/or agents at one time, representing different NHL hockey teams who watched him play hockey. When they approached him, and they always did, he would kindly tell them to contact Marty Pelham if they had an interest in him.

Because he was able to stay at home for most of his training needs, Peter, always looking for something to keep himself busy, decided that he would apply for admission to the Purdue University School of Engineering. He loved civil engineering, and he understood, perhaps better than most athletes, that he needed something to do after his sports career ended. Niki concurred, and they made plans to visit Purdue. Peter talked at length with his wife about the university, because he did not want her to be uncomfortable or sad in visiting the school where her brother, Joey, had died many years before during a football game.

"I would not want to cause you any discomfort or sadness, Niki. Please tell me how you really feel about going to West Lafayette with me."

"This trip will be a happy one, Pete. I have finally come to understand that what happened to Joey was really no one's fault. It was a terrible accident, that's all. And now, more than anything, I want you to realize your dreams. You deserve to have your dreams come true."

His voice was soft as he replied, "My dreams *have* already come true, Niki. I am here with you and Nicholas, and Katya, too. And…you are now my wife, and we are expecting our second child. I am blessed beyond measure." Peter put his arms around his wife and kissed her deeply. "Thank you, Niki, my love," he whispered.

On a sunny Sunday afternoon, Niki drove Peter and Nicholas to West Lafayette. Katya was with Ron for the afternoon, and had gently declined an invitation to go with them. "Enjoy yourselves, and when you return, you can tell Ron and me all about your trip."

The campus was striking in early November, with a few trees still bright with unfallen leaves. Peter liked the architectural design of the School of Engineering buildings. He was always fascinated with structure, design, and the materials used in buildings, and he was not disappointed with those at Purdue University.

Nicholas turned his head back and forth as he watched college students walking, jogging, running, biking, or skateboarding along the streets and common areas. There was *so much to see.*

Peter was as excited as Nicholas. He smiled down at Niki, "Isn't this a wonderful place, this university? I never dreamed that someday I might be able to attend classes, earn a degree, in such a place. It has always seemed beyond my wildest dreams, and yet, here I am with my beautiful wife and my wonderful son, touring the university that I will attend. Niki...it is all because of you...this realization of my dream."

She smiled back at him, "It isn't just my doing, Pete. *You are the one who had the dream.* And I am so grateful that you want to share it with Nicholas and me." She leaned over and kissed him on the cheek.

As they slowly drove through the campus, Peter asked, "This is the university that Neal Armstrong graduated from, isn't it?" He was in awe of the aerospace program.

"Yes, my love, Purdue is the place. Did you know that this university is world-renowned for its curriculum *and its alumni?"*

Peter nodded his head, "Of course, Niki. And...if I am not mistaken, the Soviet Union copied Purdue's program for aerospace engineering. But perhaps you already knew that...am I correct?"

"Imitation is the highest form of flattery, Pete. Why reinvent the wheel, or in this case, the rocket? Much of the world, however, thinks that Neal Armstrong's moon walk took place in a studio here on earth. Was that also the Soviet line?"

"Yes, of course. But they scrambled, anyway, to put their own astronauts there, too. When the Kremlin saw that they had lost the space race to the Americans, they funneled a great deal of money into their space program, much to the detriment of the daily life of common Russians. Food and the necessities of life became hard to get in the Soviet Union. There were only so many rubles to go around, and the Party...the Communist Party...was very selfish. And so, almost everyone, except the most powerful officials, suffered."

"Papa?" piped Nicholas, "I'm hungry. Does this big school have a place where we can eat?"

Peter turned to answer his son, "Yes, I'm sure they do. Will you keep a lookout for a good restaurant for us Nicholas?"

"Yes, Papa!"

Niki shook her head and marveled at her men, one small and one tall. As it happened, they ate lunch at "Sarge's," a restaurant in West Lafayette that specialized in steaks and salads. Nicholas loved both, and enjoyed himself immensely. Peter had to admit that, except for the St. Elmo's restaurant in Indianapolis, the steak here was among the best he had ever eaten.

On their way home, Niki asked her husband, "What do you think about the campus, Pete? Did you like what you saw?"

"Absolutely," Peter nodded vigorously. "I will do the testing and whatever it takes for application to Purdue. What do you think, Nicholas?"

Nicholas rubbed his sleepy eyes and told his parents, "I liked it, too."

Niki lookeded at Peter with wide eyes, and an even wider grin. He returned her look. Their son brought a great deal of happiness to both of them.

At home in his spare time, Peter started cooking some meals for his family. Often, Ron was invited to the 'test kitchen,' too. Peter found that he enjoyed cooking, and did his share of meal preparation. Niki began calling him her Grill King, because he liked to experiment with grilling meats and vegetables, and he made different sauces and marinades that were delicious. Katya liked to help her brother with his sauce preparation, and their collaboration provided some gourmet meals with a decidedly Russian flair. Ron told Katya that he was now 'converted' to Russian food, and that she and Peter could cook for him anytime, which pleased her very much.

The Genchenko family settled into a happy daily rhythm. Niki was back to working two mornings a week, Tuesday and Thursday, in the orthopedics and sports medicine clinic with Ron. She took Nicholas with her because there was now a day care center in the clinic, and he had a wonderful time with the other children. Niki was happy that her son was becoming very socially adept. There was even one little girl, a year older than Nicholas, who obviously enjoyed playing with him, and sharing her snacks with him, too. This turn of events made Niki giggle a little, and wonder what the future might hold for her son? He has his father's charisma, she decided.

Katya always went to the clinic with Niki and Nicholas, much to

Ron's delight. When he discovered that she was an experienced bookkeeper, he hired her to work the mornings that she came in with Niki. Everyone, it seemed, was happy with the two mornings a week schedule.

Most afternoons after Niki finished working in the clinic, she, Nicholas and Katya went to see Peter practice at the arena. They always packed a lunch, and enjoyed their meal while they watched Peter skate. Niki brought Peter's lunch, too, and he was ready for it when he left the ice at two o'clock.

The Genchenko family sat in the stands together eating, laughing, talking, and having a wonderful time. Some of the Indy hockey players came to sit with them because they liked Peter, and, more important, they found Katya irresistible. Niki noticed their interest, and commented on it to Peter, who thought that it was hilarious.

"What do you think Ron would say if he knew about this?" Peter laughed as he spoke to Niki about his very beautiful and alluring sister.

"Well...he might ask her to marry him sooner!" Niki's grin was impish.

Each day when Peter finished his hockey practice at the arena, Niki checked him over for injuries or other problems. *This man of mine is amazing...he's just amazing.* She was pleased that he was regaining his strength and stamina. She could see it as he skated with the Indianapolis team. No one, not one of them, could keep up with him, or stop him when he went in for a goal.

The coach had jokingly asked Peter whether he might want to play with the team, but then said that he knew better. He knew that this man was good enough to play with the best, and that Peter would probably be signing with a top team soon.

Marty called toward the end of Peter's fifth week of workouts with the Indianapolis team, "Peter, the Polar Banners want you to come to Pittsburgh and practice with them on Thursday and Friday of this coming week. They have finished their pre-season workouts, and they're now back in Pittsburgh. They are really interested in you, especially so because I gave them your stats and the videos from the International Winter Games. Can you get to Pittsburgh next week to work out with them?"

Peter held the phone away from his ear, "Niki! It's Marty, and he wants me to go to Pittsburgh to work out with the Polar Banners next Thursday and Friday!"

"Oh, Pete, that's *wonderful.*" Niki's face was aglow and she nodded, *yes, yes, yes.*

"Yes, Marty, I can do that. Will you be there?"

"I wouldn't miss it for the world, Peter! While we are there, I'll give you a history of the team, and I think that you will find it interesting. The PB's are quite a club and with you as their Left Wing, I really think that they'll have a shot at the Stanley Cup. I really do. We can talk with their coach, Bob Johannsen, about money after he gets to see you play. Right now, I'm thinking they may go as high as six figures for you if all goes well during your practices and workouts with them, and they decide to ask you to play for them."

When the telephone call ended, Peter sat for several moments as if in a trance. And then he shouted and leapt into the air, arms outstretched, in excitement.

He swept Niki up in his arms, lifted her off the floor, and spun her around, "The Polar Banners, Niki, it's the PB's, and they're interested in me! Can you believe it?"

Of course she could. She knew all along that Peter would get a chance to play with a team in the NHL. How could he not? Anyone with half a brain could see how special he was.

She put her arms around Peter's neck and looked up at him, "Yes, Pete, I can believe it. I had no doubt that Marty would find a place for you. And you deserve this opportunity…you really do!"

Nicholas came running, his little feet making 'thump, thump, thumping' noises on the hardwood floor, as he ran into the room to see what was happening. He grabbed his father's legs at the knees and put his arms around them.

Peter swung him up onto his shoulders, "Papa is going to play hockey, Nicholas!"

Katya followed Nicholas into the room, "What…what is it, Petrosha?"

"I've been invited to practice with the Pittsburgh Polar Banners." His smile was wide as he hugged his sister and shared his wonderful news with her.

Katya gave her brother a congratulatory kiss on the cheek, "That is wonderful news, Petrosha! I am so happy for you, so very happy."

Chapter 36

The following evening, the Genchenko family was just sitting down to supper when the doorbell rang. Peter excused himself and got up from the table to answer the door.

When Peter opened the door, he was, literally, speechless. Marc Terenoff stood before him on the wide porch, hands in pockets, a cigarette, unlit, dangling at the corner of his mouth. There was a cab in the driveway, with its engine running.

Terenoff spoke in Russian, "Hello, Peter, I've come a long way. Aren't you going to ask me in?"

Peter recovered quickly, moved away from the door and extended his hand inward, "You *have* come a long way for a visit…come in, come in."

Terenoff looked around the great room, "Well, Peter, you have done very nicely for yourself, I see."

Peter folded his arms, cocked his head to the side, and smiled, "You didn't come all this way to tell me that."

Terenoff laughed and then coughed a short, perfunctory smoker's cough. "No, but I did come to give you something. I didn't trust anyone in Moscow enough to see that you received this, so, out of a sense of duty, and a little curiosity, I guess, I am here to present you with a cashier's check for the first of many payments of your father's book royalties."

When Peter saw the amount printed on the check, he looked quickly at Terenoff, his eyes wide with surprise, "Is the amount correct? I mean, all of these zeroes…?"

"Yes, Peter, it is correct, and it is just the first of many payments that you will receive from the Swiss bank account that was formerly Vasiliy Arnov's. You and your sister are now millionaires."

"But, how…?" Peter sat down heavily on the nearest chair.

Niki came into the room and saw Terenoff. And then she saw Peter, a stricken look on his face, sitting in a chair. She turned back to Terenoff, and her eyes, blazing with anger, raked across him.

She quickly went to Peter, took his hand, and knelt down in front of him, "Pete, what's wrong?"

Devoted, thought Terenoff, that's the word to best describe these two. He watched Niki as she knelt in front of Peter, obviously concerned for him. Terenoff saw the anger, the protectiveness, in her eyes when she had glared at him as she first came into the room. She must have thought that I brought bad news for Peter. How fortunate Peter is, and how rare this kind of devotion is between a man and a woman. Perhaps this relationship will make up for all of the things that Peter has endured in his life because of his father.

Peter looked at Niki, his eyes still wide, as he handed her the check. "Nothing is wrong," he spoke barely above a whisper, "but this is not to be believed."

Niki gasped when she saw the amount written on the check, "*Pete! Oh…my…God!*"

Katya came into the great room carrying Nicholas on her hip, "Petrosha...Niki?"

Niki handed her the check, "Look at this Katya. Isn't it *wonderful?*"

Katya looked from the check to Peter and Niki, then Terenoff, and back to the check, her mouth open in incredulity, "I don't understand. What? How?"

Peter got up from the chair to put his arm around Katya's shoulders, "Do you remember Chief Investigator Marc Terenoff?"

"Yes, I remember him," Katya looked timidly at Terenoff over her brother's shoulder.

"This is wonderful news, Katya...*wonderful news!*"

Peter then took his wife by the hand and told Terenoff, "You have met Niki before, Marc. We are now married."

"I apologize for my behavior a few moments ago. I thought that you had come to harm Peter...or something..." Niki was embarrassed as she reached to take Nicholas from Katya.

"Given Peter's history, and all of the things he's been through, you had every right to be suspicious of me." Terenoff's hooded, usually somber, dark eyes actually twinkled with mirth.

At Peter's invitation, Terenoff paid the cabbie, dismissed him, and joined the Genchenko family for dinner. The tale he told them during their meal was nothing short of amazing.

Once Vasiliy Arnov was arrested, Terenoff began searching for Arnov's hidden bank accounts. With the cooperation and help of Interpol, he was able to find some of what he was looking for in Switzerland. It took some time, Terenoff told them, to trace the sources of money coming into Arnov's three different accounts at Banca Suisse. Then, when Interpol put pressure on the book publisher of Ivan

Genchenko's three books, Interpol was finally able to trace the royalty deposits to Arnov's accounts in the bank in Switzerland.

"Several of my colleagues in Moscow didn't want Ivan Genchenko's son or daughter to receive any of the money that we found in Arnov's accounts, but Interpol was involved, and so the authorities in Moscow had no choice but to give to you what is yours." Terenoff had a sardonic smile on his face as he spoke.

"Actually," he continued, "my Interpol contact, Armand Dupres, gave the first bank draft to me and asked me to deliver it to you. He was as suspicious of my colleagues as I was, and we both wanted to make sure that the money got to you, Peter, and to your sister. I wouldn't have been able to afford to come here on my own, so Dupres made me his Interpol Courier. Besides, the Soviet Union is collapsing all around us; you are aware, of course, of the fall of the Berlin Wall on November 9th?"

"Da," Peter nodded. "Will you be all right?"

"Of course…well, at least I think that I will be able to protect my family…" Terenoff's voice trailed off, he shrugged, and then continued, "Nonetheless, as soon as you can establish a bank account, Dupres will have the rest of the money wire transferred here to you. I don't know the exact amount, but I do know that the book publisher will begin transferring royalties into your bank account as soon as we notify them of the wire transfer information. The publisher has committed to assuring that all of the royalties will go to Ivan Genchenko's family. This card has all the information that you need regarding bank and publisher contacts. And…if you have any difficulties whatsoever, do not hesitate to contact me." He handed the card to Peter.

Niki invited Terenoff to stay the night, as it was getting late, but he declined, telling her that he had a room at the Holiday Inn at the airport, and that he had an early morning flight to catch.

"I wish that I could stay, Mrs. Genchenko…uh…Niki, and I'd like to get to know this young man better." He smiled at a very sleepy Nicholas.

Niki put her arms around Marc Terenoff and kissed him on the cheek. "Thank you from the bottom of my heart for what you have done for Peter and Katya. I know that it took extraordinary courage on your part, and I truly thank you, and your family, too. It was a dangerous thing that you did, but you took the chance because you are a decent and honorable man, just like my husband. I wish you a safe journey home."

"You are welcome. And I *will* have a safe journey home, because my spirit is much lighter now that justice has been served for Ivan Genchenko's children."

Terenoff insisted on calling a cab for the return to his hotel. "All of you have a great deal to discuss, and you should more than likely celebrate your newfound wealth a little, too."

When the cab arrived, Peter shook Terenoff's hand and then embraced him for several moments. "I will never forget what you have done for my family, Marc. Please know that, if you are ever in need, I will be there for you and your family. *Thank you.*"

Marc Terenoff hurried out the door, turned and smiled at the Genchenko family as they waved goodbye, and with a farewell wave to all, got into the cab and then disappeared down the driveway.

The only person in the Genchenko household that slept much that night was Nicholas. Even though they put on their pajamas, Niki, Peter, and Katya sat in the great room in front of the blazing fireplace for several hours, wide awake, drinking hot tea, feet up on the huge coffee table and ottoman, talking about the wonderful turn of events that Marc Terenoff had brought their way.

"Unbelievable, this is just absolutely unbelievable," said Peter, for perhaps the hundredth time since Terenoff's departure.

Chapter 37

At around nine the next morning, Peter showered with Niki and shaved while she dried her hair. When Niki was set for the day, she went downstairs and found that Katya was already dressed for this special day in a light blue dress and matching heels. Katya was in the kitchen, and had put on an apron to prepare a quick breakfast for Nicholas and the rest of the family.

"Coffee," said Niki as she entered the kitchen, "I really need some coffee this morning."

She stretched and yawned, and then bent to hug and kiss Nicholas. Niki wore a navy pantsuit with navy heels. Her hair was pulled back from her face, held by a silver barrette at the base of her neck, and she wore pearl earrings.

Nicholas had been dressed in his Sunday best outfit by his Aunt Katya, "Are we going to church, *Mat?*"

"No, Nicholas, but this is a *very special day*. We are all going to the bank together." Niki again hugged Nicholas and kissed the top of his head.

"Are you sleepy, Niki?" Katya smiled gently at her sister-in-law.

"Yes, but I'm excited, too. Sometimes there *is* justice. But if it hadn't been for Marc Terenoff…"

"He's unusual, isn't he? And he's also a very brave man. Good morning everyone." Peter, dressed in a dark gray suit, white shirt and conservative blue tie, chuckled for a moment as he came into the kitchen. My handsome husband, thought Niki, as she watched Peter come into the room. Having him here with Nicholas and me still seems like a dream sometimes.

Peter kissed his wife on the cheek and hugged her as she looked up at him and smiled. He loved to see her smile. Her happiness meant everything to him. He moved across the room and also gave Katya a hug and a kiss.

"Papa, will you sit next to me?" Nicholas called to his father from the table.

"Yes, in a moment Nicholas. I'll sit next to you and we will eat a good breakfast together."

Peter gazed out a kitchen window toward the woods, "I would never have guessed, in the beginning, that Terenoff was an honest man. He was actually very intimidating the first time that I met him. And I was convinced that he hated me because of Ivan. He knew who Ivan was immediately, and told me so."

"An honest man…can you believe it?" Katya's face was somber as she spoke.

"Yes, and he made it possible for us to leave Russia, Katya. If he hadn't helped us with the Magistrate, we might still be waiting for our passports."

Peter took off his jacket and placed it on the back of the chair as he sat down next to his son at the breakfast table. Nicholas wriggled with delight as they enjoyed their oatmeal, toast, and juice together. Peter loved his son almost to distraction, and the knowledge that he and Niki were going to have another child filled him with happiness. *Will we have a boy or a girl*, he wondered, *or one of each?*

He was getting used to being happy. His days of sadness and misery were unbelievably over, and were now becoming a distant memory. And the cold, aching place inside him, that had been with him since his childhood, was now gone. Niki's love, and the love of his son and sister, had banished that cold place, making it disappear forever.

Peter watched Niki as she helped Katya with the kitchen chores. My beautiful wife, how did this ever come about? And Katya...perhaps Ron was the answer to her prayers; at least Peter hoped so. His sister truly deserved to be happy, and settled, too.

After breakfast, Peter backed the car out of the garage for Niki. He still hadn't gotten a driver's license, but he intended to, when he found some time to practice his driving skills. The thought of Niki, sitting next to him, slightly nervous, but helping him while he was driving, made him laugh a little. She is so patient with me...how can she be so patient with me?

His answer came when she walked out of the front door, Nicholas in hand, and gave Peter one of her lovely smiles, just for him. Her smile told him everything that he needed to know; she loved him as much as he loved her.

Niki drove them to the downtown Indianapolis Bank One, where she had checking and savings accounts. She and Peter had talked about it, and they had decided together that it would be easier to keep all of their financial business in one bank.

The bank manager came out to help the Genchenko family because the teller who started the application for the new account began to stutter and stammer when she saw the amount of the certified check to be deposited. Peter and Katya wanted to put the account in all of their names, even Nicholas's. They wanted to be sure that, if something happened to either, or both, of them, the account would still be available to Niki and Nicholas. The problem, they soon found out, was that the only ones in the family with Social Security Numbers were Niki and Nicholas, and it was necessary to have one to open a new account.

The bank manager shrugged his shoulders and told them, "It might be best to just deposit this check in the existing savings account, Mr. and Mrs. Genchenko, and Ms. Genchenko, and then decide later if you want to put it in an IRA, CD, or some other high interest-bearing account, because you could probably live off of the interest without touching the principal, if you wished to do so."

"Well," said Peter thoughtfully, "we can just use the savings account that Niki already has, and then, when Katya and I become citizens, and have Social Security Numbers, we can do things a little differently if we want to. Is that all right with everyone?"

Nicholas, in his father's arms, said emphatically, "Yes, Papa, and can we go home now?"

They were still laughing at the certainty of Nicholas's pronouncement as they left the bank. It was a fine, a wonderful, moment, and Peter knew that this was another day that he would not forget. It will always be the day, he decided, when I knew that I could finally provide for my family. I can keep all of them sheltered, well-fed, warm and safe…from now on. *How could life be any better than this?*

Chapter 38

It was a wonderfully heady, exhilarating feeling for Peter as he skated out onto the ice with the Pittsburgh Polar Banners. He was playing his usual Left Wing position in this practice game, and he felt as if he had played in this arena before. He didn't know what to expect, but he had done some research on his new teammates-to-be, and knew that he was in good company.

The bracing first breath, as he had taken the ice, geared him up for the battle at hand. Peter Genchenko never considered hockey to be anything other than a battle between seasoned warriors with sticks for weapons. He had explained this to Niki during one of their heart-to-heart talks, and she hadn't laughed, because, she told him at the time, she had been a witness to many of his battles/games.

Marty Pelham and Sheldon Levin were standing with Niki, Katya, and Nicholas when Peter first took the ice to practice with the Pittsburgh PB's. It was truly a marvelous exhibition of Peter's skills. They watched him, time and again, and seemingly effortlessly, move the puck up and down the ice, skating in and out of the paths of other players on the team, *no matter who was trying to catch him,* to make attacks on goal.

Marty couldn't contain himself when Peter scored his third goal during practice. It was a beautifully executed play; a perfect example of what Peter could really do, and as natural for him as breathing. Even Teril, who was on the 'opposing team' of players during the practice, wasn't able to take the puck away from Peter, and could not prevent him from scoring.

Marty grabbed Niki by the shoulders, "Did you see that? *Did you see that?"*

Niki's smile was radiant, and her eyes were shining, as she replied, "Of course, Marty, this is Déjà vu! I've told you before, a long time ago…there is nothing, no one, like *Pete on ice.*"

After the practice game ended, several members of the team, Kelley, Craig, Steven, Boris, Collin, Jordan, Besso, Ruchoi, Trotter, Mullins, Murphrey, Francois, and Samuel came up to Peter, surrounded him and took turns shaking his hand in welcome. Coach Bob Johannsen had not wanted any of his players to interact with Peter Genchenko prior to his initial practice with the team for reasons that only Johannsen knew.

Therefore, when the players came over to welcome Peter, it was their first meeting off the ice. Needless to say, they were all very glad to have a 'walk-on' the likes of Peter Genchenko. Peter was overwhelmed at first, but soon warmed to these men who would be his teammates.

Coach Johannsen joined his team in welcoming Peter, "It's great to have you, Genchenko. I couldn't believe at first what Marty Pelham was saying about your abilities, but then I watched the tapes he sent, and I decided that you, along with the rest of a very strong team, were just what the Polar Banners needed right now." Coach Johanssen shook Peter's hand with a strong grip. "I've just finished talking to Marty, and he's got a lot to tell you. For right now, all I can say is…*welcome to the team."*

Marty took Peter high up into the stands to talk to him about the Pittsburgh PB's history, and to bring him up to speed on what the franchise was willing to offer Peter to sign with the team.

"The PB's," said Marty, "have a long history. Right now, they're in the Eastern Conference, Atlantic Division. The club, under other names, the Predators in the twenties and the Wasps in the thirties to the sixties, got a boost when Pittsburgh was one of seven places that got to have a second team when the NHL expanded, actually doubled, during the sixty-seven, sixty-eight season.

"The owners searched a little while to find a good name for the new franchise, and finally decided on the Pittsburgh Polar Banners. You know the old saying, "a banner day?" Well, I have heard many stories as to how they arrived at that name, but the best one, I guess, is about the place where they would be playing. The Pittsburgh Civic Center looked like a big igloo, and the owners thought Polar Banners, you know, a flag on the igloo, would capitalize on that." Marty smiled and shrugged his thin shoulders. "Anyway, once they decided on their name, they went to work on a logo for the team.

"In 1980 the team went to red and gold, old colors used very early on in the franchise, and they got some criticism for it, but they kept the colors. As for the logo…a Polar Banner with a hockey stick insignia in a triangle of ice…get it? As I said a moment ago, the Pittsburgh Civic Center looked like a huge igloo, hence the name, Polar Banners…the flag flying from the igloo with a triangle around it, is thought to be a tribute to the three rivers converging in Pittsburgh." He laughed, "Well, it's a stretch, but it's probably, at least in part, true."

Peter replied, "Polar Banners are on the ice at both poles, Arctic and Antarctic…it was a good choice. Anyway, I've done some research on the team, too, and they've had their ups and downs; some difficult times."

Marty nodded and looked down on the ice from their perch high up in the stands. "They were dogged by bad luck for some time, Peter. The PB's got to the playoffs only twice during their first seven years as a hockey franchise. Larry Teegarten, the first general manager, had a hard time getting talent. A lot of their first players came from the minor leagues. Sully Hill was the head coach for just two seasons. Then they found Terry Mungovan to do the job. Have you heard of him?"

"He's in the Hockey Hall of Fame, isn't he?"

"Yeah, he's the one…but he didn't have an easy time with the PB's, either."

Marty looked directly at Peter. "You make it look so easy out there on the ice, skating and hockey, but you and I know that it's not easy at all."

Peter smiled briefly, "No, it isn't, but I love playing, just the same."

It was Marty's turn to smile, "It shows, Peter. I predict that someday your name and jersey will be in the Hockey Hall of Fame, too."

Shrugging, Peter said, "That would be wonderful, Marty. But for now, I just want to play hockey. Niki and I know that my career could end at any time with some injury or another, but she is behind me completely. Everything that we do, every decision that she and I make, is a joint effort. We both agree that it is my time to play my sport. But as a backup, I have applied to the Purdue University Engineering Program. When I 'grow up' I want to be a civil engineer." This time, Peter smiled broadly.

"You're into engineering? That's great, Peter. A lot of athletes don't look beyond the next game, but you're preparing for a future after sports; good thinking"

"As I told you, Niki and I discuss everything. Much of what you call "good thinking" on my part actually starts with Niki."

"There is no question that you are a very lucky man, Peter, no question at all. Niki has been your best advocate ever since the International Winter Games in eighty-six."

"Yes...she has..." Peter's heart filled with gratitude for the life that he and Niki now had.

"Well, let's talk about salary. I'm still negotiating with the owners. But I can tell you, after what they have seen that you can do on the ice today, in spite of their best players, I think they'll up the ante a bit more."

Peter was puzzled, "What is 'ante'?"

With a short laugh, Marty told him, "Peter...ante is a word used in gambling, but it's also slang for getting you the very best, and highest, salary that I can squeeze out of the owners. They will always low-ball an offer at first, and then it's up to the agent to get the athlete what he really deserves. In your case, I think that you are worth the highest six figures, or more. You have everything going for you; talent, speed, strength, charisma, and, by golly, you're a good-looking guy, too, in spite of your battle scars. But you're not just some handsome sap who's made it to the big ice. You've earned your way, *fought* your way, to the top, and it shows. You will be a great box office draw for the PB's when the *media* discovers you! The folks at the Pittsburgh Post-Gazette and the Tribune-Review, and WPCW Channel 19, not to mention WSDX and WBGG radio, are really going to like you." Marty leaned toward Peter for emphasis.

"Well, I've tried to work hard in the past Marty, and I'm willing now to do whatever it takes to help the Polar Banners get to the playoffs. My family is behind me one hundred percent. Niki couldn't be more helpful than she is now. How many hockey players have a wife who is a sports medicine physician? As I said before, how lucky can a man be? I am blessed."

"Niki is one-in-a-million, Peter. Yeah, I'd have to agree that you are blessed in that way, too, very blessed." Marty put a hand to his forehead for a moment, "Okay...where was I?"

"You were giving me a history lesson on the PB's...and then you started talking about salary."

Marty nodded, "That's right, I was talking salary. But let me bring you to the current season from where the PB's have been, okay?"

"I think that I have some knowledge of where they have been, but it's good to hear it from your perspective, too, Marty."

"The seventies were not good for the PB's, Peter, and here's why...one of their best players, and a favorite with the fans, was injured in a freak accident and never came back to play. He died more than a month after the accident."

"Was he injured on the ice?"

"Oh no...it was on a motorcycle." Marty was shaking his head, "His last name was Birely...uh...Keith Birely, a really great guy."

By the seventy-three and seventy-four season, the PB's were close to the bottom of the league. Kenny Kirby was named General Manager after the bad season. Kirby was a smart cookie, and almost had the PB's in the playoffs by the end of seventy-four.

"Things still didn't go too well for them, though, because around seventy-five or seventy-six, the PB's had built up some debt that they had to pay off. The team was rescued by a group of guys that included some former hockey players like Tim Tryon, but they had some problems, too. When Kirby was named general manager, everyone thought that they could put the bad times behind them, but it didn't work out that way.

"Well...by the early eighties, things didn't look any better. The PB's had the basement in the league in eighty-three and eighty-four. There was, however, a light at the end of their dismal tunnel in eighty-four. The light was none other than Teril Ruchoi, and you just played a practice game against him, Peter. Every team in the league wanted Ruchoi during the draft, but the PB's hung onto him. He's the reason that the PB's are still playing hockey, really. But in spite of Ruchoi, they haven't had a playoff berth in this decade."

"I didn't realize that they'd had such a bad time, Marty. Maybe 1989 will be a good year for the PB's...who knows?" Peter looked sideways at Marty and smiled at him.

Marty returned Peter's smile with a broad one of his own, "With you on the team, they can bank on it!"

Chapter 39

The Genchenkos' lives changed drastically when the hockey season started in earnest. Peter was at home Monday through Thursday most weeks, and then traveled to Pittsburgh by passenger jet out of Indianapolis for home games. The owners and head coach of the Polar Banners cut Peter a little slack by letting him travel directly by air, not with the team, to games in the region. This arrangement for an athlete was highly unorthodox, but Peter was producing at each game. He usually had at least two goals per game, and had his share of hat tricks as well. He became, as his teammates called him, the "king of the slapshot" for the PB's in record time.

Peter and Teril Ruchoi played very well together early in the season, and made some great plays for their team that seemed to be harbingers of a better future. But then the PB's were dealt a crushing blow when Ruchoi suffered a hairline fracture of his left femur.

Peter understood that Ruchoi was the true sparkplug of the team, and he, himself, didn't have enough experience with the other players to take Ruchoi's place. Playing professional hockey was light years apart from the exhibition hockey games that Peter had played for the Red Army Hockey Team. Still, Peter's steely determination to go all-out, 'balls-to-the-wall' to play and win games earned him the respect, and more importantly, the trust, of the PB's general manager, coach, and his teammates.

Niki attended as many games as her clinic schedule would allow because Ron saw to it that her patients were well taken care of in her absence. Quite often, Niki's friend, Stephanie Trent, would assist Ron if he needed help with Niki's patients.

"You go, girl," Stephanie would tell Niki. "Take good care of that gorgeous man of yours!"

Niki always took Nicholas and Katya with her when she traveled to see Pete play with the PB's. The Genchenkos were becoming seasoned air travelers. One of the best times that they had on the road was when they traveled to New York for a Rangers home game with the Pittsburgh PB's. Niki and Katya planned far enough ahead that they got tickets to see the matinee performance of "Cats" on Broadway with Nicholas and Peter during his down time in New York.

When Peter had to go to Madison Square Garden for practice before his game, Niki and Katya took Nicholas shopping with them. He loved seeing the oversized stuffed toys at FAO Schwartz, and the fantastic erector sets and miniaturized construction equipment there. He said that he wanted to be a Civil Engineer just like his father was going to be when he graduated from Purdue. Even though Nicholas was very young, his father often talked about civil engineering projects with him. The two even worked together on three-dimensional puzzles, and Nicholas's ability surprised and delighted both of his parents.

Peter joined his family for lunch before heading to the arena for wrapping and taping in preparation for the game that would start at seven o'clock. He thoroughly enjoyed listening to his son's excited recitation of the wonderful things he had seen with his mother and aunt at FAO Schwartz.

"Papa, the bear was *this big!*" Nicholas raised his arms in the air to demonstrate the size of the bear.

While Niki beamed at her son and husband, and Katya laughed out loud, Peter swooped down and lifted Nicholas high above his head.

"Was the bear *this* big, Nicholas?"

"Yes, Papa…he was even bigger than this!"

When Peter returned to the training room assigned to the PB's, Coach Bob Johanssen was gathering his players for a pre-game pep talk. He was very animated as he told them that the Rangers were as tough a team as they would meet on the road. He told them that his PBs' bench was deep enough, but he wanted the team to know that Ruchoi's absence would drastically change the way the team was going to have to play their game tonight.

Something about this training room reminded Peter of the training room in Market Square Arena in Indianapolis. Memories swirled and passed before his eyes. He remembered vividly the first time that he had set eyes on the beautiful Dr. Nikola Kellman. He had been ill, mostly as a result of contracting his father's final illness, pneumonia, and to his everlasting chagrin, had fainted when he had first arrived in Indianapolis from Russia. Dr. Kellman had worked miracles, and had gotten him ready to play hockey with his team, the Red Army Hockey Team, competing in the International Winter Games in Indianapolis in 1986. It was in a training room not unlike this one where he first fell in love with the woman he now called Niki…his wife.

"Genchenko, what are you smiling about? Do you have something that you'd like to share with me and the rest of the team?" Coach Johanssen was puzzled and a little irritated by Peter's seeming inattention.

"I think the term is 'Déjà vu,' Coach. This place reminds me of another training room, several years ago…well, it seems like a lifetime ago, that's all." Peter was still smiling.

"Let's just concentrate on this game, okay? We're going to have to work hard if we want to pull a win for this game tonight." Coach Johanssen was all business, and wanted no pre-game distractions.

Niki hoped that she would be able to keep Nicholas awake through the first period of the game. Even though hockey games were noisy because of the crowd, the announcer, and loud organ music, her son was a sleepy-head who asked for his bath and bed at eight-thirty, or so, every evening.

She and Katya had seats right behind the PB's bench, and she was grateful to Coach Johanssen for allowing her to have such great seats. At the back of her mind, there was always the thought that, if Pete was hurt during a game, she would be there to help him. Niki and Coach Johanssen had discussed the issue, and he had agreed, "in theory," he said, to allow her to assist the team doctor if the need arose. But, in fact, Peter Genchenko had a clause in his contract that stipulated that his wife, if she were in attendance during a game where he was injured, would have full control over his treatment and care.

The Pittsburgh Polar Banners took the ice as the announcer introduced them. As Peter went out onto the ice, he looked back at his family and gave them a 'thumbs-up' gesture and a smile. Delighted, Nicholas waved his arms in the air in a salute to his father. On the ice, Peter sucked in a great gulp of icy air. This was invigorating to him, and always quickened his pulse in readiness for the battle to come.

The spectators gave the PB's a smattering of applause, mostly polite, but low in decibels. However, when the Rangers took the ice, the crowd exploded, standing, jumping up and down in time with the loud music, and screaming their approval of their team.

Peter skated with his teammates in a looping figure eight backward formation, turning forward at the top of the loop, skating all out, and then reversing again. Peter had introduced this formation to the PB's. It was one of the things that Grigory Serov, his coach on the Red Army Hockey Team, had used to 'psyche out' opponents, and it worked. The crowd got quiet as they watched the PB's doing their warm-up skate.

As he skated, Peter took the measure of the Rangers as they maneuvered on the ice, and noted that they were using 'banana blades' on their sticks. The curvature of the blades allowed for more control of the puck during play. He knew that they were a tough, 'rough-and-tumble' team, and he wanted to see who would give him eye contact with implicit threats. How many would challenge him directly? He got reactions from three Rangers, in particular, and he understood that these three, at least, had probably been assigned to keep him scoreless. Peter smiled to himself as he decided, *we shall see about that*. His smile got a reaction from all three players, who glared at him. Peter chuckled, *gotcha!* It is wise to know one's adversaries. And since ice hockey is a game of strength and speed, he intended to be the best at both.

Peter gazed out at the familiar 200 foot long and 85 foot wide rectangle of the rink where the red Center Line divided the rink into two equal parts, and the two Blue Lines on either side of the Center Line indicated the End Zones. Center Ice, he knew, was where play is usually fast-paced and furious, and is the neutral zone between the Blue Lines. He was trying to determine if there was anything different, unusual about this arena, this ice, just as he had taken the measure of the players of the opposing team. He saw the blue spot at Center Ice where play starts, and the eight red spots where play would resume after stopping as the result of a call. He saw the red lines placed at the curvature of the boards, the Goal lines, where the Goals fastened into the ice. Peter was systematically mapping out his strategy for this game.

As Left Wing, Peter was part of the forward, offensive, line. His position, combined with that of the Center and Right Wing, made him a forward. Two defenders, the Defensemen, and the Goalie, rounded out the starting six for the game.

Although Peter's jersey did not have the letter 'C,' for captain, affixed to it, that was Teril Ruchoi's designation, Peter nonetheless had an 'A' as 'alternate.' This was an important designation, because the captain and his alternate(s) are the only players allowed to speak to any of the officials when a questionable call is made. The coach, who must always stay on the bench, has to depend on the team captain, or his alternate, to inform him of the rulings of the officials.

Peter was given the responsibility of representing his team for the face-off, and one of the three opposing players that had glared at him during warm-up stood opposite him in the large blue dot in center ice. The crowd hushed for several moments as the referee held the puck. Both players held their sticks on the ice in readiness, and then the referee dropped the puck. Peter swept it to Francois, his PB's center, before the Ranger's player moved his stick. The crowd went wild.

Niki felt an electric excitement as she watched her husband on the ice…well, here we go again! *Dear Lord, please keep Pete safe.*

The Rangers had, indeed, assigned a 'policeman,' an intimidating player, to harass Peter. However, it didn't matter at all, as Peter moved in and out of the Ranger players' formations at will. When the policeman got too close, Peter deked, turned the other way, and usually took the puck with him, leaving the attacking player far behind, or lured into the boards. When the policeman didn't work, the Rangers sent in a 'chippy,' an excessively rough player, to enhance the effects of the policeman's efforts against Peter.

Even with two aggressive players dogging his every move, Peter, in a breakaway, scored his first goal a minute and fifty seconds into the game. The crowd became quiet as they waited for their team to respond, and, as it turned out, it was a long wait.

At the beginning of the second period, the scoreless Rangers were in possession of the puck. Peter and Kelley were streaking up the ice after the attacking Rangers. Peter could see that the PB's Goalie, Murphrey, was ready for whatever came his way, with his blocking glove out in front of him, and his stick at the ready. Jordan poke checked the puck away from the Ranger's right wing at center ice and sent it in a backhand pass to Peter, who deked, went behind two of the Ranger's forward line, and sent the puck back to Jordan in a give-and-go pass.

The two PB's then crossed the Blue Line together, passing the puck between them into the Rangers' attacking zone where the Goalie nervously skated back and forth in front of the net, trying to determine which of the attacking players would try to make a goal.

The Rangers' defensemen scrambled to keep up with Peter, but could not. They repeatedly tried to charge Peter, and then Jordan when he had the puck, but the two managed to deke before bodily contact. Peter decided to freeze the goalie by seeming to move and shoot the puck. It worked, and Peter did a drop pass so that Jordan could pick it up and shoot the puck into the goal.

"SCORE...the Polar Banners have scored again!" The announcer

yelled over the roar of the crowd. Unwittingly, with his microphone still open, he shouted at his partner in the booth that the PB's were getting the best of the Rangers. The arena became very, very quiet. The Rangers' coach immediately called a time out in an attempt to interrupt the rhythm and forward momentum of the PB's.

Peter sat with his team, a bottle of water in his hand, a towel on his head, listening to Coach Johanssen's assessment of the game, so far. Peter turned and winked at his son, whose smile was radiant. Both Niki and Katya blew him kisses. It was wonderful to have them here, and Peter understood very well how fortunate he was.

Play resumed with a faceoff between the PB's Trotter and the Ranger's 'policeman' who had been trying to injure Peter. Trotter hammered the puck to Mullins, who sent it to Besso as they skated furiously toward the Ranger's goal. Peter, as left wing, literally flew up the left side of the ice, being careful not to cross the blue line before his teammates advanced the puck into the attacking zone.

The Ranger's 'chippy' was trying to keep pace with Peter, but Peter maneuvered, deked, and came around behind him before streaking past in full-out stride to join his PB's teammates for the attack on goal. The 'chippy' attempted to hook check Peter as he passed, but his stick chopped the air instead of Peter. The linesman jumped up on the boards as Peter roared past him. As he reached the attacking zone, Peter was ready for whatever play his teammates had put together.

Peter saw the policeman assigned to him raise his stick in an attempt to butt-end him and deked quickly away, leaving the policeman off balance with the ferocity of his attack. Peter swung into the slot and received a flip pass from Craig, which he slapshot past the goalie's blocking glove. *Goal!*

The third period was hard fought on both sides. The Rangers answered the PBs' goals with two of their own. Peter was boarded once, but immediately got up off the ice because he understood Niki's anguish when he got hurt. The last thing that he wanted her to do was worry about him. This was especially so in her present condition.

The Ranger's 'chippy' and 'policeman' had spent minor penalties in the penalty box, and the PB's had received one minor penalty, as well. All in all, however, the game was as clean as any professional hockey game could be.

With forty-five seconds left on the clock in the third period, Peter hook checked the puck from the Ranger's center and, flanked with his forward line teammates, with their defenders right behind, made a last attempt to score against the Rangers. He passed the puck to Besso, who was close enough to have a shot at goal, but the puck was diverted by the Goalie into the corner behind and to the right of the goal. The spectators were standing and shouting at this point.

Three Rangers and two PB's were mucking in the corner for the puck, digging to gain possession. Here again was a Déjà vu experience for Peter. When the puck came free from the mucking players, he took possession of the puck, swung to the side of the goal and flipped it in, just as he had in 1986 during the International Winter Games in Indianapolis. The red light behind the goal lit up, and the crowd gave a loud, collective groan. And then the ending buzzer sounded. The game was over, and the PB's had prevailed! Even though there were loud hisses and some booing from the spectators at the end of the game, the Rangers' fans were mostly well-behaved, even in defeat, and began to make their way quickly to the exits in Madison Square Garden in an orderly fashion.

Peter's teammates all slapped him on the back jubilantly for his good game. The victory was sweet, so sweet.

Niki hugged Peter tightly as he came off the ice, and then Katya hugged him, too. Unbelievably, Nicholas had fallen asleep during the game, and was cuddled with his blanket in his seat behind the PB's bench.

Chapter 40

By mid-season, sportscasters from all over the country were predicting that Peter Genchenko was going to win the Stanley Cup for the Polar Banners, in spite of the loss of Teril Ruchoi. However, when Peter was interviewed, he always downplayed his role, telling his interviewers each time that he was only one player on the team, and that everything that happened during games the PB's played was a team effort.

"Hockey is a team sport. It's rough and fast, and it takes the contributions of all the players to win a game. A hockey game cannot be won by just one player. You must remember this when you write your story." Peter's response was emphatic.

It was a roller coaster time for Peter and his family. He loved playing hockey, but he also loved being at home with his wife, son and sister. He decided that he would hold off on his pursuit of an engineering degree long enough so that he could eke out some time at home with his family.

Niki could no longer hide her pregnancy. Her abdomen was beginning to be nicely rounded, although the baby wasn't due until late June or early July

One night toward the end of February, Peter lay on his side in bed talking to Niki, who was nestled comfortably in the crook of his arm.

"You probably shouldn't be on the road so much with me now, Niki. I worry about you when you're driving or flying...and even though Katya is usually with you and Nicholas, I don't know what I would do if something happened to any of you, or the baby." He patted her abdomen gently as he spoke.

"Pete, you don't need to worry about me. I'm fine, and the baby is fine, according to Dr. Leonard." She was quiet for a moment, and then continued, "But when you're gone, I feel so terribly lonely...I feel lost without you." Tears welled up in her eyes.

"Would it surprise you," he asked, "if I told you that I feel the same way, lonely and lost, when I can't hold you in my arms at night? Those are the nights when I have nightmares...about losing you."

"Oh, Pete, I didn't know that you still have dreams like that."

"Hush," he said huskily. "Just let me hold you now. Let's be quiet and enjoy this wonderful closeness. You are so soft and warm when I hold you like this."

*"Yes...*it's wonderful..." her words trailed off as she fell asleep.

Early the next morning, Peter packed for Detroit. The PB's were playing the Red Wings, as tough a team as any they had on their schedule, and he wanted to be ready for whatever they were going to throw at his team. Peter had promised his coach that he would be dressed and ready for practice at 3 o'clock Michigan time. Since Indiana stayed on Eastern Standard time throughout the year, it was sometimes challenging to make certain that he would arrive on time for his Michigan, Ohio, and Illinois games.

Peter hated the alarm clock. He always felt deprived when he had to leave his bed when Niki was still sleeping there, warm and cuddling up against him. She needed more sleep when she was pregnant, he knew, and he always hated to disturb her if she was sleeping.

Katya was already downstairs in the kitchen brewing some hot tea. "Petrosha…you are up so early. You don't have to leave for another hour and a half."

Peter smiled at her, "I could say that you are up early, too. Is Ron coming over this morning? I thought you mentioned something last night about going downtown with him."

"We are going shopping for an engagement ring, and the required two gold wedding bands for our *Ohr Somayach,* our wedding ceremony, Peter." Katya's smile was shy, and she looked down for a moment.

"How wonderful! I didn't realize that things had progressed this far with you and Ron." Peter hugged his sister, and kissed her cheek.

"You have been so busy with your hockey team, and I haven't had the chance to tell you before now."

"Have you told Niki, yet?"

Katya shook her head, "I didn't want to say anything until I could tell you the good news, Petrosha."

"Well, I should have known that something was going on. You have visited Ron's parents several times in Chicago, and they must have fallen in love with you, too. Congratulations, Katya, I'm so very happy for you and Ron."

"Who would have thought that you and I could have such a wonderful turn of fortune? Sometimes at night I think of our old apartment in Lyubertsy. And sometimes, too, I dream of waking to find that I have grown old in that apartment. Do you think my dreams are odd?" Katya's beautiful face was somber.

"*Nyet*…because sometimes I have dreams like that too…and I

waken in the middle of the night. But then, Niki will put her arms around me, and the sorrow, the fear, the dread, goes away. It evaporates…" Peter spoke in a quiet voice as he described to Katya how he, too, felt at times.

"Papa?" Nicholas came into the kitchen rubbing his eyes, his puppy-faced slippers scuff, scuffing along.

"My son, what are you doing up so early?" Peter lifted Nicholas above his head and then lowered and hugged him.

Nicholas looked into his father's eyes, "You're leaving today, and I wanted to say goodbye. *Mat* told me last night that you had to play hockey again." He looked to be on the verge of tears.

"I do, Nicholas. But I wish that I could stay here with you and your *Mat* and Aunt Katya."

"You do? Don't you think it's fun to play hockey?"

"Well, Nicholas, it's really more like a job. I have to work, and so I play hockey. Your friends' fathers all have to work, too, but they have other, different kinds, of jobs."

"Papa's right, Nicholas," Niki came into the kitchen stifling a yawn with her hand. "Hockey is very hard work, but your father loves his job." She yawned again, smiled, and said, "Good morning, everyone."

"Good morning, Niki…" Katya smiled back at her sister-in-law.

Still holding Nicholas, Peter extended his other arm as Niki came into their family circle. "Good morning to you, too." Peter kissed her cheek.

She looked up at him and asked, "You're driving today, aren't you? Is it okay if Nicholas and I tag along? Katya is going shopping with Ron, and he told me in clinic yesterday that they're going out to dinner afterward. Stephanie has the clinic all set up, too. This is the week the medical residents are working, so I'm not scheduled to work today. Nicholas and I can go with you and hang out at the hotel until the game. You know how Nicholas loves to swim, and your hotel has a huge pool that will keep him busy up until game time. What do you think?"

"Papa, I *love swimming!*" Nicholas was excited at the prospect.

Peter smiled, "How can I say no to such exuberance?" He turned to his sister and continued, "There is some wonderful news that Katya has to share with everyone."

Katya's face shone as she shared her news, "Ron and I are going to shop for my engagement ring, and our two plain gold wedding bands today."

"Oh, Katya…how wonderful!" Niki put her arms around Katya, "how truly wonderful!"

Chapter 41

With Teril Ruchoi's injury taking him out of twenty-two games in the '89 and '90 hockey season, and other, more intangible factors, the PB's didn't earn a playoff berth. But it wasn't because Peter Genchenko didn't try mightily to get them one. The 'buzz' in the media about Peter was becoming more of a roar. Everyone, it seemed, loved Peter Genchenko and his unorthodox skating style. "Sports of Today" did not often put a hockey player on its front cover, but they made an exception of Peter. He was touted as one of the hottest new talents in the National Hockey League in 1990.

In mid-April, Sheldon Levin called Peter to congratulate him on making the "Sports of Today"cover. "It's great, Pete, just great! I talked to Marty a few minutes ago, you know he's in Hawaii this week, and he said he was going to call you this afternoon. He thinks you're the greatest thing on two skates!"

Peter laughed, "Whatever that means...thanks for calling, Sheldon. Niki and Katya are very excited, too. And Nicholas has the cover photo pinned to the bulletin board in his room. Our family is very happy about the whole thing."

"Well, you and your family have every right to be happy. You really deserve the honor and the publicity, Pete. I don't know of anyone who deserves it more."

"Thanks, Sheldon, thanks so much. Oh…by the way, have you received your invitation to Katya and Ron's wedding?"

"We sure have, and it's great news! We sent our RSVP a couple of weeks ago." Sheldon was always exuberant, "Your sister is a beautiful woman, Pete, and Ron's a very lucky guy. My wife and I will certainly be there on their special day. If I remember correctly, the ceremony is in Chicago, isn't it?"

"Yes, Ron's parents live there, and they have lots of family and friends in the area. It's actually easier for our Indianapolis family and friends to go to Chicago."

As Niki walked by, Peter reached for her hand and smiled. "Sheldon, I'm going to have to let you go, now. Niki, Nicholas and I are going to have our final wedding costume fittings in an hour, and we've got a half-dozen other things to do today to get everything ready before we leave for Chicago."

"Okay, Pete…I look forward to seeing all of you there. Tell Niki and Nicholas that I said hello."

"I'll do that, Sheldon…and thanks for calling about the "Sports of Today" photo and article."

Peter, who now had his driver's license, hurried out to the car and slipped into the driver's seat. Niki sat in the back seat with Nicholas, who was in his car seat. "Your 'precious cargo' is ready to be chauffered to Broad Ripple," she said, with a lilting laugh. Niki knew how much her husband loved to drive.

Peter still felt excited when he got behind the wheel. He was a careful driver at all times, because he had seen many an accident on the Interstate highways going through and around Indianapolis. He hummed along with a Beach Boys tape of "California Girls," a favorite of his son's, as he drove his family to the wedding boutique in Broad Ripple, an artist's community within Indianapolis. Although he had been driving for several months, he still felt nervous inside when he had to drive on I-465. He considered it to be a race track, and had laughed with Niki many times about his 'exciting' experiences on the beltway.

Stephanie had picked Katya up earlier because they had to be at the boutique more than an hour before Peter, Niki, and Nicholas were scheduled for their final fittings. And it was very nice that Stephanie had a calming influence on Katya, who was more than a little nervous as her wedding day drew near.

On this special day, Niki was bubbling over with excitement. "This is truly so wonderful, Pete. I love the bridesmaid's dresses that Katya has picked out. We will be wearing soft spring colors; blue, pink, lavender, yellow and green. Stephanie feels so happy that she's been invited to be a bridesmaid. The friends that Katya has made in the clinic, Tina and LeeAnn, can't talk about anything else, and Tina's little girl, Lynn, will be the junior bridesmaid. She is such a beautiful child with her dark hair and big gray eyes."

"Katya has told me the same things…well, I guess it *is* exciting to be in the kind of extravagant wedding that Ron's parents, and we, are planning for them; the *Ohr Somayach*, the Jewish Wedding Ceremony. And I think that Chicago is an exciting city, Niki. Ron told me that there will be people coming from *all over the world* to attend the wedding, and the Drake Hotel is the perfect setting for the occasion."

"Ari Michael is in the banking business in a big way, internationally, so I'm not surprised," Niki replied.

Nicholas was kicking his feet up and down in his car seat, his excitement very evident. "Aunt Katya wants me to stand next to Papa in the wedding, and I'm going to wear a grownup suit!" Nicholas clapped his small hands together with glee.

"My two handsome men…you will both look great in your tuxedos." Niki looked first at Nicholas and then at Peter as she smiled.

Katya was waiting for them when they arrived at the wedding boutique. It was less than a week before the wedding, and Ron and Katya, as *kallah,* groom and *chosson,* bride according to the Jewish Wedding Ceremony, must be kept apart for the week prior to their wedding. *"Absence makes the heart grow fonder."*

The previous Friday, Niki and Peter had hosted a small reception, called the *vort,* in their home in Indianapolis. Ron's parents traveled to Indianapolis for the *vort,* and Niki's parents, as stand-in parents for Katya, attended also. Ron and Katya, along with their families, signed the *tenaim,* an agreement that sets forth the date of the wedding and the obligations that both families must meet for the new couple. Ron's parents were quite happy with the arrangements, and had thanked Peter and Niki for their *shidduch,* matchmaking of their son with Katya. Niki and Marina prepared a wonderful Kosher meal for the *vort* that they served promptly at three in the afternoon following the signing of the *tenaim.*

Of course, Nicholas was actually the 'star' of the reception. Everyone enjoyed talking with him during the meal. And afterward, the men helped him build his "Lego" buildings in the great room in front of the fireplace. Peter, and then Ron, followed by Klaus and Ari, got down on the floor with Nicholas.

Miriam was delighted with the way her husband was enjoying himself. "I have never known Ari to be so happy as he is now," she told

Niki and Marina as they worked in the kitchen.

When Niki, Nicholas, and Peter arrived for their wedding costume fittings, Peter was delighted to see the glow of happiness on his sister's face. She was happy and relaxed as she told them, "Andrea is ready to tell us all about the wedding preparations."

Andrea was a tiny, fair-haired, nicely-coiffed and well-dressed woman who wore three-inch heels that matched her sky-blue suit. In spite of her diminutive size, she had a very strong presence as she welcomed Peter and his family.

"Hello, you must be the Genchenkos. The wedding party is in the second studio, so come along, and we will get started." Andrea was the wedding planner, and she flashed her professional smile at them and led them to studio number two where the bridesmaids were already gowned. Stephanie was in lavender, LeeAnn in yellow, Tina in pink, and little Lynn was in soft green.

"Oh, everyone looks so *lovely*." Katya was pleased with her bridesmaids' dresses.

Andrea pointed to a private dressing area, "Niki, your dress is ready for you to try it on, and I'll help you." She turned and said, "Peter, Nicholas, you can both walk through the arbor over there, and Kenneth will assist you."

Niki was filled with trepidation because she had begun to blossom in the beginning of her third trimester. She was concerned that she would look too pregnant in her Matron of Honor dress, but Katya had wisely chosen a softly draped empire-waist dress with cap sleeves and a small train that balanced the look. All of her bridesmaids, including the junior bridesmaid, would wear the same dress, in different colors.

"There," said Andrea as she fluffed the train out after helping Niki into her dress. "It's perfect! Blue is your color. Look in the mirror, Niki."

"I can't believe it…it doesn't…I'm not so…well, I didn't expect…" Niki was at a loss for words.

"We left a little expansion room at the back of the dress, Niki, but as you can see, you look quite lovely in your dress."

"Katya was right when she told me not to worry about this final fitting, Andrea. Thank you for being a miracle worker!" Niki's relief was quite evident.

"Beautiful, oh, you look so beautiful!" Katya entered the dressing room, and her smile was huge as she gently patted Niki on the shoulder.

Peter and Nicholas came into the studio in their finery, and there were "oohs" and "aahs" from all of the bridesmaids.

Andrea told the group, "Ron's brother, Zeke, has had his final fitting in Chicago, and so have Ron's cousins Abe, Daniel, Samuel, and David." She held up a hand and began counting off on her fingers, "Let's see…the Bride and Groom's mothers have their dresses, and their fathers are all set, too. Am I correct, Katya?"

"Yes, Andrea, you are correct." Katya's delight was almost palpable.

Andrea then summed everything up. "We will be packing the dresses and tuxedos for transport to Chicago on Wednesday of this week. That includes everything down to the suspenders, cummerbunds, shoes and socks for the men, and the shoes, headpieces, and underpinnings for the ladies' dresses. When I checked with my assistants earlier this morning, they told me that everything is ready for the Jewish Wedding Ceremony in Chicago, from the flowers, music and decorations, to the catering, and the Drake Hotel arrangements for all of the out-of-town…and all of the international guests. Does anyone have any questions?"

"None," said Katya. "You've thought of everything, Andrea, and Ron and I are very pleased with the way that you have handled our wedding preparations."

That evening, when the Genchenko family had all enjoyed a good meal, and were sitting comfortably in the great room at home, the conversation turned to the events of the coming weekend…the wedding. Nicholas sat, sleepy-eyed, in his Aunt Katya's lap, listening to the adults' voices. Peter had an arm around Niki, with his head resting against the back of the sofa. Niki held Peter's other hand in hers, nestled against her round abdomen.

Peter spoke in an emotion-filled, yet quiet, voice, "Katya and I…never dreamed…that our lives would be so happy, now. It seemed so impossible to us…such a short time ago." It had been his fondest dream that Katya, too, would find happiness, and now this dream was also coming true.

Chapter 42

Peter hugged his sister one last time before she boarded the plane that would take her to Chicago. *Katya is going to be married.* The thought gave him more than a moment's pause, but it also made him smile at her good fortune. He knew that Ron would be loving and kind to her; of that there was no doubt. He had watched carefully as Katya's relationship with Ron had bloomed. But Peter had taken care of his sister since they were very small, and now, he realized, her marriage would take some getting used to. She would be Ron's wife. Tears filled his eyes, and he slowly wiped them away. *She is in Ron's hands now…*

Peter understood that, as a Jewish woman, Katya had requirements that she had to fulfill before the wedding ceremony, not the least of which was the ceremonial bath, the *Mikvah*. Katya had been studying the *Ohr Somayach* since Ron had proposed to her. And she told her brother that she had discussed, at length with her husband-to-be, the Mitzvahs that she must perform before their wedding.

Peter knew that Katya was going to be picked up at O'Hare Airport in Chicago by Ron's sister-in-law, Eve, with whom she would stay until the wedding ceremony. Miriam Michael had asked her daughter-in-law to assist with the arrangements for all of Katya's *Mitzvahs* that she must accomplish prior to her *Ohr Somayach*.

Earlier in the morning, Niki had gone to the clinic to see her patients, and Nicholas was with his grandparents, so Peter had taken Katya to the airport. His feelings were bittersweet as he watched his sister walk into the jetway. It made him think of another time, when he was the one departing, his heart broken, because he had to leave Niki. He remembered Niki's tearstained face, and he understood all too well that she, too, was brokenhearted that he was leaving.

Peter had to remind himself sometimes, that his memories, though painful, were only that; memories. His life, and his sister's life now were light years away from what they were back then.

On his way home, Peter thought of some of the things that had been included in the wedding preparations. Ron and Katya agreed to allow Peter and Niki to give all of the bridesmaids and their families airline tickets and rooms at the Drake Hotel for the Michael wedding. Niki had broached the subject with Peter early in the wedding preparations, and he agreed that it would be helpful to ease the costs of the out-of-state wedding for Katya's bridesmaids. Ron had hesitated at first, but Katya had pointed out that it would be helpful to her bridesmaids and their families because of the expenses in Chicago.

Ron, who would do anything to make Katya happy, decided that this was an important issue for her, and acquiesced.

Stephanie Trent was the only bridesmaid to decline the offer. "*Nik,*" she laughed, "I don't have many expenses, and my career in medicine has been very profitable. And I don't even have any outstanding student loans! It's wonderful that you can help out the other bridesmaids, because they have families, but I only have me to worry about, just little old me."

"Okay, Steph, but I didn't want you to feel left out…" Niki hugged her best friend.

Niki left the clinic just before one o'clock, and made a quick stop at her parents' home to get Nicholas. "I've got to go home and finish packing, Mom, but please ask Dad if you can stop by the house to say goodbye before you leave."

"We will, Niki. Your father and I have to finish our last minute things, too, and then we will come over for a bit." She bent and kissed her grandson, "Nicholas and I have had a wonderful time today."

At home, Peter, who was returned from the airport, offered to take Nicholas with him to pick up some drycleaning and a few other items. "I know that you've had a busy day, Niki."

He was very protective of his pregnant wife, and wanted to do whatever he could to make things easier for her. He couldn't help himself. He worried about Niki. Perhaps his guilt over not being there with her for the birth of Nicholas was the source of his worry, and he accepted it.

Niki stood on tiptoe to kiss him on the cheek. "You are the sweetest man, and I love you. I'll see you two in a little while." She then kissed Nicholas on the cheek, too.

She used the quiet time to finish packing for her two men. Let's see…I've packed pajamas, underwear, socks, shirts, pants, shoes, toiletries…what have I forgotten? After checking their things a second time, she was sure that Pete and Nicholas had everything that they would need in Chicago. She did the same for herself, and decided that she had forgotten nothing. Okay…we are ready. *What a relief!*

Niki wanted to put her feet up and relax for a few moments. The baby had been very active since she had gotten home, and she hoped that sitting quietly for a little while would have a calming effect on her little one. A dinner casserole was in the oven, and Niki had prepared a salad to go with it, so dinner was ready to go when her men returned.

Niki was already missing Katya's company, and she knew that everything that had come to be commonplace, Katya in the great room, reading a book, or in the kitchen, at dinner, or lunch, or breakfast…being there to talk to, to laugh with, to confide in, as if they had been born sisters…would now change. A bit of sadness crept into her heart for a moment, but then she also felt gratitude for all of the time that she and Katya had shared together, and the sadness melted away. Katya and Ron would be living in Indianapolis, and she would see them often. After all, she and Ron were partners now in their sports medicine clinic, and Katya managed their office.

Niki understood that things would be different for her, and for Peter and Nicholas, too, but their family was actually expanding. Ron would now be their brother-in-law. The thought of it made her smile.

The doorbell rang, and Niki let go of her reverie. "Mom and Dad," she smiled at her parents at the door. "Are you all packed and ready to go to the airport?"

Marina and Klaus stepped inside. "We have just dropped Duchess off at the kennel, and she has given new meaning to the words, hang dog look," said Klaus.

"I'll bet she was "hang dog" because she's so spoiled!" Niki hugged both of her parents, and then asked, "Would you two like a cup of tea before you head to the airport?"

"Yes…that would be wonderful, Niki." Marina looked a little tired.

They went into the kitchen and Marina helped her daughter with the tea preparation. Soon, there were three cups of steaming, decaffeinated

Earl Gray tea, and a plateful of homemade cranberry-orange muffins on the kitchen island.

Niki took a sip of her hot tea, "Dad, how are you holding up?"

"I think that your mother and I are ready to get on the airplane." He held his cup of tea with both hands, "Once we are in Chicago, we will be very happy to go to our suite at the Drake and put on our pajamas."

"Do you have time to have dinner with us? I know that Pete and Nicholas would be very happy to see both of you, and I've got a casserole in the oven."

"Well, Niki, your casserole smells delicious." Marina hesitated and looked at Klaus, "Ordinarily, we would love to have dinner with you, but we probably should go on to the airport, because our plane takes off in less than two hours."

"Oh…that's right. You have to put your car in the long term parking area, and it always takes longer than you think to get your bags checked and your boarding passes."

Klaus chuckled, "Always…it always takes longer than one thinks to get all of those things accomplished before flight time."

Peter and Nicholas came into the kitchen through the garage entrance, and Nicholas immediately ran to his *babushka.* "Papa and I went shopping!" He put his small arms around his grandmother's legs.

Klaus opened his arms, "Come here, little man…"

Nicholas lifted his arms to be picked up. "Are you going to fly in a big airplane?"

"Yes, I am, and so is your grandmother."

Peter laughed as he told his in-laws, "Nicholas has talked of nothing else since we told him that we were going to fly in an airplane."

"I think Nicholas remembers very well the long flights we had coming and going to Russia." Niki smiled at her son.

Klaus looked at his watch, "It's time for us to go to the airport, Marina."

Peter, Niki, and Nicholas waved at Klaus and Marina from the veranda as they drove away. When they could no longer see the car for the Pine trees, the Genchenko family went inside to have dinner.

Later that evening, when the dinner dishes were cleaned up, Nicholas had his bath, and was in bed asleep, Peter and Niki sat on the red leather sofa in Peter's study. They were holding hands and talking quietly.

"I know that you must be tired, Niki." Peter bent toward her and kissed her cheek.

"Oh...not so much, Pete...I'm doing okay, and I'm really looking forward to going to Chicago. Ron and Katya's wedding is going to be spectacular, don't you think?"

Peter nodded, and his thoughts turned to his sister for a moment. When he answered his wife, his voice was filled with emotion. "Yes, their wedding will truly be spectacular, Niki, just like ours was."

Chapter 43

Peter and his family boarded their plane at ten o'clock in the morning. At around five o'clock, there had been some mild thunderstorms, but they had rumbled through Indianapolis and had quickly gone to the east with their lightning flashes, dark clouds and rain, allowing the sun to shine through the overcast sky.

In the boarding area, Peter sat looking at Niki's lovely profile. She knows me too well, thought Peter. She understands my reluctance to fly in bad weather, but I know that she worries about it, too. He looked down at Nicholas, in his arms. My son, you seem oblivious to the weather. But Peter noticed that Nicholas was clutching his favorite stuffed bear against his chest.

When their row was called by the boarding agent, Peter took Nicholas by the hand and lightly patted Niki's shoulder as they walked up the jetway into the airplane. When she turned to smile up at him, his heart turned over. *Oh, my beautiful Niki.*

Their flight was a bit bumpy crossing Lake Michigan, but there were no delays or holding patterns required before their plane touched down at O'Hare International. It had been a short flight, a "hop-skip-and-a-jump," according to Klaus, who was waiting for them in the area for arrivals.

"Where is Mom?" Niki was surprised that her mother hadn't accompanied her father to pick them up.

"Your mother is getting a facial, manicure, and pedicure this morning, Niki, so I volunteered to gather the Genchenko family at the airport and bring you all downtown to the Drake."

"So, Mom's getting 'the works,' huh?" Niki smiled wryly.

"Yes, Niki, even though I told her she really didn't need to go to such trouble, she is beautiful just the way she is, she insisted that she wanted to look nice for Katya's wedding." Klaus shrugged his big shoulders and gave Nicholas a kiss on the top of his head.

"We had a good flight, even though there were some bumps along the way. And Nicholas took a nice, long nap." Peter held his sleepy son in one arm and shook Klaus' hand with the other.

"Actually, our flight was very smooth yesterday. It was better that way for Marina's sake." Klaus raised his craggy eyebrows and then winked at Peter.

In the baggage area, Nicholas was shifted to his grandfather's arms while his parents searched for their luggage. It turned out that they were very fortunate on this day, because all of their luggage pieces were intact and accounted for. Peter saw that Niki was greatly relieved to find that this was so, and he relaxed, too.

"If everything is good, let's get in the car and go downtown." Klaus, who had been waiting more than an hour for them, was ready for action.

Chicago traffic was a revelation to Peter. At stoplights, he watched as cabs inched into crosswalks, trying to intimidate scurrying, oblivious pedestrians into moving aside. Horns sounded; bleating horns, shrill horns, *loud* horns, and horns that could have sounded warnings to ocean-going vessels.

And the *buildings*...the Sears Tower, the John Hancock Building, the myriad of skyscrapers made of steel, concrete, and whole facades in glass and aluminum...a civil engineer's dream! In spite of the heavy traffic and noise, Peter decided that he liked Chicago. And then he saw *the lake*...Lake Michigan, and he was in love with this Windy City. Peter reached over, took Niki's hand, and squeezed it. He wanted her to know how thrilled he was with this huge city. With Nicholas sleeping, nestled on her lap, she returned Peter's hand squeeze and smiled at her husband. Without saying a word, she had conveyed the thought that she, too, was thrilled.

The Drake is a magnificent hotel, thought Peter as he and his family headed toward the registration desk. A Bellman had taken their luggage at the entrance to the hotel, thus freeing all of them up considerably. Klaus had Nicholas in his arms, and Peter held Niki's hand as they inched forward. The main lobby was full of people, and judging from the manner of dress of many of them, Peter knew that they were probably not Americans. *Are all of these people here for my sister's wedding?* And then he chuckled at this irrational thought.

Their suite of rooms was situated next to Klaus and Marina's suite on the third floor of the Drake. Peter tipped the bellman generously. There was a great deal of luggage to wrestle with, and the Bellman had handled his job with courtesy and aplomb.

"Enjoy your stay," he told them, as he exited the suite.

Klaus gently placed Nicholas in his father's arms, "I'm going to check on Marina, and then I can give you some idea of the dinner arrangements for this evening. I do know that Katya will dine with our family and the bridesmaids' families, and Ron will dine in a separate dining room with his family and groomsmen. Ari has told me that we are all following the Jewish Wedding laws and customs regarding the separation of the groom and bride prior to their wedding."

"Call us as soon as you know the timing. I think that we are going to need a little time to freshen up…that is, if we can ever get Nicholas fully awake again." Peter smiled at his father-in-law and then lightly mussed his son's hair.

There was a tap on the door, and Niki went to answer it. "Mom, wow…you look great! Dad told us that you were doing the 'spa thing' today."

"Well, Niki, I think that they did the best that they could with what they had to work with…" Marina kissed her daughter's cheek.

Klaus turned to his wife, "Is there anything further regarding dinner arrangements this evening?"

"Yes, Katya is staying in this tower of the hotel, and we will all gather at seven o'clock in the private dining room on the third floor. This dinner isn't part of the wedding ceremony; it's just a way of making sure that everyone has a good dinner. So far, I've been able to contact all of the bridesmaids and their families. Everyone will be there for the dinner…including our Michael!"

Niki was ecstatic, "Mikey's here? Oh, I'm so glad that he made it on time!"

There was another tap on the door. This time, Peter answered it, "Hello, Mike, come in, come in. Niki and I are very happy that you could come for Katya's wedding."

"I wouldn't miss it for the world, Pete." He turned toward Niki, "How's my little sister? And Nicholas, my gosh, you've really gotten big!" Mike swung Nicholas up into his arms and gave him a gentle squeeze as Nicholas squealed in delight.

It was a happy, noisy, and sometimes tear-filled, gathering. Their dinners were all cooked according to Kosher Law, as required. Nonetheless, everyone remarked on the delicious meal. Nicholas cleaned his plate, and even asked for some of his mother's meal, which she gladly gave to him.

Peter watched as Katya's inhibitions, her shyness, her nervousness, melted away. She absolutely shone, her face alight, as she basked in this wonderful, preliminary celebration to her wedding. Her brother could not be happier for his beloved sister.

Chapter 44

It was after eleven o'clock when Peter and Niki finally had their shower prior to crawling into bed. When they bathed Nicholas, he had made no complaints as they put his pajamas on. And he didn't even mind getting into a strange bed. In fact, he seemed quite relieved to have his parents pull up the sheet and blankets as he snuggled down into the sweet-smelling, down-filled pillows.

"Niki…" Peter spoke quietly as the warm water swirled around them in the shower, "do you think that we could…?" He put his arms around her, and kissed her deeply on the mouth. *"I need you so much."*

His lovely wife surrendered to his kiss, and then smiled up at him, her dark hair dampening into a darker shade in the softly falling water, her breasts pressing against his chest, her skin glistening in the spray, "Oh…yes, Pete…I've been looking forward to this wonderful shower all day." Her voice held the familiar lilting, musical quality as she answered him.

Peter had always been gentle with Niki when they made love, even when his need was great. And now, with her abdomen rounded with their second child, he was even more careful not to press her too deeply.

He gently lifted her onto him, *"Niki, my sweet Niki."* They slept until the alarm went off at seven o'clock. As Peter rolled over to shut it off, he was surprised to find that Nicholas was snuggled up against him.

Niki sat up when she heard her husband chuckling softly. "Pete? What's so funny?"

Peter turned to her, "Of course, I'm sure that you will never guess who has joined us in our bed."

"Nicholas Petrovich...our little man." It was her turn to laugh.

Niki reached across her husband's broad chest to lightly caress her sleeping son's cheek. As she did so, Nicholas opened his eyes and smiled at his mother.

Nicholas sat up in bed and slowly stretched one arm over his head, and then the other, "I'm very hungry...do you think that we can have pancakes this morning?"

"Let's order room service for breakfast, Nicholas. We don't have too much to do today until the wedding and reception, and it will be nice for just the three of us to have a quiet morning." Peter liked the thought of a pancake breakfast.

"Papa, I really like room service!" Nicholas had become a very sophisticated little traveler when his father played hockey.

"My wonderful men...that's a great idea." Niki, still tired from yesterday's travel and the dinner that ran into the late evening hours, was thankful for a little more quiet time with her family.

As they were sitting down to their breakfast, still in their pajamas, there was a tap on the door. Peter got up to answer it, and found Ron, smiling widely. "If Katya is with you this morning, I won't bother you, but I have some great news that I want to share."

"Come in, Ron. Katya isn't with us right now, so tell us...what's the good news?" Peter was curious.

Still excited with what he was going to tell them, Ron spoke rapidly, "My parents are going to give us a Caribbean cruise for a wedding present, and I wanted to make sure that Katya would like to do something like that. I just didn't want to spring it on her, only to find later that she might not like to do a cruise. What do you think?"

Niki's reaction was immediate, "Oh, that's great news, Ron! I'm sure that Katya is going to love a Caribbean cruise honeymoon."

"Perhaps you wouldn't mind some company?" Peter's grin was machiavellian.

Ron was startled momentarily, and then began to laugh, "You got me that time, Peter! No...I don't think that we need any company on our honeymoon."

"Uncle Ron," piped Nicholas, "would you like some of my blueberry pancakes?"

Ron ruffled his soon-to-be-nephew's hair, "They look good Nicholas, but I've already had my breakfast."

Later that day, Peter and his family were ready for Katya and Ron's wedding. Here we are, thought Peter, the Genchenko family, dressed and ready for the occasion. Peter looked at his beautiful wife and handsome son, and told them that he was certain that no other family attending this wedding could be any more handsome together. They were standing at the entrance to the main ballroom of the Drake Hotel, and Peter was going to join Zeke, Ron's brother, to witness Ron's signing of the marriage contract, the *ketuvah.*

Ron came quickly over to Peter and his family, "I think everything is ready for the signing of the *ketuvah.*"

He looked a little shaky, which was completely understandable, thought Peter, who vividly remembered how nervous he, himself, had been on his wedding day.

"I'll be back in a few moments, Niki, Nicholas…Ron needs me right now."

Peter grinned at Niki and his son, and then turned and walked with Ron toward the ornate document standing on a large golden easel in one corner of the ballroom. Zeke was waiting for them, and took Ron's arm as he patted him on the back.

Peter and Ron had previously talked at length about all of the things that must be accomplished during the *Ohr Semayach*, and the *ketuvah* was one of the most important of them. Ron told Peter that the marriage contract, a legal document, is written in Aramaic. While he spoke, Ron held up one hand as he counted off on his fingers the obligations of the husband to his wife. The most important of these, he said, were delineated as: a dwelling for shelter, food for sustenance, clothing for warmth and comfort, and pleasure in the marriage. The wife would have the opportunity to place a lien on all of her husband's property in order to receive what she is due if he should divorce her, or die before she does. Peter commented to Ron that he had no idea that the *ketuvah* was so important, and that it was actually key to the married life of the Jewish man and woman.

"Although Jewish Law allows divorce under certain circumstances, Peter, it is understood that the woman in a marriage will more than likely be the one to suffer in the event of a divorce. Thus, the marriage contract, the *ketuvah*, spells out exactly what the wife's rights are." Ron took the entire process seriously. "My *kiddushin,* my dedication and marriage to Katya, is something that I hold dearly."

"How interesting," Peter observed, "that the *mitzvah* of *kiddushin* was so well-understood by those who wrote the Jewish Laws. The Sacrament of Marriage in Christianity could benefit from many of the things that you have just told me."

Ron was anxious to sign his *ketuvah,* and took pen in hand. Peter and Zeke stood as witnesses for the ceremonial signing; the groom, with two witnesses. Many wedding guests, who had come to see this *mitzvah* carried out, were also there to witness the signing. After Ron signed the marriage contract, there were hors doeuvres and drinks served to all of those in attendance. Many *lechaims,* were called out to Ron as the celebrants enjoyed their strong beverages.

Mike Kellman, who had started the toasts, came to Ron and shook his hand. "Congratulations, Ron. You have made a wonderful choice in Katya."

Peter, standing next to Mike, heartily agreed, and added, "Katya has also made a wonderful choice."

Zeke clapped his brother on the back as he downed his second glass of *Chivas*, "To life, Myron! *Lechaim!"*

Ron's face was wreathed in smiles and reddened as he, also, drank a second glass with Peter, Zeke, and Mike.

"Now, we must find my father and Klaus for the *bedekin."* Ron was the picture of the anxious groom.

Peter called out to the wedding guests, "Ron and Katya need all of their male guests to witness the veiling of the bride. Also, the two violinists chosen for this part of the ceremony must come to play the music for the *bedekin."* Peter called, "follow us…" as he fell into step with Ron, Zeke, Mike, Ari, and Klaus.

Katya was receiving her guests in the 'Bride's Room' where her family and friends, the bridesmaids, were in attendance. She was seated on a tall, satin-covered chair, with a lace-bedecked footrest, and looked as though she might be royalty, she was so beautifully dressed and coiffed.

When Peter entered the room, his eyes immediately searched for Niki. When he saw her, he gave her a bright smile as the violinists began to play the beautiful wedding music for the *bedekin* ceremony. *What a lovely day to be here with the most important women in my life, and my handsome son,* thought Peter, as he held out his hand to Nicholas, who came running to him.

Marina stood with Miriam to the side of Katya. Both women smiled and acknowledged their husbands as they came into the room.

Peter and Zeke followed Ron as he approached Katya for the veiling ceremony. Both men had their hands on Ron's shoulders as he stood before his bride. Peter felt Ron's shoulder trembling, and patted him gently, as did Zeke. The room became quiet, except for the music of the violins. Ron reached for Katya's veil, and Peter saw the look on his sister's face as she gazed up at Ron. *She's happy now…so happy.*

It had been a week, Peter knew, since Katya and Ron had seen one another, as prescribed by Jewish Law. How wise the Mishnaic Law seemed to be in this matter.

After the veiling, it was now time for Ron to go to the canopy, the *chuppah,* in the company of Ari and Miriam. This part of the wedding ceremony would be held outside in the open air on a wide terrace off the main ballroom of the Drake Hotel. Ron put on his *kittel,* a white robe that signifies the start of a new life, a life where all past sins are wiped away as the bride and groom become one. It was now Ron's obligation to pray for his unmarried friends, that they might find their own perfect love, while he awaited the appearance of Katya in the company of Marina and Klaus.

The cantor began to sing verses from the "Song of Songs" as Katya came onto the terrace with Marina and Klaus on either side of her.

Peter, standing nearby with Niki, Nicholas, and Mike, was enthralled by the unfolding ceremony. He reached for Niki's hand and squeezed it gently. *Our lives, Katya's and mine, are just beginning now, with our beloved partners by our sides.*

Katya, with Miriam and Marina now at her side, circled Ron seven times as he prayed. The significance of the number seven had to do with the seven days of creation, and the new creation of the man and woman as they came together as husband and wife.

Rabbi Gelman stood behind the center of the canopy under the starry heaven facing Katya and Ron as they came up to stand under the canopy. He held a glass of wine and recited a blessing over the wine praising the Lord for Jewish Laws regarding the sacred life of Jewish families. After the blessings, Katya and Ron drank from the cup of wine that was the symbol of the Lord's Blessings.

Niki and Zeke, who came forward to stand as the witnesses of the marriage ceremony, watched as Ron placed a band of gold, without ornamentation, on Katya's ring finger. Ron recited the ancient verse, "Behold, you are betrothed to me with this ring, according to the Law of Moses and Israel."

Peter stood and read the *ketuvah* to the bride, groom, and wedding guests, and then carefully rolled the contract, tied it with a ribbon, and handed it to his sister.

Wine was poured and the *sheva brachos,* seven blessings, were recited by Rabbi Gelman over the wine as required by Mishnaic Law. Ron and Katya were as Adam and Eve, the first couple in the Garden of Eden. They both again then drank from a common glass, after which Ron broke the glass under his heel. This signified the Diaspora, the separation of Jews from Jerusalem and the destruction of the Temple, which celebrants and wedding guests alike must reflect upon, and mourn, even in joyous times.

For several moments, quiet reigned, and then the orchestra began to play, and the wedding guests, separated by curtains, male separated from female, began to dance. Voices lifted with *Mazaltov* greetings to the new husband and wife. Katya and Ron were then taken by Peter and Zeke, as witnesses, to their *cheder yichud,* the private room, where they could lock the door and be alone together for their first dinner as husband and wife. Each had fasted on this wedding day, and, now very hungry, they thoroughly enjoyed the food provided to them. Ron kissed his new wife deeply before, during, and after their meal, much to the delight of both.

At the same time that the new couple were enjoying their first married meal, the wedding guests sat down to a fully Kosher dinner provided by the families of the bride and groom. Rabbi Gelman performed the washing of hands and blessing of the bread before the meal was served.

At the end of their dinner in the *cheder yichud*, Ron and Katya returned to their wedding guests, and were introduced as, "Mr. and Mrs. Myron Ari Michael," for the first time by the Rabbi. Katya and Ron, arm in arm, beamed as they circulated throughout the ballroom, stopping to speak to their many wedding guests.

Marty Pelham, his wife, and Sheldon Levin and his wife came up to Katya and Ron, "Mazaltov, Mazaltov, you two," said Sheldon.

Still beaming, Ron held Katya's hand as he told them, "Thank you…thank you both so much. This is the happiest day of my life," he looked at his wife, "and, I hope, Katya's, too."

Blushing, Katya nodded her head and kissed her husband's cheek.

"Of course, dear Ron, it truly is."

Across the ballroom, Niki tugged at her husband's sleeve to get his attention, "Pete...Pete, everyone...I mean, *everyone, even those from all over the world,* are talking about Ron Michael's beautiful bride. Some of these people are dripping with diamonds and wearing designer clothes...very sophisticated...and they are commenting on how beautiful Katya is!"

Peter nodded, smiled down at Niki and caressed her cheek with his fingertips, "I, too, have heard many comments like that about Katya. But I must tell you, my dear wife, that I am hearing the same things about you. I have been congratulated many times, by people that I do not know, that I have had good fortune in taking such a beautiful wife as you." Peter put his arms around Niki and kissed her on the forehead. "I love you, my beautiful Nikola."

Mike, hand in hand with Stephanie, and Klaus with Nicholas on his shoulders, came over to them a few moments later after making their way across the crowded ballroom.

"Hi, Pete...Niki..." said Mike. "This wedding celebration is really something!"

"It is a wonderful thing to behold, isn't it?" Niki put an arm around Stephanie's waist to include her in the conversation.

"This is truly a spectacular wedding...and the ceremony was just beautiful," said Stephanie.

Peter nodded and told the group, "It doesn't seem that long ago that Niki and Ron came to take my sister and me from Lyubertsy, the terrible place where we lived. And now...well, just look at Katya. She and Ron are perfect together."

Mike agreed, "It really hasn't been that long ago, Pete. And you're right; Ron and Katya are a handsome couple."

Niki gave Mike's hand a squeeze and said, "And now we are in a new place, and a new time."

Klaus joined the conversation and pointed upward, "My grandson wanted to see over all of the peoples' heads because he said that he was tired of being "too short," and wanted to see what the "tall people" were seeing."

"I'm not surprised, Klaus. Perhaps someday my son will be as tall as his grandfather and his Uncle…who knows?" Peter, who had seemed a little sad for a brief moment when he was talking about the past, now smiled again.

"*Mat,* Papa, Uncle Mike, it is very *tall* up here!" Nicholas put his arms above his head and laughed.

"Hold on tight, Nicholas. Being tall doesn't mean that you can't fall down." Niki was always the protective mother.

"Achh…Niki, he is fine, just fine. I would never let my grandson fall." Klaus gave his daughter a look of mock dismay.

"Niki, our son is holding on tight to his grandfather's shirt collar. It's a wonder that Klaus can breathe."

This brought a giggle from Niki, "Okay, I know when I'm out-manned. But be careful, please."

Marina, who had been sitting and chatting with Miriam and some of her friends from Tel Aviv, excused herself and came over to her family. "This is a wonderful wedding, don't you think? And I want to tell all of you that I have been exercising my languages with many of the guests here; some Russian, some German, several French. It is an amazing group. I do so admire Miriam. She seems at ease with all of them."

"Ah, my cosmopolitan, my international, wife. You should have been a politician." Klaus put one arm around Marina as he held Nicholas in place on his shoulders with the other.

"Mom, you look beautiful tonight." Mike leaned down and kissed his mother on the top of her head.

"And you, my son, are a very handsome, and eligible, young man. Don't you think so, Stephanie?"

"My mother the matchmaker," said Mike. "You gotta love it!"

For the first time, Niki saw that Stephanie was blushing. She had never known her friend to blush. Hmmm...this is interesting, she thought.

The music started again, and this time, with the *mechitzah* still in place to separate the dancing men and women, it seemed as if all of the wedding guests were dancing, the floor was so crowded.

When the meal and dancing were finished, and the wedding celebration was nearly complete, Rabbi Gelman recited the *birchas hamazon,* the prayer after the meal, and included a recitation of the seven blessings over another glass of wine, from which Ron and Katya again drank.

Katya stood as Peter and Niki came over to say goodbye. "My dear, dear brother and sister-in-law...this has been a most wondrous, a most happy, day! And you, Petrosha, and Niki are the reasons for Ron's and my happiness, on this, our wedding day."

Peter shook Ron's hand, and held his beautiful sister close for a moment. He then held her at arms' length as he told her, "I wish you and Ron all the happiness in the world."

Niki kissed Katya's cheek, and held Ron's hand for a moment, "Congratulations to you both. And...have fun on your honeymoon cruise! We can't wait to see the photos."

Peter reached for Niki's hand and said, "Katya, we can never thank you enough for all of your kindness and help in the early days of our own marriage…and Ron's help, too. We will miss you both when we go home…you won't be there…you will be together in your own home…just as it should be."

Peter and Niki gathered Nicholas from his grandparents, and wished Marina and Klaus a safe trip home. Mike was flying back to Indianapolis with them for a short visit.

"Goodnight, Mikey," Niki squeezed her brother's hand. "Maybe we can get together before you head for California."

"Sounds good to me…" Mike shook Peter's hand, and then his nephew's. "See all of you in Indy."

The Genchenko family turned, and walked slowly, hand-in-hand, out of the nearly empty ballroom.

Chapter 45

May and June seemed to fly by, with blooming flowers and the sprouting of the vegetable garden that Peter planted with Nicholas. He had never had the opportunity to plant any kind of garden, vegetable or otherwise, and Peter found that he truly enjoyed working in the soil. Niki suggested heirloom tomatoes as a small crop, and she helped Nicholas and Peter to plant Silver Queen corn, her favorite corn-on-the cob variety. They also planted radishes, sweet onions, green peppers and leaf lettuce; an instant salad. As a bow to Niki's sense of aesthetics, Peter planted flowers in a border around the garden; Marigolds, Impatiens, Sweet Peas, Snapdragons, Zinnia, and Poppies. The flowering border was truly spectacular, and visitors commented on the beauty and success of the Genchenkos' flower and vegetable garden. Every morning, Peter took Nicholas by the hand and walked down to the vegetable garden by the lake to check on the growth of the various plants, and to weed and water them.

Peter noticed that his wife had truly blossomed, like his garden, as she got closer to her due date. He didn't allow Niki to do any work with a hoe or rake. He told her that she could boss her men around, but she couldn't get her hands dirty. This ultimatum made Niki laugh, even though she knew that Pete was right in not letting her get too physically involved with their garden.

The peerless summer days seemed to pass too quickly, and then it was time to start preparing for the second little Genchenko's arrival in mid-July. Instead of painting the baby's bedroom by themselves, Peter and Niki agreed it would be much easier to hire someone for most of the painting and carpeting work.

Stephanie helped Niki with color schemes and window coverings. Together, they decided what baby furniture left over from Nicholas could be used, and what needed to be replaced. Peter wisely let his wife make most of the decisions regarding baby décor.

Katya came to visit at least weekly, and Nicholas eagerly looked forward to her visits. They often had play dates, where they would visit the Indianapolis Children's Museum, or the library downtown. Katya was now just working part-time in Ron's clinic because they were hoping to start a family.

During many of Katya's visits, she, Niki and Stephanie consulted on the last few things for the new little Genchenko's room.

Katya was fascinated with Niki's pregnancy. She fully understood that this new little one would be another life in the preservation of the Genchenko family name.

It was just a 'twinge,' at first, while she was grocery shopping in the supermarket. Niki realized very quickly, however, because of her previous experience with the beginning of labor with Nicholas, that this was not just a Braxton-Hicks contraction. There was nothing preliminary about this 'twinge.' No…it was strong and insistent. She and Nicholas had just finished their shopping, and she was trying to push a very full cart toward her car. By the third contraction, Niki almost doubled over. *This is so different…so different than it was with Nicholas.* Fear clutched her heart.

"Mat?" Nicholas was patting his mother's hand, and he had a worried look on his face.

"It's...it's okay, Nicholas. Don't worry, little man. I just need to get these groceries in the car..."

"Ma'am?" A young man was standing next to Niki, holding her elbow. "Are you all right? Here, let me help you get your groceries into your car."

"What...? Oh...thanks...I'm not feeling too well, just now. I think it's the baby...Pete, I need to call Pete." That was the last coherent thought that Niki had.

Peter was driving much too fast...*Niki...Niki.* The call had come when he had just finished working in his vegetable garden. He was washing the dark, loamy soil from his hands when the telephone rang.

"Mr. Genchenko...Mr. Peter Genchenko? This is Brent Talbot with IPD..."

IPD, what is IPD? The police? Why are the police calling me? "Yes...what...?" His voice faltered. Peter immediately thought of his wife and son, and he nearly dropped the telephone.

Patrolman Talbot heard the panic in Peter's voice. "Hold on, Mr. Genchenko...I just want to let you know that your wife is in labor..."

"Is she all right? And what about my son...?" Peter was sick at his stomach.

"They are both okay...and I just want to let you know that your wife is at Indiana University Hospital in the obstetrics unit, and your son is being looked after in the hospital childrens' daycare center..."

Peter got into his car, took several deep breaths, and turned the key in the ignition. He hadn't called anyone before he left the house because he didn't want to delay any more than he had to. His heart was pounding, but he knew that he had to be careful, he had to drive very carefully, so that he would be there for Niki.

He started praying; begging God to take care of his family...*Please, God, help us. Please keep Niki and the baby, and Nicholas safe.*

She was pale, so pale. Fear gripped Peter's heart as he reached for Niki's hand. When he touched her, she opened her eyes.

"Niki, I'm here..." He squeezed her hand gently.

"I waited for you." Her smile was wan and brief.

A tall woman in blue scrubs, haircovering and mask took Peter by the elbow, "Here, take this jumpsuit, cover your hair with this cap, and put on these shoe covers and mask. This room is called LDRP, and that stands for labor, delivery, recovery and postpartum. We do everything here, and that's why you have to 'dress out' to be in here during the delivery." The nurse was no-nonsense as she told Peter to go into the anteroom to 'dress out.'

He had never dressed more quickly in his life. He pulled on the jumpsuit, hopping from one foot to the other as he donned the shoe covers, pulled on the cap and put on the mask, before running back into the LDRP.

"Where is Nicholas? I've been so worried about him." Tears rolled down Niki's cheeks as she looked up at Peter.

"He's fine. I called the daycare center, where they're keeping him, and asked them to get in touch with your parents."

Her eyes were closed, but she smiled, nodded her head and whispered, "Thank you, Pete...I'm so glad that you're here with us."

Us...she said "us!" A new little Genchenko to add to our family. Peter's heart was pounding.

The nurses were busy getting the room set up for the delivery, and a young man's face peered in the door to the room, "Hi everyone, I'm standing in for Dr. Leonard…I'm Keith Byron…uh, Dr. Keith Byron. Is everything ready for the delivery?"

Lisa, the delivery room nurse spoke up, "Yes, Dr. Byron…but has the Ultrasound Department contacted you with their findings?"

Dr. Byron's eyebrows arched in question for a moment, "Uh, yes…we have a placenta previa marginalis here, don't we?"

As the nurse answered the doctor, Peter's heart pounded even harder, and he bent to whisper into Niki's ear, "Niki, do you know what they are saying? Is something wrong?"

She looked up at her husband with eyes that were calm and seemingly without pain, "It's okay, Pete. There is a small amount of the placenta, you remember, it's part of the sac that holds the baby, that is covering my cervix, the opening into my uterus. That's why there was some bleeding earlier…but it's okay right now. Please, Pete," Niki took his hand in hers, and brought it to her lips, "don't worry about me or the baby. We are doing okay right now."

In spite of Niki's reassurances, Peter was feeling the pinpricks of fear moving up his spine. I can't be afraid…I've got to be strong for Niki, he thought. With great effort he tried to remain calm. *What's taking that doctor so long out there in the hall?* He wanted to go out into the hall and drag the doctor into the room.

"Okay everyone, let's bring this little one into the world." Dr. Byron, a mask covering his face, opened the door with his shoulder and strode into the room, forearms up, with water dripping from his elbows.

A nurse, clad in a long gown, a mask and eye shield, gloves and a cap covering all of her hair, handed the doctor a towel from the sterile field on her back table so that he could dry his hands and forearms. She then helped him into a long gown, and gloves.

Peter watched as the nurses lifted Niki's legs up into what they called stirrups that seemed to have miraculously appeared from beneath the end of the bed. Once her legs were in the stirrups, the end of the bed folded under. The nurses scrubbed her abdomen and pelvic area, and then draped Niki from the middle of her chest to the upper thighs, leaving a 'tent' into which Dr. Byron slid himself on a rolling stool.

"Okay, Mrs. Genchenko," Dr. Byron called from beneath the drape, "I'm going to put a quick pudenal block in so that you won't feel any pain…there, it's all finished. I'll wait just a couple of minutes…*oh, the cervix is now completely dilated, and I'm seeing some crown. Nurses, please raise the head of the bed to about thirty-five degrees…okay…raise it!* Dr. Byron lifted his head above the drapes, and there was a question in his eyes.

"Doctor, the bed isn't lifting at the head. We're trying to see what's wrong…" Two of the three nurses in the room seemed to be scurrying around beside, and then beneath, the bed.

Peter decided quickly that if the bed wouldn't raise up, then he was going to have to help Niki and the baby. He slipped into the bed behind Niki, his long legs dangling over the sides, and told the doctor, "How high do you need my wife to be lifted?"

"Well, uh, put your arms around her, under her breasts and above her belly, so that she can push back against you. She's going to need to start pushing right about *now.* "

Peter was greatly surprised by the strength of Niki's body as she pushed back against him at Dr. Byron's direction. He was absolutely in awe of her strength, and that she was not crying out in pain. This labor, this hard work of delivering their child was something that he had understood imperfectly. All of the reading and viewing of videos on childbirth had not prepared him sufficiently for this moment, but Niki, his beautiful Niki, was taking it in stride, without complaint.

"Let's wait for the next contraction…there it goes…okay, now *push,* that's it, that's it."

Peter felt tears rolling down his face, but he didn't change the position of his arms around Niki to wipe them away. His heart was in his throat as Dr. Byron kept coaching Niki along.

"You're doing great Mrs. Genchenko…just a little more…that's good, now rest a moment. Here we go! Push, push, push. Oh yeah…it's a boy…no doubt about this one! Just look at that package." Dr. Byron was delighted with this very healthy baby boy, "He will probably go more than nine pounds, and I'm guessing that he's at least twenty-two inches long…and just listen to that lusty cry. That's a big boy for a little mom! Good work, Mrs. Genchenko!

Dr. Byron placed the squalling baby across Niki's abdomen and then he ducked back under the drapes, "Just a few more things here…" And he was quiet for several moments.

Niki gently stroked her baby's cheek, "Pete, oh Pete…he looks just like you. Look at his wild man hair! And he's really got a good set of lungs." She was crying and laughing at the same time.

Peter, overwhelmed with emotion, was barely able to speak, "Yes," he croaked, "he's a wonderful baby, Niki. Thank you, my love, my Niki…" He bent and kissed her cheek.

"Placenta is out and it's got three vessels, and the uterus is pulling down nicely. I'm tying off the cord. Just a minute here…okay, that's done! Well, Mr. Genchenko," Dr. Byron said as he finished and stood up, "do you want to hold your son?"

"Yes, yes!" Peter was thrilled at the prospect.

One of the nurses draped Peter's arms with a sterile blanket, and then handed the newborn to his father. His son wasn't crying anymore. Peter was amazed that this tiny little man was looking around the room, and then he turned his head, and his eyes, as they met his father's, looked into Peter Genchenko's soul.

Chapter 46

Niki got to go home on June 30th, the second day after her delivery, and it was a momentous occasion for the Genchenko family. Nicholas was very excited to have a baby brother, and was thrilled when his *Mat* and Papa let him hold his little brother in his lap.

Deciding on a name for the baby had been a family effort while Niki was still hospitalized, because the hospital had to provide a birth certificate before the mother and baby could be discharged. They all had an idea what the littlest Genchenko's given name should be, and everyone had a vote. After much discussion, the name Josef Petrovich Genchenko was bestowed upon the new arrival. Peter and Nicholas had prevailed in the voting, and Niki was very happy with their choice, although she had leaned toward the name Mikhail for a short time.

Marina and Klaus were waiting for them when they came home. Katya and Ron arrived soon after, and it was a lovely afternoon of quiet celebration over the arrival of little Josef.

Marina, Katya and Stephanie were going to take turns helping out while Niki regained her strength. Peter had also invited Klaus, Marina and Duchess to stay with them for the first week, and perhaps longer, if they wished. There was more than enough room in the Genchenko house to accommodate them.

Niki was breastfeeding the baby, but she also pumped some breastmilk for interval feedings, sometimes at night, so that she could get some rest and regain her strength.

In their first two weeks at home, Peter got up to do the midnight feedings, and Nicholas often got up with his father, sitting close by his side, while little Josef drank his bottle. On this early, very early, Sunday morning, Peter sat contentedly as he watched his two extraordinary sons interact. Peter understood that the bonds forged by siblings were lifelong, just as his bond with Katya was. Brothers…my sons, thought Peter. How wonderful it would have been to have had a brother as well as a sister. For a moment, he thought about the Garringer Marines, Zachary and Ryan, who had been so pivotal in helping to rescue Katya and him. Having a relationship like theirs would have been truly wonderful.

Peter was still holding Josef while Nicholas slept beside them, when Marina got up to start the day at five o'clock. He smiled at Marina, and, as she took Josef in her arms, Peter whispered to her that he was taking Nicholas upstairs to his own room for another hour or two of sleep.

Peter stepped lightly on the stairs, and after tucking Nicholas into his bed, he crept quietly down the hall to crawl back into bed with Niki. He pulled up the light sheet and blanket, and snuggled up behind her as he slipped an arm under, and the other around, her.

"Good morning, Pete…I guess it's time for me to get out of bed," she whispered in a sleepy voice.

"Not yet, Niki. Just let me hold you for a little while. Josef is with your mother, and Nicholas is back in bed. I want to hold you…I need to hold you…for just a little while."

When Peter awoke, he was alone in bed. Sunlight was coming in around the shades in the bedroom, and when he glanced at the bedside clock it was almost nine o'clock. The house was quiet, and momentarily, he wondered where everyone might have gone?

He quickly shaved and brushed his teeth, hardly glancing in the mirror. He didn't need to see the tired man reflected there. Lately, he had felt tired quite often. It was an odd sensation for him, as he had always had a great deal of energy. But lately…well, a new baby is a challenge, he decided. Niki is the one who is truly sleep-deprived, he realized. It had been so kind of Marina and Klaus to come to stay and help with Josef and Nicholas. Otherwise, he wondered what he and Niki might have done?

After throwing on some of his old gardening clothes and making the bed, Peter opened the bedroom door and the wonderful scent of a fresh pot of coffee wafted toward him. He quickly descended the stairs and was greeted by his oldest son.

"Papa's awake," called Nicholas, who had been sitting with his grandmother in the great room while she read to him.

"Good morning, Pete. Niki is in the kitchen bathing Josef, and Klaus has taken Duchess for a walk." Marina pointed toward the kitchen as she spoke. "Were you able to finally get some rest?"

Peter smiled, ruffled his son's hair, and said, "Yes, I did, and now I'm following the aroma of coffee…I think it's just what I need this morning."

"Pete?" Niki called from the kitchen, "We saved some breakfast casserole for you…and I'll make some toast, too, after little Josef is diapered and dressed."

As he came into the kitchen, Peter noticed that Niki had put on some 'real' clothes today, jeans and a blouse. His wife was nothing short of remarkable, he realized. Her tummy, as Nicholas called it, seemed to have flattened to her pre-pregnant state in this second week after she had given birth to Josef.

Peter kissed his wife on the nape of her neck. "I love your perfume, Niki."

"Silly," said his wife. "The fragrance you are attributing to me is actually baby lotion."

"Well, whatever it is, it certainly smells good on you." Peter kissed her cheek, and patted her bottom gently with his hand.

Their days were idyllic during this perfect summer; gardening, baby and toddler care, and visits from family and friends for lunches, dinners and play dates kept the Genchenko family happily busy. Marina came two mornings a week when Niki worked in the orthopedic clinic she and Ron had established. On those same two mornings, Peter pursued his civil engineering degree at Purdue University. Little Josef and a very active Nicholas didn't mind, because their grandmother was a loving and integral part of their lives.

In the third week of August, Peter received the mid-September hockey practice schedule from the PB's coaching staff. But now, instead of actually looking forward to playing hockey, he wished that he had some ordinary job that would allow him to be at home every night with his family. Of course he still loved to play hockey; that wasn't the question at all. But he realized that the heavy travel schedule would begin in early November, and his heart was heavy at the prospect.

Late one night, when the boys were both sound asleep, Peter raised the issue with Niki, and they discussed how best to meet their childrens' needs, because they wanted their sons to have a good start, and in their minds, that meant both of them being with their boys as much as possible.

"I could drop one day a week in the clinic, Pete. That would make one day less that I would be away from the boys." Niki understood and shared Peter's concerns about having adequate time with their sons.

"No, Niki, I can't ask you to do that. You are a wonderful doctor, and you deserve to practice medicine. We don't have any money worries…with my father's book royalties, and other assets that we have been fortunate enough to accumulate. But I feel that the window is closing on my hockey career, and I'd like to have one or two more seasons with the PB's. I'd like to help them win the Stanley Cup, if possible. Do you think that I'm being selfish?"

Niki raised her hand to caress her husband's cheek, "No, Pete, you aren't being selfish at all. In fact, there isn't a selfish bone in your body. I have never known a more giving, loving man than you…and I understand why the start of the hockey season is weighing heavily on your mind. I know that you are going to miss Nicholas and Josef terribly."

"And you, Niki, don't forget that I will miss you, too." Peter smiled gently at his wife.

"But Pete…you have to do something for yourself, too. I could never ask you to stop playing hockey. You deserve to play and win." She smiled as she told him, "There is no one like my Pete on ice…and I have said it many times to many people. You are an exceptional athlete in your chosen sport, Pete. I want to see you and your team win the Stanley Cup, so maybe *I* am the selfish one. And I truly believe that you can do it, Pete. You are one in a million, my darling Pete, and you belong to Nicholas, Josef, and me."

Peter reached for the bedside lamp and turned it off. "Niki," he gently ran his hand up and down the soft, smooth skin of her arm, "do you think that we can...?"

Instead of answering him, she sat up in bed and pulled her nightgown over her head, tossing it to the foot of the bed. Niki lay back down, turned, and kissed her husband for a long moment on the lips.

"I'll take that as a yes!" There was delight in Peter's voice.

His heart turned over, just as it had from the very beginning with Niki. Their coupling was familiar, yet deeply pleasurable and intensely satisfying; he knew her body, and she, his. Their need, their passion, one for the other, knew no bounds. This had been so from the very first time that they had made love.

Two births, two babies, thought Peter, as he penetrated the warm depths of his wife, and she is still the same. "Niki..." He kissed her deeply.

Chapter 47

It was September, and the garden had become all but dormant. There were a few heirloom tomatoes left on the vines, and a pepper plant was still producing, but the lettuce, radishes, cabbage and kohl rabi had mostly given up. In contrast, Nicholas and Josef's pumpkins were still growing larger by the day.

Peter and Niki read books about Halloween and Thanksgiving to both sons, even though little Josef was much more interested in his mother's breast, or the bottle at feeding time. But both parents believed that it was never too early to start reading to their youngest son.

Niki was busy planning a birthday party for Nicholas. Marina and Klaus were helping with the planning of the birthday party as Peter geared up for the PB's practice schedule. Mike Kellman told his sister that he would take a week away from his business for the birthday party, and to meet his newest nephew, Josef. Everyone looked forward to Mike's visit; it had been too long since the Kellmans and Genchenkos had last seen him.

"We will have such a wonderful birthday party for our Nicholas," Marina told Niki.

"He's at a great age, Mom...his excitement over his birthday is wonderful to see."

"Will we be able to work out a time and date when Peter can be home? He was telling your father just recently that his team has a very tough practice and game schedule this year."

"They really do, Mom. Sometimes I wish...well, I guess that I'm just being selfish...but there are times when I miss Pete so much, that I wish that he didn't have to travel at all..." Niki's voice trailed off.

"That is the way life is in a marriage, Niki. You aren't being selfish...you just miss your husband. There were times, when you children," Marina hesitated, "when you and your brothers were young, and your father was traveling all over the world for the company, that I was terribly lonely. Do you remember those times, Niki?"

"Sort of, I guess...but you worked, too, Mom. We had a wonderful nanny, but she couldn't hold a candle to you."

Marina was surprised, "I was always a little in awe of your nanny. She seemed to be able to do everything with ease and spirit. Perhaps I was a little jealous of her in some ways, too, Niki."

"You need not have been...it was you, and of course, Dad, that we missed, and although we enjoyed our nanny's company, we were always ecstatic when you and Dad were at home...always."

Marina brushed a tear from her cheek, "I never knew that, Niki...I just thought...well, I don't know what I thought..."

Niki hugged her mother, "Mom, it's okay. I know how hard it is to be a parent, now. I want to do so much for my boys, but it isn't easy to find the time for everyone and everything. It seems that there are so many choices and tradeoffs."

"You are right about that, Niki. And I guess that women, in general, who have to work, or *want* to work outside the home, have to strike a good balance, somehow, between raising a family and working. It isn't at all easy, is it?"

"No, it's not, Mom, but Pete is truly the key to everything that is important to me. I feel as though we got a second chance to love one another when he and Katya came here to live with us. I can remember, vaguely, how lost I was when he went back to Russia. Nothing seemed to matter to me at all until Stephanie came to my rescue." Niki held up her hand, "I know that you and Dad were heartbroken by the way that I acted at the time, but you have to understand that I was nearly out of my mind with grief when Pete had to leave."

"I did feel helpless, Niki. I didn't know how to make it better for you. I just didn't understand how much you loved Pete, and how much *he* loved *you*. But now, look at how wonderful your life is with him and your sons. I pray every night that all of you will be safe and happy."

"Thanks, Mom. You and Dad have been there for me and my family every step of the way, and I love you all the more for it." Niki again hugged her mother for several moments.

Everyone, it seemed, had been invited to attend Nicholas Genchenko's birthday party. Uncle Mike arrived a day ahead of the actual party, and his arrival sparked a great celebratory meal at Ruth's Chris Steak House on Keystone. Marina and Karl sat next to their son, who was seated next to Niki's friend, Stephanie. Peter noticed that Stephanie brightened considerably when she found herself seated next to Mike. Peter mentioned his observation to Niki, who was delighted to hear it.

"Wouldn't it be fantastic if the two of them got together, Pete? Maybe Mike will even come back to live in Indy…who knows?" Niki's smile was broad as she looked up at Peter.

"It would be wonderful for all concerned, Niki, but right now, it's just speculation, and nothing else."

"Of course you're right, Pete, but I know that my parents would be *so* happy if Mike returned to Indiana. And…if Stephanie's reaction means anything, *she* would be very happy, too."

The next day, the Genchenko house was filled with well-wishers and birthday presents There were more than forty people inside the house and spilling out the big French Doors to the buffet on the veranda. Niki, Marina and Katya had prepared a wonderful stand-up buffet that included delicious dishes for children and adults, alike.

Uncle Les and his wife both commented on the Beef Wellington. "You ladies are very talented. Maybe you should go into the catering business? We'd throw a party just to get you to prepare a buffet for us."

"That's a great idea, Uncle Les, but, with everything else going on, it isn't really feasible."

"Ah, yes…reality can be a bitter pill to swallow," laughed Les, as his wife gently elbowed him.

"Well, it's almost time to light the candles and cut the cake, so I'd better get busy." As Niki started up the steps, she noticed that Mike was following Stephanie, walking toward the lake. *It would be wonderful to have Mike here with us, and to add Stephanie to our family.*

There were more than a dozen children who had come with their parents to celebrate the birthday of Nicholas Genchenko. Peter and Ron checked in on some of them who were in the playroom, and saw that, although there was much exuberance, everyone was getting along quite well. They noticed too, that even though Nicholas was just turning three, he seemed to be leading his little friends as they played.

Ron laughed as he remarked, "By golly, Pete, it looks like Nicholas is a born leader."

Peter nodded his head, "A born leader, perhaps, but I hope that he doesn't choose politics as his life's work!" *How extraordinary,* thought Peter.

Every time that Peter saw his wife, it was at a distance, and the baby was in her arms. He decided to seek her out so that he could take baby Josef off her hands for a little while.

Peter tapped Niki on the shoulder, "May I have this dance?" He chuckled as she reacted.

"Maybe later, Mr. Genchenko…but right now, I have my hands full."

"I have noticed…so let me hold Josef. I feel like going up to his bedroom and rocking with him. Of course, I'm being selfish, because I will more than likely enjoy sitting in the rocking chair just as much as our Josef."

"It would be perfect for both of you. Go enjoy your son, Pete." She gently placed Josef in his father's arms, stood on tiptoe and kissed Peter and Josef before she hurried away to help Marina and Katya with the rest of the buffet food.

Klaus called up the stairs more than an hour later, "Peter, it is time to sing happy birthday to Nicholas."

Peter stood, and then placed Josef in his little bed. Father and son yawned at the same time, and when Josef was settled in his bed, Peter headed for the stairs and more birthday revelry.

Chapter 48

Peter's flight to Pittsburgh was bumpy on this late September afternoon, but he was too tired to be concerned. It seemed that playing hockey, instead of being just a game, was becoming a physical challenge. He still loved playing, and it was very rewarding monetarily, and personally. He also liked everyone on his team. They were all professionals, and had collectively helped him to bring his game to the level of a professional, too.

As always, when he was traveling, Peter thought of his family, and how difficult it was to leave them. It was getting harder and harder to do so. He didn't want to miss any of his sons' milestones…the important things…because he had missed so much of Nicholas's first two years. He and Niki, and Nicholas, had been separated by thousands of miles during that time. And Peter still considered it a miracle that he, and Katya too, were here in this wonderful country, married to wonderful people, and happy beyond anything that they could ever have imagined.

The Delta 'puddle jumper,' as Peter's father-in-law called the commuter line from Indianapolis to Pittsburgh, bounced and bumped along in the air corridor between the two cities. Although, by now, Peter had logged thousands of miles in flight, he still felt uncomfortably vulnerable in the air.

Peter put his head back against the seat, and tried to adjust his long legs into a fairly painless position. He didn't mind the 'no frills' lack of service on the airplane because he usually had what Niki had referred to as 'butterflies' in his stomach whenever he had to fly anywhere. He thought about his wife, and all of the extra responsibilities that she had when he was not there to help her. Marina had been wonderful to them all, and was always there to lend a hand. Nicholas's very successful and very happy birthday party had been only one of the many, many things that she had helped Niki to put together. And Peter's gratitude extended to his father-in-law, too. Klaus was absolutely crazy about his grandsons, and was always available for whatever task there was to be done.

When Peter thought about his son's birthday party, he chuckled aloud, causing the female passenger next to him to glance at him briefly. Oh well, thought Peter, she probably thinks that I am a little odd. Well, so be it, and he shrugged his shoulders and continued to smile.

My wonderful Nicholas, thought Peter, is so very special. His birthday party, complete with his pre-school friends and their parents, and his own family, including Uncle Mike, had been a resounding success. It wasn't just the gifts that Nicholas enjoyed; it was interacting with his friends and family. How truly blessed Niki and I have been, to have such a warm and loving son.

Peter's thoughts then turned to baby Josef. He loved the crooked little smile that Josef gave him when he was being fed. The light in his tiny son's eyes was wondrous to behold. Blessed, yes, Niki and I are truly blessed.

When the plane circled the airfield several times and then finally landed, Peter grabbed his carry-on bag, and headed down the aisle. He was relieved and happy to be escaping the confinement and cramped quarters of the interior of the plane.

What will this day bring, he wondered? He understood that practicing with his team, the PB's, was almost as important as actually playing an opponent. His comfort level with his team members continued to be very high. Everyone on the team, and certainly the coaches, wanted the same things; to win games, and ultimately, the Stanley Cup. They all wanted to bring the Stanley Cup home to Pittsburgh.

In the locker room, Peter spoke to many of his teammates, and listened to the laughter, chatter and exuberance of those around him. Always the observer, he liked to see and hear the reactions of the other players as they got into their gear. He realized, too, that these men had very different childhoods from his own, for the most part. What would it have been like to live in an atmosphere of love and acceptance? Of course, he would never know, but he was determined that his children would have a loving, caring environment in which to thrive. He and Niki would see to it.

When he was fully dressed in his practice uniform and skates, he literally catapulted himself out onto the ice, took in his customary several deep breaths of the cold air coming off the ice, and prepared to carry out the instructions that the coaches had given the team as they prepared for practice. They were trying several new formations and tactics today, and Peter was ready for whatever came his way.

Let the good times roll…and he smiled as he raced around the oval of the ice, with one of his teammates, Jordan, in hot pursuit, trying to catch him.

Chapter 49

Halloween at the Genchenko house was a busy time for the family. While Niki painted the faces and designs on the pumpkins, Peter worked on carving out the half-dozen pumpkins for Nicholas and Josef. Peter, according to Niki, was the pumpkin 'surgeon.' Klaus and Marina joined in the festivities as they took many photographs of the big pumpkin display. Of course, their grandsons were the central focus in all of the photos.

One photo, in particular, Peter had decided to enlarge and have framed for his 'gallery' wall in his study. It was a photo of Nicholas holding his tiny brother, Josef, with Duchess sitting erect and very alert behind them. Every time Peter looked at the photo, he had to smile at the happiness and delight shining from Nicholas and Josef's eyes.

Unbelievably, in the rush of time, it was now the busy week after Thanksgiving. It seemed as though he had just put away all of the Halloween decorations, and disposed of the disintegrating pumpkins. Peter's life, he decided, was on the oft-stated 'fast track,' as his teammates called it. Dividing his time between his family and playing hockey had most certainly put him on the 'fast track,' thought Peter. But Niki, his sweet Niki, never complained. And Peter understood why that was so; his happiness was hers...and she loved to see him play his sport.

The PB's were playing the Chicago Blackhawks tonight, a little more than a week past Thanksgiving. Peter knew that the Blackhawks were a very strong team, and he was excited at the prospect of matching wits and outskating them, if he could. The Blackhawks were more than just tough, they were very skilled, as well.

Out of habit, he looked up into the stands, hoping to spot Niki, even though he knew that she would not be there. Things were so different now…Niki was at home with their sons, where she needed to be. He wished that she were here, though. Am I just being selfish? They had talked about the difficulties that each would face when they were not together. Peter's travel schedule was going to be hard on all of them, but especially so for Nicholas and Josef.

As always, the loud music and even louder spectators before the game, helped to energize Peter, preparing him for battle. He always thought of hockey as a battle…a controlled battle, what with the referee and linesmen, but a battle, nonetheless.

His coach called out the starting players' names, and Peter Genchenko was one of them. As the announcer introduced the Polar Banners starting players, they skated out onto the ice to the loud boos and hisses of the local fans. They were playing the Blackhawks in Chicago on this night in late November, this very snowy and cold November night.

Early this morning, as he traveled in his Chevy van on Interstate 65 from Indianapolis to Chicago, he had been reminded of his Lyubertsy days…cold wind and blowing snow. The difference, however, was that he was now driving a reliable vehicle with plenty of gasoline, and with a heater that actually worked.

As he drove, he thought of the last time that he had seen his friend, Misha. It was Misha who had driven him to the Sheremetyevo airport to catch a plane to the United States. Peter clearly remembered that it was December, 1986. The car that Misha had borrowed for the trip was barely roadworthy, and Peter recalled that he and Misha had been uncomfortably cold in the old Zhiguli because the heater didn't work. Misha had many things to say, most of them laced with profanity, regarding Yevgeny's old Zhiguli automobile. I miss you, Misha. You were the kindest, most understanding friend anyone could ever have. And then sadness engulfed Peter's heart. Misha had died so needlessly at the hands of evil men. *God rest your soul, my friend.*

The game, indeed, was a battle on this night, and Peter was in the thick of it. He and his teammates, because of their camaraderie and endless practice, were able to interpret each others' moves quite well. At the end of the first period, Coach Johanssen had praised the way that his team had played, thus far. He told them that they were one point ahead of the Blackhawks, but that could change at any moment. The coach called on all of the team to "dig deep" for better plays.

"You are doing well, right now," he told them, "but we should be ahead by more than one point."

When the buzzer sounded the beginning of the third period, Peter was through the door of the bench and out onto the ice like a shot. One of the Chicago players, a 'chippy,' so-called because of roughness and sometimes illegal play, tried to attach himself to Peter. In the face off circle, Peter easily sent the puck to Murphrey, who played right wing for the PB's. The Chicago player who was facing off with Peter, the 'chippy,' actually tried spearing Peter with his stick blade, when he couldn't take possession of the puck. But he was stabbing air, because

Peter, in his left wing position, was hurtling up the ice in a breakaway toward his opponent's goal.

In the final minute of the game, Kelley, one of the PB's defensemen, traded the puck back and forth with Murphrey and Peter as they swiftly went up the ice to the restlessly moving Blackhawk goalie. Boris and Collin, two PB's players who were out to prove their worth by hard work on the ice, followed Murphrey, Kelley and Peter as they came into the attacking zone.

Peter saw an opportunity, in spite of the 'chippy' who was trying mightily to stop him, and sent the puck to Kelley, who made a game-ending slapshot on goal, just before the final buzzer sounded.

There was a collective groan as the local crowd saw the puck fly past their goalie and into the net. Peter lifted his stick above his head with both hands in celebration, and Kelley did likewise.

Peter sensed that this could be the season…everything was coming together so well…perhaps the PB's could bring home the Stanley Cup this season. And Peter was oh-so-right.

The Pittsburgh Polar Banners went to the playoffs against the Minnesota North Stars in the 1990-91 season, and swept the playoffs in six games. It was a wonderful, hard-played season for his team, Peter knew, and he would always remember the day that the PB's cinched the Stanley Cup. One of the things that he had promised himself a long time ago was that he would call Moscow to tell Grigory Serov, his former Red Army hockey coach, if the PB's won the Stanley Cup. Peter had never forgotten that Grigory had believed in him when Peter didn't even believe in himself. I owe Grigory a debt of gratitude, thought Peter, for all of the opportunities that he opened up for me.

The media in Pittsburgh could not get enough of the quiet and handsome Peter Genchenko, whose humility surprised everyone. Someone had coined the phrase 'media circus,' which Peter believed was quite accurate, but he did not buy into it, and maintained his cool at all times around the media.

"Is this guy for real?" asked one sportscaster during a sports telecast. "He really has a lot to brag about, but all he can talk about are his team and his coach. What a guy, that's all that I can say."

Marty Pelham and Sheldon Levin attended all of the PBs' playoff games. And no one, not even Peter and his wife, were any happier than were Marty and Sheldon over the fantastic six-game sweep that the Polar Banners pulled off against the Minnesota North Stars.

Marty and Sheldon ran down the stairs from their seats in the third row behind the PB's bench and onto the ice to congratulate Peter. A very hoarse Marty hugged Peter as Sheldon waited his turn. "You did it! I knew that you could make a difference if you only got the chance, Pete, and you really did it!

Sheldon gave Peter a bear hug, "Do you remember doing your workout in the exercise room at the Westin in Indy back in '86, Pete? I thought that you were like Superman then, and you've just proven it now."

"Yes, I remember Sheldon, but I could not have predicted this." Peter pointed to the scoreboard high above the ice.

Sheldon laughed, "You might not have seen this coming, Pete, but everyone who has ever seen you play hockey will tell you that you have worked hard, and you deserve this."

Before he gave an interview to anyone, Peter ran on his skates into the stands to celebrate with his family. Nicholas was so excited that he reached for his father from his Aunt Katya's arms, and almost fell, but

Peter caught him. Peter hugged Nicholas, and bent to kiss little Josef, who was in his mother's arms.

Niki, Nicholas and Josef, Klaus and Marina and Katya and Ron were there to witness the PB's triumph over the Minnesota North Stars to win the Stanley Cup. There were kisses, congratulatory handshakes, backslaps, more kisses, and many tears shed on the part of Peter and Niki. He couldn't help himself…when Peter took Niki in his arms, his eyes filled with tears of happiness.

"I never expected that this moment would come…I just never expected it, Niki." He whispered in her ear as he held her close. "It's unbelievable…completely unbelievable, and I have you to thank for it."

"Pete, you did this yourself. It's so wonderful, and I'm so happy that you want to thank me, too, but *you did it, Pete!* You've helped the Polar Banners bring the Stanley Cup home to Pittsburgh!"

But it was Niki that Peter focused on…she was everything to him, and he had looked up at her in the stands time and again as he played hard. "You were there in the stands many times, Niki, and I took my strength from you. Every time I looked up at you, I felt stronger. It has always been that way since we first met."

The media frenzy was in full swing when Peter made his way back to the ice as his coach beckoned to him. Many, if not most, of the sports commentators were calling Peter Genchenko's name, but Peter pressed one, and then another of his teammates forward to be interviewed. Finally, there was no one else, and they pounced on Peter Genchenko, the man they all wanted to talk to.

Early the next morning, Peter made an international telephone call to Grigory Serov. He wanted Grigory to know how much he appreciated everything that Grigory had done for him, and he knew that Grigory would be very happy to hear that one of his Russian players had played on the winning team that took the Stanley Cup in the U.S.

"Zdrassfitye...*hello?*" The voice on the other end of the line was unmistakeable in timbre and volume. It was Grigory.

"Zdrassfitye to you, Grigory. It's Peter...Peter Genchenko, and I have some news to share with you."

"Ahh...I know it is you, Peter. Your voice, I know your deep voice well. How are you and your beautiful wife and son?"

"It's now sons, Grigory. Niki and I have two sons, Nicholas and Josef. We are blessed."

"Indeed you are, Peter. *Two sons now?* Privaskhodny...*wonderful!*" he boomed.

"And how are your beautiful wife, Hoda, and your seven lovely daughters, Grigory?"

"I thank God that they are all safe and well, Peter."

"Good, I'm glad to hear that. Are you sitting down, Grigory?"

"Da...*yes,* Why do you ask?"

"The team that I am playing for, the Pittsburgh Polar Banners, just swept the Stanley Cup series to win the NHL championship."

"That is truly privaskhodny, Peter! Your team swept the series? You didn't waste any time once you got to America, Peter. Schastleevy *happy,* I am so very happy for you."

"Have you received my cards and letters, Grigory? I know that everything is upside down in Russia right now."

"Well, Peter, no one is sure of what is going to happen, but I believe that our military losses in Afghanistan, which go hand-in-hand with monetary losses, have started a downward spiral for the Soviet Union.

There are many rumors…the military, the political, the working class…that indicate that no one is being paid by the government. If this continues, the Soviet Union will fall, and Russia will be ruined. There is evidence of hunger and homelessness everywhere."

"I'm very sorry to hear that, Grigory. The American President Reagan urged Russian President Gorbachev to tear down the Berlin Wall, and it happened November 9th, but I didn't really know how bad everything else was until you told me just now. Is there anything that I can do to help you and your family, Grigory?"

"Nyet…there is nothing to be done, but my family is safe. Hoda is a good manager, and we have everything we need, even wood for the fireplace, so we can hold out for more than a year…a year, Peter, if things get really bad. But thank you for offering to help. More than likely the mail service will be the next thing to fail, so I may not get your correspondence. I also think that the telephone service is just running from day-to-day, so we may be out of touch for some time. But don't worry…Hoda's family lives in Grosny, Chechnya, and we can go there for a while. Most Russians are afraid to go to Chechnya, and for good reason." Grigory laughed halfheartedly.

"There is a bad history between the two countries, even though the Soviet Union considers Chechnya to be one of its provinces since the Second World War. I agree with you. Very few Russians would even think of going to Chechnya because of serious safety issues." Peter understood Grigory's dilemma.

"Hoda and I will survive, and so will our daughters. Do not worry about us. But…a few prayers might help." Grigory was resigned to the situation.

"We always include you and your family in our nightly prayers, Grigory."

After a long and busy day at home, Peter and Niki talked, as they usually did, after they were in bed. "When I called Grigory this morning to give him the good news about the Stanley Cup, he was very happy for me. He asked about you and Nicholas, and I told him about our little Josef. He offered his congratulations on our expanding family. He also told me that the situation in the Soviet Union is getting worse by the day."

"Some of our news media are reporting on the situation there, Pete, but I don't put much stock in what newscasters say. I think the news that we get is sketchy and rather distorted sometimes, and it also depends on who is reading it, and what they choose to emphasize."

"True," he replied, "but I wish that I could help Grigory and his family. He insisted that they are fine, and that they have stockpiled the things that they need to get by. But it will be a long and cold winter for them if they only have their one fireplace to keep them warm. Russian winters are bitterly cold, Niki."

"I know, my love, but is there anything that we can do to help them?"

"Grigory said that their mail service is in serious trouble, and that the telephone service isn't far behind. I'm not sure what, if anything, we can do right now."

"Perhaps Uncle Les can help us to help Grigory? He could open some diplomatic channels…"

"I don't think that's possible right now, Niki. Grigory did say, however, that he might take his family to Chechnya. Hoda's family lives in Grosny, and Grigory told me that most Russians, and certainly the Gorbachev government, would not pursue them there."

Niki lifted her head from the pillow and craned her neck to look at him, "Chechnya? Who in their right mind would even consider such a thing?"

"Remember the old saying, Niki, "Desperate times call for desperate measures," and he pulled her down close to him and put his arms around her.

Chapter 50

Life in the Genchenko household was truly never dull. In fact, Niki began keeping a journal, complete with photographs, of all the cute, funny, crazy things that were happening day-to-day with Nicholas and Josef, so that Peter could keep up with everything. His travel schedule with the PB's had been heavy during the NHL hockey season, but Niki made sure that Peter could share in the wonderful daily life of their sons.

Klaus and Marina, with the blessings of Peter and Niki, bought a parcel of land from them across their lake in the spring of 1991. They had been discussing it for several months, and decided that now was the time to 'down-size' from their huge home on Geist Reservoir.

"We just don't need that much room, anymore. And besides, the yard work is getting harder every year." Marina smiled at her daughter, "You know that your father won't hire anything done in the yard if he can help it."

"Well, it's really for our retirement home," Klaus told his daughter and son-in-law, looking askance at his wife, "and we want to be close enough to help out with our grandsons whenever you need us."

Peter was amazed at how quickly the Kellmans' house went up. He loved architecture and engineering, and he and Klaus had their heads together all of the time regarding how best to proceed to the next step in building what Marina called her, "new little dream home."

The women went to work, too. Niki and Marina thoroughly enjoyed the interior process of bringing the new home to occupancy. They shopped for scaled-down furniture for the great room, dining room, and all of the four bedrooms. Marina and Klaus wanted Nicholas and Josef to have their own rooms when they came to visit. And the kitchen, "the heart of the home," as Marina called it, was a farm-style, eat-in kitchen, with bead-boarded walls and ceiling, and everything in white, even the floor, which was a bleached pine.

"I love a big, clean kitchen…and this one is a dream come true for me." Marina's happiness was palpable.

The kitchen shared a common wall with the great room, and Klaus designed a double-sided fireplace, for warmth and ambience in the great room and the kitchen. Peter really liked the idea, and asked Niki if she might ever agree to doing something similar in their own home.

"Someday," she had told him with a smile, "maybe someday."

In early May, the Kellmans and Duchess moved into their new home, just in time to set out the gardens. Peter helped turn the soil with Klaus while Marina planted all of her favorites in front of the house; lillies, hydrangeas, crepe myrtle, tulips, Pampas Grass, poppies, phlox and Columbine. There were also two northern Magnolia trees, three Dogwood trees at the back of the lot, two Redbuds, and several Bradford Pear trees lining the long driveway.

Peter designed a foot bridge across one end of their little lake that would shorten the distance between the Kellmans' and Genchenkos' homes considerably. He incorporated safe railings into the design for the protection of his boys. Ron came to help with the project one

Saturday in mid-July and immediately discovered that his carpentry skills were not really adequate, at least for building bridges. He was amazed at Peter's strength and his ability to lift large pieces of lumber into place, and understood that what Peter was doing was something that he could never do. Nonetheless, Peter and Ron enjoyed their work together. And Ron's skills improved greatly over the course of the afternoon under Peter's tutelage.

Katya came along with Ron so that she could visit with Niki and her nephews. But it wasn't just a 'visit.' As she and Niki prepared dinner, she confided in her that she was expecting a baby. For Katya, it was like sharing her secret with a sister.

"Ron and I are very happy, Niki. But, of course, he won't let me do very much in the house, now. He's afraid that I'll 'overdo it'." Katya laughed her gentle laugh.

Niki put her arms around her sister-in-law, "That's wonderful news, Katya! I'm so happy for you. Are you going to tell Pete tonight at dinner?"

"That is my plan, Niki. Ron can't wait for me to officially tell everyone. He tells me every day that he is so happy about the baby. And, you know, his happiness is mine." Katya had a faraway look in her eyes.

Niki wondered, briefly, if Katya was thinking of Mikhail Preslov, Misha, her fiancé in Russia? Pete talked about Misha sometimes. He had told Niki about the terrible things that had occurred in Lyubertsy during the time that he was in the United States for the 1986 International Winter Games, and Misha's murder was the worst of them.

Niki remembered her own terrible heartache when Peter had to return to Russia after the games. And she couldn't even begin to comprehend what it would be like to lose a loved one the way Katya had lost Misha. Just thinking about it made her shiver.

"You are cold, Niki?" Katya had noticed that Niki was trembling.

"Oh…no, Katya…I was just thinking about something that happened a long time ago." Niki gathered herself, "Well, let's get cooking, Mrs. Michael. Our men are going to be starving when they get here after all of their hard work."

Katya replied, "They *will* be hungry, won't they?"

"Do you have a due date yet?" Niki was thinking ahead to having a new little one in the family.

"I'm just two months along, Niki, but I am already beginning to lose my waist!"

"Well, just wait, Katya. You won't believe what you will see in the mirror five months from now. By seven months, I couldn't see my feet anymore without holding onto something and bending forward."

"I can't imagine, I just can't imagine it, Niki." Katya was now giggling, a hand to her mouth.

The women, including Marina, who had arrived with Klaus shortly before dinner, served a farmer's repast to their men, small and tall, at dinnertime.

They served fried chicken, mashed potatoes, home-canned green beans and salad. Unbelievably, Nicholas and Josef loved salad greens, and were gleeful, too, when they were served mashed potatoes and sliced chicken. Nicholas was less messy at the table, but Josef seemed to enjoy his food more. His mother had cut everything up for Josef into tiny pieces, so that he could eat quite well even though he had only four teeth; two up and two down.

Marina had baked two of the most delicious cherry pies that Peter and Ron, with guilty looks at their wives, said they had ever tasted.

Klaus, pointing a finger at them, said, "I told you that Marina could bake a cherry pie better than anyone else that I have ever known!"

Ron, his mouth still half-full of pie, managed to say, "You're right about that one." His response started a round of laughter, after which Ron asked for another slice of pie.

Before the women got up to clear the table, Ron used his spoon to tap on his water glass. "I have, no, *we have*, an announcement, everyone."

"Yes?" said Peter. "And what would that announcement be?" Peter looked at Katya, who was blushing and laughing.

"Katya…?" Peter stood and reached for his sister.

Ron could contain himself no longer, "Tell them our wonderful news, Katya."

"We are pregnant…" Katya's blush got deeper.

"How wonderful…so wonderful for you both!" Peter hugged Katya, and then grabbed Ron in a bear hug.

Nicholas asked a question after everyone calmed down, "Is this a birthday party?"

Peter patted his son on the head, "Yes, of a sort, it is, Nicholas. But it will be a while before we bring the cake and gifts."

Marina, and then Klaus hugged Katya, and Klaus shook Ron's hand vigorously. In unison, they said, "Congratulations…congratulations to both of you!"

Josef, his mouth still coated with his last bite of mashed potatoes, put his hands up in glee and screeched his delight.

"I think Josef approves, too. Katya…Ron, I think that I speak for everyone here when I say that we are all so very, very happy for both of you." Peter couldn't contain his wide grin.

Chapter 51

They were now in the fullness of summer…late June. Josef's first birthday would be celebrated on the twenty-eighth. Peter and Niki had established a happy routine. Each morning, weather permitting, they took their early morning coffee out onto the veranda facing the lake. Waterfowl, herron, geese, ducks of several varieties, and a pair of swans with three cygnets greeted them from the water on this warm summer morning with its lovely sunrise. Peter raised his cup in a toast to his wife, and she returned the favor. Their sons were usually up and about by seven, so they had quietly brewed some coffee and crept outside before six-thirty. Niki knew that, as every married couple with children will attest, it is quite nice to share an early morning quiet time with your spouse before the kids wake up.

They sat on a large swing that Peter had built for just such an occasion. As the swing moved back and forth slowly, he spoke softly, his arm around Niki. "I love it here…it's wonderful. You chose this place with the idea that someday we would share it…but I still don't understand how you knew…?

"I was pregnant with Nicholas when I first laid eyes on this house, and it just seemed right, Pete. I didn't, couldn't, give up hope that somehow we would be together again. Sometimes the heart sees things, knows things, that we don't consciously understand. All that I can tell you, is that I never gave up hope. Nicholas and I were living here in this house that I put together as much as I could, in the way you and I had talked about it." She turned to look up into his face, "I spent a lot of time in your study, Pete. I felt the closest to you in that room because you had described it to me, and I created it from your words."

Peter set his coffee cup down on a side table, turned and took Niki's cup and set it down, too, and then kissed her deeply. "You are my heart and my soul, Niki."

She gently stroked his cheek with her hand, "And you mean everything to me, Pete, everything."

They heard it at the same time…giggling. Their sons were awake, and now the day would start in earnest. Niki turned to her husband and giggled, too, "Well, here we go again."

Breakfast was orange juice, scrambled eggs, muffins, and turkey bacon. Peter told his wife that he didn't mind going without the other, tastier, less healthy meat, but he wasn't being completely honest with her, and she knew it. The boys, however, enjoyed their meal, because they didn't really like the saltier, fatty bacon that their father preferred.

All in all, it was a great start to a wonderful summer morning. Niki was expected in her sports medicine clinic by nine-thirty, and Marina and Klaus were going to take Josef and Nicholas to the Indianapolis Children's Museum at nine. Peter had a conference call scheduled at one o'clock with several sportscasters and reporters who had been dogging him for several weeks for an interview.

"Sometimes," Peter told Niki, "I wonder why they are so interested in talking with me? I am only one player on the team. At least this time they started with the Coach. I told Hayley Benton of NBC that I wouldn't speak to anyone until Coach Johanssen gave me the okay on the interview."

"Well, Pete," Niki replied, "just consider this as a boost to your team. All you have to do is bring up the PB's name and the names of your teammates throughout your interview, and at least some of the media will 'get it.'"

"Why is fame, or the perception of it, so ephemeral, Niki? One day you're a 'hot property' and the next day, you're not. I know that this thing called 'fame' will be short-lived. But it stands to reason that these sportscasters know that one man, one player, on a team has to have help, and lots of it, in order to win games."

Niki slipped her slacks on and zipped them up. Peter looked appreciatively at his wife's lovely body for several moments and then smiled at her. "uh…now, what were we talking about?"

She pulled a shirt on over her shoulders, and smiled back at him. "Lost your train of thought? My goodness…"

Marina called up the stairs, "Niki, Pete…we're ready to go. Do you have time to kiss the boys?"

"Ah, reality," sighed Peter as he looked longingly at his wife.

"We'll be right down, Mom." Niki gave Peter a quick kiss on the lips, tucked her shirt inside her slacks, slipped on her shoes and hurried down the stairs.

"It's probably good that you got here a little early, Mom, Dad, I still have some things to do before I leave for the clinic." Niki, as usual, seemed pressed for time.

"Early is always better than late," Klaus said philosophically.

With kisses all around, and goodbye hugs, Nicholas and Josef were loaded into their car seats, and Klaus and Marina were inside their van.

"We'll bring the boys home to our house a little after two this afternoon, and they can take their naps there. Is that going to work for you and Peter?"

"That's a splendid plan, Mom. Pete's got his conference call with the media today, and a quiet house will help him out."

"What about dinner…should I fix something?"

"I have a crockpot of vegetable soup going, and I made cornbread this morning. There's enough for everyone, so you're invited to supper, say…around six. How does that sound?"

"Great!" said Klaus, who liked his daughter's delicious vegetable soup.

"Bye, everyone…" Niki waved at them as they headed down the driveway and disappeared behind the huge evergreen trees.

Peter had been waving at them from the front door, as he was still in his pajamas. He watched Niki as she quickly climbed the stairs onto the porch. He had become aroused as he had watched his wife dressing a few minutes before, and hope, among other things, rose inside him.

He held the door open for Niki, closed it behind him, and leaned against it. "Niki?'

"I've got twenty minutes, Pete, before I have to leave for the clinic," and she bolted up the stairs.

Shirt, slacks, pajamas and underwear lay in a tangled heap on the floor of their bedroom. "I'm glad that I didn't have to wait until tonight to make love to you, Niki."

"And so am I, Pete. *This is wonderful.*"

As their love had deepened, unbelievably, since they first fell in love, so had their hunger for one another. Their mutual physical pleasure was ecstasy.

They lay for a few moments afterward, holding onto one another, and then Niki told Peter, "I've got just enough time for a quick shower. Today is definitely a ponytail day. It takes my hair forever to dry."

In the shower, Niki was soaping up her body, and then she noticed that Pete was standing in the doorway to the bathroom. She opened the shower door, "Get in here, Peter Genchenko, and mister, this had better be fast."

It *was* fast, but deliciously, passionately so. "I love you so much, Pete...so very much."

He cupped her wet face in his hands and kissed her, "And I love you..."

Niki was only ten minutes late for her first clinic visit. "Traffic is always such a mess," she told Ron and Stephanie upon her arrival.

She could see that Ron 'bought it,' but Stephanie smiled widely and complimented her on her "rosy complexion" and her "cute, but wet" ponytail.

Niki gave her friend a rueful smile, and then quickly ran to do her first clinical assessment of the day.

Peter had insisted that his coach be included in the conference call interview, and got his way. Coach Johanssen told Peter that he appreciated the opportunity, because, he said, the media could be a little forgetful and inaccurate when reporting an athlete's interview.

The telephone rang, and Peter put it on the speaker function. The caller represented a sportscasting conglomerate, and he was key to the setup of the call. "I'll put you on hold while I get everyone else connected, Pete. Is that okay?"

"That is fine," replied Peter.

"Okay, Pete, we have Jerry Mains of "Sports Today," Linda Hyer of

"USA Today," Mel Reasor of "Sports Weekly," and Renee Solomon of "Hockey Digest" on the line. Is everyone ready?"

"Have you included Coach Johannsen?" asked Peter.

"I'm here, Pete."

"That's good...well, let's start with Renee, then Mel, Linda, and Jerry. I want to limit each interviewer to three questions, and then I'll move on to the next one. Does that meet with everyone's expectations?"

Each of the interviewers agreed to Peter's terms. Coach Johanssen said that he would stay quiet unless Peter asked him to help with questions on the Polar Banners' history, or questions regarding game strategies.

"Renee...? I'm ready when you are," said Peter.

That evening, after the boys were in bed, Peter told Niki that a conference call was an unusual device. "I actually felt more relaxed without the media pushing their microphones in my face the way they do after a game. I wouldn't mind doing this kind of interview from now on."

"It will never happen Pete, because they love to take videos of you after a game. They love to run those videos on the nightly news, and put some still photos in the newspaper and their magazines. You sell tickets, Pete. That's the name of the game, my handsome husband. *You sell tickets.*"

"Coach Johanssen didn't have to rescue me from any of the sportswriters, Niki. It surprised me, but they all seemed to be curious about me, rather than trying to get some scoop, or dirt, like they do when they ambush some other poor schmuck. They didn't do that with me, and I was very relieved."

Niki smiled, "Well, Sweetie, they've probably tried to dig up something on you, but you don't hit the party scene, or drink and do drugs. Other than your amazing ability to play hockey, you are pretty tame."

Peter grinned as he reached for his wife, "*Most* of the time, I'm pretty tame, but *you've* seen the tiger in me, Niki, many, many times."

Chapter 52

They read the newspapers, three of them, and watched the newscasts for several days after Peter's conference call. The magazine sportswriters promised Peter that he would receive a copy of their magazines when they came out with his story.

Niki, who was in the kitchen feeding Josef and Nicholas, was excited about the publicity, "Pete, look at the nice layout and story in USA Today...it's great!"

In fact, Peter was very surprised at the photos and story about him. "They have been kind and quite generous in their praise. How amazing is that?"

"Your dreams, Pete...remember the things you told me when we were alone during the blizzard back in eighty-six? Your dreams, and therefore my dreams for you, have all come true. Isn't it wonderful?"

Nicholas came in to sit in his father's lap as Peter looked at the layouts for his interview and photos, "Niki, it's more than wonderful...I can't really explain how I feel about all of this attention. But, it is making it more and more easy for me to support my family on my own, the way that I have always wanted to." Peter's smile and the look in his eyes pleased his wife greatly.

"Papa, you look so big in your hockey uniform!" Nicholas put his arms out to the sides.

"There is a lot of padding beneath my jersey uniform, Nicholas. It protects me from getting bumps and scratches." Peter ruffled his son's dark, thick hair with his big hand.

Niki, with Josef in her arms, came into the great room and reached out and caressed her husband's cheek, "Here's another memory…it was the time that I said you would look good in a gunny sack, Pete. You have that 'certain something,' call it charisma, that attracts people to you. I hadn't been with you an hour when you came to play hockey for Russia in the U.S. competition in Indy, but I fell for you, really hard, and I knew, I just knew, that I wanted to spend the rest of my life with you, although, at the time, I wouldn't admit it to myself."

Katya called to congratulate her brother, "Petrosha…such wonderful photographs, and a wonderful story about you in the newspaper. Ron and I are very happy for you."

Ron put the phone on speaker, "This is fantastic, Pete, just fantastic. You've made it to the top, now."

Peter thanked his sister and brother-in-law, "I'm truly pleased, and surprised, that the media is treating me so kindly."

"Katya, are you feeling well? What does your obstetrician say about you and the baby?" Niki asked.

Katya laughed, "He says that I am as healthy as a horse, Niki. Now what else can I say after a comment like that?"

"That says it all, dear one, and we are glad that you're doing well." It was Niki's turn to laugh.

Peter changed the subject, "Ron, I'd like to come in for a thorough check-up before the hockey season starts this fall."

"Is there anything in particular, Pete? Are you having any problems?" Ron's tone became serious.

"No…" Peter glanced at Niki, "my wife, the doctor, keeps me healthy with diet and an excellent exercise regimen, but it is probably time to do all of the blood work and treadmill studies again, don't you think?"

"Well, yes, but if you're not having any problems, why don't we wait until mid-September to do the work-up? Is that acceptable?"

"That's fine, Ron. I'll ask my sweet wife," he looked at Niki as she came back to sit beside him, "and then she can set me up for 'the works' when she's in the clinic."

Actually, Peter was concerned about his level of energy. He was tiring much more easily in the last two months than he could ever remember. Well, of course there was that time that he had been shot in Russia, but he didn't think that his present state was anything near what he had suffered then. He mused, I am getting older, and I have more responsibilities. Maybe I should cancel the rest of my summer classes at Purdue? There just never seems to be enough time for everything that I want or need to do. I'll have a conversation with Niki, he decided. Both of us are really running hard, even with Klaus and Marina's help. I know that Niki understands me completely. We have no secrets from one another, of that I am certain. If I can just get through this hockey season, maybe I can settle on something else to do that won't take me away from my family so often. I love playing hockey, but I love my family more…so much more.

That night, he actually had an uninterrupted good night's sleep. When he awoke the next morning, he was refreshed, and his outlook was more hopeful. I can get through this. I know that I can. And he reached for Niki to give her a good morning kiss.

As was now the norm for the Genchenko family, breakfast was busy and quick. Peter would have liked to sip on a cup of coffee out on the veranda, but he had taken charge of dressing his boys as Niki put together their meal. Marina was coming this morning to take the boys to the Indianapolis Zoo. Peter wondered how he and Niki could ever manage as well as they were, if not for Marina and Klaus? Their decision to build a house close to their daughter's family had proven to be a wonderful thing for all of them...the boys, Niki and Peter, and, of course, Klaus and Marina, who dearly loved their grandsons.

When the house was quiet, with Niki heading to the clinic, and the boys with their grandparents, Peter set about putting all of his hockey gear together. There were things that he had to replace, he knew, and he looked at his skates, gloves, helmet, and the like, so that he had some idea as to what he needed. Of course, the PB's outfitted all of their players for professional play, but Peter used his own equipment when he practiced with the the local Indy team.

In his study, Peter sat at his desk and called in a small order for the heavy socks that he wore with his skates, and also ordered another pair of practice skates, size 14, to accommodate his heavy socks. Niki liked to tease him about his "big feet" and he smiled as he thought about her.

Let's see, he thought. I've got to call my professor at Purdue regarding the rest of the summer schedule...and I'm going to have to adjust some times for my classes this fall. He held his engineering course syllabus in one hand, compared it with the PB's hockey schedule in the other, and realized that it was going to be difficult to mesh his personal and professional responsibilities.

Professor Merrill was Peter's advisor in the Purdue Engineering program, and he had always been very helpful regarding timeframes in which Peter could finish projects. Today was no exception, and Peter's heart rose in gratitude.

"Pete," said Professor Merrill, "you don't need to worry. All of your previous projects and tests have been excellent, and I have no problem with allowing you a certain amount of latitude."

They agreed on the timing of several required projects, and Professor Merrill told Peter that he could take his tests at any time, just as long as they were all completed before the end of the current semester.

"I thank you very much for your understanding, Professor Merrill. I love engineering, and I want to finish my coursework and projects so that I can finally graduate and go to work for a firm."

"I don't often tell a student this, Pete, but in your case, I truly can. You are destined for good and great things, and it is a pleasure to be your advisor."

Peter was very surprised, and answered, "Thank you…this is all a dream come true for me."

The walls of Peter's study were lined with family photographs and professional accolades. Niki has been busy, he chuckled, as he put his head back against the cushion of his chair and looked around. We will run out of wall space very soon. Well, this isn't getting my chores done, he thought, and stood up quickly.

Peter looked around for a box of tissues…his nose seemed to be running, but he hadn't had any signs or symptoms of a cold. He noticed with surprise when a droplet fell onto the back of his hand…blood…a nosebleed? When was the last time that I had a nosebleed?

It didn't last long, and Peter quickly forgot about it. When Niki came home, Peter didn't even mention to her that he had a nosebleed earlier in the day.

Chapter 53

Peter marveled at the passage of time. It was now mid-November, and the PB's first away game was with the Detroit Redwings. Peter felt fit and rested after a four-day hiatus in the schedule, and he was ready for this game. As alternate captain of his team, he wanted to do everything that was required, and more, in order to give them a good start for this 1991-92 season. It didn't hurt that the PB's were coming off of a home ice win over the Chicago Blackhawks, either, and that his team seemed more than ready to defend their Stanley Cup win last season.

Motor City...Motown, thought Peter as he drove through Detroit. This city is the birthplace of many of my favorite singers, male and female, and musicians, too. He smiled in remembrance of his dance with Niki, back in 1986, when Aretha Franklin's "Chain of Fools" played, and he had first danced with Niki...held her in his arms. He was completely out of his mind in love with Niki then. But not as much as he loved her now. It's deeper now, he thought. But at the time, he knew that he had never loved anyone the way he loved Dr. Kellman, his Niki.

Practice went well, but Peter still missed Coach Johanssen very much. Heart disease, thought Peter, is a terrible death sentence. How strange life can be, with its twists and turns, its ups and downs. No one on the PB's team has been prepared for the loss of Coach Johanssen to a heart attack…not a single one of us.

Peter liked the new coach, Sam Heckman, but it seemed strange not to hear Coach Johanssen's voice in the training room, exhorting the team to "dig deeper" to win. Echoes, I will always hear echoes of Coach Johanssen's voice when I think about game strategies, thought Peter.

The PB's were well-prepared when they took the ice for this game against the Detroit Redwings. The team as a whole was dedicating their efforts today to the memory of Coach Johanssen.

The arena was packed on this afternoon…just a week before Thanksgiving. As always, the noise level was many decibels above what the Federal Government allowed in most workplaces, but hockey was different. Hockey fans, as far as Peter's experience went, were very different from basketball fans and football fans. He had read many articles that indicated that hockey was more a working class sport, while it took much more money to attend football or basketball games. As he thought about this, Peter shrugged his shoulders. Well, hockey is for the masses…there is nothing elitist about it, and the players' salaries are not so astronomical as football and basketball, so it keeps ticket prices within the range of most fans.

Game time…Peter was ready for the faceoff, and he was looking directly into the eyes of one of the largest hockey players he had ever seen. This is going to take some finesse, he decided. As the two waited for the linesman to drop the puck, Peter quickly looked to his left, and the Redwings player's eyes followed Peter's. The puck went down, and Peter swept it to the right, and quickly skated past his huge opponent.

The crowd roared in dismay as their player stumbled and fell flat out as he tried to turn and skate after Peter Genchenko.

The Redwing's policeman, who could also be called a chippy

because of his roughness, tried again and again to slow Peter's play down, but Peter would just deke, swing back behind, or to the side of the player, and keep moving toward the Redwing's goal. The policeman reached out his hockey stick and attempted a slashing maneuver. The linesmens' whistles blew simultaneously. However, the policeman had not gotten the opportunity to slash Peter, as he deked away at the last moment, and sent the puck to his teammate, Besso.

When play resumed, the PB's still had possession of the puck, and Peter, with the help of Francois and Samuel, split the defense of the Redwings and scored a goal. It was the first time that Peter had ever witnessed a completely silent arena during a hockey game. Even the organist quit playing for several seconds. The Redwings' fans were in shock, but it didn't last for long, as they began shouting and stomping in the stands, and the organist began playing a dirge.

The score remained one to nothing in favor of the PB's until the last five minutes of the third period, when Peter and Craig teamed up to get another goal against the scoreless Redwings.

Peter, who had been resting on the bench, watched the play on the ice closely, and noticed that there was a weakness in the Redwings' play. Their left wing player almost always swung around and behind the goal, whether it was his own goal, or his opponent's. Peter understood that something that was habitual could easily be elicited under pressure, and perhaps might be used to score another goal on the Redwings.

Coach Heckman tapped Peter's shoulder, and he went in on the fly as Steven came out. Trotter had possession of the puck, and he made a snap pass to Peter, who headed toward the opponent's goal with the Redwing's left wing player trying mightily to catch him. In a breakaway, Peter and Trotter traded the puck back and forth, until they split the defense once again, and Peter made a flip pass back to Trotter. Peter then skated over to his left wing position and waited for the Redwings left winger to catch up to him, and to begin his swing around and behind the goal. Disconcerted, the left winger tried to maneuver away from Peter, but he didn't want to change his course. This decision was his undoing, as Peter body checked him into the boards, while Trotter slapshot the puck into the goal.

Later that evening, when Peter and his teammates were reviewing the game, their coach pointed out the play that had caused all hell to break loose; Trotter's score as Peter board checked the Redwing's left winger. They all agreed that the game had truly ended there, although there was almost a minute left on the clock. It was as if their opponents had lost heart, and the PB's felt that it was odd for that to have happened.

"Oh well, a win is a win, even when it's not pretty," Coach Heckman told his team.

Peter headed south on I-69 at about eight o'clock. He had a five-hour drive back to Indianapolis, but he wasn't at all sleepy, or even tired. It was his usual post-game high. Too much adrenalin, he speculated. There was one thing, though, that he had noticed during his shower. He had some bruising along his right thigh, and wondered how he had done it? He had been checked and board checked many times in the fast-paced game, but that was nothing different for him. His all-out style of play brought contact with other players, and it had always been so.

He knew that Niki would be waiting for him with a cup of her hot chocolate ready for him to sip on. They would discuss the events of their day, and then turn in, that is, if the boys were sleeping. Otherwise, it could be an interesting night. Peter chuckled aloud. He knew that being a father required a lot of energy and dedication.

It was just as he had imagined during his drive home. Niki was there on the sofa of the great room, and there was a fire in the fireplace. He even smelled the hot chocolate when he came in from the garage into the kitchen, and walked into the great room.

"Congratulations, Pete. Your name and face were on the sports news tonight. You did, however, share the spotlight with Trotter."

"And that is as it should be." Peter sat down beside his wife, took her hand in his, and brought it to his lips for a kiss.

"Have you gotten any sleep, yet?" Peter asked.

Niki nodded, "I got under the comforter in bed around eight-thirty after I got the boys in bed, and then I got up about eleven-thirty and took my shower. I timed everything right, because I even fixed some hot chocolate for you."

Peter slipped out of his jacket, tossed it on a nearby chair and sat down beside Niki. "Hot chocolate sounds very good to me right now." When Niki smiled at him, he felt warm inside.

She talked to him from the kitchen, "I'm so glad to have you at home. I always worry when you drive home after a game. I watched some of the footage of the game during the sportscast on the late night news on Channel 13, and I saw how hard you played. You are really something out there on the ice, Peter Genchenko." Niki came in from the kitchen and handed him a steaming cup of hot chocolate.

Peter grinned, "Well," he said, "on the ice, I keep moving, because if I did not, I'd be run over like a rag doll."

"Is that so?" said Niki, who grinned back at him and patted his cheek.

After Peter finished his hot chocolate, Niki took his cup and rinsed it in the sink, after which she put it in the dishwasher. She called out to Peter, "How does beef roast sound for dinner tomorrow?"

"It sounds good to me, and the boys like it, too." Peter gathered his coat and picked his shoes up from the floor. "Are you ready to go upstairs?"

Niki covered her mouth and yawned as she turned out the kitchen lights, "I am more than ready…"

Peter quickly got into his pajamas and brushed his teeth while Niki turned down their bed and crawled in. They had both peeked in on their boys before they came into their own bedroom. The boys were sleeping quietly and peacefully.

Peter pulled Niki close to him as he got into bed and put his arms around her. She didn't make a sound, and he knew that she was already asleep. This brought a smile to his face. *My beautiful sleepyhead.*

Mentally, he ran through the things he had to do tomorrow, ticking them off one by one: Purdue project, haircuts for the boys, repair the squeaking stair on the main stairway, clean out the rest of the garden…but he fell asleep before he finished his list.

Chapter 54

It was a festive Christmas, 1991. The Genchenkos entertained their neighbors with two buffets early in December, and then they hosted a party at their home for the PB's when the team was playing in the area. Marina, Katya, and Niki went all out on the smorgasbord for the athletes, serving them some of their requested favorites; pickled herring, borscht, caviar, roast goose, smoked salmon, and the most wonderful variety of salads, vegetables, breads and desserts that the three cooks could create.

Klaus played host, with an assist from Ron during the buffet party for the PB's as Peter enjoyed his teammates, rather than just trying to mingle a little with them. The men took over the dining room, the great room, and spilled over into Peter's study.

"Who plays the piano…?" Sam hooked a thumb at the beautiful instrument, because he was curious about the grand piano in the great room.

Peter turned and gave Niki a beckon call, "We do."

Trotter smiled and asked, "Will you play something for us?"

Peter's teammates began clapping their hands together, "Let's hear it for Pete and Niki…!"

As was their usual practice when they played, Peter took the left and

Niki took the right side of the keyboard. "Niki leaned over and whispered in Peter's ear, "Hallelujah Chorus?"

"Perfect…" Peter whispered back.

They ran the keys up and down, did a few intricate scales, and then began to play the "Hallelujah Chorus" for their guests. Handel's powerful composition filled their home with joyful music.

Klaus held Nicholas on his shoulders and Marina cradled Josef in her arms. They were enthralled, and couldn't help but sing the words to the music. Soon, Katya, with Ron behind her, holding onto her shoulders, and then most of the PB's players, were singing, too.

With the last "Hallelujah" ringing in everyone's ears, the entire party began to applaud the fine performance of the music. Niki, and then Peter, stood and bowed in thanks for the applause of their guests.

"What a wonderful evening it was," Niki later told Peter as they straightened up the house together.

"It couldn't have been more perfect, Niki." Peter put his wet and soapy hands on Niki's cheeks and kissed her mouth gently. "It was a perfect party in every way."

Mike flew in from San Francisco for the Christmas week celebration with his family. "Will Stephanie be here some of the time, Niki?"

"Oh, yes, Mikey, and she has been asking about you, too." Niki smiled up at her big brother.

"Does she know that you call me 'Mikey,' Niki?" Mike's eyebrows were raised in mock apprehension.

"And what if she does…will that be a problem?" Niki was being smug.

Peter, with Josef in his arms, jumped into the conversation, "Niki always calls me Pete, and now most of my teammates do, as well. It's something like a term of endearment, I think, but I don't know what it's called in hockey." Peter laughed after this pronouncement.

"Yeah…? Well, it's okay, I guess…" and Mike gave his little sister a bear hug, much to her delight.

Nicholas tugged at his uncle's pantleg, "Uncle Mike, Uncle Mike, welcome home!"

Mike reached down and scooped his nephew up onto his shoulders, to squeals of delight from Nicholas. "How's my big man?"

"I am great, Uncle Mike…just like my Papa!"

Marina and Klaus hosted Christmas eve dinner in their home across the lake. It was their first big celebration in their new home, and Marina went all out in decorating for the season. In keeping with a 'down home' Christmas, she decorated with natural things like grapevine wreaths, colorful dried flower arrangements, and dried fruit, nuts and berries strung on ribbons for her live tree. Niki and Katya loved the charming effects of an old fashioned Christmas. They even helped to string the cranberries and popcorn for tree decorations.

Klaus and Marina made a huge wreath for their front gate as the first welcoming Christmas decoration.

"Mom, Dad, I just never knew that the two of you were so creative. Our home on Geist Reservoir was always very formal, and I didn't realize that you liked this homey and beautiful décor, too." Niki was delighted with her parents' Christmas decorations.

"When Irina and I were small, our parents couldn't afford expensive decorations during the holidays, so our best memories are of gathering colorful things from nature. Our wreaths were made from things that we found in the fields and forest around our home in the outskirts of St.

Petersburg. Papa always took us in the sleigh that our old horse, Vladimir, pulled. Our mother tucked heavy blankets around our laps, legs and feet so that we would not get cold." Marina smiled in remembrance of her childhood Christmases.

The doorbell rang, and Nicholas ran to the door and managed to pull it open. "Merry Christmas," he said to his great aunt, Irina and great uncle, Karl.

"Hello, hello everyone!" Karl was in a festive mood.

Klaus embraced his brother and kissed Irina's cheek. "We are so happy that you could come to stay with us this week. We are having an old time Christmas, and Marina is certainly enjoying herself."

The doorbell again chimed its mellow notes, and this time, Mike went to answer the door. When he opened the door, Stephanie was standing there in her Christmas finery; a long red coat and black boots.

Immediately, Mike's face lit up, and he told Stephanie to, "Come in…come in out of the cold. I think you might find some hot, spiced Christmas tea inside. We can look together for it."

He helped her out of her coat, and turned to his family, "Stephanie's here, everyone."

Niki looked at Peter and smiled, because Mike's face said it all. He was very, very happy to see Stephanie.

The Kellmans' Family Christmas Party was a success. The traditional meal that Marina served, the drinks that Klaus made…were perfect, according to their guests. After dinner, the hosts and their guests sang carols A cappella by the fireplace. Everyone agreed that Stephanie must have perfect pitch, because she was able to start them all out on the right note every time for each carol.

Josef and Nicholas were the happiest of the family members, and their bright eyes, giggles, and sampling of cookies that their grandmother had made, entertained everyone.

It had started snowing in late afternoon, and by the time that dinner was served, and the caroling afterward was done, the snow was more than three inches deep on an already snow-covered road. Since Karl and Irina were staying with Klaus and Marina, Mike would be staying with Peter and Niki.

Niki saw that Mike was concerned that Stephanie was going to have to drive home by herself in the deepening snow. Stephanie shrugged nonchalantly and told Mike that she would be fine.

Peter touched Niki's shoulder and asked her if it would be all right to invite Stephanie to stay at their house. "Mike would not be worried about Stephanie if she agrees to stay with us."

"Good idea, Pete." And Niki turned to invite Stephanie to stay at their house for the night. "You can call your folks to let them know that you'll be staying with us, Stephanie. How about it?"

"I don't have any pajamas or toiletries with me, Niki, so I probably should go on home." Stephanie was a little embarrassed for a moment.

"I have extras, and you'd be making Nicholas and Josef happy if you stay." Niki was persuasive.

"I'd feel much better if you didn't get out onto the highway tonight, Stephanie." Mike gave her a hopeful look.

Stephanie tilted her head to the side and smiled, "Okay, I know when I am licked. I'd be delighted to stay overnight if you don't think that I'll be in the way."

Ron and Katya said their goodbyes, telling everyone that they only had a few short miles to get home.

"Katya, Ron…we have an extra bedroom if you want to stay," said Klaus.

"That's very kind of you, but I don't think we will have any trouble getting home. We'll call to let you know that we arrived safely," Ron told them.

Niki, Peter, their sons, and Stephanie and Mike put on their boots and heavy coats, and waved farewell, first to Katya's family, and then to Klaus, Marina, Karl and Irina.

Later in the evening, after Niki had put the boys down for the night, she put out fresh pajamas, a robe and slippers for Stephanie to wear. "I've turned down the bed in the second guest room for you, and once you get comfortable, we'll all have hot chocolate in front of the fire. Pete and I love to do that, and tonight it will be extra special with you and Mike here with us."

Unexpectedly, Stephanie's eyes filled with tears, "You are the kindest, most considerate person I know, Niki, and I want to thank you for including me in your family's Christmas celebration."

Niki smiled, and hugged her best friend. "I had an ulterior motive this time, Stephanie, and his name is Mike Kellman. He really wanted to spend time with you, and you graciously accepted our invitation."

Peter watched from the kitchen as Mike and Stephanie sat together on the sofa in the great room, talking quietly. My wife the matchmaker…and he smiled at Niki as he helped her with a tray of steaming mugs filled with hot chocolate.

Chapter 55

The '91-'92 hockey season was a tough one for the PB's, and especially so for Peter. He forced himself to play as hard as he always had, but he often felt weak for more than a day or two after a hard-fought series of games.

Now, in January, he knew that the PB's had a shot at another title, and he wanted, more than anything else, to help them do so. Sam Heckman was a good coach, and Peter wanted to see him repeat the Stanley Cup win of last year.

Peter promised himself that this was to be his last year on the ice. He had family obligations that he felt he should meet. He wanted to spend more time with his sons...and he wanted to be with Niki...he missed her so much when he was on the road. His heart ached for all of the things he was missing while he pursued his career in hockey. And...he had not, as yet, told Niki that he was not feeling well. He didn't want to frighten her. Besides, he believed that the way he was feeling of late was transient. He had always bounced back after injury or adversity, and playing hockey was definitely not difficult for him. He loved his sport. But it is time, Peter thought. It's time that I paid more attention to the most important people in my life...my wife and my sons.

Peter got out of the car in his garage and checked his watch. It's almost three-thirty in the afternoon; what a day. It had been an eventful road trip for him, what with the three games he and the PB's had played in the last week, and he was anxious to see Niki and the boys. Actually, he had been filled with anticipation ever since he had crossed the state line from Illinois into Indiana.

"Niki," he called as he entered the house from the garage. There was a wonderful aroma wafting from the kitchen…was it a chicken in the crockpot? Niki used her crockpot often to cook meals when she knew that she would be busy. He listened for a moment…there were no little boys' sounds, no music, no laughter. "Hello…hey, where is everybody?"

The house was very quiet, and Peter went from room to room downstairs, and was starting up the stairway when the front doorbell rang. Klaus was standing on the front porch, and smiling widely when Peter opened the door.

"I thought I saw your car come up the driveway. There is good news to tell you, Peter. Katya has just delivered a nine-pound baby boy! Niki brought Josef and Nicholas to our place, and then went downtown to Indiana University Hospital to see Ron and Katya's new little son. She left about an hour ago, and she asked us to keep an eye out for your return. She didn't want you to worry."

"That's fantastic news, Klaus! Did everything go well for Katya?" Peter was elated and concerned at the same time.

"Ron told Niki that everything was fine, and that Katya's labor was only three hours." Klaus slapped Peter on the back, "Well, Uncle Peter, what do you think about all of this?"

"It's the best news Klaus, it's really the best…" Peter's smile was wide as he nodded his head up and down. "Now I am Uncle Peter!"

"Niki said that if you came home while she is at the hospital, that I should tell you to join her there."

"Is that okay with you and Marina, Klaus? If you have any plans, I can just bring the boys home and wait for Niki."

"Oh, no...no, we are just enjoying our grandsons. Go join your wife and your sister and her family. Marina and I couldn't be happier if it were a new little one for you and Niki." Klaus patted Peter's shoulder. "Go on, now, Peter. Join the celebration at the hospital." Back in the kitchen Peter checked the timer on the crockpot, set it for the warming mode, and hurried out to his car in the garage. What a happy event, he thought. Katya is now a mother. He smiled as he thought of his gentle, sweet sister in the role of mother. She will be a wonderful mother, my sister. Ron is a very lucky man, and so is their newborn son. His smile widened as he wondered how Ron had survived the birth of his first child?

Peter was very lucky, as he found a good parking place in the parking garage close to the elevator into the hospital. When he arrived in the Indiana University Hospital LDRP area, he found his sister's room and peeked around the door, then stepped inside to greet everyone.

Niki came to his side quickly and took his hand, "Welcome home, Pete. Isn't this a lovely surprise?"

"Yes, it is." He turned to Katya and then to Ron, "How was it...uh...was everything all right?"

"Textbook," said Ron, beaming with pride, "Katya's delivery was textbook."

Katya, sitting up in bed with her son in her arms, asked, "I wonder what the gender was of the person who wrote the 'textbook' on birth?"

This comment caused some laughter, especially from Katya and Niki, and Ron's face reddened. "Well," he said, "I should have been more tactful, I guess," and smiled ruefully.

Niki took Peter's arm and led him to Katya's bedside, "Isn't he beautiful, Pete? He has Katya's coloring and Ron's curly hair. And his eyes, just look at them; he has eyes the same color as his mother's and yours."

Peter leaned over and kissed his sister on the cheek, "Congratulations to my sister," he turned and included Ron, "and her very brave husband."

This remark also brought a ripple of laughter to the room that started with Ron, "For a while there, I didn't feel very brave, and Katya actually comforted me, rather than the other way around."

"I don't think a man truly understands how strong his wife is until the birth of their first child, Ron. Niki has told you and Katya of the mishap with the delivery bed that happened when she was delivering Josef, hasn't she?"

Katya nodded and Ron followed suit, "That had to be exciting and a bit scary for both of you," said Ron.

"You are right on both counts; exciting and scary, but I discovered just how much strength there was in Niki's diminutive body. She pushed and pushed against me as I sat behind her on the bed, and finally, little Josef made his appearance. Was it scary? Yes, very much so, but Niki took it in stride. Women are made of very strong material, Ron; stronger than men."

"After today, Pete, I do not doubt that one bit!" Ron's expression was one of sincerity mixed with awe as he agreed with his brother-in-law.

Niki asked, "Have you chosen a name for the littlest Michael family member?"

Ron, standing at the bedside said, "Katya and I have agreed on the name Ari Myron Michael. Do you like the sound of it?"

Peter and Niki nodded in unison, as Peter replied, "Perfect…that is a perfect name for your first son."

At the dinner table later that evening, Niki said, "I couldn't believe how heavy the traffic was on the way home from the hospital, Pete."

Peter shrugged, "It's the sales season, Niki. Everyone is out shopping for bargains."

Nicholas spoke excitedly about his new cousin Ari, as they ate dinner. "What does he look like, Papa?"

Peter had to grin at his son, "Not *what*, but *who* does he look like, Nicholas? And the answer to that is, he looks a lot like Aunt Katya, and a lot like Uncle Ron. He looks like both of them, son."

Niki, who was helping Josef with his dinner, smiled at Pete, and nodded her head at her son, "Papa is right, Nicholas. Little Ari Myron Michael looks like both of his parents, and also like your Papa."

The evening passed quickly, and Peter bathed the boys as Niki cleaned the kitchen. He laughed with his sons as they splashed and 'swam' in the bathtub. How quickly, thought Peter, time is passing so quickly. My sons are growing too fast! He recalled a hymn, "Slow Me Down, Lord," that the choir and congregation at their church often sang during Sunday services. He wished he knew of a way to slow down the passage of time so that he would not miss any of his sons' milestones, but he knew in his heart that there was nothing that he could do about it. *I'm going to quit playing hockey after this season.* I cannot, I must not, allow this wonderful time in my sons' lives to slip by without my involvement.

Dressed in pajamas, with fresh glasses of water at their bedsides, Peter tucked his sons into bed and called down the stairs to their mother, "Niki, it's time for prayers and goodnight kisses."

There was a musical lilt to Niki's voice as she called back, "I'll be right there, my men."

Chapter 56

The Michael family celebrated the Bris of little Ari Myron according to the ceremonial timing of the circumcision to be performed by their Rabbi. Niki remembered vividly how upset she had been with the circumcisions of her own two sons, even though there were no problems, and her heart went out to little Ari. She spoke to Peter about her feelings, and he assured her that it was the hygienic practice of the Jews that kept their people from some of the strange and terrible illnesses suffered by Gentiles over the millennia.

Niki smiled at her husband, "Who is the doctor here, Pete? Of course I know and understand how important circumcision is for hygiene, but it breaks my heart to hear the cries of pain. I just…I almost can't stand it, Pete. And when it was our sons under the knife, I felt like the knife was cutting into me both times."

Peter leaned down and kissed her forehead, "My tenderhearted wife," he said, "I understand your feelings, I really do, and I would be very surprised if you didn't feel this way."

Peter and Niki were hosting a celebration of Ari's Bris, and were excited to hear that Ari and Miriam Michael were coming for a visit with their son and his family.

Miriam told Niki during a telephone conversation that she and her husband had attended many religious celebrations over the years, and that this special event would be the high point for them "This will be all the more special to us because little Ari is our first grandson," Miriam told Niki.

As always, Marina and Klaus were involved in all the details of the celebration, large and small, Their son, Mike, had an entire week that he was going to spend with them, and of course, with Stephanie, too. Marina had high hopes that her son was finally interested in settling down, and she loved his choice. Stephanie was like a third daughter, after Niki and Katya, of course.

With the holidays and Ari's Bris behind them, the Genchenko family got back to the routine of daily life. Peter's schedule was hectic, to say the least, and he was on the road much more than he felt that he should be. But he knew that it was a tradeoff. Hockey was a time-consuming job. However, his guilt over not being with his family as much as he wanted to was taking its toll.

One night after he and Niki made love, Peter lay on his pillow facing her. The afterglow of their lovemaking was always wonderful, and on this night, it was even more so. They were so in tune with one another in most ways, but their physical love was the most powerful connection for both of them.

"Niki," Peter said softly, "I want to retire from hockey at the end of this season. I've come to this decision because I want to spend more time with you and the boys. What do you think?"

Niki was quiet for a moment, "I know that it has been hard on you, Pete. I can see it in your eyes when you come home after a week on the road. And about your decision…we don't have any financial worries…and you've still got your courses at Purdue. So, retire, if that's what you want to do, Pete. I am all for having you here with us. Our boys are growing so quickly! It seems that every time I measure them, they've grown more than I expected."

Peter chuckled, "And they have gotten heavier, too. I used to be able to lift both of them over my head, one in each hand, and now it's not so easy to do that."

It was Niki's turn to laugh, "I agree…just getting them in and out of the van is like going to the gym for a workout."

"Are you reconsidering your commitment to a large family, Niki?" Peter's amusement was evident in his voice.

She sighed, "Not at all, Pete, not at all. In fact, I've been thinking, ever since Katya had little Ari, that it would be nice to have another baby."

Peter put his hand to her forehead, "Well…you're not feverish…are you serious about wanting another baby?"

"Yes, Pete, I am." Niki spoke barely above a whisper.

"We certainly don't have any problem conceiving…so I'm ready whenever you are."

"How about right now?"

"Again…and no protection this time?" he asked.

Niki repeated Peter's words, "I'm ready whenever you are."

"I hope we don't wake the boys up with all this activity," said Peter as he threw back the sheet and blanket, and balanced himself above his wife.

Niki called to Peter, "Pete…we've overslept…I'm going to call Mom and ask her if she can help out this morning."

Peter rolled over in bed, and sat up on the edge for a moment before he replied, "I think that we might have been too busy last night, Niki," and turned to gaze at his wife with a devilish grin.

"Oh, poor baby," she patted the top of his head. "Have you been exercising too much, lately?"

Peter shook his head, "I never get tired of our exercise regimen, Niki."

Marina arrived when Niki was in the shower, and Peter answered the door in his pajamas, "Hello, Marina. Thanks for coming over so quickly. I don't know how we could have overslept…usually I set the alarm before I get into bed, but I'm not sure what happened last night." Peter told a white lie to cover up for the amorously busy night that he and Niki had enjoyed.

In a few moments, a wet-haired Niki in her bathrobe came down the stairs carrying Josef in her arms, with Nicholas trailing behind. "I'm so sorry for the short notice, Mom…you are a lifesaver!"

Peter caught Niki's eye and raised his eyebrows momentarily. She seemed to understand that he must have explained why they were late, and she turned to smile at her mother.

"It's perfectly all right, dear. Your father and I have no plans for today, and we will have lots of fun with our grandsons."

Nicholas was obviously delighted that his grandmother was going to take him to school today, and Josef, in his mother's arms, was kicking his legs with happiness, and reaching his arms toward his grandmother.

Marina started breakfast for the boys while Niki and Peter went upstairs to get ready for the day. Niki dried her hair as Peter shaved, and they looked at one another in the mirror, smiling broadly.

"We may have lost some sleep last night, Niki, but I think it was worth it, don't you?"

Niki, with hair now dried, turned and leaned against his shoulder, "Yes…it was *wonderful.*"

Chapter 57

The end was in sight, and the PB's were eyeing the Stanley Cup for this '91-'92 season. Tomorrow they would play what Peter hoped would be their last game against the Chicago Blackhawks. The Stanley Cup hung on that game. If the PB's won tomorrow, they would sweep the Chicago Blackhawks and win the series. He wondered if the PB's would be able to pull it off, but he knew that his team had proven to be unstoppable this season under the coaching of Sam Heckman. Their momentum was great, and they were steamrolling into what could be the last game.

I think that we can do this again, Peter thought. Wouldn't it be fantastic to bring the Stanley Cup home to Pittsburgh again for another year? It stirred his heart and soul. We can win…I know that we can win!

Niki mostly followed Peter's games on television this season because of her responsibilities at home, but they talked every night after eleven o'clock. Nicholas and Josef were always in bed, and Peter's games were usually concluded by that time, so they could talk without interruption about how their days had been.

Sometimes, Peter sensed that Niki was close to tears as they talked. At these times, his voice became gentle, and he would ask about their sons. Niki always brightened, and she would bring him up-to-date on milestones, accomplishments and achievements.

Tonight, she told him, "Josef has another tooth, Pete. He is going to have big, beautiful teeth like yours. And Nicholas just loves his school teacher. He also mentions a little girl by the name of Natasha. He says that she looks like me, only smaller." Niki laughed.

"Natasha?" said Peter. "I wonder if she is named after someone in her family? Maybe she is Russian, who knows? I think that Russian women are beautiful; especially when they have some German mixed in."

"Oh, you're just saying that to flatter me, Peter Genchenko, but I've got your number."

He laughed and told her, "Yes, you do, Niki. You certainly do. Always."

"Good luck tomorrow, Pete. Marty called first, and then Sheldon called, too. They both said that they would be in the stands cheering you and the PB's on."

"I'll wave at them, Niki. Well, my love, I'll say goodnight. Tomorrow is going to be a busy day."

"I love you, Pete. Take care…please take care, and come home to your family in one piece."

"I will, Niki, and I love you, too."

After they finished talking, Peter got into the shower. He had already showered earlier, but he wanted to wash away the smell of tobacco and alcohol that he always seemed to pick up when he and his team had dinner together. It didn't matter where the restaurant might be. Peter always seemed to get stuck near some chain-smoker. For a long while, he had tolerated the smoking because it reminded him of his mother, and if he really wanted to admit it, of his father, too. But anymore, he was much more sensitive to the odor, and it irritated his throat.

Peter disrobed and stepped into the shower wearily. He stood under the hot, sharply spraying water for several moments, and then noticed something very unusual. The white tile floor of the shower stall seemed to be turning pink. What is this? He rinsed the soap off of his body and got out of the shower. When he put a towel to his face, it startled him as he took it away. There was blood on the towel. Peter looked into the mirror, and saw that his nose was bleeding…again. What is this?

As he stood in front of the mirror, he noticed several more bruises on his arms, torso, and legs. He hadn't been hit that hard recently, so it surprised him to see the new bruises. There were several others, old bruises, that were turning yellow as they were absorbed. I should ask Niki about this, thought Peter. I'll ask her when I get home. And he put it out of his mind.

As was his custom when he was on the road, he wore no pajamas to sleep in. At home, he often would wear only pajama bottoms, but he always kept a pajama top nearby in case one of his sons needed him during the night. On this night, Peter fell into the deep sleep of exhaustion almost immediately.

Peter's dream was another variation of a recurring theme. He would see Niki in a crowd…this time she was high up in the arena seating, watching him play hockey. In his dream, he puzzled as to why she was not down lower, behind his team's bench. As he turned to look around, however, he realized that he was in the old Red Army Hockey Arena in Moscow. He glimpsed Misha…yes, it was Misha, in the stands, and he was waving at Peter. He seemed to be cautioning him about something, but Peter couldn't understand what Misha was trying to tell him.

Peter looked behind him for activity on the ice, and realized that there were no hockey players there. Where has everyone gone? And then he caught sight of Tom and Mickey, his friends, who were Athletic Trainers during the International Winter Games in '86. They were coming toward him with a gurney. Their faces were sad, sorrowful. Peter wondered, why are they here…how did they get to this God-forsaken place?

As they got closer, he realized that they were coming for him, and he looked down. There was blood on the ice, and he understood that it was his blood. When he looked up into the stands, he could no longer see Niki, and fear clutched at his heart.

Peter sat bolt upright in bed, panting, with sweat covering his face and chest. He looked around the room, not recognizing anything for a moment, and then he knew that he was in a hotel room. When he looked at the clock beside the bed, it was almost six o'clock. The alarm was set for six, and would sound at any moment, so Peter shut it off.

Almost in a daze, he got up to the bathroom. I need a shower, another shower, he thought. The room was cold, and his skin now felt cold and clammy. I want to go home…I need to see Niki and my sons. But he knew that today was going to be the deciding game for the Stanley Cup. He was thankful that it was an afternoon game. I'll see my family tonight, and he felt a small bit of hope rise within him. Peter thought of the training table that would start at seven. How am I going to be able to eat something when I feel like this?

By game time, Peter had gotten control of himself physically and mentally. He had called Niki and talked with her for a while this morning. She was his anchor, his good luck charm, his beloved. Hearing her voice, lilting and happy, raised his spirits considerably. He didn't tell her about his dream of the night before. And he didn't mention his nosebleed or bruises, either. He didn't want her to worry about him, and he didn't think that the bruises were important, anyway.

"How are Nicholas and Josef behaving?" he had asked.

"Peter, you know that these two sons of ours are little angels, don't you?"

Niki made him smile. "Of course they are." *My dear, sweet Niki has given me so much to be thankful for.* And gratitude swelled in his heart.

Game time! The hockey fans in the Pittsburgh Arena were ramping up the noise to a fever pitch. For the PB's, everything was riding on this game if they were going to sweep the Chicago Blackhawks to win the Stanley Cup. Peter Genchenko fervently hoped that they could do so, because he wanted this to be his last game. He had reached that decision this morning after the terrible night that he had endured. He was surprised by his own attitude, however, because hockey had always been such an outlet for him, a blessing that had kept his mother and sister in their little apartment in Lyubertsy, with enough food to eat, and warm clothing for the winter. But he knew that he was ready for the next phase of his life. He was now a husband and a father, and he wanted, more than anything, to be with his wife and children. He also wanted to earn his degree in civil engineering and begin the life of a man who could dream things, build things, and perhaps leave his mark on the world.

Coach Heckman picked his starting players, and again, Peter was among them. Before the start of the game, the coach reiterated the strategy that he and his team had decided upon for this game. He told them that he believed that the Blackhawks would expect some of the plays from previous games, but he wanted to totally throw them off in this game. He congratulated each of his players for their efforts, thus far. He knew, he said, that they had all worked hard to get here for what he knew could be their final game. It's the Stanley Cup, he told them, and he was certain that they could bring it back to Pittsburgh this year.

The Chicago Blackhawks were a tough team coached by a canny coach who left nothing to chance. Peter was well aware of their prowess, as he had studied the statistics and team styles of every professional hockey team in the U.S. before signing with the PB's. He and Niki had pored over the information with Marty Pelham, and the three of them had decided that when the PB's offered Peter a place on their team, they were the team for Peter. It was Peter's good fortune that the PB's felt the same way about him.

This has been a wild ride, and I will forever be grateful for the opportunities that I have been given, and for the acceptance and camaraderie of some of the best hockey players in the NHL. No one could ask for more.

As always, Peter turned and looked up in the stands before he catapulted himself out onto the ice to do battle. He was, of course, looking for Niki, although he knew that she wasn't there, but he couldn't help himself. And he always dedicated each game to her with their secret signal, a tight circle on the ice and a wave of his hand. Quite often, Niki commented to Peter when he got home that she had seen him give her the signal. And it delighted Peter that the media had tried to figure out just what he was doing when he signaled Niki, but were completely unsuccessful.

Steven would do the face off for the PB's, and he nodded at Collin, as if to indicate that he would send the puck to him. However, Peter was actually the one who would get the puck if Steven was successful in controlling the face off. And their ploy worked; Peter received the puck and in a breakaway, went up the ice toward the Blackhawks' goal, with Steven by his side, and Collin swiftly following them.

Peter gave Steven a flip pass over one of the Blackhawk defenders, and Steven then sent the puck to Boris. When Boris attempted to freeze the goalie, he did a drop pass for Peter, who immediately and successfully went for a goal. The red light flared behind the Blackhawk cage and pandemonium broke loose in the stands.

Marty and Sheldon, sitting behind the PB's bench, joined the shouting and stomping, and Niki, at home, let out a loud, "Yeah, Pete!" much to the surprise of her parents, and Katya and Ron, who had joined her to watch this championship game. Nicholas sat with his brother on his mother's lap and put his arms around her neck in jubilation, because he knew that his father was the reason for her excitement.

"I have a feeling, boys, that your Papa is going to be a big help in winning this game for the PB's!"

"You've got that right, Niki," said Klaus, who thoroughly enjoyed watching his son-in-law play hockey.

At the high point of their celebration, Niki saw that Peter was board checked by one of the Blackhawk's chippy players. A one minute boarding penalty was called on the offending player, and Peter, now up on his skates, used the PB's man advantage to put together another goal, this time teaming up with Francois.

Whenever Pete was boarded or checked in any way, Niki always got upset. The next closeup of her husband showed that his nose was bloodied, and he was skating toward the PB's bench. The blood had reached his jersey, and a sense of dismay bloomed in Niki's heart. What caused this, she wondered? When he was boarded, he didn't hit his face, so why would he have a nosebleed?

The PB's coach called a timeout while the athletic trainer worked on stopping Peter's nosebleed. It took him several attempts at tamponade, putting a special 'plug' in Peter's left nostril, before he got the bleeding under control. By that time, play had resumed, and Peter was left on the bench. Whenever the camera swung his way, and it did so quite often, Niki could see how much Pete wanted to be back out on the ice.

The sportscaster talked about Peter's style on the ice for a moment, filling in the lull in activity as play finally resumed. "You've got to hand it to Pete Genchenko, Melvin, he's all about hockey, and he's tough. If he keeps up his present statistics, he's going to be a candidate for the Hockey Hall of Fame, mark my words."

"Oh, Jack, I agree with you wholeheartedly. Genchenko is really something on the ice; he plays clean, he's fast, and he's smart. That combination in a player is wonderful to watch. He and his teammates do quite well together, too."

Klaus patted Niki's shoulder, "Peter is fine, Niki, so don't worry. I also think that the sportscasters know what they are talking about."

Coach Heckman sent Peter in on the fly, replacing Besso on the ice. The chippy that had sent Peter into the boards started toward him, but Peter deked, received the puck from Collin on a pass, and streaked up the ice with Craig at his side in a breakaway. Peter was going for goal again. If he made this shot, he would have a hat trick. Peter liked that idea, and literally flew into the attacking zone. However, he didn't have a clear shot, but saw that Jordan was wide open, and Peter sent the puck to him in a flip pass over a Blackhawk player's stick.

Peter checked the chippy who was still trying to injure him, and sent the player flying into the boards as Jordan sent the puck home. At that moment, all hell broke loose in the stands.

Peter was surprised to see his coach jumping for joy, and when he looked above and to the left, he caught Sheldon and Marty celebrating with high-fives and back slaps. Peter grinned, and the television camera recorded it for posterity.

Niki loved the shot of Peter grinning at the stands, and was glad that she was recording the event so that when their sons were older, they could see how their father played hockey. It was a stellar moment in the Genchenko household.

When the final buzzer sounded, the Pittsburgh Polar Banners were victorious. They had swept the Chicago Blackhawks to win the Stanley Cup! Confetti rained down on the ice, much to Peter's surprise, and he wondered, momentarily, who was responsible for all that paper? The media grabbed Besso and Steven, and then they swarmed around Peter and his coach. When it was Peter's turn to speak, he congratulated his coach and his teammates on the great game that they had played, which ended up with another win, a back to back win, of the Stanley Cup.

"Pittsburgh will be proud tonight," said Peter, "and they should be. This is wonderful, just wonderful, and I can't thank my fellow teammates enough." He turned, faced the camera, and blew a kiss to his family.

At home, Niki saw her husband blow a kiss to her, and couldn't help but cry tears of joy. "I'm so proud of him...he's such a fantastic athlete...and yet he has true humility. My handsome, wonderful man. You've done what you worked so hard to do, and now you can come home to your family."

Katya agreed with Niki in regard to her brother, "You know, he is so grateful for the opportunities that he has been given. I am so happy for both of you." Katya gave her sister-in-law a hug.

Klaus, Marina, and Ron, in turn, hugged and congratulated Niki, too. And then the party began winding down. Marina was helping Katya with little Ari as Niki prepared a light meal for her boys.

"Would you all like to stay for supper? I can whip something up pretty quickly."

Ron was the first to reply, "How can you think about supper, when we have all snacked so much? If I eat anything else tonight, I'm going to burst."

"I think that Ron is right, Niki. We have all had as much snacking and excitement as we can stand for one day." Katya's smile was bright as she spoke.

Klaus and Marina made it unanimous, "Dear," said Marina, "I've got to get your father home so that he can relax in his favorite chair. I don't think he's even going to want any dinner after your delicious snacks."

Katya began packing up all of little Ari's necessities for the traveling baby. He was sleeping quite comfortably in his father's lap. Nicholas and Josef were sitting on the sofa with their grandparents, and Josef was leaning into Marina as if he wanted to take a nap.

Uh-oh, thought Nik. I'd better feed my boys and get them ready for bed. They're not going to sleep too well if their tummies aren't full.

"While Katya and Ron are packing up, I'll give my boys their supper," said Nik.

"Good idea, Niki," said Klaus. "Our little men are probably hungry. They didn't eat a lot of the things that their elders ate."

"I'm going to warm a bottle for Ari, so the boys can all eat together," Katya was smiling at Ron.

"Niki…? Can I help you in the kitchen?" Marina stood up with Josef in her arms.

"You can come out and keep me company, but I really don't need any help, Mom."

Sweet-tempered little Ari finished his bottle at about the same time that Nicholas and Josef were done eating their dinners. And then it was time to say goodbye.

"Thanks for coming…I'm so glad that you all came to help my boys and me cheer Pete and the PB's on to win the Stanley Cup," Niki was smiling and happy as she waved goodbye to everyone.

When she closed the door, she spoke to her boys, "Your Papa and his team are winners, boys. What a wonderful day this has turned out to be!"

Nicholas hugged his little brother, and Niki knelt down to hug both of her little men. "Okay, it's bath time, you two."

Chapter 58

Niki was waiting in Peter's study, sitting on the sofa and watching for headlights in the driveway. Nicholas and Josef had their baths, and Niki had read a book to them before tucking them into bed for the night. To her delight, they fell asleep almost immediately. Peter always said that they were just like their mother...sleepyheads, and thankfully, he was oh, so right.

When Niki saw the driveway light up, her heart lit up, too. *Pete, it's Pete!* She ran to the garage entrance into the kitchen before he activated the door.

As the car rolled slowly into the garage, Peter saw that Niki was smiling at him from the doorway into the kitchen. *My sweet, my beautiful Niki!*

Peter got out of the car, left the door open, and rushed to his wife. He took her in his arms, and lifted her off the ground. "I'm so glad to be home, Niki...so glad," and he held her tightly against him.

"Congratulations, Pete...you did it, you and the PB's won the Stanley Cup! The family, our boys, Katya, Ron and Ari, and Mom and Dad, were here to watch you make history. And Mike called from San Francisco, too!"

He gently set her on her feet, cupped her face in his hands, and kissed her deeply. For several moments after he kissed her, he stood looking down at her, and then told her, "As of tonight, I am retiring from hockey, Niki. I want to be with you and our sons…I don't want to miss out on anything in our lives; not anymore."

Peter's announcement so surprised Niki that she couldn't say anything for several moments. When she recovered her composure, she put her arms around his neck and told him how happy she was with his decision.

"I know that we've talked about this before…it will be wonderful to have you at home, Pete. I've often told you how lonely I am when you are on the road, but is this really what you want? I wouldn't be able to forgive myself if you felt that you had to give up your dream of playing professional hockey for me."

"Niki, no, it isn't you…it's me. This is truly what I want to do. We don't need the money. The money isn't important to me, to us, and we have everything that we need, and much more. I have been playing hockey because it has been the realization of a dream, and now that I have had my dream come true, I want to get on with the rest of my life. There is so much that I want to accomplish besides playing hockey. Does that make sense to you?"

She nodded her head, "Yes, Pete, it does, and it's the most wonderful news…"

Peter kissed her again, and whispered, "Thank you, Niki, for understanding. I didn't want to disappoint you…I would never want to disappoint you."

"I know, Pete, I know it, and I can't think of anything that you might do that would cause me to be disappointed in you."

He went to the car and closed the door as he popped the trunk. "I've got some things for the boys and you," he smiled, "and I've also got some laundry." His smile became rueful.

Niki helped him carry the boys' gifts into the kitchen, and asked him to just leave the laundry in the bag out in the garage until morning.

Peter sat down on a kitchen stool and leaned his elbows on the countertop for a moment. He didn't want to tell Niki how tired and weak he felt. *Soon, I'll talk to her about this…whatever it is…I'll tell her soon, but not now, not tonight.*

"I asked Coach Heckman if I could get out of most of the interviews the PB's had scheduled after the game today, and he told me that I could, but that I'd have to do the Stanley Cup victory celebration in Pittsburgh tomorrow. I am happy that we won, Niki, very happy, but I wanted you to be there during the celebration, and I wasn't sure that you could be with me. It sounds self-centered, if not selfish, of me to expect you to go with me…"

"Pete, I'll go with you. Mom and Dad will be happy to take the boys; they always are. So there is no question but that I will go to Pittsburgh with you for the celebration."

There was such a look of relief on Peter's face with Niki's pronouncement that it surprised her. He had often told her that she could read him like a book, but this time, he had truly taken her by surprise.

"Pete…are you okay?"

"I'm a little tired, Niki, that's all. This has been a tough season."

"It really has, Pete. When we were all watching the game today on television, it looked like the Blackhawks had a vendetta against you, specifically, not just the PB's as a team. Ordinarily you don't get boarded, but they were really after you during this game, and boarded you more than once."

Peter smiled and nodded, "Well, Niki, the stakes were very high. We wanted the Stanley Cup, and the Blackhawks were doing their best to prevent us from winning it."

"Have you told your coach about your retirement, yet?"

"No, Niki, I didn't want to say anything to dampen the celebration. I'll tell Coach Heckman after the Stanley Cup celebration. Don't you think that would be best?"

Niki was thoughtful for a moment, "Yes, and I think that you should talk to him as soon as possible after the celebration, Pete, before the media get wind of it. It's always better to be up front about something as important as the impact of someone of your caliber leaving the team. He, and the team as a whole, might not take the news very well, Pete, because you have been a valuable player, and one who is consistent in his scoring. They are really going to miss you."

Peter cocked his head to the side, smiled, and replied, "I will miss them, too, Niki, very much. And you are remarkable for your insight, and so much more. You have summed it all up quite well, and I am going to approach my retirement announcement exactly as you have just laid it out."

It was Niki's turn to smile, "Well, thank you, Pete...but I think that you had it all figured out, too. You, my darling husband, are a 'class act.'"

"Come here," Peter, still sitting on the kitchen stool, held his arms open, "I just want to hold you again for a moment."

As he embraced her, she lay her head on his shoulder, and it was a déjà vu moment for him, harkening back to the awards dinner dance after the International Winter Games in 1986. For some reason, it made him feel stronger momentarily...perhaps because he knew, even then, that he wanted to spend the rest of his life with Niki, and this dream, too, had come true.

Niki raised her head, "Are you hungry, Pete? I've got some of my homemade vegetable soup, or I could grill a steak for you."

"A bowl of soup, I think, would be good." Peter's voice was subdued, as if he didn't have the energy to speak in his normal, deep and rich tone.

"While I'm heating up the soup, you could go upstairs and look in on the boys, and you could take your shower..." Nik, with her back to him, was already looking into the refrigerator for the soup container.

Peter turned and gave his wife a wicked grin, "What...? Does this mean that you're not going to join me in the shower? I thought that we could do a little celebrating...perhaps a little working on baby number three?"

His wife's laughter, as always, was music to Peter's ears. And he wondered for perhaps the hundreth, no, it was more like the thousandth, time, just how he had gotten so lucky to have this woman, this lovely woman, for his wife?

"Peter Genchenko...!" Niki laughed, facing him, "Are you making an indecent proposal to me?"

He lapsed into Russian, "Nyet...nyet...there is nothing indecent in the way that I feel about you, my love."

Peter took the container of soup out of Niki's hand and put it back in the refrigerator. "Let's go upstairs together to check on the boys, Niki. And then, you can help me with my shower. I can never scrub my back well enough, and you do it so nicely." He smiled at Niki, took her hand, and started toward the stairs.

Chapter 59

Peter and Niki first looked in on Nicholas, and he was sleeping on his side, his dark hair quite striking against the white pillowcase. Peter bent over and pulled up the bedcovers a bit, and then he kissed his son's cheek gently.

In Josef's room, little Josef, in his baby bed, was dressed in a blue fleece 'onesie' with feet. Niki was the one who had instituted the use of the all-in-one pajama because Josef always kicked off his covers, and she was afraid that he would get chilled during the cold winter nights.

Peter was tall enough to bend over the railing of the bed, and lightly kiss Josef's dark blond curls. Niki stood by, basking in the beauty of her husband's love for his sons.

They walked hand-in-hand to their own bedroom, where Niki turned down the bed. "Pete, would you get a couple of towels and washcloths out of the linen closet?"

"I've already got them, Niki."

Peter was in the bathroom, where he lit the many candles on the countertops and around the Jacuzzi. He didn't want direct lighting for their shower. He had too many very obvious bruises, and he didn't want Niki to worry.

Candlelight is good...the better to keep everything dreamy and romantic. I'll talk to Niki tomorrow about the bruises. Maybe on the way to Pittsburgh, it won't seem so serious. At least I am hoping that it won't.

"Shower's ready, Niki." Peter stepped into the shower quickly so that Niki would not get a good look at him.

"Ohhh...the candles are a wonderful touch, Pete." Niki quickly shed her robe and opened the shower door. "This is so-o-o nice, my love."

They bathed each other, just as they had from the beginning of their intimacy, and Niki's touch brought the desired response from Peter. Incredibly, even though he thought that he was near exhaustion, Peter easily lifted Niki onto him, and they slowly moved together as one, the warm spray of the shower a delightful and sensual accompaniment to their coupling.

Niki closed her eyes, lifted her chin, and let her lips part as she vocalized her excitement and pleasure as she and Pete made love to one another.

Her response delighted Peter, and heightened his own pleasure. "Niki...my wonderful Niki," he whispered in her ear as he held her close to him, moving, moving, moving toward their mutual release.

At her moment of fulfillment, Niki opened her eyes wide, and told Peter in a breathless voice, "I love you...I love you so very, very much, Pete!"

Peter followed her into ecstasy, "And...I love you, too, Niki..."

Marina and Klaus arrived shortly after Niki called them the next morning to help with Nicholas and Josef. "This is so exciting, Niki," Marina was almost as excited as her daughter in regard to the celebration in Pittsburgh.

"It is, Mom. Pete's not nearly as excited as I am, but he rarely acknowledges how much he has contributed to his team. Sometimes, I think that he feels he shouldn't take much credit for what he does, but he is so special…"

Peter came into the kitchen. "My ears are burning again," and he gave a wry smile to his wife.

"And well they should, Peter," said Klaus. "These women have been talking about you since Marina and I arrived a few minutes ago."

This statement brought a round of laughter from everyone, Peter included. When things calmed down, he went to the table where his sons were starting their breakfasts.

"What are you having this morning, boys?"

Nicholas swallowed his mouthful, "Pancakes, and bacon, and peaches," he said, raising his fork in the air.

Little Josef, his face smeared with syrup and butter, waved his baby fork in the air, too. The smile on his face was nothing short of cherubic.

Peter saw that Niki was already dressed, and he admired her wardrobe choices. She was wearing the PB's colors, red and gold, and he had never seen anyone look so lovely as she did in those colors. She wore a soft gold, fitted dress that skimmed her curves beautifully, and she wore a red demi-jacket with the PB's trademark logo on her lapel. Her dark hair softly flowed, cut at chin length, and moved gracefully as she turned her head. She called it her 'easy do' because, even if it was windy, her hair did not seem mussed as it lightly swung back into place.

Peter wore black slacks, and a red sweater under a gold jacket; the PB's road 'uniform.' Niki looked at her husband appreciatively. Such a handsome man, she thought, and so loving, too. How lucky I am.

In the car, Peter told Niki, "I'm glad that we packed an overnight bag. I hope the weather stays clear, but you never know…it's going to be cold in Pittsburgh. The coats and boots that we are taking with us should be enough to keep us warm, though." He reached over and touched Niki on the cheek.

"I am so proud of you, Pete, so very proud. And I'm thankful, too, to know that you won't be on the road traveling with the team anymore. I know that you love hockey, and I know that you have forged some great friendships with your teammates, so your decision to be with the boys and me is all the more wonderful…for all of us."

Peter took I-475 south to I-70 east, and set the cruise control on seventy. He calculated that it was going to be about a seven- or eight-hour drive, but the roads were clear, and the sun was rising as they drove east. It's a bright sunrise, and this will be a good day, Peter told himself. He had enjoyed a good night's sleep after he and Niki had showered. This thought brought a wide smile to his face. *I love our showers.*

"What are you thinking, Pete? I recognize that big smile," and she smiled back at him.

He reached over and took her hand in his, "I was just thinking that this is going to be a good day, Niki."

And Peter was right; it *was* a good day. There was a triumphal motorcade through the heart of the city, with noisy and jubilant fans lining the streets as they passed the Golden Triangle on their way to the arena. After the team appeared before the media, and after all of the requested interviews and photographs had been taken, the PB's, their coaches, their wives and friends sat down to a gala dinner together. Niki watched how easily Peter fit in with everyone. It made her feel warm inside. Pete is finally getting the attention, the praise, the friends that he so richly deserves. I'll always remember these moments that we are sharing today...always.

Peter took his coach aside after the festivities, and asked him if they could have a serious talk. He wanted to get through his announcement quickly, and didn't want Sam Heckman to be upset, although he understood that Sam probably would be.

Heckman wrinkled his forehead and then smiled at Peter. "Of course, what's up, Pete?"

Niki walked to a corner of the ballroom near one of the huge open doors and sat down on a bench as the tables were being cleared of all remaining dishes and silverware. And then the tablecloths were stripped methodically and quickly. It amazed Niki at how efficient the hotel staff were at their jobs. Serving hundreds of guests all at once is a big job, thought Niki, but these people make it look easy.

She kept an eye on Peter and his coach, in a far corner of the room, and judging from the coach's body language, Peter had already given him the news of his wish to retire. The coach leaned forward, his elbow on the table, looking at Peter with a glum look, Niki saw. He seemed to be trying to talk Peter out of his decision, but Niki knew that when Peter made up his mind, he held to his position. She felt sorry for the coach, but she was very relieved when Peter shook hands with Sam Heckman and nodded his head toward her.

It's all said and done, she realized, her heart lifting. Pete's going to be close to home from now on, and tears filled her eyes. They were tears of joy for Pete, for their boys, and for herself. There will be no more sad and lonely nights separated from one another...Pete's coming home to stay!

That night, they stayed in a hotel. It was late when the dinner finally ended, and Peter had spent almost an hour talking to his coach. He and Niki agreed that another seven or more hours' drive to get home was probably not going to be a good idea. Niki had called her parents earlier to see if they could stay with Nicholas and Josef until tomorrow, and Klaus had laughed and told his daughter that, of course, they would be happy to stay with the boys.

"How was the celebration, Niki?" Klaus wanted to know.

"Well, Dad, it was fantastic, but I think that Pete is actually worn out with all of this celebrating. He told me that all he wants is a hot shower and a comfortable bed tonight, and I think he deserves both after the tough season that he's played." She wanted to tell her father that Pete was retiring from hockey, but she knew that Pete should be the one to tell Klaus and Marina about his decision.

"You are right, Niki. Go pamper your husband, and don't worry about your sons. Your mother and I don't have any plans at all for tomorrow, and you two deserve a quiet night together."

"Kiss them both for Pete and me, Dad, and tell Mom that we are so-o-o grateful for this quiet night together."

Peter had no control over the lighting in the hotel room, and in particular, the bathroom, and he knew that Niki was going to see his bruises. In one way, it bothered him that Niki would be worried when she saw the bruises, but in another, it would be a relief. Peter was beginning to understand that something wasn't right...the bruises, his fatigue...what does all of this mean, he wondered? Niki will know what to do. She always knows what to do.

"We were right about the overnight bags, Niki," Peter was pulling out a pair of pajamas from his bag. "This has been a long day, and I'm ready to relax."

"Shower first?" asked Niki, as she pulled off her dress.

"There's no question about that one…" Peter got into the shower and set the temperature of the water as Niki finished undressing and hung her clothes in the closet.

"Ready or not, here I come!" She quickly ran to the shower, pulled the curtain aside, and jumped in.

Everything in the bathroom was white. The floor, walls, countertops, commode, and shower curtain were all white. It was on this bright background that Niki first saw Peter's bruises in various stages of healing, dark blue, purple, reddish-pink, and finally, greenish-yellow.

Niki swallowed hard, and her eyes widened as she looked first at Peter's torso, and then his arms and legs. She turned him around to see his back and buttocks. It seemed as if the bruises were too numerous to count.

Her face became a mask of apprehension, "Pete…I don't understand…what's happening here?"

"I honestly don't know, Niki. I have never bruised like this before…but playing professional hockey is much different than the amateur version of the sport."

"I know, Pete, but what I am seeing can't be just from contact or boarding…it's too widespread." Niki put a hand to her mouth, and for a moment, she felt abject terror. *"Pete, oh my God!"*

"Niki…I'm all right; don't be afraid, please don't be afraid," and Peter put his arms around her.

He turned off the shower and helped Niki out of the tub as he grabbed a towel to wrap around her. She was trembling and breathing heavily, and he didn't know what to do to help her except hold her in his arms until she calmed down. Finally, she seemed to relax a bit, and he reached for a towel to dry himself off. The hotel room was not warm, and Peter felt chilled to the bone.

Peter led Niki to the bed, sat down with her on the edge, and turned to her, taking both of her hands in his. There were no sobs, no crying aloud, but it wrenched his heart when he saw that tears were streaming down her face. It was as if she was in a daze.

He started to speak, but his voice faltered at first. When he got hold of himself, he tried again, "Niki, I should have told you sooner about the bruises, and how tired I've been, but honestly, all that I wanted to do was to get this hockey season over with. I wanted to put hockey behind me…and then I was going to tell you about what's happening to me. I know that something is wrong, but I don't think that it can be anything serious."

"How long…?" Niki's words had a hollow sound. "How long have you been feeling weak and had this bruising problem, Pete?"

He was quiet for some time, and then told her, "I noticed that I started bruising about a month ago, Niki. And I also had a couple of nosebleeds that had nothing to do with physical contact during a game. I didn't really think much about any of it until I started feeling so tired, so very tired. If the last game that I played is any indication of what is going on, then I am really in trouble. I was completely exhausted at the end of the game."

Niki put her head on his shoulder, "Why didn't you tell me, Pete?" She let go of his hands and brushed tears from her eyes with her fingertips.

"It was selfish of me, Niki. I was focused on having another Stanley Cup win, and I thought that I would be all right until the end of the season. But I didn't want to worry you, either, Niki." He brushed her wet hair gently away from her forehead.

She lifted her head from his shoulder, put her hand under his chin to turn his face toward her, and said, "Pete, we have to act quickly on this. When we get home tomorrow, I'm going to start calling some of my colleagues for information. I have some good contacts at Krannert, you know, the Cancer Pavillion. And we can go from there…"

Peter's voice was barely above a whisper, "Cancer…do you think that I have cancer?"

"I don't know, Pete, but your symptoms…" Niki couldn't finish the sentence.

They didn't sleep much that night. But they were holding onto one another as if for dear life, and Peter was so very glad to have this brave little woman with the heart of a lioness, who was the mother of his children, in his corner. *We will find a way to beat this, whatever it may be.*

Chapter 60

Four days after the Stanley Cup celebration, Peter and Niki were driving to the Krannert Cancer Pavillion together to see the doctor that Niki had chosen as the best specialist for what she had diagnosed Peter's problem to be. She had ruled out all but two diagnoses; lymphoma and leukemia, and she fervently hoped that she was wrong, wrong, wrong for either one, but the physician in her realized that it had to be one or the other.

"Hi, I'm Ted Clinton." The doctor, a frail-looking, bespectacled African-American, was a full head shorter than Peter. He looked up at Peter with intense hazel eyes and a friendly smile, and offered his hand to him.

"Hello…" Peter shook the doctor's hand and was able to muster a reasonable facsimile of a smile, but just barely. "Thank you for seeing me so quickly. Niki has told me how tight your schedule is." Peter was surprised that the doctor had available clinic time to see him.

Dr. Clinton nodded his head toward Niki, "Your wife has a lot of good friends in the Indianapolis medical community, and I was happy when she chose me to work with you on your diagnosis and treatment." Peter glanced at his wife, and his heart ached. She had lost weight, he thought, almost overnight…he had overheard her parents talking about it, and how much they were worried about their daughter and son-in-law. But in truth, her beauty was now more ethereal, and her skin had the look of fine porcelain. *My beautiful Niki.*

"From what I have read regarding your recent medical history, Peter, you have had bruising, nosebleeds, fatigue and some shortness of breath. So," he paused for a moment, "I am ordering tests that will, hopefully, give us an idea of what we are looking at in regard to your symptoms."

He thumbed through several pages, "Based on your physical examination, I see that your spleen is enlarged, your temperature is elevated, low grade, but elevated, and you look quite pale. I've seen pictures of you...I guess the one that was on the cover of "Sports Today" I remember most...and there was no pallor to your skin at that time.

"For right now, I am just going to order the simplest of tests, a complete blood count, a CBC, and that will tell me quite a bit about what direction to take. Based on the CBC results, I may request a bone marrow biopsy."

Peter was looking at Niki when Dr. Clinton mentioned the bone marrow biopsy, and he saw her flinch as if she had been struck. He reached for her hand and held it against his chest. He knew that she understood, only too well, what his diagnosis might be. From the time that they had arrived at home after the Stanley Cup celebration in Pittsburgh, Niki had quickly found the doctor that she considered to be one of the best in the field of hematology/oncology. And here they were, in the Krannert Cancer Pavilion, less than a week after he had told her about his illness.

Peter hated the sound of the word cancer, but he was fully aware of the fact that he could not deny what was happening to him, and he knew that Niki was very frightened for him. At night, she sometimes sounded as though she was crying in her sleep. He, himself, had not been able to sleep very much as he struggled with his demons again. The nearly forgotten cold place inside him, the dwelling place of fear and dread, began to spread in his chest. In the long dark nights when he heard Niki crying, he pulled her close to him, and whispered to her how much he loved her. If she awakened, she would turn toward him and lay her head on his shoulder, and the cold place inside him would disappear for a time.

On the way home from their first visit to Dr. Clinton's Hematology/Oncology clinic, Peter spoke quietly to Niki about his illness and its ramifications. "Dr. Clinton's assessment and examination of me today was very thorough, Niki. For some reason, I felt comfortable with him immediately. He seems so caring...are there many doctors like him?"

Niki smiled wistfully, "He's the best, and his diagnosis and cure rate are at the top of the statistical comparisons of doctors nationwide."

"How difficult is it to have a bone marrow biopsy, Niki?" Peter didn't want to say, "painful."

"Well, it isn't easy, Pete, but from my own observation, it is the quickest way to pinpoint a diagnosis and get your treatment underway as soon as possible. We don't want to delay anything, Pete...not now. I don't want to frighten you, but we have to be realistic. Time is an important factor in any cancer cure rate. We have to be aggressive and start right now to fight whatever this thing is." At that point, Niki's voice broke and tears started at the corners of her eyes. "I'm scared, Pete...I don't want to lie to you, or sugar coat anything."

"We are in this together, Niki. And if you haven't noticed, I'm scared, too. I'm used to fighting my own battles alone…or at least I was until you and I got back together. But I know that I couldn't have anyone more capable and willing than you are to go through this with me. Niki, you mean *everything* to me, and you know that I will fight this thing for you and for our sons."

"We will both fight it, Pete." Niki rubbed her forehead with one hand and asked him, "Have you talked to Katya and Ron, yet? It's going to be very hard to tell them, Pete, but we have to be realistic, and they need to know."

"I'll call my sister in the morning. I don't want her to be upset, or have a sleepless night." Peter's voice had a ragged edge to it, as if he were very tired.

When they arrived at home, Peter pulled the car into the garage slowly. All he wanted to do was get into the shower, put on his pajamas, and get into bed. He felt weak and lightheaded, and he wasn't hungry. In fact, he felt somewhat nauseous, but he didn't want to tell Niki these things. He wanted to spare her as much as he possibly could. *I can't burden her with all of this.*

They walked into the kitchen together, hand in hand, and saw that Marina and Klaus had just finished dinner with the boys. Immediately, Nicholas and Josef began laughing with delight, and both reached their arms up toward their parents for a hug. Peter, and then Niki, kissed each of their sons on the top of their heads.

"Oh, I am so glad that you are home…I made a chicken noodle casserole, and saved some for you two." Marina smiled, but there was sadness in her eyes as she looked first at her daughter, and then at Peter.

Klaus stood up and lifted Josef from his high chair, "These boys have been very well-behaved today, I want you to know, and they even picked up all of their toys, too."

Peter hugged Nicholas against him and reached for Josef. "I'm sure that they kept both of you very busy, too, if I'm not mistaken."

Klaus couldn't deny it, and laughed, "They will keep me young, to be sure. I'm getting a good amount of exercise."

Duchess, her stump of a tail wagging so hard that her hips wiggled, leaned against Peter, looked up at him, and whined. He reached down and rubbed her ears gently, and Duchess gave a satisfied growl. This brought a round of laughter from all of the adults.

"I think she's jealous, and wants you to notice her, too, Pete." Niki's laugh was gentle.

Her laughter was music to Peter's ears. *Ah, a sense of normalcy has crept back into her voice.* "All right, Duchess, I've rubbed your ears, and now I have to eat some dinner." He stroked her back for several more moments, and then turned his attention to what Marina was asking.

Marina set places for Niki and Peter, "Would you two like some milk with your casserole and vegetables?"

"Can we wash our hands, Mom? It will only take a moment." Niki slipped out of her coat and hung it over the back of a chair.

"All right, but hurry…the casserole will get cold." Marina didn't want to serve them a cold dinner.

Nicholas asked, "Papa, will you help Josef and me with our baths tonight? We miss you…"

Peter's heart melted, "Of course I'll give you and Josef your baths. Just let your mother and me eat a little dinner, my son, and then we can go upstairs for your baths."

Klaus cleared his throat and made an announcement, "Niki,

Peter…Marina and I have moved into one of the spare bedrooms upstairs near the boys' rooms. We intend to be here with you until you have figured out something regarding Peter's health." Klaus was always very straightforward.

Peter closed his eyes for a moment, *God Bless you both,* he thought. You are going to be wonderful additions to our household in the days and weeks ahead. And Niki is going to need your help with our boys if…or more than likely, when, I am hospitalized.

"Dad, Mom, that's great! We can't thank you enough…I don't know what Pete and I would do without the two of you." Niki put her arms around her mother, and smiled up at her father.

Peter concurred, "This is so generous of you…it lifts my spirits to know that the boys will be with their grandparents when Niki and I can't be with them."

Marina said it all, "We are family, and we will get through this together."

Although Peter wasn't at all hungry, he managed to eat some of Marina's delicious casserole. She had made a loaf of bread, and the crust was crunchy…European style, just the way he liked it. He slathered a slice with butter and offered a bite to Niki, who then nibbled at the corner of the bread.

"Thanks, Pete…Mom's Russian bread is delicious, isn't it?"

"Da…it truly is," Peter responded in Russian.

Marina and Klaus went into the great room with Josef and Nicholas so that their daughter and son-in-law could talk to each other without interruption during their meal. Marina had always enjoyed her 'grownup' time with Klaus, after their children were in bed for the night, and she understood, especially in the present circumstances, that

Niki and Peter very much needed this 'grownup' time for discussion.

Peter and Niki sat next to each other, rather than across the table. As they ate, they talked quietly about their day, and what the coming week might bring. Niki leaned a shoulder against her husband while they stirred their food around on their plates. Neither was truly hungry, but eating together allowed them to feel a small sense of normalcy.

"Dr. Clinton sent a stat order for your labs, but the clinic laboratory won't reopen until Monday morning, Pete, so tomorrow will be just an ordinary Sunday for us. Would you like to go to church in the morning…do you think that you'll be up to it?"

Peter nodded his head and told his wife a white lie, "Of course I'll go to church, Niki. Right now, though, I'd like to bathe the boys, put them to bed, and get into the shower with you." He mustered a wry smile for his wife, his beloved Niki.

She touched his cheek with her fingertips, "I like that invitation, Pete, and I accept."

It didn't take long to bathe their two very active boys, but Peter felt his energy ebbing rather quickly. He could see, in the actions of his sons, how much they had been missing him lately, and it tugged at his heart. I didn't understand, he thought, how much my absences have affected my family. Niki has been carrying the burden of daily family life, and working in her clinic, too, while I have been playing a game. Hockey is a game, after all. He looked over at Niki as she sat toweling off little Josef. When she looked back at him and smiled, his heart swelled with a deep and abiding love for her. My Niki…my love, what are we going to do now?

Chapter 61

Today is the day that I find out what is wrong with me. Momentarily, a current of fear coursed through Peter from head to toe at the prospect of "finding out." He had to admit that the weekend had gone well…they had all attended church, and had enjoyed a delicious roast beef meal that Niki and Marina had put in the oven early in the morning. The afternoon and evening had passed quickly; too quickly to Peter's way of thinking. And he couldn't postpone the arrival of *Monday,* with all of its ramifications.

Peter was up and dressed, sipping coffee at the kitchen bar and waiting to take Nicholas to school. Niki was upstairs getting the boys ready for the day. Klaus, a coffeecup in his hand, was reading the newspaper in the great room next to a crackling fire in the fireplace. Well, thought Peter, the fire could be called 'cheery' if I didn't feel as if I were a condemned man. But condemned by what? His thoughts were flitting from one thing to another, without much coherence. I have to stop this! It isn't doing me any good.

Marina was just returning from a walk with Duchess, "Did you enjoy the bran muffins, Peter? I used Niki's recipe, but she is a much better cook than I am."

"They are delicious, Marina." Peter told his mother-in-law, "Niki learned her culinary skills from her mother."

Marina returned his smile, and said, "Thank you, Peter…that is a very nice thing for you to say to me."

She then turned and began taking off the harness that kept Duchess in check during her walks. When Duchess was free of her leash, she bounded over to Peter for a neck and ear rub.

"Did you enjoy your walk, Duchess?" Peter's voice was subdued.

As if she could understand Peter's words, Duchess whined and licked his hand. Even though Duchess was actually Klaus and Marina's dog, it was obvious to everyone that she loved Peter best.

"All right, Duchess, you have had your walk, and it's now time that you have your breakfast." Marina was laughing as she called her dog.

Peter looked at his watch, saw that it was seven-fifteen, and wondered if it was too early to call Katya and Ron to tell them about his situation? No, that is not completely true, and I have to be totally honest with myself, first, before I tell them about my health. This isn't just a 'situation.' And Peter knew that he had to tell his sister, even though she would be heartbroken. My sweet, tenderhearted Katya…how will you take this news?

Most parents of a little one will be up at this hour, he decided, and reached for the wall phone next to the kitchen bar. After three rings, his sister answered the phone, and Peter asked, "Hello, Katya? Did I awaken you?"

His sister laughed, "Oh, Petrosha, you know better than that, don't you? Little Ari has been up since five-thirty."

Her laughter warmed him inside, "Well, I guess that I do, although Niki has done more than her share of early morning feedings with our boys. But I do have some experience with that, too."

"Ron does, also, Petrosha…but he is mostly the late-night shift. He has told me that he does better at night than in the morning," she laughed again, "and he is right. He is not a morning person at all."

Peter swallowed hard, "I…have something to tell you and Ron. Is he there with you right now?"

Katya hesitated for a moment, "Yes, he's having a cup of coffee here in the kitchen…"

Peter took a deep breath, "Could you put the phone on speaker, Katya? I need to talk to both of you…"

He heard Ron's voice, "What's up, Pete?"

"Niki and I are going to go back to see my doctor…you remember that we saw him last week?"

"Yes, but she didn't say much more than that, so I thought that it was something routine. What's going on, Pete?" Ron's voice took on a serious tone.

"My doctor is Ted Clinton, Ron…" Peter waited for a response.

After a short silence, Ron asked him, "At Krannert…is Dr. Clinton at Krannert?"

"Yes, Ron…is Katya still there in the kitchen with you?"

"She's right here, by my side, Pete."

Peter stammered, "I…we…Niki and I…decided that I have a problem…a problem with my health. I didn't want to worry anyone, but Niki insisted that I call you to let you know."

"Oh, Petrosha, what is it?" There was fear in Katya's voice, and Ron could be heard in the background trying to comfort her.

"We don't know, yet, but I have had some tests, and Dr. Clinton told us to come back today for his report."

For several moments, there was silence on the other end of the line, and then Ron said, "Okay, Pete. Katya and I will help in any way that we can."

"For right now, I don't know what is going to happen, but we should know something later on...hopefully today. I didn't want to say anything until I was sure what my problem is, but Niki convinced me that I should tell you both now. She is right, of course, but I don't want you to worry about me needlessly."

"Moy brat, *my brother*, you are precious to me, so very precious...Ron and I will do anything and everything that we can to help you and Niki."

Peter could hear the emotion in his sister's voice, "Please don't worry, Katya. I know that everything will turn out fine. But, as I said, Niki was right about telling you...what is going on. If I learn anything today, I'll call to let you know."

"Okay, Pete," said Ron. "We will wait for your call."

Peter and Niki both drove Nicholas to school. It was just a short drive from their home. When they arrived at the school, Niki took Nicholas by the hand and went into the school with him.

The architecture of the building was modern, yet somehow echoed some features that seemed pure Frank Lloyd Wright. Peter had liked the building the first time that he saw it. What would it be like to sit down with an architect and plan such a building together? I'm going to have to contact my adviser at Purdue, Peter felt a momentary sense of dismay, because I don't know if I'm going to be able to continue my engineering studies. In fact, there are many things that I'm not sure about. He felt a wrench in his gut; another stab of fear.

Niki returned to the car quickly, "We should probably go on over to

Krannert. It doesn't matter if we're a little early, and maybe if we're lucky, they'll take us sooner."

Peter looked over at her, and saw her luminous dark eyes that he loved so much. It caused him physical pain to see how sad they were. *Niki...Niki...how can I protect you from all of this?*

"Okay, Niki, let's go." There was the sound of resignation in Peter's voice.

Chapter 62

Dr. Clinton was actually a little late in arriving at the clinic, and the delay was excruciating for Peter. He wanted to get this over with. He wanted to find out what he and Niki would be facing in the days, weeks, perhaps months, to come.

The waiting room had started to fill up after he and Niki had gotten there, and Peter didn't like to be in close quarters, and especially not close quarters where there were more than twenty people sitting cheek by jowl. He felt too warm; he knew that his face must be flushed. His heart maintained a staccato beat. If it weren't for Niki, he might have bolted from the clinic without seeing the doctor. *Dear God, please help me…help us…this is too much…to endure.*

Niki reached over and took his hand, "We are going to get through this together, Pete, no matter what."

She smiled at him, but it was a very sad smile. Briefly, irrationally, Peter wondered if Niki had ever wished that she hadn't met him? After all, their separation when he had to return to Russia after being with her during his recuperation…when they had finally admitted their love for one another…was excruciating, and Niki had told him that her heart was broken when he left.

I have caused her so much pain, thought Peter. And our reunion and happiness have been shortlived. But I am feeling sorry for myself, and I have no right to be so selfish. My sons…our sons…have brought us both joy beyond measure. If I am no longer here to be with them, I know that Niki will raise them well. She has strength, so much more strength than I have.

"Genchenko…Mr. Genchenko?" A young woman dressed in blue scrubs called his name from one of the many doors set in the wall behind where Peter and Niki were sitting.

Peter jumped up, and was dizzy momentarily. Niki stood next to him, and let him lean against her. For a moment, only a moment, he flashed back in his memory to the first time that he had met Niki. He had been ill, and hadn't been able to travel with his team to the U.S. When he finally arrived, he was lightheaded from dehydration and lack of food, and he fainted and fell against her. It was a very inauspicious beginning to their relationship.

"Are you okay, Pete?" Niki whispered so that no one in the waiting room would hear.

He nodded his head, "Da…da…I am all right, Niki. I just shouldn't have jumped up so quickly, that's all."

The nurse reached for Peter's other arm and helped him into the treatment area. Peter was no longer dizzy, but cold fear tightened around his chest.

"I am fine, thank you," said Peter. "I can walk on my own." He was embarrassed by the spectacle that he had just made in the waiting area.

"Dr. Clinton wants you in room four, Mr. Genchenko." The nurse pointed toward the end of the corridor.

It was several minutes before the doctor came into the treatment room, and Peter spoke quietly to Niki, "I wish that I had your courage,

Niki. If I knew what I have to face, perhaps I could do better. I need to know the enemy, and not knowing is…difficult for me."

"I know, Pete…it's the 'not knowing' that scares me, too. But let's not borrow trouble until we know what we are facing." Her eyes were bright with unshed tears.

The door to the treatment area opened and Dr. Clinton slipped inside the room. "Peter," Dr. Clinton shook Peter's hand, and turned to ackknowledge, "Niki," nodding his head toward her.

Dr. Clinton sat down in a chair across from the Genchenkos. He always hated to begin a patient appointment with bad news, but he couldn't change what he had seen earlier regarding Peter's laboratory blood test results.

He leaned forward, elbows on knees, hands clasped together, a serious look on his face, "The simple lab tests that I ordered last week have come back, and the results are…indicative of Acute Myelocytic Leukemia. Peter, you are neutropenic, a low white blood cell count, anemic, a low red blood cell count, and thrombocytopenic, a low platelet level. Usually, platelets are found during lab testing to number 150,000 to 450,000 per microliter. Yours were less than 110,000."

Peter looked over at Niki to see how she was taking this very bad news, and he saw fear in her eyes. *Niki…how I wish that you didn't have to hear this.*

The doctor continued, "I don't like having to give you this bad news…but don't lose heart or hope. There are many things that we can do to treat this condition, if it is, in fact, what is causing your symptoms, Peter."

Niki spoke first, "This is a very time-sensitive diagnosis in regard to treatment, isn't it Dr. Clinton?"

"Yes, it is, Niki, but I want to do something else that might help me pinpoint Peter's diagnosis. I want to do a bone marrow aspiration and biopsy. This is the only way that I can really know what the best approach to treating Peter's illness will be."

"How soon…?" Peter asked.

"Tomorrow morning, I have you scheduled in our outpatient clinic for the bone marrow aspiration and biopsy, Peter. We need to get started as quickly as possible. The old saying, "time is of the essence" is very apt in your situation, Peter. And there is another reason, too: the bone marrow aspiration and biopsy will tell me whether you have AML or APL. I am hoping that it is the latter, because APL, Acute Promyelocytic leukemia, has the highest cure rate. I am also ordering a panel of blood tests; liver enzymes, renal function, B12 levels, folic acid levels, and erythrocyte sed rate…uh…sedimentation rate…to rule out other diagnoses."

"The treatment is different, too, for APL, isn't it Dr. Clinton?" Niki was back. Her face was set in concentration as she took in everything that Peter's doctor was telling them.

"It is, Niki, and the subtype, M3, for Acute Promyelocytic Leukemia as listed in the classifications for France, Great Britain, and the U.S. is the most treatable. I don't want to give Peter any false hope, but the prognosis for APL is much better than it is for other leukemias."

"What time is the bone marrow biopsy and aspiration scheduled for in the morning?" asked Peter, who, by now, felt the old, familiar and terrible grip of cold in the center of his chest. He was beginning to feel like a bystander at his own funeral.

"It's at eleven o'clock, and the scheduler will tell you what you need to know in preparation." Dr. Clinton stood up.

Peter stood, too, and towered over the slightly built doctor, who looked up at him, and then shook his hand again. Peter looked directly into the doctor's kind eyes, and found no subterfuge there.

"You have been in excellent physical condition most of your life, Peter, because you are an athlete. Your activity levels have, no doubt, been very high, given the strenuousness of your sport. These things are definitely in your favor." Dr. Clinton fell silent as he gazed first at the very quiet Niki, and then at Peter.

"But…?" countered Peter. "What things are not in my favor? Where do we go from here?" He put an arm around Niki's shoulders and pulled her close to him, awaiting what he knew for a certainty would be more bad news.

"After the procedure tomorrow morning, Peter, I will be able to tell you much more than I can at the present time. But I can say that, given what the hematologist saw during microscopy on your blood sample of last Friday, there is a broad ray of hope that you could have the most curable of the leukemias; APL. For now, that is all that I can give you. I wish that there was more to say…but there isn't, at least for now."

Peter drove and Niki leaned her head against his shoulder on the way home. For the most part, they were quiet, lost in their own thoughts. But every few moments, Peter looked down at his wife and smiled his sad smile. He didn't know what to say to her at this juncture, except the words that were so deeply felt within him.

"I love you, Niki. I love you so very very much."

"I know, Pete…and I love you…"

Chapter 63

When Peter and Niki returned home, Duchess was waiting for them. Peter rubbed her head and ears, and put her outside to romp for a while. Niki went into the kitchen where she found a note on the kitchen counter written in Marina's elegant script, with a few Cyrillic flourishes due to her Russian heritage.

> Dear Niki and Peter,
>
> We have taken Josef shopping with us, and will return after we pick Nicholas up later this afternoon—probably after three, or so.
>
> Please let sweet, little Duchess out when you get home, and give her some kibbles for lunch.
>
> Love,
>
> Mother and Dad.

Niki smiled wanly when she read the note and turned to Peter, "They just wanted to give us some time alone, Pete. They're being very kind…"

Peter replied, "More than kind, Niki…they have been wonderful to us. I'll let Duchess in…" and Peter opened the back door to let Duchess leap back into the house. He wiped her down quickly, and then filled her bowls with food and water. "Okay, Duchess, you need to be quiet and sweet. This has been a hard day for Niki and me."

It was almost as though Duchess understood exactly what Peter was telling her, and she settled down to eat her lunch.

"Let's go take a nap, Niki…" Peter needed the solace of physical closeness with his wife.

Without another word, Niki started up the stairs and Peter followed, holding the hand that she extended back to him. At the top of the stairs, he pulled her into his arms, and she began to cry tears of helplessness.

"Niki…Niki," he whispered. "I am so sorry for all of the pain that I have caused you since we first met."

"The joy that we have shared far outweighs the pain, Pete. Besides, we aren't the only family to have something terrible like this happen to them."

"No, we aren't, it's true, but right now, I feel," he groped for words to describe what he was feeling, "so terribly sad for you. You know and understand what Dr. Clinton has been saying, but I can't get my mind around it."

She nodded, "I think that not knowing is worse, though, because doctors throw these big words around, and the poor patient can't understand, can't cope, can't hope. I'm not faulting Dr. Clinton in any way, and I think he did a good job of explaining to you what to expect…but it is mind boggling."

"You already know what to expect, though, Niki." Peter said quietly.

She trembled for a moment, "Yes, I do…and I will be by your side every step of the way."

This time, it was Peter who took Niki by the hand and led her into their bedroom. He pulled back the comforter and blanket, closed the door, and began to undress. "Let's lie down together for a little while. Your parents aren't going to be home for several hours, and I'd like to hold you close…nothing between us…just skin to skin."

In their bed, facing one another, it soon became obvious that Peter was fully aroused. He whispered, "Niki…could we…?"

"Pete, do you feel up to it?" Niki was very surprised.

It was his first true smile of the day. Peter lifted the covers and asked, "What do you think?"

Their lovemaking was slow and gentle, yet deeply fulfilling, in spite of the circumstances. They took solace in one another, and if it were possible, their bond, their connection, grew even deeper with this new threat.

It was dark outside when Peter woke up. He twisted his head to see the time on the LCD clock radio on the bedside table, and was amazed when he saw that it was almost eight o'clock. He turned to look at Niki, and found that she was no longer there in the bed. He could hear muffled sounds coming from other parts of the house, and realized that his sons were probably getting their bath. I should get up, he thought. I want to see my sons, I want to be with them and their mother.

His body ached in places he had never had pain before as he rolled over to sit up. *This is worse than playing hockey.* Peter opened a dresser drawer and pulled out some underwear, socks, and sweats. Thinking ahead, he wondered if Niki would agree to a shower tonight? This made him smile in spite of his pain. The thought of her, covered in soap bubbles…well, that will have to wait.

Peter came down the hall slowly and looked into the boys' bathroom where all of the commotion was coming from. "Good evening," he said, and smiled at his sons.

"Papa!" Nicholas jumped up from the water to give his father a wet hug.

Niki was toweling Josef off as he sat on her lap, and she looked up at Peter, a tender smile on her face. "Hi, sleepyhead."

Little Josef raised his arms to his father, "Papa, Papa!"

Peter, with Nicholas in one arm, reached down to pick Josef up. When they were both in his arms, he held them close and bowed his head for a moment to say a silent prayer. *Please, Lord, let me be with them for a while longer. I can't bear the thought of leaving them.*

Niki's heart ached with the knowledge of what was to come…and yet her men, the three of them, made a wonderfully loving tableaux as she watched. Pete is such a good father to our sons. *Let him stay with us, please let him stay with us.*

Nicholas told his father, "We saved some dinner for you, Papa."

"Thank you, son. I'm sorry that I missed having dinner with all of you tonight. I guess that I was just very sleepy."

Niki stood on tiptoe and kissed her husband's cheek, "And you had every right to be sleepy, Pete."

Downstairs, Klaus and Marina were watching television, with Duchess at Marina's side. Duchess was the first to notice Peter coming down the stairs, and jumped up to greet him.

Klaus called out to his dog, "Duchess, behave yourself."

"Peter, we saved a nice plate of dinner for you in the warming oven. I'll come out to the kitchen to help you." She looked up at her son-in-law and smiled.

"There is no need for you to do that, Marina. Niki is coming down soon. We said our prayers with Nicholas and Josef, and she said that she would join me while I ate."

"Are you rested, Peter?" Klaus asked.

Peter hesitated a moment, thinking about his little 'nap' with Niki, and what had gone on before he fell asleep, "I am…and thank you for taking such good care of the boys and keeping our household going so well. Niki and I can't thank you enough."

Klaus raised one hand, "We are your family, Peter, and we are happy to be able to help you and Niki."

She was on the stairs, and Peter watched her come down. In spite of everything, Niki's so beautiful, he thought, but so thin. How can I protect her from what is to come?"

"Hello everyone," her voice sounded as calm and as sweet as it usually did.

Peter held a hand out to her, and she came to him for a hug. "Did you have a nice nap, Niki?"

"Yes, my dear, I certainly did," she looked up at him with an angelic smile. "When I heard Mom and Dad come in with our boys, I realized that you were still sleeping, so I got up as quietly as I could and sneaked downstairs. You should have seen the boys eat their dinner, Pete. They were little 'eating machines' tonight."

"They are growing so fast. It's hard to comprehend…" Peter's face held a sense of wonder.

"In our experience," said Marina, nodding at Klaus, "we felt the same way…especially with our sons."

Peter was surprised when Marina spoke openly of her sons. Usually, she didn't mention her own Josef, the son who had been injured and passed away many years ago, but tonight she spoke, no matter how obliquely, of him as well as Mike. She had said, "sons."

He had not had much appetite lately, but Peter felt hungry tonight.

His mother had always told him that a little exercise was good for him, and she was right. He chuckled, remembering his mother's words.

"What...?" Niki was looking at him with eyebrows raised. "Is there something that I'm missing here?"

He shook his head and gave a short laugh, "My mother always said that a little exercise was good for me. Actually, tonight I feel some hunger; a good sign, I think, and it proves that my mother was right."

"She was...and she raised a good son, too, Pete."

"Should I be eating this much so late in the evening, Niki? I love your mother's pasta and tofu, but should I eat just a small amount?"

"It's okay, Pete. Eat what you like. They just want you NPO, you know your Latin, *nil per os*, nothing by mouth, after twelve midnight. It's only because of the conscious sedation that you will have for the procedure. Some patients get sick to their stomachs and have esophageal reflux or vomiting when they receive any kind of anesthesia, so the NPO order is to help prevent these things."

A little after nine, Marina and Klaus came into the kitchen to say goodnight. Peter had told them earlier about the procedure in the morning, and both said they would be up early to say goodbye, and to get Nicholas and Josef ready for their day.

"Niki tells us that you won't feel any pain because you will be under anesthesia, and that is good to know. Nonetheless, you have our prayers, Peter." Marina's face was somber.

Peter hugged his mother-in-law, and said, "*Spaseeba,* thank you,"

Klaus patted his shoulder, "We will be thinking of both of you, Peter."

When her parents had gone to their room, Niki asked, "Have you called Katya and Ron yet, Pete?"

"I don't really know what to tell them, Niki, and I don't want to worry them unnecessarily."

"True, Pete, but I can tell you that Katya is very worried about you…and she truly needs to know what's happening with her brother."

Peter bowed his head for a moment, "All right, I know how I would feel if Katya was the one who was ill. I'll call her now," and he stood up.

"Sit down, Pete, I've got the phone…" Niki dialed Katya's number, and handed the phone to him.

On the third ring, Katya answered, "Hello…"

"Hello, Katya?…you are still up…is Ari doing well?…Good, it's good to hear that he is…and Ron, he's doing well, too?…Niki has told me that I must give you and Ron an update on things…Well, tomorrow I'm scheduled for a bone marrow aspiration and biopsy…Niki tells me that it is going to be under conscious sedation…Yes, I think that is most important…Dr. Clinton at Krannert is excellent…He has been thorough, and has given us much to ponder…He has run several blood tests that showed some unusual characteristics in my test results, and so we are progressing to the bone marrow aspiration and biopsy…No, it won't necessitate an inpatient stay…Niki and I will call you about the results…Is Ron able to handle the load at the sports medicine clinic?…Good…Niki has been concerned about it…She told me that Stephanie has hired an additional physician to carry the load, and it's working…It's getting late…yes, I love you, too, my sister…Niki and I will call you as soon as we know anything…Goodnight."

As Niki and Peter straightened up the kitchen together, she told him, "Cleaning up the kitchen with you is another reminder of that winter storm back in eighty-six, Pete, when we were alone for several days. It's sort of déjà vu, isn't it?"

"Da *yes*, Niki, and at the time, I never realized that we could ever be together again when I had to return to Russia. Yet here we are, married, with two beautiful sons…I am so grateful for everything.

Chapter 64

Dr. Clinton came into the pre-operative holding area and saw the Genchenkos, "How are you today?"

Peter smiled ruefully and replied, "I'm perhaps a little nervous, but otherwise okay."

Niki had some questions for Dr. Clinton, "You ordered several blood tests on Pete…liver enzymes, renal function, B12 levels, and erythrocyte sed rate. What can you tell us about the results?"

"All of the tests, with the exception of the very low erythrocyte sedimentation rate, were in the lowest so-called 'normal' ranges. Therefore, I believe that doing the bone marrow aspiration and biopsy will yield a definitive diagnosis, I'm still thinking Acute Promyelocytic Leukemia, and we can then start therapy quickly after we get our results. What I want to determine with the biopsy is whether the decrease in platelets is due to a peripheral problem, or a deficit in production. Once we have the tissue sample, the flouorescent in situ hybridization method will be used to differentiate between AML and APL. It's an excellent method for this purpose."

"And the therapy…what will your approach be, Dr. Clinton?" Niki wanted to know what to expect.

"Acute promyelocytic leukemia is actually a subtype of acute myelocytic leukemia, as you know, Niki. APL is more treatable, with a higher recovery rate, somewhere around ninety percent, than some of the other leukemias. Some oncologists, including me, use the ATRA, all-trans-retinoic acid treatment, that is sometimes combined with Anthrocycline chemotherapy. There is also treatment with Arsenic trioxide that has shown to be a promising approach to remission. If these treatments are not successful, then allogenic stem cell transplant will be considered. For right now, though, let's get this procedure underway. Based on what we find, Peter, we will start aggressive therapy as soon as possible." Dr. Clinton placed his hand on Peter's shoulder.

Peter listened to Niki's and Dr. Clinton's discussion, but most of it was meaningless to him. It was as though he was trapped inside a bubble; something that kept him from fully participating in the things that were about to happen to him. And the cold and painful, yet familiar numbness in the center of his chest, the feeling that, not long ago, he had thought was gone forever, had returned.

The study and practice of medicine are very complicated; of that I am certain, thought Peter, as he watched Niki's reaction to Dr. Clinton's intended approaches to treatment. He realized that she was stressed far more than he had previously understood. Niki knew exactly what had to be done, and he was relieved that she would be there, as she said, "every step of the way." But Peter fervently wished that she would not suffer, too, because of him. *She doesn't deserve this heartache.*

"I'll see you in a few minutes, Peter." Dr. Clinton pulled the privacy curtain aside and pulled it back as he departed.

"How are you doing, Pete?" Niki gently caressed his cheek with one hand.

"Niki, I must tell you...I have been better. I will be very glad when this day is over."

Two scrub clad surgical nurses came into the patient pre-surgical unit and wheeled Peter out of the small cubicle after checking his arm band and asking him his name and what type of procedure he was going to have. His last glimpse of Niki pained him to the very core of his being. Her eyes were red-rimmed, and she mouthed the words, "I love you," and blew him a kiss as his gurney rolled past her.

Inside the procedure room Peter immediately remembered what it had felt like to be placed on a cold operating table, and this present experience, although he wasn't in pain the way he was when his appendix had burst, he still felt very uncomfortable and a little disoriented. He was placed in a side-lying position on the thin-cushioned operating table, with his left hip facing upward, and he was uncomfortable in this position. Perhaps his pre-procedure medication was responsible for the way he felt? He truly didn't know at this point.

A nurse in a gown, mask and gloves in the procedure room asked him to identify himself and the procedure that he was going to have. Once she was satisfied that Peter was her patient, she spoke briefly to another surgical nurse that everything would be ready for Dr. Clinton after she prepped the site.

Peter couldn't believe how roughly the nurse scrubbed his hip, and then she poured something cold over the area, but he couldn't see what it was. It smelled like Iodine, he decided. Iodine was used a great deal in Russia because it was cheap, but he wondered why it would be used here?

I must behave like a man about all of this…I know that. But I can't lie to myself; this is very serious, and I am truly afraid. Peter started praying…asking God to have mercy upon him and his family. Dr. Clinton seemed hopeful when he talked to us. Maybe he is right. Maybe I have the more treatable kind of leukemia. Just thinking of the word leukemia, however, made Peter feel a stab of fear in the center of his chest. How did this happen to me?

Dr. Clinton had questioned Peter early on about exposure to toxic chemicals or radiation, and Peter had immediately told him about the factory where he had worked in Lyubertsy. He remembered that there were chemicals and solvents that were used on the automotive axles in the department where he worked. Dr. Clinton was silent for several moments, had looked at Niki, and then turned to Peter to tell him how quickly toxic solvents could pass through the skin and into the blood stream. If that was what happened, Dr. Clinton hypothesized, then Peter's leukemia could have been caused by his exposure to solvents over a timespan of several years.

There was something reminiscent of the torture perpetrated in the Dark Ages when Peter's bone marrow biopsy procedure got underway. Although he had been sedated, Peter nonetheless felt the terrible pain of the passing of the large aspirating syringe through the periosteum and bone, into the center of the iliac crest for aspirating the semi-liquid marrow. When the aspirating syringe was withdrawn, the trephine, a larger bore instrument, was passed through the same opening into the posterior iliac crest to obtain a solid piece of bone marrow. Peter knew that he would never forget the sound of the trephine as it passed through the bone with a 'crunch,' or the searing pain of the instrument as it was passed into the center of his hip bone. When he was only fifteen years old, he had been shot mistakenly by one of his father's enemies, and the searing pain of the trephine reminded him of the terrible pain of being shot in the abdomen. *Lord, have mercy on me.*

Peter could just barely hear Dr. Clinton speaking to someone, another man whose voice was deeper than Dr. Clinton's, about the pale color of Peter's bone marrow. They were speaking quietly, but Peter's sense of hearing was acute. "At Peter's age, there should be more red than yellow marrow. It's leukemia, no doubt…and now the hard work begins in the laboratory to determine the differentiation of the cell type of the leukemia." Dr. Clinton's voice was somber.

Niki was pacing up and down in the surgical waiting area. She couldn't sit still, because she knew how painful the bone marrow extraction process could be with a trephine passed through the periosteum, compact bone, spongy bone, the haversian canal, the trabeculae, and into the marrow cavity of the iliac crest. Her physical body ached for Peter, but her very soul seemed to cringe at the thought of the pain that he would have to endure. My love, my love, she repeated over and over, her mantra to ward off the total collapse that she felt would certainly come if she didn't hear something soon from Dr. Clinton.

Peter was fully alert when the nurse asked him to maintain a supine position, lying on his back, for at least ten minutes so that the procedure site was compressed. She explained that he couldn't go back to the recovery area until she was assured that there would be no bleeding at the site. She also explained that he could resume normal activity in a day or so, but if there was pain, he could take non-aspirin analgesics for comfort. The nurse stressed that he report any side effects, such as bleeding, pain at the site, elevated temperature, or heat and redness at the site, to his doctor.

The last time that she checked Peter's wound, she told him that it looked good, and that he was ready to go to the post-anesthesia recovery unit. "You have been, by far, the best patient that I have ever had for a bone marrow biopsy, Mr. Genchenko, and I applaud your courage." The nurse patted him on the shoulder, and then handed him off to an orderly for transport to the outpatient recovery area.

When Peter saw Niki, she put a hand to her mouth to keep from crying out, he knew. Her eyes were large and luminous with unshed tears, and Peter believed, in spite of her tears, that she was still the most beautiful woman in the world. He managed a smile, and reached out a hand to clasp hers. She lifted his hand to her lips, just as she had done several years before, after he had an appendectomy, when he was already in love with her, but didn't know that she was in love with him.

Chapter 65

In the post-anesthesia recovery unit, Dr. Clinton was all business as he told Peter and Niki, "In comparison to bone marrow aspiration, which is quickly accomplished, a bone marrow biopsy, although it takes more time to test in the laboratory, is indicative of all cells. For now, Peter, you will be sore around the biopsy site, so take it easy. I know that most of the literature regarding post-procedure bone marrow aspiration and biopsy tells patients that they can resume normal activities within a short time. However, I always recommend at least twenty-four to forty-eight hours of limited activity in patients who may have a leukemia diagnosis. So, Peter, Niki, it's TLC for a while, and that is a good thing.

"Peter, do you know how lucky you are to have such a wonderful wife as Niki? She knows and understands what we have done, and what we are about to do for you, and she is a perfectionist when it comes to her patients. She treated my son, Andrew, after he suffered a torn anterior cruciate ligament, and brought him back to playing form after his difficult surgery. My son is now playing soccer for Indiana University, and I will be forever grateful to Niki...and so will Andrew."

"I do know that Niki is wonderful, Dr. Clinton, and she means the world to me. I trust her intuition, and her skill, and now I am in the good hands of both of you."

"You will call us when you get the lab and pathology results Dr. Clinton?" Niki's voice betrayed her weariness.

"I will...and then things will speed up very quickly, because the earliest treatment possible is the best approach." Dr. Clinton hurried out of the recovery area, and waved at his patient as he passed through the automatic doors.

At home, Duchess leapt for joy, as always, at seeing Peter. "I think she wants to go outside, Niki..."

"I'm sure that she does. But let me help you onto the sofa first, Pete, and then I'll take care of Duchess." She helped him as he walked slowly over to the sofa, and then gingerly sat down. "Is this okay, Pete?"

"I'm fine, Niki, so go take care of Duchess." Peter wasn't fine, but he didn't want Niki to know.

"Come on, Duchess, it's time to go outside, sweetie." Niki beckoned to Duchess and headed for the back door.

Niki filled Duchess's bowls to overflowing as she waited for Duchess to come back to the house. Now what did I do that for, she wondered? Could it be that I'm a little distracted...or something else? "Okay, big girl, come back in here," she called out the door.

After Duchess was settled down, Niki got to work on preparing a downstairs room for Peter. I'm not going to let him climb up and down the steps...at least not until tomorrow.

Peter was very happy that Niki was making a bed for him on the large sofa in his study. He wasn't sure whether or not he could climb the stairs to their bedroom, and her foresight in setting up a bed downstairs was nothing short of brilliant.

Marina and Karl were with the boys for the birthday party of Nicholas's best friend Autumn, and that meant that Peter and Niki had the house all to themselves, at least until after six o'clock. The good souls that they are, Marina and Karl, thought Peter, with gratitude.

"Pete, I called Ron while we were still at the hospital and filled him in on how things were going. Do you want to call Katya and talk to her a little bit?"

"Yes, I need to call her, Niki. Could you hand me the phone?"

She turned and grabbed the phone from its base, "Here you go, Pete."

Peter smiled at Niki as he dialed Katya's number. After four rings, the answering machine picked up, and Katya's warm and sweet voice asked her caller to, "Please leave a message...thank you."

"Katya, I just wanted to tell you and Ron that I survived the procedure today...no, seriously, it wasn't so bad as I thought it would be. Niki and I will probably hear from Dr. Clinton in the next few days, and we can tell you more at that time. Kiss little Ari for me, and tell Ron that I am hanging in there, as they say. I know that you both are very busy, but if you find yourselves out near our place, please come and visit us. I love you all. 'Bye."

Peter was moving slowly. Every step felt as if the trephine was again stabbing into his hip. He was grateful to Niki when she brought his pajamas to him.

"Thank you, my dear wife, for understanding that blue jeans are harsh against bruised skin and damaged bone."

"Here, let me help you with the bottoms, Pete. You really shouldn't lift your left leg very high, because it's going to aggravate your hip on that side."

As Niki knelt on the floor in front of Peter to help him get into his pajamas, she looked up into his eyes, and took his breath away, as always. "Niki, my sweet Niki…what are we going to do now?" He cupped her chin in his hand.

For a moment, she hesitated, and then regained her composure, "We wait to hear from Dr. Clinton, Pete. Until then, we are sort of in suspended animation…we can't go forward, and we certainly can't go backward, so we just wait. The nice thing is, we will be waiting together. As long as I draw breath, Pete, I will be at your side."

Peter bowed his head, and then looked up, "I haven't been alone since I first kissed you. And even though we became separated by thousands of miles, you were in my heart. When you told me that we had a son, I made room for him in my heart, too. And now we have two sons, so the three of you," he held his hand over his heart, "are always with me."

Niki was still kneeling in front of him, and rested her head in his lap. Peter stroked her dark hair away from her face, "strands of silk," he said. "Your hair is like beautiful strands of dark silk,"

"Thank you," she managed to whisper.

"Why don't we cuddle up together under this soft blanket, Niki? When your parents bring the boys home, we will be more rested, don't you think?"

"You always have the best ideas, Pete, but aren't you hungry?"

"Not yet…are you?"

She shook her head, "No, I just want to lie next to you and feel your arms around me."

They cuddled together 'spoon fashion' on the overstuffed sofa. Peter lay on his right hip, he couldn't stand any pressure on his left, and Niki curled up against him. Duchess crept into the room quietly and lay on the floor next to the sofa.

Niki slipped out of Peter's embrace, hoping not to awaken him. It's time to get dinner started, and even though Pete says he's not hungry, he needs to eat something. In the great room, she looked at the grandfather clock, an heirloom from her father's German grandmother, and was surprised that it was almost five-thirty. Gosh, I'd better get busy, she thought, as she entered the kitchen. Tonight is a vegetable soup kind of night, she decided. Pete likes vegetable soup, and so do the boys and Mom and Dad. She opened the freezer door, took out two large containers of her homemade soup and placed them in the microwave to thaw. Let's see…I think that there's a loaf of homemade bread in the freezer, too, and she again looked inside the freezer. Yup, there it is…good.

She heard Nicholas first…his voice calling, "Papa's home!"

And then the hungry hoard descended upon Niki. "How was the party?"

Nicholas told his mother, "It was very noisy, but we had lots of fun."

Josef reached out to his mother from his grandmother's arms, and Niki took him, giving him a hug and a kiss before she put him on her hip. "Is everyone hungry?" She gave a brave smile to her mother.

Klaus laughed, "Well, I am, even after the birthday cake. Whoever heard of a late afternoon birthday party?"

Marina, with furrowed brow, told her daughter, "The boys ate very little cake, so I'm sure that they will eat some dinner. But tell us, please, how is Peter?"

"He's okay, Mom. I made a bed for him in his study so that he wouldn't have to climb the stairs tonight, and he was still a little sedated when we got home, so he's taking a nap right now."

"I'll help the boys to wash their hands, Niki, and then we can feed them." Marina looked a bit tired.

"Let me do that, Marina…you have had a busy day." Klaus smiled at his wife and took the boys in hand. "We will be right back."

Marina put her arms around her daughter. Neither spoke…they didn't have to. Niki put her head on her mother's shoulder for several moments and let out a long sigh.

This time when Niki smiled at her mother, the smile twinkled in her eyes, too. "Thanks, Mom, I needed that."

Peter poked his head into the kitchen, "Am I invited to the feast?"

Nicholas, with Klaus carrying Josef, entered the kitchen from another door. Both boys shouted almost in unison, "Papa, Papa!"

Duchess, her stump of a tail wagging her entire backside, leaned into Peter for a little attention, too.

Peter rubbed her head for a moment and then stooped to gather up his sons. He felt a sharp stab of pain in his hip, but he didn't let on that he was in pain. Klaus came over to pat Peter on the back gently, and Marina stood on tiptoe to kiss his cheek.

"When will you hear something, Peter?" Klaus asked.

Peter shrugged, "Dr. Clinton didn't give us a definite timeframe for the lab studies, Klaus. My guess is that it will be at least two, if not three, days."

The table was set, and Niki started dishing up her "world famous vegetable beef soup," as her husband, and her father, called it. "Okay, everyone…find a spot at the table and have a seat. Josef still gets the booster chair." She forced herself to be upbeat as she called the family to dinner.

Duchess dived under the table to snag whatever might fall to the floor, as she usually did. She always made her way to where Peter was sitting, and often put her head on his knee, but Peter never minded her attention, and always found something to reward her with.

Niki's bread had a wonderful European crust; crunchy on the outside and tender on the inside. She had even thought ahead and taken the butter out of the refrigerator so that it would spread easily. Josef reached over onto his mother's plate and retrieved a nicely buttered morsel of bread. This action on the part of the smallest one at the table made everyone, including Nicholas, and Josef, himself, laugh.

Peter sat watching his family interact, and it filled his heart to overflowing with love for all of them, Marina and Klaus included. I…we…can laugh in the face of adversity. There is always something worthy of laughter in this loving family.

While Marina straightened up the kitchen, Niki took Nicholas and Josef upstairs for their baths. "Come on, boys. It's after seven-thirty, and you both need to be in bed by eight."

Klaus took Duchess for a walk. She had earlier come into the great room dragging her leash in her mouth, and started toward Peter. "No, Duchess, you must walk with me this evening. Peter is recuperating, and you'd only pull him all around. Sit…sit, Duchess, while I put on your harness."

Peter felt lightheaded and tired, and decided to go back into his study to rest. He wished that he could help Niki bathe their sons, but he truly didn't feel up to it tonight.

Slowly, very slowly, Peter lowered himself onto his sofa 'bed,' trying to avoid placing any pressure on his hip, and succeeding fairly well. The next thing he knew, he was awake and drenched in perspiration. The house was dark, except for a nightlight in the hall near the door to Peter's study. He sensed, not heard, Niki's quiet breathing, and wondered if he might be dreaming? Where is she? He was still on the sofa, but he was covered by a thick blanket. Again, he strained his ears to listen. There…she's over there, and he realized that she was sleeping on the little cot that they used from time to time when they had a houseful of company. He hadn't heard her come into the room or set up the cot. He tried rolling over to the edge of the sofa, and it took several false starts before he made it into a sitting position.

Niki called softly to him, "Pete…are you okay?"

He took a deep breath, "I am…and I apologize for waking you up, Niki. I know that you are stressed and tired. You need your sleep, and now I have awakened you."

She came to him and placed a hand on his forehead, "You've got an elevated temp, Pete."

"You are right, Niki, and I'm wet from head to toe."

"Let's see…" Niki was trying to remember if she kept any aspirin-free analgesics that had temperature-lowering properties.

Once she found the acetaminophen, Niki poured a cold glass of water for Peter. "Don't take the medication just yet, Pete. I want to get an accurate reading of your temperature."

After several moments, Niki took the thermometer from Peter's mouth. "It's one hundred two and two tenths, Pete. Go ahead and take the medicine…"

He swallowed the tablet, and the ice water felt good on his parched throat. Niki brushed his hair back from his forehead with her fingertips, and Peter smiled up at her and leaned his head against her breast.

"I'm going to put you in our downstairs shower for a quick rinse-off, Pete. While I was getting the thermometer and the meds, I grabbed some pajamas and a towel and wash cloth. Can you stand up without being dizzy? I don't want you to fall, and, if memory serves me right, I wasn't able to hold you up one time when you fainted. Remember the first time that we met?"

Peter smiled and replied, "I will never forget it, and the beautiful Russian face of the woman who rescued me. I thought that you were Russian, Niki, because of your lovely features…"

Chapter 66

Niki got into the shower with Peter and gently washed him, while she kept his hip wound dry. "When we finish in here, I'll check your temp again. Hopefully, it won't be as high as it was a few minutes ago."

"Thank you, my love. I don't know what I would do without you." Peter felt dizzy, but didn't want to tell Niki because he didn't want to frighten her.

Niki got out of the shower and wrapped a towel around herself, and after she helped Peter out of the shower, she toweled him off. She then dried his hair with a hairdryer so that he wouldn't take a chill. He loved the warmth from the hairdryer that helped to dispel the cold that had seeped inside him, in spite of his elevated temperature. And aside from that, as always, he loved having Niki so close to him.

"Would you like some hot tea, Pete? If you're still cold, hot tea will help to warm you up." Niki's voice was gentle and calm as she brushed his hair.

All Peter wanted to do was lie down and rest, but he didn't have the heart to tell Niki. He knew that she was already very worried about him, and he didn't want to add to that worry.

"A cup of hot tea will do nicely, Niki." He turned and smiled up at her.

"While the water heats, I'm going to check your temperature again, Pete. You probably think that it's strange that you can be cold even though your temperature is elevated."

This made Peter smile, "You are the expert Niki...but I have experienced just such a phenomenon as this when I was a child. I knew that my mother was worried, I could see it in her expression, and I wondered how I could be hot and cold at the same time?"

Niki slipped the thermometer between Peter's lips, "It's your immune system that's raising your temperature when your body senses a threat. Most living organisms, except those that are poikilothermic, you know, cold-blooded, have a rather narrow temperature range in which they can live. If the temperature gets too low, they..." Niki hesitated, not wanting to say the word, die. "They can't multiply...and if it gets too high, the same thing happens. That's why your immune system heats up your body temperature when an infectious organism tries to get in."

This rather lengthy explanation to his question made Peter smile again, even though the thermometer was still in place. I have my own living, breathing, medical encyclopedia, he thought.

Niki took the thermometer from Peter's mouth and checked it under the bright kitchen lights. "It's still elevated, Pete, but it's below 100 now, and that's good. Let's have our tea."

Niki carried both cups of steaming tea as they returned to Peter's study. This is so reminiscent of our time together back in 1986. Everything was so uncertain then...but now...here we are with a family, and what might look like an enviable life to an outsider. Yet we struggle still to keep it all together. What will Dr. Clinton find out about Pete's illness? A stab of fear passed through her, and she nearly dropped one of the cups of hot tea.

"Niki…are you all right?" Peter reached to steady her.

"I wasn't paying attention, Pete. I guess I let my mind wander; not a good idea when you're carrying hot tea."

"Nyet," he answered, as he carefully sat down in his big chair and put his tea on the desk.

Niki hesitated, sipped a bit of her tea, and then spoke, "We should know something in the next day or so, Pete. Right now, we don't know what we are facing…"

"I know, Niki, but whatever it is, I can handle it with you by my side."

"And you know that I will be there." Niki looked over the edge of her tea cup at him, and her eyes were soft and loving.

It had taken the laboratory three days to send a final report on Peter to Dr. Clinton, who immediately called Niki to bring Peter in the next day. The doctor came into the treatment room slowly, said hello in a quiet voice, and sat down to tell Peter and Niki what the laboratory had found.

It's bad news, thought Peter. I would not want to be a physician, who, more often than not, has to give patients bad news. How does Niki do it, he wondered?

"Peter, Niki, I have the results of the bone marrow aspiration and biopsy. There are several things that I want to tell you both, and I know that Niki will understand. But I want you, Peter, to ask as many questions as you want, so that you will understand everything, too, and then we can go from there."

Dr. Clinton shuffled the papers in the thick folder in front of him back and forth, drew out several, and began to speak again, "We did an immunohistochemistry on the solid bone marrow extracted during your procedure, Peter, and it was found, using the Wright-staining technique, that you have leukemia. This is a certainty, and I want both you and Niki to fully understand the implications here."

He was quiet again as he pulled several more sheets of paper from the folder, and then he continued, "You have acute promyelocytic leukemia, Peter. It's important that you remember that the remission and cure rates for this leukemia cell type are in the ninety percent range. Therefore, I want to start treatment with the ATRA, the All-trans-retinoic acid therapy, immediately. You will have to be hospitalized while you are under ATRA treatment, because you will need to be in a reverse isolation room as we weaken your immune system during treatment."

Peter found his voice first, "What is 'reverse isolation,' Dr. Clinton?"

"The air in your room will be slightly pressurized; it will flow out from your room, and there will also be an anteroom for pressure equalization and putting on the necessary gown, gloves, mask and haircovering by caregivers and visitors. With reverse isolation, you will be protected from the environment while your immune system is weakened. Does this make sense to you?"

Peter nodded, "Yes, I understand." He turned to look at Niki, who had been very quiet up to this point.

"When you say, "immediately," do you mean that Peter will be hospitalized today?" Niki's voice was flat and without inflection.

"Yes, I do, Niki, and you know, of course, that the quicker we get treatment started for Peter," he nodded in Peter's direction, "the quicker we can begin to see progress toward remission."

Peter reached for Niki's hand, and held it in his, "I didn't pack a toiletry kit or anything, Dr. Clinton, but I'm ready to stay and get things going."

The doctor smiled, "Even if you had brought things from home, we wouldn't let you use them, or store them in your isolation room, Peter. The things that we consider to be most clean, our clothing and personal items, even bed clothes, are covered with contagion, so you can't even have your own pajamas."

"How...how long is the course of treatment, Dr. Clinton?" Niki's voice was hesitant.

"The lab results will tell us that, Niki. These things are very different for each individual, and at this point, I don't really know what the length of treatment will be."

Dr. Clinton stood up, "Are you ready to go, Peter, or do you have any other questions before we start the admission process?"

Peter stood, and helped Niki to stand, holding her hand and steadying her. "We are ready, I think. Niki...?"

"Yes," she said, and all that she had the strength to do was bow her head and follow Peter out of the room.

Chapter 67

"Dad...Pete's going to be hospitalized today...no, right now... Dr. Clinton wants to get started on Pete's treatment immediately...Pete has something called acute promyelocytic leukemia, and Dr. Clinton says that there is a ninety percent cure rate, so we will keep our hopes up...I just wanted to let you and Mom know what to expect today...If I find out anything more, I'll let you know...Yes, I miss the boys so much...Well, right now, Pete is going through the admissions process, so I'll know a little more when I call you the next time...Please tell Mom that I'm sorry that we won't be there for supper...I know, I know, Dad, but Pete and I feel as if we haven't been fair to you and Mom, or to our sons because we've been gone so much...Thanks, Dad, we don't know what we would do without your help...Once I get Pete settled in his room, I'll come home and talk to the boys about their father...Give everyone kisses from us...I love you, too."

Niki wiped away the tears from her cheeks. I don't want Pete to see me like this. I've got to be strong for him. But fear clutched at her heart, and she felt sick at her stomach. I can't give in to this self-pity, thought Niki. And in her mind's eye she pictured her sons playing, wrestling, laughing with their father. It will be that way again; I hope and pray that it will.

I have never given into fear, thought Peter, and I do not frighten easily. How could I, with the life I led as a child? Everything was uncertain when Katya and I were around our father. Ivan's temper was always near the surface when he had to deal with us. We learned very early in our childhood to stay out of Ivan's way. But now…what will I do? Will I have the strength to get through this dark time? I don't want Niki to worry, but I know that she does. I have seen it in her eyes, in her weight loss. What can I do to help her? And our sons…how can I protect them if I am sick?

There were so many conflicting emotions running through Peter as he went through the hospital admitting process, that he felt almost detached, like a ghost passing through rarefied air. *Dear God, please give me the strength to get through this, and please protect my family, when I cannot.*

"Pete…" Niki called softly to him, "I just talked to Dad, and he and Mom will get supper for the boys. I told him that I would be there after supper, and that I'd talk to the boys about what is happening."

Peter, in a hospital gown, was already in bed, and connected to all sorts of sensors for pulse oximetry, electrocardiogram, blood pressure, pulse and respirations. An intravenous line had been established in his left brachial vein.

"Niki," he smiled and reached for her hand.

"It didn't take them very long to get you all set up, Pete." Niki looked at all the electronics and lines, and felt overwhelmed.

"Come here, Niki," Peter still held out his hand.

She pulled a chair close to the bed and took his hand, "I want to be brave and strong for you, Pete, but right now, I just want to crawl up into that bed with you and have you put your arms around me. I feel like such a coward."

Peter scoffed, "You are not a coward. In fact, you are the bravest woman that I have ever known, in spite of your small size. If we were in a battle, I would want you at my side." Niki's reaction to his words made Peter smile, in spite of the heartache inside him.

She took his hand and told him, "We *are* in a battle, Pete, and I will fight for you…"

Peter closed his eyes for a moment, and then agreed with her, "You are so right, Niki, but Dr. Clinton, although he was very serious when he told us about my leukemia, did say that there is a ninety percent cure rate for what I have. I am buoyed up by the cure rate statistics, and I am very hopeful of a good outcome."

"And so am I, my love." Tears filled Niki's eyes again, and she lowered her head as she tried to hide them from her husband.

Peter gently put a finger beneath her chin and lifted her gaze, "I have been told by an excellent source, my mother, that tears are a necessary part of the healing process, Niki. You don't need to hide your tears from me."

They were quiet for a while, hand in hand, waiting for what would come next. The door to Peter's room was open, and Niki understood that he would be moved to another room where reverse isolation, a pressurized room with out-flowing air, to protect an immunocompromised patient, would be used. This would be where he would spend a week, two weeks, or more during his initial chemotherapy.

She wasn't sure how she would be able to give their sons the attention they needed from their mother, and still be here when Pete needed her, until she thought of Susan Anderson, the private duty nurse who had cared for Ilya, one of Peter's teammates on the Red Army

Hockey Team during the International Winter Games in 1986. To Niki that seemed so long ago, now.

"Pete," said Niki, "Do you remember Ilya's nurse, Susan Anderson, when Ilya injured his knee and had surgery during the International Winter Games?"

For a moment, Peter was silent, and then responded, "Yes, she stayed with Ilya during his recuperation in the hospital. Why do you ask?"

"I want someone that I know and trust to be here with you when I can't be…and I was very impressed with Susan. If I contact her, would you mind if she stayed with you during my absences?"

Peter smiled at his thoughtful wife, who left nothing to chance, "I think that it is a wonderful idea. I have been worried about you, not eating, not sleeping, not having enough time with our sons, and Susan could be invaluable to both of us. I don't want you worrying when you aren't here with me, my lovely wife."

There were other things that Niki needed to discuss with Pete. Katya had called early this morning to see what type of treatment her brother was going to receive, and Niki had told her that, until Dr. Clinton had a definitive diagnosis, everything was up in the air. Katya offered to come and stay with the boys, and Niki had told her that she appreciated the offer. The boys were doing okay with their grandparents, Niki had said, but there would be times that they might need some help.

"Ron and I want to help you and your family, Niki, and you know that my brother means the world to me. We will do anything for you…just tell us what you need, and we will help."

"Right now, Katya, we have everything taken care of, but it would be wonderful to see you, so come any time. And I promise that I will let

457

you and Ron know if we need help."

"Niki…I want to ask a favor of you…I know that your mother and father are staying with Nicholas and Josef, but I truly want to help, too. In fact, Ron and I have talked about coming to stay at your house during the time that Peter is in treatment. Please forgive me if I have been too forward, but I talked to your mother about helping, and she said that if Ron and I and Ari came to stay with Josef and Nicholas, she and your father would be "right next door" as she said, and we could all help you and Peter. It would be so much easier for your family, Niki. And…since I am not working, I can share the car-pooling duties with your mother and father, Ron can continue his usual duties at the clinic, and you can also work in the clinic, if you see the need."

Niki realized that Katya wanted to be near Peter and his family during this time of crisis, and she was choked with emotion for a moment. "Oh, that would be *wonderful,* Katya! I've been afraid that I've been taking advantage of my parents, and I've been torn between helping Pete and mothering my sons. The boys love to be with you, Ari, and Ron…so this could be an answer to Pete's and my prayers. He's been so sad about not being able to be with them."

"You can discuss this with Peter…" Katya started to say.

"He will be so happy when I tell him, Katya. Pete will have no problem at all, and he will get to see you, too, more often. His life, our lives, have been so busy up until now…and he has said many times how much he misses seeing you."

"We will gather our things tonight, Niki, and we will see you in the morning. Tell my brother that I love him, and that my family will be with your family for as long as you need us."

Niki talked to Peter about Katya's offer of help. He seemed stunned at first, and then put a hand to his forehead and began to cry quietly.

"Pete…it's okay…Katya and Ron have discussed this, and they want to help in any way they can." Niki's heart fell, because she thought that she had hurt Pete in some way with what she had thought was good news for their family. She put her cheek against the top of his head and gently rubbed his back.

When he was able, he used the heels of his hands to wipe away his tears, and reached for his wife. "I didn't want to burden Katya with my illness, Niki, because she has had so much sadness in her life. Even so, I am not surprised that she would make such a generous offer. Your parents have been wonderful, but they will need help when…when things…are not so good…so I am very happy to accept my sister's offer to help. Should I call her to thank her?"

"No, Pete, there is no need to call her. She and Ron and Ari will be coming to our house in the morning, and you can call her then."

Chapter 68

Dr. Clinton stood outside Peter's isolation room and spoke with Niki, "We will start the ATRA treatment in about thirty minutes, Niki. He's not going to feel very well about an hour into the infusion, just so you'll know, but we have medications that will take the edge off of his discomfort."

She nodded, "I'm going to 'dress out' with the gown and mask, and such, and I'll stay with Pete until the infusion is finished. I've asked a nurse, Susan Anderson, to do private duty when I'm not here. Susan has previously worked private duty for one of my patients, and she does an excellent job. Pete is well-acquainted with her, too. She will be coming in for the evening shift while I go home to have dinner with our sons. But…Dr. Clinton, Peter will have more than "discomfort" won't he? I've been doing some research, and the ATRA treatment is quite tough on patients."

Dr. Clinton, having been chastised by his colleague, said quietly, "Yes, Niki, he's going to have more than just discomfort, and I apologize for minimizing the effects of the treatment. But you have to know that it is his one best chance with this subtype of acute myelocytic leukemia. Promyelocytic leukemia, in spite of the published cure rates, is a very serious disease."

"I know, Dr. Clinton," Niki answered in a small voice.

"We will use a PIC line today, you know, a peripherally inserted catheter, to deliver the treatment. In the morning, Dr. McLaughlin, our cardiovascular surgeon, will insert a port in the right subclavian vein for better, and certainly less painful, instillation of the medication. Do you have any other questions, Niki?"

She didn't answer him immediately, because she was trying to absorb and accept what he had just told her that they were going to do to Pete in the morning. Niki wanted to cry out in dismay, but controlled herself. She knew that inserting a port in the subclavian vein was going to be very painful for Pete.

Finally, she stammered, "Uh...no, I don't, no...I have no more questions right now Dr. Clinton. Thanks for all that you are doing for Pete."

In the anteroom to Peter's reverse isolation room, Niki quickly put on a gown, mask, headcovering, shoecovering, and gloves. When she entered the inner room, the air pressurization and equalization sounded like the entry into a space ship.

Peter looked up from his bed, "Is that you, Niki? Ah, yes, I can see your beautiful dark eyes."

"It's me...how are you doing?" She reached for his hand with her gloved hand.

"Any moment, I think, a nurse will be coming in to start what the admissions nurse called a catheter. Why do they want to put a catheter in me, Niki?"

"Oh, Pete...it's not *that* kind of catheter. They are going to start an intravenous line, and those are called catheters, too."

Peter felt greatly relieved to know that he wouldn't have a urinary catheter. He remembered that one had been inserted when he had surgery for his appendix and hernia a long time ago…in 1986…when Niki had been so kind and wonderful to him when he was ill. He truly did not want to have another urinary catheter ever again, and the admissions nurse had inadvertently scared him at the mere mention of the word, catheter.

They both heard the 'swishhh' of the outer door, and then the inner door to Peter's room, as someone dressed the same way that Niki was, came into the room.

"Hello, Mr. and Mrs. Genchenko, I'm Su-Lin Wi, and I am going to start Mr. Genchenko's PIC line. I'll also do the actual administration of the chemo, too."

"You don't have to call me Mr. Genchenko. You can just call me Pete. However, my wife is a medical doctor, and you may wish to call her Dr. Genchenko."

Su-Lin was startled at first, and then began to apologize, "Please accept my apology, Dr. Genchenko…I had no idea…"

"Don't worry about it, Su-Lin. You can call me Niki, or "Pete's wife," or something like that. Pete and I are easy to get along with."

"Have you ever watched a PIC line insertion Dr…uh…Niki? If not, I'll show you how we do it here at I.U. Med Center."

Peter watched his wife and this young nurse interacting, and understood that Niki would always make absolutely sure that things would not get out of hand. How many times had he prayed today…six…seven? He couldn't remember, but he realized that this PIC line thing might need another prayer, or two, and he immediately thanked God that Niki was here with him while the nurse put the line in.

Su-Lin proved to be very adept at placing a PIC line, and within fifteen minutes, Peter's chemotherapy infusion was underway. He closed his eyes for several moments, retreating inside himself, as the fluid entered his body. He didn't know what to expect. Would he feel pain in his arm or in his chest? Even though he and Niki had talked about what his treatment would be like, Peter still felt a certain amount of uncertainty. Give me a 'chippy' or a 'policeman' hockey player on the ice, thought Peter. I can take high-sticking or boarding when I'm on the ice during a game. But this chemotherapy is delving into the unknown. Nonetheless, I can't let Niki see that I am frightened.

Niki observed that Dr. Clinton was right about the 'discomfort' that Pete would feel about an hour into his infusion. She saw Pete's brows knit, and his hands tighten into fists. He said not a word, and continued to keep his eyes closed, but Niki knew that Pete was in pain. If only I could help him. I'm just a bystander, if I can't think of something to help him…but *I don't know what to do!*

Peter concentrated on good memories as the pain of the chemotherapy infusion became almost unbearable. He had many memories to think about with Niki and his sons…there was the reunion when Niki had come to Russia to rescue Katya and him, and the unforgettable rush of love as he held his son, Nicholas, for the first time. He relived their wedding…Niki actually had accepted his proposal…and it was a perfect day. And the feelings that had run through him as he helped Niki through her labor with Josef…he loved her even more after that experience, and he had a second son to love and cherish. He thought of his sister…and of course, their mother…but he couldn't resurrect any good memories of his father. No, there were no happy memories there. But he smiled for a moment when he thought about his friend, Misha, when they were young and in secondary school. My good friend, Misha...perhaps we will meet again sooner than I knew? And with the thoughts of his dead friend, Misha, Peter wondered if they would see each other in the afterlife? He hadn't really thought of death in terms of heaven and hell. Nevertheless, he hoped that Misha would be there to greet him in heaven, if their lives were worthy of a heavenly reward. And there were so many wonderful memories of Niki...their first meeting, and the slow realization over the short time that he had been in Indianapolis with her, that he was in love with her. Our dance on the night of the awards banquet...that was when I knew for certain that I loved her. He smiled at the thought of how beautiful she looked, and how wonderful it felt to hold her in his arms.

Niki sat a few feet from Peter and watched the outward signs of emotion on his face. It amazed her when she saw him smile, yes, smile, a few times. She wanted to reach out to touch his hand, but knew that any form of stimulation would only cause him more pain. If I only had some way of comforting him, she thought, but there was nothing, really, that she could do. Inside...her heart was crying out to him...but outwardly, she had to sit by while Pete was suffering, and she didn't know if she could bear it.

Su-Lin came in to check on the progress of Peter's infusion at least every ten to fifteen minutes. She was very quiet, and did not attempt to engage Niki in any conversation. When she came in to terminate the chemotherapy infusion, she spoke to Niki in the softest of whispers, and beckoned her to come out into the anteroom.

"Your husband has come through his first treatment very well, Dr. Genchenko. Ordinarily, patients present outward signs that they are having difficulty, but Peter doesn't follow that pattern. Some of my patients are made of 'sterner stuff' which seems to be the case with Peter. He is going to be sleeping now, since I discontinued his infusion. One of the things that we do is flush the line and then add a light sedative that also acts as an anti-emetic; just as a precaution against nausea and vomiting."

Niki nodded, "Thank you, Su-Lin. You have been wonderful, and I know that Peter will tell you the same thing when he is able to."

Su-Lin's eyes were smiling, even though Niki couldn't see the rest of her face because of her mask.

"Has Dr. Clinton told you that a private duty nurse, Susan Anderson, will be staying with Pete on the second shift? She will be doing private duty from now until he is discharged." Niki was trying to make sure that everything would be all right for Pete.

"Yes, he has, and I have had excellent experiences with Susan. She is one top-notch nurse, but I am sure that you already know that." Su-Lin nodded her head as she spoke.

"That is good to hear, Su-Lin." Niki looked at her watch, "I'm going to have to hurry to have supper with our sons tonight. I told Pete that I would come back this evening around ten o'clock. Will his sedative have worn off by then?"

"Let's see...it's five-fifteen now, and Peter will start to wake up in two or three hours...so he should be wide awake when you get back."

Niki looked at the closed door to Peter's room, "I feel as if I should kiss Pete goodbye. Would you please tell him, when he wakes up, that I will come back to see him? I don't want him to worry..." her voice trailed off.

Su-Lin smiled, "I understand how you feel. So many of my patients' families feel guilty when they have to leave a loved one in order to meet their obligations to other family members."

"Yes…and I won't be able to kiss him for a while…at least not while he's on chemo, and it seems so strange."

Niki hurried home to her sons. Her heart, no, her very soul was in turmoil, as she tried to think of a way to tell her sons that their father was in the hospital. As young as they were, would they understand what was happening, and if so, would they be frightened as much as she was? I have to protect them from the worst, but I need to be able to explain things…I don't want them to feel abandoned.

The house was a busy, noisy place when she came in through the kitchen door from the garage. Katya, Ron, and Ari were already there in the great room, Niki saw, and Nicholas and Josef were raptly listening to a book that Katya was reading to them. Marina and Klaus had dinner preparations well under way.

When Marina saw her daughter, she quickly came to her and put her arms around her. Neither said a word; none was needed. Klaus came to them and put his arms around his wife and daughter.

"Mat…Mom…is Papa with you?" Nicholas came hurrying into the kitchen when he saw his mother.

Ron followed Nicholas and bent down to gently touch his shoulders with his fingertips. "The boys have been asking about you and Pete, Niki."

She nodded, "I know how they are when Pete is on the road playing hockey…" I can't cry. No, I can't let Nicholas see me cry. And she managed a smile for her son.

Katya joined the rest of the family, Ari in her arms and Josef toddling at her side, "Right after we arrived and got settled, Niki, we have been enjoying the books this evening. Your boys picked out their favorites, and Ron and I have been taking turns reading to them." Her eyes searched Niki's, but she didn't ask any questions.

Niki did her best to smile as she reached down and picked up Josef, "Let's all have a nice dinner together, and then we can sit down and I'll tell you about Pete."

Peter awakened slowly, as if he were floating up out of a deep chasm. He looked around the hospital room, his eyes searching for Niki, but she wasn't there. His gaze came to rest on a nurse, in full isolation garb, sitting in a chair near the door.

"Hello," he said quietly.

"You're awake…and hello to you," replied Susan Anderson.

Peter hesitated for a moment and asked, "Are you Susan?"

"I am, and I will be here with you on the second shift every evening as long as you are here in the hospital. How are you feeling?"

Not so good, thought Peter, but he answered, "As well as can be expected, I think. Niki, my wife, told me that Dr. Clinton said that I would have "some discomfort," but that was a bit of an understatement."

"True…I should say, very true, and I don't understand why most doctors say that when they are explaining chemotherapy treatment. Sometimes, I think that they don't want to unduly frighten their patients. But after the first round of chemo, the patients always know the score."

The anteroom outer door 'swishhhed' as someone entered, and within a few minutes, Niki came into Peter's room. "You're awake…that's great. You were snoozing pretty well when I went home to have dinner with the boys. Everyone was there; Katya, Ron and Ari,

467

and my parents, too, so we ate at the big dining table." She turned to Susan, "Hello, and thanks for coming on such short notice. I…we…feel very fortunate to have you."

"I'm glad to be here. Peter has been sleeping for most of my shift, and just woke up completely a few minutes ago."

Niki went to Peter's bedside, "Would you like something to eat, now, Pete? Are you hungry at all?"

"I'm more thirsty than hungry, Niki. Maybe I could have something cold to drink? My throat is a little dry."

"Dr. Clinton wrote, 'diet as tolerated' in his orders, but I want to get a clarification. You two can visit while I go check the chart and order something to eat for Peter. Is there anything special that you like…maybe a shake? You could use the calories." Susan wanted to make sure that her patient got some form of good nutrition.

"I like malted milk shakes, Susan. Do you think that the kitchen has something like that?"

"I'll do my best, Peter," and Susan hurried out the door.

Niki pulled a chair up close to Peter's bed, and began telling him how her talk with the boys, and the rest of the family, too, had gone. "The boys took it well, but they're so young, Pete, that I don't know how much they understood. Of course, Nicholas had lots of questions, and I answered them in such a way as to minimize what is happening right now. I didn't want to be untruthful, but I didn't want to scare him, either."

"And what about Katya and Ron? Were you able to talk to them after the children were in bed?"

Niki nodded, "I did, Pete, and they understand the…" she hesitated briefly, "gravity of your situation. Ron was explaining things to Katya

468

as we talked, and she realizes what the next few weeks and months will be like. They both assured me that they are going to stay with our boys for as long as it takes to get you healthy again."

Peter reached and took Niki's latex-gloved hand in his, "I truly wish that everyones' lives weren't being turned upside down over this," he stopped for a moment and then continued, "situation of mine."

"Hush, Pete…you are loved very much by your family, and we are all in this together."

Chapter 69

Two weeks into his treatment, Peter's hair started to fall out. His hair had always been thick and unruly, so this new development caused him some consternation. Am I just vain, he wondered? But the clumps of hair lying on his pillow seemed to be harbingers of what was to come. He wasn't sure how much weight he had lost, but he knew it to be considerable, because he had no appetite, and felt nauseous much of the time.

Just when he thought he could rest, someone from the laboratory, the nursing staff, or the epidemiology staff, would come in to draw blood or take a urine sample, or ask him how much he ate during a meal, or whether he had a bowel movement, or to check on whether the 'reverse isolation' air flow was working properly. It seemed as though there was a constant stream of people coming through his room.

He cherished Niki's visits, and was so grateful that she was with him when the subclavian port was put in place. It wasn't as painful as the bone marrow aspiration and biopsy, but it was close, he thought. She had even assisted the surgeon who did the placement, and Peter trusted her completely to make sure that everything would go well.

Dr. Clinton came in at least once, and most often twice, a day to update Peter on his progress. He even altered his schedule to meet

Niki's, when he could, as he felt that she deserved to be with her husband when they discussed Peter's treatment.

"Right now, according to your most current blood work, Peter, there has been…no change." The doctor's face was a study in consternation. "We have other options, certainly, but let's give this treatment another week. Niki, what do you think?"

Niki was silent for several moments, digesting the "no change" words from Dr. Clinton. "I agree that we should continue with what we have for another week…but can you tell us what needs to be done if there is still no change after another seven days?"

It was Dr. Clinton's turn to ruminate, and then he said, "We need to consider the possibility of a bone marrow transplant if we aren't seeing any progress with the ATRA treatment."

All that Peter could see of Niki's face were her eyes, and he again saw the look of fear in them. He fervently wished that he would never see that look in her eyes again, but he had no ability to prevent it. He was now having daily nosebleeds, and he knew that time was running out for him.

"I'm going to suggest that you go so far as to ask Peter's closest relatives to undergo Human Leucocyte Antigen, you know, HLA testing and typing in order to find a suitable donor in preparation for a bone marrow transplant. If this next week on the ATRA doesn't bring the desired results, we need to be more aggressive." Dr. Clinton's voice trailed off.

That same night, long after Niki had left, and Susan was on duty, Peter lay in his bed trying to think of some way to soften the blow to Niki regarding his failure to respond to his chemotherapy treatment. Susan was in and out of his room several times, and when she came in to say goodnight at the end of her shift, she seemed to be rather subdued. Peter wondered what might have happened to cause her to be that way? But he was too weak, too fatigued, too sad, to invest any energy in worrying about it.

I didn't tell him, thought Niki, as she drove home by the quickest route she knew. It's after nine o'clock, and I wanted to see my boys before they got into bed, but they're sound asleep, now. She was too tired to think clearly, and had been so most of the day. I know what's wrong with me, but how am I going to tell Pete? He has enough to worry about right now. What sort of future, if any, do we have? What right have I to have been so selfish?

Peter lay on his side in his hospital bed, peering out at the night sky through the tall and narrow window in his room. Well, it's actually early morning, thought Peter, very early morning. He craned his neck to see the clock behind him. It's two o'clock. The sky looks cold and forbidding, and yet it is beautiful, too. The moon makes the snowflakes sparkle as they fall from the sky. This observation sparked a memory in Peter. The first time that I kissed Niki was on a night like this. It warmed his heart to think of it, as he continued to look out of the narrow window. But then he thought, this is the time when I feel most lonely. If I could only hold Niki in my arms again… His need was a physical ache that had nothing to do with his illness.

"Mom, Dad, I'm going straight upstairs, take a shower, and crawl into bed. I'll kiss the boys before I turn in, and I'm not going to have any trouble falling asleep." Niki felt close to exhaustion.

"Katya and Ron said to tell you goodnight, Niki," Marina said. "Can I help you with anything? Are you hungry? You know that you must eat, too, so that you can be strong for your boys."

Niki didn't take exception to her mother's words; she was too tired, "I know, Mom."

Klaus cleared his throat, "Mike called earlier, Niki, and we told him that there wasn't anything new to report. He's going to call again on Saturday."

Mike...Mikey...my big brother, she thought, and for some unknown reason, tears filled her eyes. I wish that my big brother could be here with me. "I hope that I'll be here when he calls."

"I told him that you usually have dinner with Nicholas and Josef, so he said that he would call around seven, or so." Klaus's voice was gentle as he spoke to his daughter.

She nodded, "That's a good time, I think. Well, goodnight," Niki kissed her mother's cheek and hugged her father for a moment, and then started slowly up the stairs.

The shower must have awakened me, thought Niki. She was lying in bed, and had been tossing and turning since she got in and pulled up the covers. Pete's not here with me...how can I sleep without Pete by my side? The clock on the bedside table showed one-fifteen in bright green numbers. She threw back the covers. Enough...I've had enough. She got up and started dressing.

Peter heard the 'swishhh' of the anteroom door, and expected one of the nurses to come in for whatever task she, or he, had to do. Instead, a few moments later, as he heard the hissing change of air pressure as the door opened into his room, a familiar fragrance wafted toward him...*Niki*...is it Niki?

"Pete?" She felt uncertain as she came into the room, dressed in isolation garb.

"Niki, God does answer prayers! I was looking out of the window

473

just now at the moon and the snow falling and glistening in its light. It reminded me of the first time that I kissed you. Do you remember that night?"

"Yes...how could I ever forget it?"

He reached his hand out to her, pulled back his covers with the other, and patted the bed, "Come here, Niki."

She lay down in front of him, and he curled up behind her, as he pulled the covers over both of them. He slipped one arm under, and the other around her in spite of the gown, gloves, and mask that separated them.

He gently kissed the nape of her neck as he held her, and murmured, "Niki, my sweet, beautiful Niki..." The longing, the aching, the sadness inside him melted away as he held her close.

"I have something to tell you, Pete, and I should have told you sooner, but I didn't want to worry you. Remember when I said that it would be nice to have another baby after Katya had Ari?"

Peter said slowly, "Yes, I do, but..."

"I went to see Dr. Leonard last week, and he told me...he told me...that I'm pregnant. I wanted to tell you, but there never seemed to be a right time with everything else that's been going on."

With his arms around her waist, Peter placed one hand gently over her abdomen and Niki put her hand over his. They lay there quietly for several moments, and it was Peter who spoke first.

"You and I...we...are amazing, aren't we, Niki? Another little one; how wonderful! This is just what I needed to hear to pull me up and out of the depths of my self-pity."

Celia Jackson, a young registered nurse who had stayed on the hematology/oncology unit much longer than anyone could have predicted, given the difficulty of treating cancer patients, looked up when the resident physician on nights approached the nurses' station. Celia was the youngest child in her family, and the first to attend college. Although most of her colleagues didn't know that she graduated first in her nursing program with the highest grade point average her instructors had seen in a decade…not bad for a black child from the wrong side of the tracks…they nonetheless respected her for her good judgement and the excellent care that she provided to her patients.

"Hello, Dr. Beams, what can I do for you?"

"Uh…let's see, I need the chart for," he hesitated as he looked at his notes, "Genchenko, Peter Genchenko. I'm supposed to check on him."

Celia's heart constricted when Dr. Beams mentioned Peter Genchenko. She had seen his wife, Dr. Genchenko, go into his room a few minutes ago.

"Dr. Beams, would it be possible for you to do some of your other rounds before you see Mr. Genchenko?"

"No, it would not," the young, and very tired, resident replied. "Please pull his chart for me."

Reluctantly, Celia handed Peter's chart to the doctor, knowing that Dr. Beams could be a 'pain' when he wanted to.

However, after thinking it over for a few moments, she decided that it didn't matter if he was irritated with her. The Genchenkos needed to be alone right now. She had seen her patient's heart rate and respirations rise quickly on the monitor in the nurses' station, and although she didn't know exactly what had caused the rise, she observed that his vital signs had now begun to return to baseline. It had made her chuckle, even though Peter was in protective isolation. They must love each other very much.

With these thoughts in mind, she left the nurses' station and ran to catch up with Dr. Beams, who was striding rapidly down the hall.

When she caught up with him, she got in front of him and turned around to face him, "Dr. Beams, Mrs. Genchenko, *Dr. Genchenko,* is with her husband right now, and they deserve to have their privacy."

"What are you talking about?" Dr. Beams was all set to be cross with this nurse.

"They got some bad news today, and they need time to talk it over. Their lives have been turned upside down, and they must be feeling very sad right now. Please, Dr. Beams, just come back later…let them have some privacy."

Dr. Beams frowned, but he replied, "Okay, I'll just come back before I leave my shift. How does that suit you?"

Celia's bright smile rewarded him, "That's so kind of you, Dr. Beams, and I thank you."

This night was a turning point for Peter, and for Niki, too. Each had seemed on the edge of endurance, but now, with baby number three on the way, there was another wonderful reason for Peter to continue fighting his illness, and Niki was fighting the battle with him, every inch of the way.

After Niki left his room, Peter thought about his life, and how so many things that had happened to him seemed random…even his coming to the U.S. in 1986 seemed somehow accidental. But he could not deny that meeting Niki, and falling in love with her, was the best thing that had ever happened to him. The most incredible thing, then, was the revelation that she loved him, too. I am blessed, so blessed in so many ways…Niki and I have two wonderful sons, and having Katya here with us…and now she is a wife and mother. A few short years ago, I could not have dreamed of such a life.

He decided that when he was able, he would finish his degree in engineering at Purdue. I want to build buildings, and leave a positive legacy for my sons. Hockey has been good to me, but it is not a life's vocation. Niki and I are a good team, and together, we can do something far greater than I can, alone.

He was now happy on this cold, early morning after holding his wife in his arms for the first time in several weeks. He was smiling as he fell asleep, happy in the knowledge that he was going to be a father for the third time. I wonder what we will have…another boy…or a girl, perhaps? I have so much to live for…

Niki came home before her family got up to start their day, and she showered, dressed, and went downstairs to have a cup of tea…Gray's English tea, decaffeinated of course, with lemon and honey in it. She needed something to keep her awake, but decided that she should avoid caffeine altogether because of the baby.

Before long, she heard one, and then another, alarm clock begin to 'sound off.' The shower in the upstairs guest bedroom started up, and in spite of her tiredness, Niki smiled. *Another new day is here, and maybe it will be better than the last.*

Ron came hurrying down the stairs about twenty minutes after she first heard the shower, and came into the kitchen. "How are you doing, Nik?" Without thinking, he called her by the name that she had used when he first met her.

She smiled a tired smile, "Okay, I guess, and Pete's doing just 'so-so'. Dr. Clinton said that we are going to have to look at bone marrow transplant as the fall-back plan. Pete's lab numbers aren't changing quickly enough to suit Dr. Clinton, so he wants to progress to the next level of treatment for him."

His still-wet hair, dark and curly, gave Ron a 'little boy' look that he hadn't seemed to outgrow, and his bright blue eyes, earnest, yet penetrating, added to the look. "A bone marrow transplant...? Is Pete already listed with IOPO, the Indiana Organ Procurement Organization?"

"I know what IOPO means, Ron," Niki laughed gently, "and yes, he's listed, but he's also at the bottom of the list...and you and I both know how slowly that whole transplant list moves."

Ron sat down next to Niki at the kitchen bar, "Well, the next step is to get all of our families tested, don't you think?"

Niki bowed her head to hide the tears that had come to her eyes, "It seems like the right thing to do, but I'm not sure that Pete would ever allow his boys, or Katya, for that matter, to suffer the agony of providing enough bone marrow to help him. He's very protective of his family, Ron."

Ron's usually smooth brow furrowed, "I know...but if it's the only alternative..." He didn't finish the sentence, and it hung in the air like a verdict for the hangman.

"You and I both know only too well as physicians, Ron, what Pete is up against. But the final decision for any treatment will rest with him, no matter what."

The telephone rang, and Niki jumped as if she had received an electric shock. *Pete...has something happened to Pete?*

"Hello?" She was shaking so hard that she had to use both hands to hold the receiver. "Oh, Marty," she said, relief evident in her voice..."Pete's doing okay right now...how did you hear about his illness?"

"The Pittsburgh Post-Gazette, and the Pittsburgh Tribune-Review believe it or not, have front page articles about Pete this morning." Marty's voice held concern for his friend. "The articles say he has leukemia."

"Are you serious? Why would they print such a story?" Niki wasn't ready to discuss Pete's health issues.

"I don't know, but Peter has lots of friends, Niki, and everyone's been wondering why he up and quit the PB's at the end of a great hockey season, and after winning the Stanley Cup. There aren't too many MVP's who quit hockey after winning the Stanley Cup, Niki. So, now we know…well, at least I can say that *I* understand why he quit the team."

"He did the best that he could, Marty, and both of us, but especially Pete, are very grateful to you for helping him to get a chance to play professional hockey. And Marty…Pete didn't tell me right away that he wasn't feeling good, and when I found out, I took him to the best hematology/oncology doctor in the country, so Pete's chances are much better than they might have been if we hadn't acted quickly."

"I talked to Sheldon this morning, and he's going to be in Indy next week. Is there any chance that he might get to see Pete?"

"Pete's in reverse, uh…protective isolation, Marty, because of his weakened immune system, so he can't have visitors right now. But I will keep you and Sheldon well-informed on his progress. And Marty, if you can consider being a bone marrow donor, or anyone else you know…it would help Pete greatly."

"You've got it Niki! I'll spread the word, so that maybe someone will be able to help Pete. I'm going to call the PB's, too. Who knows…maybe someone on the team can help?"

"Thanks, Marty…thanks from the bottom of my heart." She hung up the phone slowly and bowed her head for a moment.

Ron saw how pale his sister-in-law was, and asked, "Nik, do you think that maybe you should go lie down?"

Niki shook her head, "Not right now, Ron. There are so many things that I need to do."

"I wasn't eavesdropping, Nik, but I couldn't help hearing about the bone marrow transplant donors for Pete that you talked to Marty about. I want you to know, right now, that Katya and I, and even Ari, will be tested as soon as you tell us when and where."

"Ron…you need to talk with Katya about the donor testing. I can't ask you to do this."

"You haven't asked me, Nik. I volunteered, and I'll talk to Katya about it, too. You know that she won't hesitate one moment if it means that she can help her brother."

All that Niki could reply was, "We would be so grateful, Ron…"

Katya came downstairs with a noisy and hungry Ari in one arm, and Josef holding her hand, "Good morning," but her attempt at cheeriness didn't lift Niki's spirits.

Niki gave the early risers a reasonable facsimile of a smile, and reached down to pick up Josef, who immediately threw his arms around her neck. "Where is Nicholas?"

"Oh, he's been a sleepy-head lately, and I've been having to coax him out of bed in the morning. It's all right, though, Niki, because it is still very early, and he doesn't have to leave for school for more than an hour." Katya was smiling as she filled Niki in on Nicholas.

"I've been taking Nicholas to school in the morning, Nik, and he's been very prompt when I call him to get in the car." Ron rubbed Josef's head and then Ari's as he grinned at one, and then the other.

"You have both been wonderful in helping Pete and me, and my parents. I was concerned that the boys were getting to be too much for them, but I didn't want to cause any stress for you two, or little Ari, either."

Katya put her free arm around Niki, "We are here to stay until you tell us to leave, Niki, and even then, we might not go so easily." With this pronouncement, Katya laughed softly.

Ron laughed, too, "My wife is a gentle soul, Nik, but she has a backbone of steel. Let us help as much, and as long as we can. We're glad to be able to do so."

Chapter 70

Niki helped Katya dress the three boys, and fed everyone a good breakfast, thanks to Marina and Klaus. They brought a delicious egg casserole with them when they arrived, and the boys gobbled it up. Ron took Nicholas to school while Niki drove downtown to their sports medicine clinic.

Niki was able to spend three uninterrupted hours working with her patients in the clinic that she and Ron now owned together. Unbelievably, she felt a sense of renewal and fulfillment working with the athletes. For these few hours, as she was intently involved in injuries, treatments, and management of rehabilitation; she was a doctor again. And her patients were making good progress, too, thanks to Stephanie's pinch-hitting when Niki couldn't be in the clinic. And the fact that her patients were doing well was the best feeling of all from her perspective as a doctor.

At three o'clock, Niki wrapped up for the day. She peeked in on Ron to tell him that she was heading out to see Pete, and she reminded him that her next work day would be on Friday, from nine to twelve. "Oh, and remember, Mom and Dad are bringing Nicholas home from school."

"Okay, Nik." He paused for a moment, "I'm going to talk to Katya tonight about the donor process for Pete. If Dr. Clinton gives you any information for that, will you share it with me ASAP? It takes time, as you know, to do the typing and cross-matching for organ donations. Oh, and I'll see you tonight at suppertime"

Despite her tiredness, Niki gave Ron a radiant smile, "I will share everything from Dr. Clinton with you, Ron, because you and I both know that there is no time to waste. And, again, thank you from the bottom of my heart…see you at supper."

Peter was happy, very happy, to see his wife. The day had seemed endlessly long until she came into his room. She lit up the room, somehow, every time that she visited. He wished that he could see her smile, but understood the necessity for the mask. Their shared secret, baby number three, warmed his heart, and gave him an even greater reason to fight for his life.

He was delighted when she sat down on the edge of his bed, where she had been only a few hours before. "Welcome back," he said, and reached for her gloved hand.

"Thank you, Pete," she smiled, because he could see it in her eyes. "I'm the bearer of good news…there are several people who want to have HLA testing and typing to find out whether they might be donors for you. Ron and Katya, of course…and Marty Pelham, who is going to tell Sheldon Levin about it…and so on. And Marty is going to let the PB's know that they can be tested, too, if they want to."

It was Peter's turn to smile, but he smiled through tears, "That's wonderful, a wonderful thing for Marty to do, Niki. But I must tell you that I don't want our sons, or little Ari, to be tested. I don't think that I could stand by and let the little ones in our family make such a sacrifice. It is too painful…and I just couldn't live with the knowledge that our children, or our nephew, might suffer because of me."

Niki didn't say anything for several moments, and then slowly began to speak, "Pete, I understand what you are saying, but time is not on our side. Dr. Clinton knows it for certain. Even Susan Anderson knows…I spoke to her outside in the hall when I was coming in, and Dr. Clinton told her yesterday that the ATRA wasn't working."

"Maybe that's why she was so quiet when she left last night? She was subdued, sort of sad, when she came in to say goodnight to me." Peter rubbed his forehead for a moment.

"You're probably right, Pete. She said that she wants to be tested, too." Niki looked at her husband and saw him shake his head.

"Why would she want to do that, Niki? She certainly knows what she would be in for…"

"Yes, she does, Pete. She knows only too well what to expect. But you must know that everyone who knows you wants to help you."

He shook his head again, "Why, Niki, I don't understand why?"

"You are loved by many people, Pete, because of who and what you are. Do you remember when I first told you how special you are to me?"

"It seems almost like a lifetime…" and Peter bowed his head.

"Even Chief Inspector Marc Terenoff, who had several reasons to dislike you, admired you greatly.

Peter sat on the edge of his bed after Niki left. He still had a difficult time understanding the outpouring of concern and kindness, and the offers of being checked for tissue matching in order to give him a new chance at life. Niki's news was wonderful to him. It gave him more hope than he had even a month ago. Is it possible that I will survive this terrible thing? Hope rose in his chest, and the cold place there began to melt again.

Niki got home early enough to have dinner with the family, and she gave them an update on Pete, "He's much more hopeful today. When I told him how many people have told me that they wanted to be tested to see if they were a match, he was overwhelmed,"

Nicholas had a serious look on his face, "What is a 'match,' Mat?"

His curiosity made his mother smile, "Well, Nicholas, when people are related, they usually have the same kind of…blood. And that is a good thing. In fact, some relatives have exactly the same kind of blood; especially twins." Niki looked over at Katya, who smiled at her.

"When can we start the HLA testing, Niki?" Ron was always proactive, and ready to get started on a task.

"In the morning, I'll talk to Reid Harmon, the Laboratory Director at I.U. Med Center, and he can set up the testing procedure once he gets the names and histories of those coming in to be tested."

Klaus wanted to know, "What can your mother and I do? Are we going to be considered for testing at our age? Both of us are ready to go, and all we want to know is when and where."

"Yes, we are, Niki." Marina emphatically agreed with Klaus.

For a moment, Niki was overwhelmed with emotion, and then began to speak again, "If all goes well in the morning, we can start the process in the afternoon; one or two o'clock is my guess. I'll call you to let you know where to go."

Bedtime couldn't come too soon for Niki, but she insisted on doing her boys' baths, and getting them into their pajamas. She allowed each to pick a book for bedtime reading, and sat in the large old rocking chair, a son on each side of her, and read their books to them. It was important to her to keep to their schedule as much as possible. When it came time to put them in bed, Niki gave each of them two kisses.

"One kiss from Papa, and one from Mat," she said as she kissed and hugged Josef and Nicholas.

Having already said goodnight to little Ari and the rest of her family before she came upstairs with her sons, Niki got into the shower and scrubbed her body from head to toe. She quickly dried off and got into her softest, most comfortable nightgown. Her last thought was of Pete, and she said a prayer for him, for their sons, and for the new little life inside her that she and Pete had created.

Chapter 71

Reid Harmon was very helpful, and spoke rapidly in a nasal and staccato voice, "You can tell your family to start coming in today at two o'clock, Dr. Genchenko, and we will get started on the HLA typing. Dr. Clinton has already given me a standing order for the blood work. He came in around seven this morning. I honestly think that he doesn't need as much sleep as the rest of us, because I see him here at all hours. I work a modified swing shift as Director, so that I can be here on different shifts, and I have seen Dr. Clinton on every shift, no kidding."

"I know that he takes his practice seriously, Reid…and by the way, I've told you many times that you can call me Niki."

"Oh, I know, but I still feel that I should be more formal with the physicians I work with." Reid smiled at Dr. Genchenko.

"Thanks, Reid. I'll call my family right now, so that they can start coming in." Niki hurried off to see Pete to fill him in on the latest developments.

Although he felt weak, and had no desire to speak with his university adviser, Peter decided to call the professor to tell him what was going on in regard to his health. Three weeks ago…was it only three weeks?…Peter had called Professor Merrill to let him know his situation. Peter was surprised when the professor was very accommodating, because he had not expected it.

At the time, Professor Merrill had told him, "Pete…take as much time as you need. You're already almost a semester ahead of your other classmates, especially so with your projects, so don't worry that you might fall behind. And please let me know if I can be of any help."

Peter keyed in Professor Merrill's telephone number and got an answering machine. After the message, Peter left his own, "Hello, Dr. Merrill, this is Peter Genchenko. I just wanted to follow up with you on our last conversation. I'm still in the hospital, but I'm doing all right. The reason for my call today is to ask you for the next two assignments for the class. I have a lot of time on my hands, and it would help me if you could send some work to me. Thank you, and I hope to hear from you soon. You can call my home telephone number and leave a message with my wife or one of my family members regarding my request."

"Hello, my sweet Pete," Niki spoke as she came 'swishhhhing' through the air lock into Peter's room.

"Niki…how are you feeling?" He was very glad to see her.

"Unbelievably great Pete; the baby is cooperating, at least for now, and there's no morning sickness. But, I have so many other things to tell you, Pete…where shall I start?" She actually laughed aloud.

He reached for her hand, inviting her to sit on his bed. "Just start at the beginning, Niki." He was pleased when he heard her laugh. He hadn't heard her laugh like that in a very long time. "Just a few minutes ago, I talked with the Lab Director, Reid Harmon, and he has set up a testing program for those who want to be donors for you, Pete. It starts today at two o'clock."

"Things are moving quickly, then?" Peter felt a rush of hope as Niki told him about the lab testing.

"Yes, they are. I called Dad, and he is putting the word out. He and Mom are coming in today, along with Ron and Katya. I have been in touch with Marty Pelham, who, in turn, will notify your teammates about the donor testing. And here's another wonderful surprise, Pete; the Priest at our church spoke on your behalf on Sunday, and asked if there might be some of the parishioners who would consider the testing in preparation for donor status. Mom has a list of over two hundred people who want to be tested!"

"Niki…you mean…that all of these people are being tested because of me?" Peter was astounded.

She nodded her head emphatically, "*All of them, Pete.* But here's the most wonderful aspect of this," she struggled to find the words, "outpouring of generosity. Every one of them will now be in the IOPO transplant data base, which will help others, too. That's the other amazing thing about what is happening."

Peter sat up on the side of the bed, feet dangling, and his wife put her arms around him. Neither spoke for several moments; they just clung to one another. Finally, Peter put his fingers under Niki's masked chin, and smiled at her.

"If you weren't wearing that mask, I'd give you a kiss that you'd never forget, my dear wife."

"All of our kisses have been memorable, Pete. I hold them all right here," and she placed a hand over her heart.

"And so do I, Niki," Peter replied softly as he placed a hand over his heart.

Niki lay her head in his lap, and he patted her shoulder. He wanted to stroke her hair, but the headcovering prevented it.

"I have some news of my own, Niki. I just left a message for Dr. Merrill, my advisor in the engineering program. I told him that I'd like to work on some lessons and/or projects while I recuperate. I can't just sit here doing nothing, Niki. If I had something outside of my present situation to concentrate on, I'd have less time to worry about everything. Right now, I lie awake at night and worry about you and our sons…and the baby, and I wonder what will happen…?" Peter didn't finish the sentence.

Now I've done it, thought Peter, as he watched Niki's eyes fill with tears. "I'm sorry, Niki. I didn't mean to tell you about my worrying. You have enough to worry about without me reminding you. Please forgive me." He put his hand at the side of her masked face and caressed her cheek.

She put a gloved hand to hold his hand against her cheek, "I have the very same worries, Pete. And that's what brought me here in the middle of the night last week."

Peter bowed his head, "Ah, yes, your early morning visit…how lovely, how truly lovely it was. And your "third baby" announcement was absolutely amazing. How could we ever top such a night?"

Chapter 72

Although there were more than two hundred potential donors tested, a perfect match had not been found for Peter after two weeks of testing. Peter's best hope was that Katya would be the perfect match, but she only had two of the four HLA markers to match Peter's. When Ron's typing showed a two in four marker match, it surprised Peter, but he didn't dwell on it.

Of course, Niki's testing showed only a one in four match, which wasn't what she had hoped for. There had been no testing of the children, at Peter's request, and he stubbornly held to his feelings on the subject.

Peter was getting weaker, and Niki could see it every time that she went to be with him. She saw that he was diligent with his engineering assignments, and received excellent marks from his professor, but she feared that he was expending far too much energy on things…that might never get finished. She had to begin thinking in this way. She didn't want to, never wanted to, see this terrible thing take over Pete's life, but as the days passed without a glimmer of hope for a match for Peter's bone marrow, it seemed almost inevitable now. Her heart was slowly breaking into little pieces.

Peter rubbed his nearly bald pate with both hands. Often, when he saw his reflection in the mirror of his bedside table, he didn't recognize the gaunt, and nearly bald, man staring back at him. Nevertheless, he was determined to finish this last semester of his engineering degree. He began to work feverishly on the large project that had been so dear to him, that had given him something to do when his stark surroundings made him feel hopelessly and terribly alone when Niki could not be there with him.

His project was a building for downtown Indianapolis, a thirty-story banking and commerce center, that would fill some of the empty space at the heart of the city, *his* city. It had been easy for him to feel this way about his adoptive city.

Sometimes Peter's thoughts raced. I've got to find an architect to collaborate with me on this building. I know what type of structure I want, what materials I'd like to use, but now I need an architect's input. Peter put his layout aside and called a telephone number that he knew by heart. Les Barnes would know something about this, Peter was sure.

"Please connect me with Mr. Barnes…this is Peter Genchenko." Peter hoped that Les would be in his office today, and not in court.

"Peter…how are you doing? Niki has kept my wife and me posted on your progress." Les sounded unhurried and relaxed.

"I always ask Niki the same question, "how am I doing?" because she's the one who knows."

"Well, you've got the best in Niki, Peter, she is one in a million. What can I do for you?"

"I'm finishing up one of my engineering projects for Purdue, and I'd like to find a good architect who will collaborate with me…in fact, I'm hoping to someday see this building in downtown Indianapolis, so I need someone who is good at what he…or she…does. Do you have anyone in mind, Les?"

"Hmm," said Les as he went through a few names in his head that he knew about right off. "Peter, there are two architects that I know of, who have good reputations, and who might be interested in working with you. One, Tate Hathaway, has just put the finishing touches on one of my friends' offices. He did a great job, too. The building is on Meridian, near the St. Vincent's Carmel Hospital, and it's a standout in design and material. The other is Jason Freh, and he's a young guy, but he has had a great deal of success. He's got three buildings on the west side of I-465 that make a lot of other buildings out there look pale in comparison. If you like, I could put you in touch with one, or both, of them."

"That would be wonderful, Les. Right now, most of the collaboration would be by telephone, but Purdue has a computer program that I can use…it is known as a 'super computer' because of its capacity."

"Computers are the way of the future, Peter. I even have several in my office, now, and my staff have gotten very used to having and using them. Have you got a pen or pencil handy? I'll give you the telephone numbers for both of the architects, and I'll call ahead to let them know of your interest."

Peter wrote down the numbers that Les gave him, and felt a sense of accomplishment. "Thanks, Les. You've been a big help to me."

"Call me any time, Peter…oh, and have Niki let us know when you're out of isolation so that my wife and I can come to visit."

"I'll tell her Les. Thanks again."

Unbelievably, at least to Peter, he felt completely worn out by the short conversation that he had just had with Les Barnes. He felt as if time was running short for him, and he wanted to at least have his building planning project completed for Professor Merrill. I can do this...*I can do this!* And it filled him with a new resolve to finish what he had started for his engineering class.

That evening, near eleven o'clock, Susan came in to check on him, and to see if he needed anything before she left for the night. "Peter, it's almost time for me to go off shift. Is there anything you need before I go?"

Peter was so intent on what was laid out on the drawing board that was propped up on his knees, that he didn't hear her at first. He was working on the finishing touches to the second phase of his building, and had earlier called one of the architects that Les had suggested to him, Tate Hathaway, who told Peter that he was very interested in collaborating on the project. Time is running out, thought Peter, and I've got to get Tate Hathaway interested in this project, so that one day, it might be built. I want my sons to be able to say that their father had a hand in creating a beautiful building.

"Pete?" Susan didn't want to interrupt what seemed to be an excellent diversion for her patient, but she needed to talk to him before she left for the night.

"Oh...Susan, I apologize if it seemed as though I was ignoring you. I just had a couple more things to do on this segment of my project tonight."

"That's all right, Pete. I know this work is very important to you. I'm ready to leave, now. Do you need anything before I go?"

"No, Susan, I'm fine right now. I guess that I get a little wound up when I'm working on this building design."

Susan nodded and smiled, "It's good that you have something that you like to work on...but if you don't need anything right now, I'll say goodnight, and I'll see you tomorrow."

"Thanks for all that you do for me, Susan. Goodnight." As the door closed to Peter's room, he returned his attention to the project.

Niki, Ron and Katya came in for a visit with Peter the next day. Of course, having so many visitors in a protective isolation room was not allowed, but the nursing supervisor of the unit allowed them to break the rules for a short, yet very important, visit.

"You all look like badly dressed aliens from outer space," Peter told them as they filed into his room. "It must be a low-budget film."

Ron replied, "You're not far off the track with that observation, Pete."

Katya was quiet at first, because she was taking in her brother's appearance. He was so thin, and the fact that most of his hair was gone, even though Niki had told her what to expect, hurt her deeply. *My beautiful brother is suffering.*

"Petrosha..." she said, "We want to talk to you about something that is very important to us, but even more important to you."

"Yes, Pete...we want...we want..." Niki couldn't continue, and sat down on his bed.

"We have had Nicholas, Josef, and Ari HLA tested and typed, even though you didn't want us to," Ron said as he held up his hand. "But before you say anything, I want you to know that Ari is a perfect match. Katya and I want, more than anything, to keep you with your family, and when Ari gets older, I know that he will be happy to know that he helped his Uncle Peter to stay with his family."

There was silence in Peter's room as he digested what Ron had just told him. Finally, he replied, "No...I cannot allow you to do this. I have no right...I can't cause your child, my nephew, to be in such pain."

495

Katya spoke up, and her words were emphatic, "Petrosha, this is what Ron and I want to do, and I must tell you that I could not bear it if you didn't allow us…and Ari…to help you. If you won't do it for yourself, please do it for Niki, and Nicholas, and Josef…and the new little one who is on the way."

At this, Peter broke down and began to cry quietly. He put his hands over his face as Niki took him in her arms.

Katya continued, "Our son is precious to us, and so are you. If we can possibly help in this way, please let us do so, Petrosha. I can't even begin to think of a life without you."

"And neither can I, Pete…" Niki whispered to him as she held him close.

Peter agreed to go ahead with the bone marrow transplant procedure after talking at length with Dr. Clinton the morning following his family's visit. Katya and Ron's offer on behalf of their son was a miraculously wonderful gift. And when Peter had seen the depths of despair in Niki's pleading eyes, his heart nearly broke. Katya and Ron had stepped outside his room in order to allow him to talk with Niki, and Peter had finally understood just how deeply she, and his sons, would miss him if he were to leave them. And, too, he thought of the tiny new life that he and Niki had created only a few months ago. Months…? It now seemed like years to Peter. He felt as if this room, this protective bubble around him, had actually been a prison, and now he had a reason to hope for a reprieve, a release…and he wanted, more than anything, to stay in this life, to be in this life, with those he loved. Like Lazarus, risen from the dead, he would now have a second chance.

The next morning, Dr. Clinton came in before daybreak to speak to his patient. "We want to do this as quickly as possible, Peter. Your lab work is not good…in fact…I have been worried for several days, and then your sister and brother-in-law came to talk with me about your nephew. When the HLA testing showed that he was a perfect match, I thanked God."

"And I did, too, when I found out, Dr. Clinton…" Peter's voice was barely above a whisper.

"So now we can go forward again, Peter. Ari Michael is scheduled the first thing in the morning, at seven o'clock, and you will be prepped and follow the harvest immediately with your transplant."

Chapter 73

Three weeks post-transplant, Peter left the hospital. His blood work, after only one week, had come up to almost normal readings. And then after the second week, Peter was taken out of the reverse isolation room. He felt a rush of sheer joy as he was wheeled out the door that 'swishhhed' as it opened. He was leaving his prison; the place in which he thought he surely would die.

On the day of his discharge from the hospital, Susan Anderson came in to say goodbye, "It has been a pleasure taking care of you, Peter. And I couldn't be happier at your response to the transplant. It's just wonderful! Please tell Niki that if you, or she, needs anything…anything…I will be glad to help. But for now, I will wish you well, and say goodbye. This is the best, the most happy ending that I could think of for you, Peter. Take care, and God Bless…" She bent and kissed his cheek, and then hurried away so that he wouldn't notice her tears.

Homecoming…there was snow on the ground, and as Niki drove the car up the driveway past the tall evergreens, Peter saw how beautiful everything looked: the house with snow on the roof and smoke curling from the chimney, the frozen lake to the side and behind the house…and the family; Marina and Klaus, with Ron, Katya, and the children, waiting on the 'veranda' waving and cheering as he came home. Niki pulled the car up next to the steps so that Peter could get out with less walking distance, and Duchess came bounding down the steps to greet him.

"Hello, Duchess!" Peter rubbed her head and shoulders briskly for a moment, and then looked up to see his son, Nicholas, running down the steps toward him.

"Papa, Papa!" shouted Nicholas, his face a study in joy.

Klaus, with Josef in his arms, followed Nicholas. Peter could see the delight in both his sons' eyes. No one could possibly be as happy, or as grateful, as was Peter as he reached for Josef, while Nicholas wrapped his arms around Peter's legs, and it didn't seem as if he would ever let go.

Although he had made amazing strides in his recovery, Peter knew that he could not carry both of his sons up the steps. Klaus immediately understood Peter's dilemma, and took Josef back in his arms.

Nicholas reached for his father's hand and they walked up the steps together, with Niki following. At the top, Peter smiled at his nephew, and bent to kiss Katya, who was holding her son, and then he kissed Ari's fuzzy head.

Marina, and then Klaus, hugged their son-in-law, and welcomed him home. "We have missed you so very much." Klaus patted Peter's shoulder as he spoke.

Ron laughed and offered his hand to Peter. "It's great to see you come home, Pete, really great! Let's go inside…Katya and Marina have a small feast set up in the kitchen."

As he came into the great room, Peter saw the familiar furnishings, and tears flooded his eyes. There was a fire in the fireplace that made the scene seem as if it was from a painting by Norman Rockwell. Home…I'm home! Peter's heart swelled to near bursting with happiness.

"Welcome home, Pete, " Niki stood on tiptoe and kissed him on the lips.

"I truly can't put into words what it feels like to come home. Thank you…thank you, everyone, for all that you have done for my family and me."

Marina told him, "Peter, we are all as overjoyed to have you here with us, as you are to be at home!"

When dinner was over, everyone drifted into the family room, and Ron put a tape in the VHS player. "We have all taken turns recording the day to day activities of the family, Pete, and we'd like to bring you up to speed regarding the 'goings on' in the Genchenko household while you were away."

Peter was speechless for several moments, and then spoke quietly, "Thank you…I can't tell you how much this means to me…"

Niki started the narrative of the tape, and then Katya picked up the description of the boys' activities. It was wonderful, so wonderful for Peter to see them at breakfast, or at play, or in the tub together. They have grown so much in such a short time, thought Peter, and he struggled to stifle the tears that stung his eyes. But then it didn't matter, because Nicholas climbed up on his lap, and Niki put Josef in his arms. My sons, my beautiful sons…and the tears rolled down his face, unchecked.

After the last image faded from the television screen, Niki could see that Pete's strength was beginning to wane, and so she started gathering things up, and asked if everyone could give her an idea about what the plans would be for the next month or so. "We want to get things back to a normal routine for everyone…and we thank all of you, from the bottom of our hearts, for what you have done for us. You have all been so helpful and gracious, and selfless…" She looked at her parents, and at Ron, Katya, and Ari, and then it was Niki's turn to tear up.

Peter helped his wife, "Niki and I don't know what we would have done without you, and we are so very grateful. You have taken good care of our children when we could not, and Ari's gift to me is beyond measure. Mere thanks cannot begin to tell all of you how deeply we feel about your kindness."

Ron said that he and Katya were staying for another week to help out with whatever needed to be done, and Marina and Klaus told Niki and Peter that they would come early every day for as long as they were needed in order to get the boys' days off to a good start.

"We awaken early every morning anyway, and we love to be with the rest of the family," said Klaus.

Hours after everyone had settled down for the night, Peter lay in bed next to Niki, who was sound asleep, and held her close in his arms. He had longed to be with her every night of his hospitalization, and now, he was home. *This isn't a dream!*

His sons had clung to him at bath time, and he had assured them that he would be with them in the morning. "I'm not playing hockey, and I'm not going back to the hospital, my sons, so do not be afraid. I will come into your rooms and awaken you in the morning…I promise."

"Papa, why is your hair so short?" Nicholas had been looking at his father's very thin and short hair since he had returned home today.

Peter had to laugh, because when the chemotherapy had made him almost bald, he didn't think that he would ever have hair again.

"Nicholas, Papa is trying out a new style. What do you think of it?"

Nicholas, ever the little diplomat said, "It is very nice, but I think that I liked it before."

"Well, then, I will let it grow out again. Would you like that?"

"Yes, I would Papa…"

Peter watched as Niki, in the bathroom doorway, stifled a giggle, and he grinned at her before he answered Nicholas, "That settles it, Nicholas. I will let my hair grow until it looks like it did before."

As his strength had begun to return, so had his hope that he would be able to take care of his family. Even as a child of twelve, he had wanted to take care of his mother and sister. And now, with Niki as his wife, and two sons who needed him, he wanted, more than anything, to be able to take care of them, too. As he thought of these things, he also said a prayer for the little one, as yet unborn, that he, or she, would be as happy and healthy as Nicholas and Josef. *Please, God…make it so.* And then he drifted off into sleep.

On the following Sunday, they all went to church together. Ron, Katya, and Ari were guests of the Genchenkos and Kellmans on this day of celebration of Peter's recovery. Friends and acquaintances at the church stopped to shake Peter's hand and to tell him that they had prayed for him during his illness, and had put themselves on the donor list for organ procurement because of him.

Peter felt humbled and almost overwhelmed at this outpouring of concern and kindness on the part of his fellow parishioners. He whispered to Niki, "I never imagined that anyone but my own family would care if I recovered, or not. But these very kind people have opened my eyes. They have given me their strength, they have lifted me up, and I am so grateful…"

Niki knew that Marty Pelham and Sheldon Levin were going to visit Peter this afternoon, and she had kept this information to herself so that no one, especially Marina, would start to make preparations for company. She wanted their visit to be a surprise.

Josef and Ari were down for their naps after lunch, and the men of the house were watching the Colts play Green Bay on television. When the doorbell rang, it startled everyone in the great room; that is, with the exception of Niki.

"Well, hello you two!" Niki stood holding the front door open, "Come in…join the men in the great room. They're watching their Colts play Green Bay."

Peter stood when he recognized the guests, "Marty…Sheldon, it's great to see you!" He strode across the room and embraced one, and then the other, of his friends.

Niki asked everyone, "You remember Sheldon and Marty, I'm sure…?"

Klaus and Ron shook hands with the new arrivals, while Katya and Marina added their voices to welcome them, too.

"Come in and sit with us. We were just talking about a snack," said Marina.

"Don't go to any trouble, please, on our account. We just happen to have some great news for Peter, and we wanted to deliver it in person," said Marty.

Peter was immediately curious, "What is it? Lately, I have gotten one good piece of news after another."

Sheldon reached up to put his arm around Peter's shoulder, "We know that you have, and we are very happy that you have recovered, Peter. Our news isn't as wonderful as that, but let Marty tell you what it is…"

503

Katya and Marina hurried into the kitchen to put a little something together for a snack. But Niki stayed in the great room with the men so that she could hear the good news for Peter.

"Thursday night at nine o'clock, there will be a special announcement on ABC Sports Alive by the Administrator of the Hockey Hall of Fame. Peter, you are going to be inducted into the Hall of Fame, and your jersey will be retired." Marty's face was wreathed in smiles.

Peter put a hand to his forehead, and was silent for a moment. "Are you sure...?"

"Absolutely, Peter...we are absolutely sure." Sheldon's grin was wide.

Peter stood up and reached for his wife, "Niki...can you believe this?"

Pandemonium broke loose in the Genchenko house. The men were backslapping and shouting, and the women were squealing in delight. Nicholas was in his father's arms, and although he didn't quite understand what the fuss was all about, he nonetheless added his happy shouts to the noisy gathering.

Later that night, after a joyous and truly celebratory dinner, with Sheldon and Marty as guests, everyone in the Genchenko household bid their guests goodbye. Peter and Niki began helping Klaus, Marina, Ron and Katya in straightening up the house. With so many willing helpers, the house was cleaned, the children bathed, and stories read to the little ones in the great room by Marina.

And now it was bedtime. They all trudged up the stairs in single file, Marina in the lead, Katya carrying Ari, Niki carrying Josef, and Peter holding Nicholas's hand. Ron and Klaus checked the doors and turned off the lights before following the parade upstairs to a quiet rest.

Peter pulled up the covers for Niki and himself, and put his arm around her shoulders. "I still can't believe it, Niki. I didn't play that long with the PB's, so why am I being honored and inducted into the Hockey Hall of Fame?"

Niki had to shake her head at her handsome, and now healthy, husband. "Pete…you've seen all the video footage of the games that the media released, and you saw how the judges scored your performances, so you shouldn't be surprised at your induction."

"Just think of this, Niki. I have always hoped for this honor, even when I was playing exhibition hockey for the Red Army Hockey Team. Isn't it strange that what I hoped for, what I truly wanted, even then, was recognition in the United States?"

"I guess you were just prescient, Pete." Niki delivered her words with a warm smile as she leaned her head against his shoulder.

"But I don't think that I could even begin to see what my future might be until I met you, Niki. And even then, after I fell in love with you, I didn't know, couldn't even hope, that we would ever be together again when I had to return to Russia."

"Yet here you are, healthy, whole, a husband, a father, and an athlete whose name will forever be a part of the sport that he loves."

Chapter 74

Peter held his perfect little newborn daughter for the first time, and saw that her tiny mouth looked like a rose bud. When he mentioned this observation to Niki, she was delighted and agreed with him. Together they decided, then and there, to name their daughter Roza, a Russian word that, translated into English, means *Rose*.

Roza Marina Genchenko made her debut just before midnight on December 12, 1992. From the very beginning, Roza was a dark-haired beauty who was the very image of her paternal grandmother. Her expressive green-gold eyes looked out on a wondrous world.

The birthing suite was spacious, cheerful, and bright. Peter had even had the luxury of staying the night after Roza's birth, because the sofa in the room folded down to make a bed. When Niki changed Roza's diaper, or breastfed her, Peter was there to help. As he lay on the sofa bed, he could hear the little utterings that Roza made throughout the night, and thanked God for this experience. *Fatherhood is a wonderful thing.*

Her siblings, grandparents, uncles, aunts, and cousin visited the birthing center the day after her birth. And her proud, but very tired, parents beamed with happiness as they welcomed the first visit of Roza's extended family.

The women formed a circle around Niki's bed as she held her daughter in her arms. "I didn't think that we were going to have a baby girl," she told them. "I'm not sure why, either, because this pregnancy was so different from my boys."

"Well, Niki," Marina said, "my three pregnancies were each unique. I couldn't have predicted the gender of any of my babies."

Katya, with Ari in her arms, nodded her head in agreement, "Even though Ari kicked all the time, I didn't really know what to expect!"

Stephanie, the new Mrs. Michael Kellman, chimed in, "Mike and I thought that we might wait a while before starting a family, but gosh, it's been two months since our wedding, and just seeing little Roza makes me think that sooner is better than later."

From across the room, Mike turned toward his wife to say, "I heard that!"

"Didn't you know that having babies is contagious, Mike?" Ron had an impish grin on his face.

Klaus added, "Ron is right, Mike."

These pronouncements brought laughter from everyone in the room, including the nurse, who was there checking to see if mother or baby needed anything. It was a happy gathering. Nicholas and Josef sat on their mother's bed and gazed at their new little sister.

It was quite evident that Peter had returned to his former state of good health. He had regained almost all of the weight that he had lost during his treatment for leukemia. His hair was thick and slightly long again, but amazingly, it had darkened almost to Niki's shade.

Katya took in her brother's vibrant good health, and thanked God for Peter's survival. As she looked around the room, Ron caught her eye and smiled at her as he mouthed the words, *I love you...*

Peter saw the interaction and it warmed his heart. He was so glad that Katya had found her soulmate. *We have so much to be thankful for, Katya and I.*

The Genchenko family, Peter, the boys, Niki, and the tiniest member, Roza, went home from the hospital the following day just a little after three o'clock in the afternoon. Peter drove carefully, because he knew that his cargo was precious. Niki was very quiet, and he looked over at her several times to make sure that she was all right. The expression on her face was calm, if not serene, and it made Peter happy. But he completely understood that he and Niki were going to be very busy for the next twenty or so years raising their children. *This is truly what life is all about.* Peter's heart swelled with gratitude, and he thanked God that he had been spared, had recovered from his illness, so that he could stay at Niki's side to raise their family.

The new baby bed for little Roza was difficult to assemble. However, Peter considered the construction of the bed to be a challenge, and much easier since he had nearly completed his engineering degree. Klaus stood by to give Peter a helping hand, if one was needed, and they traded comments back and forth.

"Peter, how is it that something so small, and decidedly designed for obsolescence in a short time, be such a headache to put together?"

"Your guess is as good as mine, Klaus. When I initially read each step of the directions, I realized that the steps were not in the proper sequence. I wonder how many people have been defeated by this little project?"

Klaus laughed, "Perhaps that was the intent all along, who knows?"

Niki was getting around easily, and let everyone know that she didn't need any pampering. "I feel great, I really do. But I have to tell you, Mom, that you and Dad have been so wonderfully helpful to me and my family."

"Yes…and we have been blessed to have you nearby, so that the boys, and now little Roza, will have the benefits of your love and wisdom." Peter truly appreciated his mother- and father-in-law.

Marina patted Peter on the shoulder, "That is such a nice thing for you to say…so very nice."

Later that night, after the Genchenko family was settled and in bed, Peter and Niki lay facing one another under their warm comforter, talking quietly to one another about the events of the last several days. They agreed that time seemed to be slipping by very quickly, and that they had so much to do.

"I know that you want to keep your hand in the clinic, Niki, and it's very important to me that you are able to do so. When you feel up to it, why don't you talk to Ron about how you can still contribute to the care of the athletes?"

She was quiet for a moment, and then said, "Pete, I love my profession, but I think that maybe right now, what I need most to do is concentrate on my family. It hasn't been that long ago since you…" Niki hesitated, "were so sick, Pete, and there are still times that I wake up in the night to make sure that you are there next to me."

"I know that feeling, too, Niki. I did the same thing when I was in the hospital for such a long time."

Niki yawned and stretched before speaking again, "Let's try this, Pete; I'll stay home for two months with Roza and the boys, and then I'll get back into the swing of things in the clinic. Ron and I have talked about this, too, in regard to our clinic, and it makes sense for me to be at home to take care of our children for at least two months. Besides, the fringe benefits of having me at home will be that you and I can also have more time together. Of course, Mom and Dad want to help, too, and that's something that very few parents in our situation have, Pete."

"That's very true, Niki. Anyway…if you are going to be at home for two months, I can complete my portfolio of projects. I have to call Dr. Merrill again to let him know where my last project stands. He has been great, Niki, but the sooner I finish everything, the better my chances are for graduating in the spring, don't you think?"

Niki didn't answer. Her eyes were closed and her breathing was quiet and regular. Peter smiled when he realized that she had fallen asleep.

Goodnight my love…

Chapter 75

Jonquils, daffodils, tulips and crocuses shivered in the cool morning breeze of late April. The perrenial flowers colored the many gardens on the campus of Purdue University. Peter enjoyed the bright and colorful spectacle as he drove onto the campus and sought a spot where he could park his van. He was in no hurry, as he and Niki had divided this day into time sequences for everything that had to be done, and Peter was well ahead of his own schedule. Niki was at home with Josef and Roza, and Nicholas was in school. Marina and Klaus would be available to help Niki with whatever needed attention, too. They were going to host a graduation party for Peter on May 7th, and, as usual, they were meticulous in their preparations.

Peter felt an expectant electricity in the air. Graduation day would soon arrive, and there was a great deal of activity on campus. Ahhh…a parking spot! He swung his van into the spot, feeling a sense of jubilation at having found a place to park so quickly. Peter jumped out of the van, locked it, and gauged the distance that he would have to go to get to the center of the campus. Starting at an easy lope, running now seemed effortless, he felt blessed. *I will never again take my health for granted.*

He entered the building on campus where he would pick up his cap and gown, and followed the multitude of students vying for space in lines that were alphabetically assigned. His wait, however, was not long as the university staff were well-trained in their task of providing the gowns and mortar board caps for the graduating students, more than two thousand strong.

Peter's graduation ensemble included the tassel and sash of the Summa Cum Laude graduate. He had truly blown away his fellow students' projects with his shining example of a cost-effective, yet beautiful, fully functional and utilitarian building. Professor Merrill was very pleased with his star pupil.

For several months, Peter had been working closely with Tate Hathaway, and what they had wrought together would begin to take form in six months. It hadn't taken long to get the backing, and the money, to make Peter and Tate's building on paper into a reality. Every time Peter thought about his first major construction undertaking, he had to tell himself that it wasn't a dream; it was all coming true.

Through Ron's father, Ari Michael, Peter was able to get financing for the project. Ari Michael's banking holdings were worldwide. And the best part, at least for Peter, was that Niki and Ron's Sports Medicine Clinic would fill the entire first floor of the ten-story building. They had managed to get an affiliation with the Indianapolis Methodist Hospital, which had great potential not only for name recognition, but for referrals, as well. *We have been blessed with good fortune.*

On a sunny Graduation Day in May, Mackey Arena was filled to the top seats, it seemed, as Peter searched for his family among the multitude. He and his fellow graduates from the School of Engineering filed into the arena to the strains of "Pomp and Circumstance." *This is real...this is not a dream!*

512

The prelude to the ceremonies was the singing of "Hail Purdue" by the graduating class of 1994. Peter's favorite part of the song, written in 1912 by Edward Wotowa, was the chorus:"Hail, Hail to Ol' Purdue, all Hail to our Ol' Gold and Black.

Hail, Hail to Ol' Purdue, our friendship we may never lack,

Ever grateful, ever true, thus we raise our song anew,

Of the days we spent with you, all Hail our Ol' Purdue."

The ceremony was long, but Peter felt no tedium. He had located Niki, his children, Marina and Klaus, Irina and Karl, Ron, Katya and Ari, Ron's parents, Ari and Miriam Michael, Mike and Stephanie Kellman, and, of course, Marty Pelham, his wife, and Sheldon Levin and his wife. They were all seated directly to Peter's left, and were just below the first railing of the section. Peter waved at them, and was delighted when they all waved back.

He started to look away, and then saw a large group of people…men…stand up and wave. They were sitting behind his family in the seating. Peter did a double-take when he realized that the men who were standing and waving at him were his teammates from the Pittsburgh PB's. As far as he could tell, they were all there, including Coach Heckman. *This is amazing.*

Dr. Bash, Chairman of the School of Engineering, stood at the podium and spoke for several minutes about the "Cradle of Astronauts" as the Purdue School of Engineering is known, and then the Purdue University Orchestra began again to play "Pomp and Circumstance."

When his name was called, Peter strode rapidly up the aisle and took the steps two at a time onto the stage. This, more than any hockey game, was one of the defining moments of his life. As Doctor Bash handed him his degree, Peter shook his hand rather energetically, bringing a moment of merriment to the very large assemblage. Peter walked off the stage, waved again to his family, and blew them all a kiss. Even though demonstrations of congratulation were frowned upon during the proceedings, his former hockey teammates nonetheless stood up and cheered, which nearly 'brought the house down' as applause rippled through the audience, and was followed by whistling and cheering.

The graduation party guests spilled out of the house and onto the veranda. Some were seated at tables by the lake, while others, most of whom were Peter's former teammates, preferred the large tent where the food and spirits were located.

Peter stood at the edge of the lake with Niki, holding hands. As he glanced back toward the house, he saw that Nicholas and Josef were with their grandmother, Marina, Miriam Michael held little Roza, Irina and Karl stood with the group, and Klaus held Ari. He spotted Katya and Ron talking to Mike and Stephanie, and the senior Ari stood chatting with them, as well. Marty waved from a table where he sat with his wife and the Levins, and Peter waved back.

"Well, you've done it, Pete. You have made this dream come true, too." Niki looked up at her husband with loving eyes.

"With your help, Niki…I'll never forget how much you have changed my life…and everything good and wonderful that has come to me has been because of you." Peter knew that if it were not for her, he and Katya would still be in Russia, fearing for their lives.

Niki's laugh had a lilt to it, "I have always thought that it was the other way around, Pete. *You* have saved *me*. You have completed me. We have three beautiful children, and a loving family, too. Before I met you, Pete, I truly didn't understand the meaning of love."

"Well, I am certain that you do now," Peter bent and kissed Niki, who returned his kiss with equal ardor.

It surprised both Peter and Niki when the guests began clapping their hands, whistling, and calling out their names, "Yeah, Pete...That's the way...What a kiss...Hey, Niki...You go, girl!"

Marty and Sheldon had started the applause, and it wasn't long until everyone, even the smallest among the guests, was applauding Peter Genchenko's good fortune.

Epilogue

After the Soviet Union fell in 1991, the door was opened for Russian Hockey players to come to the United States and Canada to play their sport. For his part, Peter sponsored several young Russian athletes and their families, as they became immigrants to his own adopted country.

By mid-1997, Peter and Niki had four children, three boys and one girl. In birth order, they were Nicholas, Josef, Roza, and Klaus. Peter had the large family that he had always dreamed of, and all the love that a large family has to give, too.

Time moved swiftly, and life was never dull in the Genchenko household, or in their business enterprises. Niki continued to maintain her medical practice and part ownership of the sports medicine clinic that she and Ron Michael owned. Her best friend, Stephanie, who was married to Niki's brother, Mike, bought into the clinic the second year after Ron and Niki moved the clinic into Peter's Medical Building. It was now, truly, a family affair.

In 2000, Peter and Niki hired a wonderful nanny in order to keep up with their bright and challenging children. Mary Frances Kelly seemed to miraculously mesh the childrens' school activities, sports, and day-to-day home responsibilities.

Of course, Klaus and Marina, along with Katya, Ron and their son,

Ari, also were integral parts of the very close and loving extended family, as were Mike and Stephanie Kellman, who were now expecting their first child in October, 2000.

Peter had founded Ruska Engineering and Architecture in late 1997, and brought architect Tate Hathaway in as a full partner. Together, they designed and collaborated on several projects in and around Indianapolis. One such project, an athletic club completed in 2005 that was featured in "Architectural Perfection," had an Olympic-sized ice rink, swimming pool, and basketball court, for use by disadvantaged children from the inner city. The project received the Indiana Governor's Commendation Award that year.

Peter and Katya used the money from their father's book royalties to establish safe haven orphanages and medical clinics for abandoned or disadvantaged children in Moscow and Lyubertsy. The Genchenko and Michael families visited these clinics annually during the summer months in order to ensure that they were being administered in accordance with their established missions. The clinics and orphanages were all named "Misha's Place" after Misha Preslov, who was loved by Peter as a dear friend, and by Katya, who had been engaged to marry him before his untimely death. They would never forget him, and now he was immortalized in the charitable work sponsored by the Genchenko and Michael families.

In 2007, the dacha in Tver, once owned by Ivan and Eda Genchenko, was bought and lovingly restored by Peter and Katya's families. When their families made the journey to Russia, they always spent time at their dacha on the lake. Mike and Stephanie, Marina and Klaus, Karl and Irina Kellman, and Ari and Miriam Michael also traveled to Tver for summer visits.

Peter always sought out Grigory Serov's family, and Marc Terenoff, his wife and daughter, when he and Niki and their family came to Tver. He told his friends and their families that they were always welcome at the dacha in Tver, and they often came to visit with Peter and his family. Everyone, it seemed, loved to be at the lake in the summer.

LaVergne, TN USA
18 November 2009

164509LV00001B/71/P